PRAISE FOR THE MAP AND THE TERRITORY

Gripping, vivid, and magical, this fantasy adventure from Tuomala (*Drakon*) has a power to enchant its readers... // Tuomala tackles issues of class and power as they relate to trade and infrastructure in a world devastated by apocalyptic events, raising the poignant question of how people can or should take care of each other after the world falls apart. This impressive fantasy packs the punch of a much longer epic.

— *Publishers Weekly*, starred review

...Magic, stories, and cartography mix with romance, adventure, and philosophy. Questions such as what we owe to each other and how do we care for one another when the world is falling apart seem particularly apt for our (nonmagical) world. A stellar start to a new fantasy series, this book is highly recommended for all fantasy collections.

— Lynnanne Pierson, *Booklist*, starred review

I loved the intricate world-building and the unique magics, but most of all I loved the characters, facing the end of their world with compassion and the determination to—somehow!—find a way forward.

— Melissa Scott, legendary pioneering SFF author
and winner of multiple genre awards

A.M. Tuomala's picaresque *Map and Territory* follows the footsteps of the best traditions of secondary world fantasy travel narratives like that of Jack Vance, C.J. Cherryh, and K V Johansen. With a pair of well-drawn, queernorm characters to guide us and be our entry point, *Map and Territory* is a riveting journey across a diverse and interesting fantasy landscape that is suffering a mysterious, multi-sided cataclysm.

    — Paul Weimer, SFF book reviewer and Hugo finalist

With worldbuilding reminiscent of LeGuin, Tuomala has constructed a rich and exciting story of survival and friendship. Likeable characters and interesting twists elevate *The Map and the Territory* into an intriguing and memorable adventure.

— Jo Graham, author of the acclaimed *Numinous World* historical fantasies and *Calpurnian Wars* space operas

ALSO BY A.M. TUOMALA:

Erekos

Drakon

THE MAP AND THE TERRITORY

A.M. TUOMALA

Candlemark & Gleam

First edition published 2022

Copyright @ 2022 by A.M. Tuomala

For information, address
Athena Andreadis
Candlemark & Gleam LLC,
38 Rice Street #2, Cambridge, MA 02140
eloi@candlemarkandgleam.com

Library of Congress Cataloguing-in-Publication Data
In Progress

ISBNs: 978-1-952456-12-1 (print), 978-1-952456-13-8 (digital)

Cover art by Heeseon Won

Editor: Athena Andreadis

Proofreader: Patti Exster

www.candlemarkandgleam.com

For Caroline and Kavita, without whom

I could not have made this journey.

MAP OF THE WORLD

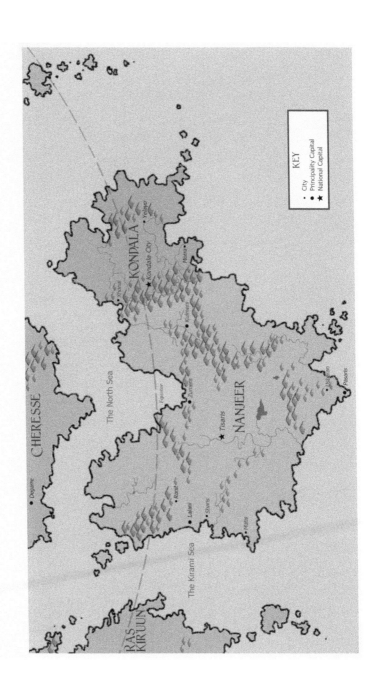

CHERESSE

KONDALA

NANJEER

RAS
KIR'UIN

The North Sea

The Kirami Sea

KEY

· City
● Principality Capital
★ National Capital

CONTENTS

PROLOGUE

Three glasses of sparkling wine, and Eshu's world got soft at the edges. A thickset godling was saying something about fate and song—they'd been on that subject all night, young wizards and new gods and wry ink-stained poets alike—but Eshu couldn't make himself focus on the words. He was enraptured by the shape of that divine mouth, those full lips pressed together for each *M* and parting around each intimate *O*. There were galaxies drifting beneath the godling's night-black skin and stars tangled in his hair, glittering silver and citrine and amethyst. When his sunfire gaze turned Eshu's way, Eshu felt like the only man in the room. He ached for something to say that would let him hold that gaze again.

He lay back on his couch and closed his eyes, feeling the pulse of the music in his skin and the warmth of the lights. If he let himself drift like this, he could track the ebb and surge of the conversation: Mnoro defying fate in high, sharp terms; the godling rumbling gently about how the force of narrative logic created heroes and monsters; dour old Usamkartha explaining that a poet shaped not the world but how it was understood.

"A wizard tells the world a story about what it is, and the world answers, *Yes*," said the godling. His voice was the distant thunder of continental plates meeting and sliding against each other; it was the music of moons in their orbits. "Eshusikinde could tell us that. What do you say, Eshu?"

Eshu's eyes fluttered open. The lights were too bright and too many colors. His eyes swam; he uncoiled from the couch, and the world whirled underneath him. The godling's gaze was hot with something more than curiosity. His fingertips caressed the lacquered wood of his chair in a way that made Eshu's pulse leap. *Njo have mercy, and let me get fucked into the ground tonight.*

He licked his lips and tried to remember how to string a sentence together in Kiruuni. "A wizard doesn't just tell the world what it is—he has to tell that story so convincingly that the world *forgets* what it was before. It forgets gravity, and distance, and how fire consumes. It forgets the shape of mountains, and how seed becomes bloom. It even forgets what he is: just a mannequin of meat telling a story that can't possibly be true."

"A remarkable con," said Usamkartha. "The power of lying on a cosmic scale."

"The power of belief," the godling countered. "The unthinking world, too, has its faith."

"As I said. Belief isn't noble in itself; it just means a susceptibility to—oh, hello, Tuuri. Sit down. Have some wine."

Tuuri. The warmth drained out of Eshu's body. He looked up and into familiar, ice-green eyes.

Tuuri with his broad hands and heavy shoulders, who crafted airship engines and built mirror-ways. Tuuri, always the first to laugh and the last to forget a slight, with his slantwise jokes that someone else always wound up paying for. The man who'd lain with his hand over Eshu's heart and promised never to hurt him in a way he didn't ask for.

It was an ugly little promise. Men like Tuuri always found a way to say other people were asking for it.

Eshu rose from his couch without a word. He stalked out of their alcove and into the main room, where music drifted over the cushions and couches; strangers laughed, touched hands, sank their teeth into figs. He couldn't stand to watch it.

A hand brushed his elbow. He turned and found Mnoro there, her blue silk shawl rucked up around her ears and her heavy-lidded eyes serious. "Come back," she said. "I'll chase him off, if you like. He doesn't have more right to be here than you do."

"I have a headache," Eshu said, which wasn't strictly true, but it was better than explaining how ugly the world felt when Tuuri was in it.

Mnoro pursed her lips. She knew him well enough to recognize and ignore the lie. "Then we'll both go. We can find a couch upstairs and talk about that comedy you loaned me. I feel like I've barely seen you since I left school. I miss you, Eshu." For those last words, she dropped into their native language, and Eshu's heart clenched at it. How many months had it been since someone had spoken to him in Kondalani?

He shook his head and answered her in kind. "I miss you, too. But I can't stay while he's here."

"Are you going back to the university?" Mnoro asked. "Or home?"

Until that moment, he had planned to go back to his dormitory in Usbaran and nurse his anger with cheap wine and weeping. But at Mnoro's question, he let himself imagine being back in his mother's house, listening to the city wake for the dawn prayer. For him and for Mnoro, *home* would always be Kondala City.

"I haven't decided," he said.

Mnoro smiled. "If you go home, tell my mama I'm planning to visit for High Summer. Tell her this time I mean it. I've warned the department head—they're not allowed to have any emergencies over the holiday."

"If I go, I'll tell her," said Eshu. He made himself smile for her. "I'll see you next time."

"All right," she said, and leaned up to kiss his cheek. "Read something nice, before then. I want you to tell me about it when you come back."

"Promise," Eshu agreed, kissing her cheek in turn. This seemed to satisfy her; at least, she let him go, which was close enough to the same thing.

He slid through the crowd toward the cloakroom by the front door, where he shrugged on his outer robe. The smooth cotton lining felt cool at first on his bare arms, but his skin quickly heated under the bulky, quilted fabric. Then back under the lights, into the scent of roasting goat meat and oranges and melons; a pair of wizards shouted after him, demanding to know where he was going when he hadn't even said hello to them yet. He wasn't sure he recognized them, so he made his excuses and slid away.

Eshu descended a brass stair worked with coiling vines, and into a cellar. Wine bottles stood racked all around him, some so old that the dust stood thickly on the glass. He crept through the well-trodden aisle between the racks, to a chamber no larger than a closet. A mirror stood there, illuminated by two lanterns with glass shades patterned like lilies. The mirror itself gave a faint blue glow, like moonlight on snow.

Eshu took a deep, steadying breath, put Tuuri out of his mind, and began to sing.

He sang the lays of secret ways—the stars that led the compass; the black currents tracing up the coast with ice on their backs. He sang the birds that spiraled home on the spring wind, and hunters shadowing the roads of ancient empires. He sang how the key knew the lock, how the tumblers clicked and turned—

—and he felt the world unlock around him.

He passed through the surface of the mirror as though through cool water. The light from the mirror behind him spread out in a long rectangle over rock and glittering sand. Beyond that, the Mirrorlands faded to twilight.

Pulling his robe closer around his shoulders, Eshu stepped out of his world and into the listening dark.

CHAPTER 1: A CRACK IN THE WORLD

R ukha was watching the horizon when she saw the lights over Sharis.

By the time the sun started to set, Rukha had been walking for several hours, and she had been heartily glad of the excuse to make camp. She'd used the last of the daylight to sight a tall tree with branches that looked stout and more or less parallel to the ground, and she'd climbed it with rope and pitons to hitch her hammock to a bough. This done, she had curled up in the cradle of it and watched the sun dip down beneath the ocean on the horizon.

It was a warm, dry night, with storm clouds patrolling the southern reaches. From her perch, Rukha could see the occasional, distant flash of lightning. The storms would blow through in a day or two, but with a little luck, she'd have made it to Sharis on the White Salt Bay by then. With a little extra luck, someone would be interested in buying plant specimens and mineral maps, and she'd have some spare money to book a berth on an airship home.

Not that it wasn't educational, she thought as she turned her gaze northward toward the distant glow of Sharis. *Can't learn about drainage basins without tramping through a few dozen of them. Lots of practice drawing streams.* But now, this close to the end of her journey, she longed for the comforts of home. Linen sheets. The sweet-hot scent of street meat fried in dough and pepper sauce. The organized clutter of the mapmakers' shop, where all her favorite inks were in easy reach. She missed her parents, too, but that was a familiar ache; it was even odds whether they'd be in port or at sea when she got back.

You'll be home soon, she told herself. And if she could manage to get passage on an airship, she'd be able to check her work from above. She imagined looking down at those rivers and streams she'd come to know intimately, that she'd drawn with care and labeled in their local and legal names—the branching arteries of the land, creeks and hollows pumping sweet fresh water down to the ocean. Rukha was still thinking about those streams unspooling when the sky cracked open.

It was almost too far away for her to make out—just a jagged, bright tear in the clouds over the glittering city. *Like when a firework goes off*, she thought, but when it didn't fade, an uneasy feeling in her gut told her that this was no firework. That light lingered like a wound in the sky, and instead, the city lights began to go out. First the darkness swallowed the lights by the shore, then it swept swiftly inward in a widening arc: a vast wave of shadow crashing over Sharis, until only the crescent of the city's edge remained.

Then a crack like thunder sounded, and the entire forest shuddered as the earth rolled beneath it. Rukha's tree swayed perilously, nearly shaking her free; in every tree, birds rose clattering and monkeys screamed confusion. Rukha gripped her hitching ropes until the tremor passed, then edged along the branch below her to check where she'd tied up her supplies. It was too dark to see, so she wrapped her legs around the bough and sorted through her belongings by feel.

Backpack, pan, cup, spare rope, scroll case—everything was where she'd left it. She sighed in relief, then eased herself up again and back to her hammock. *Maybe I should sleep closer to the ground tonight*, she thought, testing the knots of her hitching ropes again. *An earthquake like that could uproot even these big old trees.*

As she glanced back to Sharis, she saw that the lights in the

sky were gone. Although Rukha waited for long minutes to see
whether the city lights would come back, the city was still dark
when she climbed down.

She hoped they were all right.

The storms came on faster than Rukha had expected, washing out
the streambeds she'd been following and forcing her to take to high
ground. When the rain fell so thick and heavy that she couldn't
see more than a few steps ahead of her, though, she had to admit
defeat. She holed up under a stony outcropping for a few hours,
watching the rainwater pour in rivulets down the rocks to either
side of her hiding place. Since she had nothing better to do with
herself, she made a little fire to dry off her boots and whiled away
the time weaving a broad, flat hat of palm fronds to keep the rain
out of her eyes.

"If I get up in the air and find out that the whole river's shifted,
I'm not going to start over," she decided. "They get the maps they
get." Most of the time Rukha didn't mind being alone, but after
the other night, it felt a bit eerie not to have heard another person's
voice for over a week. It felt better to talk to herself, even if it was
nonsense.

By the time she finally joined the road up to Sharis, Rukha was
a day off schedule and well east of where she'd meant to be. Here,
the forest had been cut back to make room for rice terraces and
rows of taro root and ripening beans. The road was proper shell
and gravel, which was nice after a few months of tramping through
forests and bogs, and the heavy rains meant no one wanted to be on
the road. *Probably even the airships are delayed—maybe even grounded,*
Rukha thought. *I haven't seen any go by since the earthquake.*

No one came down the road from Sharis, either, which
might've been good news or very bad news. Rukha had almost

expected a few refugee caravans, after whatever had happened out there. Spooked city folk drifting back to the countryside to hide away with their cousins and wait for the trouble to pass. For their sake, Rukha hoped it was good news.

Once the rains let up, she traded her hat to a farmer for a bowl of hot spiced taro mash. After she'd thanked him, she asked whether he'd heard or seen anyone from Sharis since before the rains started.

"Not for a few days," he said. "Peddlers aren't making the rounds like they usually do. Probably a fair number of shops knocked down in that earthquake."

"Probably," Rukha agreed. She wondered, later, if she should've told him about the lights—but by then it was too late to turn around, so she kept walking toward the city.

By now, she could make out buildings: the wizards' tower spearing toward the grey slate sky, and a copper-sheathed dome that might've been some kind of university or Hall of Law. Houses, most of them wood and plaster, a few made of limestone and white shell brick. No smoke rising from them. No lights, even when the sun started to slip toward the ocean.

She tried to remember the last time she'd been through Sharis: the docks, the boardwalk lined with crab sellers and net menders and pearl fishers shaking out their wet hair. There had been a good little bakery at the boardwalk's end, where they fried fish in batter and served it so hot it was still steaming when she bit into it. The birds had chased her all the way to the fountain in the middle of town, crying for bread. Those were the kinds of places she'd always loved best, those raucous seaside streets where everyone was always doing something and you could just sort of slide into the crowd and get lost for a little while.

This close to the ocean, the air always smelled of salt and fish and rot. But now, as the evening wind swept up from the water, Rukha smelled a deeper rot that made her stomach twist.

She reached the outskirts of town just as the sun touched the horizon. A couple of stray dogs growled at her as she passed, their tails down and ears back, but they slunk away when she turned to them. Everywhere was the smell of rotting meat, overpowering the ocean's thick salt musk.

Then she turned the corner at the Hall of Laws with its green copper dome, and she stepped into the white foam at the tip of the wave. Suddenly, with a lurch of nausea, Rukha understood.

Sharis had fallen into the sea. Waves crashed against the marble face of the Hall of Laws; gouts of water blew through the broken windows with a sound like a whale surfacing. Ahead of her, the road had sheared away, leaving a steep cliff that dropped deep into the water. Far below, so far that she could barely make out the angles of rooftops and sunken verandas, lay the lost city of Sharis.

All around her floated the many-days-dead.

By now, there was little left of them—tattooed limbs rotted free of their bodies, or swaths of fabric holding a corpse together. Bright green rags, edged with thread that glittered like silver. A body half-devoured by dogs on a nearby street. Faces with eyes eaten out by fish or birds. A foot in a little silk shoe with pearls on the toe.

Rukha's stomach heaved, and she sank to her knees and retched. It had been all day since she'd eaten, and nothing came out. Tears stung her eyes; she tasted bile and spat. She couldn't stop shaking. She tried to open her hands on her thighs and hold them still, but they shook all the same until they'd shaken into fists again. Her throat hurt from crying and heaving and crying again.

She wasn't supposed to see this. It was too big for one person to witness. Sharis had never been her city; it wasn't hers to grieve.

All of it, gone. The little bakery on the boardwalk and the fountain and the pearl fishers and—and all of it, under the water with the bodies of those who'd sunken already.

Slowly, Rukha became aware that someone else was watching her. She scrubbed fiercely at her eyes and wiped her hands on her trousers, then pushed herself to her feet and turned around.

An old woman stood there, with the last sunlight spinning her white hair to gold. She was bare to the waist, muscular and heavily tattooed the way Sharisi sailors often were. *The way they used to be.* There was a belaying pin in her hand, but she didn't look like she planned to do any violence with it.

"Was this your place?" she asked. Her voice was raw, but clear and strong and carrying. Rukha shook her head. "Well, that's a mercy," the old woman said heavily. "Call me Shell."

An old superstition: when times were bad, when you didn't want to die and you could feel the Crowtaker breathing down your neck, don't give your name to strangers. Call yourself Tree, Cloud, Flower, Brick—so that if the Crowtaker pricked up her long ears, she'd pass you by. Shell was a safe name to give someone, when night was drawing down and the ocean was full of bodies.

Rukha swallowed down her own name and said, "Call me Fern." Rukha meant *rock*, and right now, she felt like the furthest thing from a rock.

"Well, then. Fern." Shell sucked in a breath through her teeth. "Sun's about spent, so it's time to get inside. There will be food for you, if you want it."

"Is there anyone else?" Rukha asked in a rush. "Is there *anyone* else alive here?"

"A few dozen that I've seen," Shell answered. She put a hand on Rukha's shoulder and started marching her back toward the edge of town. Her bare feet left a shining track on the paving stones. "The rest of 'em are holed up in the wizards' tower. Good view from the top. Seems safer than anywhere else."

"What about the wizards?" Rukha knew enough about geology to know that there wasn't a fault down the middle of Sharis, which left gods or magic. "Are they still here?"

Shell shook her head. "Went out through a mirror, probably. Leastways, they left most of their things. Can't figure out exactly when they took off. Hadn't seen them for a while, but that wasn't odd. Kept to themselves, mostly—but now I wonder. Might've known something the rest of us didn't."

Or at least, they had a better way out when they saw the lights and felt the ground shake. "Is there anything I can do?" asked Rukha. "I have lots of maps; if you need directions to anywhere—"

"No," said Shell sharply. "If we wanted to go, we'd have gone. Some did. Me, I'm staying until I find my family."

They're probably dead, thought Rukha, but as she looked at Shell's wet trousers, she realized that Shell knew already. She wasn't looking for survivors. She was looking for something to burn or bury. "I can help, if you want," said Rukha. She reached up for Shell's hand and held it, and Shell gripped her back with fingers like iron.

"In the morning."

It hurt, not being able to do anything *now*. Rukha wanted there to be something she could find or hammer or carry that would make this ugliness right; she wanted some answer she could memorize, so that she could give it when asked and make sense of what had happened here.

There wasn't an answer. There was nothing to carry. The dark came down, and it was time for supper.

The wizards' tower was in better shape than the rest of Sharis, but there were a number of cracks in the white stone walls that said its foundation had shifted. Someone had painted the walls with big black letters on the seaward side: *SHELTER. ALL WELCOME.* A couple of the bright stained glass windows were broken, but after a second look, Rukha saw that they were broken in. *The door must've been locked when they tried to get inside,* she thought. Even now, the door canted on its hinges, but Shell lifted it straight and swung it open.

In the broad central rotunda, about two dozen people had made a camp. Blankets and bundles lay everywhere, covering arcane mosaics of porcelain tile and gold; children chased each other around the blue-veined marble pillars and went skidding across the polished tile floor. The smell of incense hung on the air, driving back the stink of the dead.

"This is Fern," called Shell as she entered. "She'll stay with us a while. Find her a bowl."

"She doesn't look Sharisi," said a younger man with sailor's tattoos peeking over his collar. "Where'd you find her?"

"None of your fucking business; she's alone and needs a meal," Shell answered. "Excuse my son. He was born on a quarterdeck. No manners."

"Excuse my mother; she's got a mouth like a cannonade." The man held out his hand, and Rukha clasped his wrist. "Call me Gull. You need a blanket?"

"I've got one," she answered. "I've got a bowl, too."

"One less thing to worry about." He turned to his mother, who'd found a pipe somewhere and was lighting it to smoke. "Did you find anyone today?"

"None of ours," she said. "Thought I had, for a while—your sister's hand—but the tattoos were the wrong shape. She had arrowheads, you remember. This one was just triangles. And it had a ring I don't remember. Not that I knew every one of her rings."

"She loved that one with the green glass. Her emerald," said Gull. He took out a pipe of his own and offered it to Rukha, who shook her head. "She might not even be here. I keep telling you, she'd signed to a ship last week. She might've sailed before the lights."

"She wouldn't have gone without saying goodbye to her mother. Not her." A little girl ran shrieking past Shell's legs, and Shell watched her go with her black eyes bright and distant. "No, she's somewhere in the water, and I'm going to find her."

That night, the last people of Sharis made their supper in the tower's lavish kitchen, where a cookfire burned eternally without wood or coal. They batter-fried fish and ate it with flatbread—no one had found yeast yet in the ruins—and then drank the wizards' sweet white wine on the floor of the rotunda.

After supper, some people strung up blankets between the pillars to curtain off some private space, but most didn't. *They've lost so many people, they want to be able to see who's still here*, Rukha thought. A girl of about thirteen gathered the younger children around to tell them a story about how the Sisters found the magic feather, and she kept telling it until even the oldest had started to nod off.

Rukha sat with her blanket across her lap and her back to a pillar, watching as Gull dimmed the lamps and Shell bundled children into bed. After the long walk and the bodies and crying and retching, she wanted desperately to sleep, but even the thought of doing so made panic well up in her throat. She didn't know what she was so afraid of—not just another earthquake, but something deeper and harder to name.

This morning, she'd been on her way to Sharis to book an airship back home. Now Sharis lay beneath the waves.

But Sharis had been underwater since the night she'd seen the lights. All this time, the world hadn't been what she'd thought it was. She didn't know the shape of it anymore, and she was afraid of waking up to find that it had changed again. Or maybe that it had never been the shape she'd known.

And under all of that was a worry so deep that she couldn't even let herself think it all the way: *What if the earthquake had broken Matis, too? What if she'd lost her home?* She'd heard of earthquakes so strong that people had felt them on both sides of the Kirami Sea. Matis was so much closer than Ras Kir'uun.

After a long time sitting in the darkness, Rukha heaved herself to her feet. By now, moonlight was streaming through the blue and green glass windows, and the night was full of the whistling snores of sleeping children.

"I'm going to look at the rest of the tower," she told Shell, who sat guarding the door with her belaying pin on her lap.

"Careful," Shell answered. "Take a lamp." She passed over a lantern shielded in a stout brass cage, along with the little hand-striker that she'd used to light her pipe.

"Thank you," Rukha answered.

A spiral stair circled the inner rooms of the tower, with round windows like portholes in every cardinal direction. Rukha levered one open and found that it overlooked the sea, and she lost several minutes watching the waves curl under the waxing half-moon. When she'd been little, her father had taught her a sailor's astronomy, and now she searched for the old, familiar constellations in the sky: the Fly, the Lotus, the Dragon with Four Heads. *It doesn't look like a dragon*, she'd said, a long time ago. She'd been a little shit when she was a child.

You have to teach yourself to see a dragon, he'd answered. *Tell yourself a story about it, so that every time you look at the sky, you see the story. And then you'll find the dragon—not in the sky, but in the story.*

Before the earthquake, this window must've looked out over the city. Some wizard must've stood here, watching carts trundle down the streets and ships put in at the port, seeing the city lights come on one by one as the dark drew down.

Rukha swallowed hard, then turned away.

She lifted her lamp overhead and turned her attention to the inner wall of the stair. At each landing, there was a door, some leading to empty offices and some to sleeping chambers with the blankets and mattresses dragged out. Behind one door, she found a library full of books chained to the shelves. The chains looked heavy, and they shone ominously in the lamplight.

Every room had been rummaged through at least a little, probably by the people downstairs—*Or by the wizards, when they left*, thought Rukha, remembering Shell's suspicions. But sometimes, she found a gold pocket watch still ticking tranquilly on a bedside table, or a little bag of diamond dust lying beside a set of etching tools.

If the people of Sharis did leave, she hoped they took them. They deserved to start their lives over with something.

The door at the very top of the tower stuck, but Rukha gripped the handle the way Shell had downstairs and lifted it on its hinges until she could ease it open.

Before her feet spread out a mosaic map of the stars, with gold inlay linking the constellations and planets worked in chips of amber and comets trailing quartz tails across an onyx sky. Despite herself, Rukha gasped. She'd grown up with star charts, and once she'd even been to see the orrery at the Royal Museum of Ras Kir'uun, but this mosaic felt grander and sadder and more intimate than anything she'd ever seen before. She was alone with some artisan's great work, in a dead city, watching the gleam of her lantern kindle fire from the night sky.

After a moment, though, she realized that there was something else in the room. At the very center stood something tall and flat and covered with a sheet. *A mirror*, she thought. *Shell said the wizards left through a mirror.*

She paced across gold and quartz and amber to the mirror and fisted her free hand in the sheet, then pulled it down to puddle around the mirror's feet. In the silvered glass, she saw herself illuminated by lantern light: clothes travel-stained and shirt dusted with crumbs; round face and black hair down to her chin. Her eyes looked hollow and purple around the edges, and her lips were cracked and torn. She hadn't even noticed she'd been biting them.

"Fern," she told her reflection. When she reached out to lay a hand on the mirror's face, the glass fogged up around her palm. "Just Fern." It was harder to say, when that round Masreen face was looking back at her, but she'd get used to it.

She brushed the crumbs off her chest and turned to go. There weren't answers up here, either, but she felt a little calmer now. The panic had sunk down to her gut again, where it churned as slow and steady as a water wheel.

Then there was a shattering sound, the tail end of a scream— and something came through the mirror and knocked Rukha flying.

CHAPTER 2: THE PARTY IS OVER

Even in his coat, Eshu shivered. He probably shouldn't be walking home now, with his mind still a little cloudy with wine and anger rising off of him in waves. But he couldn't go back after telling Mnoro he was going, and he definitely couldn't face Tuuri again. *The walk will sober me*, he thought. He hoped it was true.

He sang a white light to his hand and held it aloft. All around him, the desert stretched in white waves, broken here and there by ridges of black stone or pillars of mirror-light or stunted silver trees. A long way away, mountains marked off the horizon, a smear of black beneath the deep evening blue of the sky.

For just a moment, he considered going all the way home—not back to the university, but to Kondala City's Hall of Ways. He could visit his family. He wanted to sit with his sisters at the breakfast table and let his mother lecture him about how skinny he was getting. After the dawn prayer, they'd eat soft flatbread with lentils and butter-smooth goat cheese while Sunba prepared her case notes at the table, and afterward he'd braid Kiga's hair for her and listen to Asha telling him about thousand-year comets. In the morning, he could visit Mnoro's mothers like he'd said he would, and they'd probably send him packing with a sack of almond sweets.

It would be well past midnight in Kondala City. His family would worry if he came in still half-drunk at three in the morning.

Instead, he turned toward the far-off mountains, and he fixed the university in his mind. The library with its plush rugs worn down to bones of warp and weft. The courtyard overgrown with pine and ivy. His dormitory cell with the diamond-paned window that looked out over the wooded hills.

A cold wind swept over the sands and sent them spiraling. Where the sands blew away, they revealed a path made of rough black stone.

Eshu looked back. The mirror he'd come through was only a panel of light in the darkness. Then he set his feet to the black stone path and started walking, and soon he found himself amid an ancient forest that smelled of snow and pine.

When he'd been new to the mirror-ways, he'd looked for the trick of it—the moment when the landscape changed. He'd watched the dunes from the corners of his eyes as though he could catch pine trees rearing up from the earth or see oceans rising from the valleys; he'd walked the path with his eyes closed and his hand on Tuuri's arm, listening to the slide of sand on rock as it gradually shaded into birdsong.

It had taken Eshu a long time to learn that that moment happened when he first began to look for the path. It was only his senses that took a while to catch up.

Now and then, he glimpsed other mirrors among the trees, gleaming like beacons over a carpet of dead pine needles. Colleges, he supposed, or wizards' homes, or maybe busy travel hubs like the Hall of Ways. Once, he glimpsed a stranger with a dim blue lantern step from one mirror straight to another, like a neighbor crossing an alley to borrow flour.

Then suddenly, there was a crack like thunder, and the mirrors began to go dark.

Cold dread prickled at Eshu's skin. He'd never seen that happen before. He banished the light in his hand just to be sure his eyes weren't playing tricks on him, but the deep-forest darkness immediately swallowed him. There were no other lights in the wood.

His heart lurched. *This is going to be fine*, he told himself. *This is going to be fine; I don't need any of those mirrors. I just have to get back to mine.*

He conjured his light again and pulled up the hem of his robe with his other hand, and he began to run. Branches tore at his locs and the scales and feathers framing his face, and they caught his robe and broke with a sharp sap smell that made his eyes sting. The rocks dug through the soft soles of his shoes like blades.

At last, after what might have been minutes or hours or days, he had to stop. His side had stitched up, and his chest ached from breathing the cold, dry air. The black stone path wound between the trees, and he couldn't see the end of it. A part of Eshu knew, with that irrational certainty of terror, that there *was* no end of it anymore. He bent over to catch his breath, coughing with unaccustomed exertion. The wind was loud in his ears.

Tuuri used to tell him stories about hungry ghosts drifting through the wastes, preying on those who lost their way. *They're not even eyes in the darkness*, Tuuri had used to say. *Not even claws and teeth. They're only the feeling of hunger that can never be full, and cold that can never be warm. And sometimes, when the wind blows, you hear them calling for you to leave the path.* Stupid stories meant to scare him, Eshu had always thought. Now, with the mirrors dark and the cold wind sighing through the pines, Eshu wasn't so sure.

He should have reached the mirror by now.

I'll go back, he thought. *Sleep on a couch. Try again in the morning.* The host might grumble about guests overstaying their welcome, but Eshu could deal with a little grumbling.

He tried to fix the house in his mind: a sprawling manor by the sea in Ras Kir'uun, with orange groves just dropping their petals. The host, a handsome older wizard who'd traded his eyes to a god to live three hundred years. He pictured the warmth of the lights in that central room; the smell of honey and wine and candied orange blossoms.

When Eshu turned around, the desert stretched before him again, vast and dark and empty. He could no longer see the mirror he'd come through.

He thought of the stranger who'd flitted from mirror to mirror with her blue lamp held over her head, and a cry welled up in his throat before he could hold it in. "Help! Is anyone there? I need help! Someone, please, help!"

There was no answer but the wind, rattling the silver leaves of the desert trees and whistling over the ridges. A cold thrill of fear sang up Eshu's spine. He looked down for the path and saw only sand.

If Tuuri had been here, he would have known what to do. He built mirrors; he knew how to make new paths or find old ones in the Mirrorlands. *It's possible to find or make a path, if you know what you're doing.*

Eshu knelt on the sand and laid his light before him. In its glow, he could see his own fingers shaking. "Njo, Far-Traveler, let me find the way," he said softly. "Please help me. I don't know what the fuck I'm doing."

He tried to imagine Kondala City up in the mountains, with the prayer drums and bells sounding in the morning. He remembered his mother's house, dried herbs hanging from the rafter poles and mirrored beads on her shawl. In his mind's eye, he conjured up the billowing green curtains of the Hall of Ways at the heart of the city, with its eight great mirrors reflecting each other to infinity.

He looked up and saw only white sand blowing in diamond drifts. He felt sick.

Eshu curled up in the lee of a black rock ridge, draping his outer robe over his face to keep the sand off of it. He knew he needed to sleep, but he couldn't make himself relax enough. Something was badly wrong, and he wasn't sure whether it was in the Mirrorlands or the world outside of them.

There was no dawn here, but after a long time shivering against the ridge, he made himself do the dawn prayer anyway. Knelt with his hands on his knees and sang of Njo, Laughing-Eyed, Far-Traveler, who taught her people the Way of Stories. By the end of it, his eyes stung with grit. He wiped them off with the back of his hand, and his eyeliner came off with it. *I'm a fucking wreck*, he thought, and the sheer normalcy of that thought made him laugh until his stomach hurt.

When he'd recovered himself, he climbed to his feet again and looked around him. There were the black mountains, a slash on the horizon. The silver trees. The sand. The starless sky. Not even a footprint said that anyone else had ever been here.

For a long moment Eshu stood there, letting the terror wash over him. His heartbeat throbbed hot and urgent from his temples to the tips of his fingers. He listened to the hiss of sand blowing across the dunes. It hurt to breathe, as though he was breathing in shards of glass.

He sang the scratch and sulfur of the match, the wild sheet of flame that licked down the matchstick; he sang the fiery bud that bloomed upon the wick. He sang the sun gilding the breakers on the ocean, the bright waves unfurling over shining sands. He sang the stars in points of distant flame. His voice rolled rich and deep over the dunes, and everywhere it echoed, the hills resounded with the hymn of light unconquered, light invincible.

When Eshu opened his eyes, the sands blazed with a thousand shifting hues. They caught the light that streamed from his hands and broke it into shards of red and green and gold, until each grain of sand seemed to gleam with an inner flame.

In that dazzling light, Eshu saw something moving on the sands.

It left no print or trace on the ground. The light went straight through it; it was less substantial than shadows, less even than wind. But as it passed over the ground, the diamond sand dulled briefly to white beneath it.

It had a pull like a deep chasm with no railing. The fear of falling became anticipation, so keen that it felt like a craving.

Sometimes, when the wind blows, you hear them calling you to leave the path. Eshu thought he understood now what Tuuri had meant.

Even if he hadn't been exhausted, he couldn't hope to outrun this thing. As the spirit closed in, he drew a circle around himself with the toe of his shoe and poured daylight into it. "Who are you?" he asked. "What do you want?"

At the edge of the circle, the creature hesitated. Wherever the light shifted, he caught glimpses of something beyond it—mad eyes. Fingers shriveled over gnarled bones. Pieces of something old and wild and hungry. The longer he looked, the more he strained to see it through the flickering lights, the clearer its shape became. He saw its long, stringy hair, the gory sockets around its golden eyes, its elegant sneering mouth full of shattered teeth.

He realized, too late, that he was thinking it into being.

Njo, don't let me die behind the mirror. "Who are you?" Eshu asked again. The ghost smiled. There was blood on its lips. It lunged across the circle with its eager mouth wide, and Eshu screamed and fled across the dunes.

He lost a shoe and left it in the sand. Rocks tore at his bare sole, then sand ground into the wounds; he stumbled and kept sprinting. His veins were full of ice and fire. His chest burned with every breath. *There has to be a way out*, he told himself as he fell sliding down a hillside and into a cracked-mud valley. He heard footsteps behind him and knew that the thing was getting nearer—getting *realer*—the more he ran.

Just one light, he thought desperately, as the valley began to flow with water and sucking mud clung to his feet. *Mirrorlands, give me a single light to follow—*

The cold was hard on his heels now. It reached for him with taloned fingers; he felt something graze his robe and heard it tear.

There was blood in the water, and he didn't know if it was his. He smelled salt.

Then the darkness slid in a sheet from a gleaming mirror pane, and Eshu catapulted through.

He hit someone's back and sent them—her—crashing to the ground. She caught herself on her hands and flung him off, cursing wildly as she fumbled for her lantern. *Nanjeeri*, he registered after a moment, and the relief he felt was all out of proportion to the foul things she was calling him. *She's speaking Nanjeeri.*

His university was in South Nanjeer. He'd come out somewhere vaguely close to where he'd meant to go. He was safe.

"I'm sorry that I burst in on you like that," he said, when she paused to draw breath. He spoke good Nanjeeri. He was proud of it. He could pull himself together enough to be polite in it. "My name is Eshu. I've spent the night running from things that wanted to eat me in the Mirrorlands, and I'm tired, injured, and very lost. Could you please tell me where I am?"

She blinked and sized him up, so he took the opportunity to do the same. She was compact, sturdy, with well-muscled arms and trousers tied at the knee; from the way her warm brown skin had burned across her nose and cheeks, she looked like she'd spent a lot of time in the sun recently. Not much like a wizard.

Then again, after the uncountable nights he'd had, Eshu supposed that he didn't look much like a wizard, either. "Did you come through the mirror?" he prompted, when she didn't answer right away.

"No, I walked," she said. "Call me Fern. This is Sharis—or what's left of it. You're not one of the Sharisi wizards, then?"

Sharis. All the way up the west coast. Then he registered the rest of what Fern had said, and he asked, "What do you mean, what's left of it?"

"It might be better if you see it. Or worse. Probably worse." She gestured him to follow her through an arched doorway at one end of the circular chamber.

He tried to follow. Now that he wasn't running for his life, Eshu keenly felt the cuts on his foot and the sand that had worked its way into them. His sole was dripping blood; when he tried to put his weight on it, pain boiled up all the way to his knee. White spots swam in front of his vision. Eshu hissed and stumbled back to his good foot.

Fern frowned. "Let me help," she said, coming back to slide her shoulders under his arm. "There might be someone downstairs who can fix you up, but it's a long way down. We'll take it slowly. Just one step after another."

Together, they limped out of the mirror room and onto a spiral stair. A thousand questions waited on Eshu's tongue: *Where are the other wizards? Why are you here? What happened to Sharis? What happened to the Mirrorlands?* But Fern didn't seem like she would have the answers, so he didn't try to ask. "What time is it?" he asked eventually. It seemed like a safe question.

"About midnight," she answered.

"At least it's a reasonable hour for sleeping."

"I don't think the people here care much about reasonable hours nowadays."

At a landing, Fern let him go and went to lever open a broad, round window. The smell of salt and rot poured through. "It looks worse in daylight," she said. Her voice hitched a little. "You can see what's on the shore, and even through the waves a little. But you can see enough by moonlight."

Eshu hobbled over to the window and looked out over the wreck of Sharis. He'd only ever seen illustrations of the city, cheap woodblock prints in tourists' guides to Nanjeer—but even his untrained eyes could see the crescent where the ocean floor had fallen away. "Shit," he whispered.

"Yeah," said Fern, just as softly. "Shit."

"How did this happen?"

She shook her head. "There were lights in the sky, then an earthquake. Someone downstairs thinks the wizards might have done it. You're a wizard, right?"

"I'm studying to be one. I'm at the university in Usbaran." *Shit, what's happened to Usbaran? And Kondala? Did this happen there, too? Is that why the mirrors all went dark?* "I have to get home, Fern. I have to go back."

"To Usbaran? I haven't seen an airship for a while, but maybe one will come soon—"

"To Kondala City. I can go through the mirrors." He couldn't help imagining the Hall of Ways cracked down the middle, every mirror splintered. A fault line running through his mother's house, and his sisters falling.

"Didn't something just try to eat you in there?" Fern shut the window and latched it in place again, shutting away the ruins. "Come on. You need to have someone look at your foot. And maybe sleep. You don't look like you've had much sleep."

"Neither do you," he said, but he couldn't muster any heat. He felt tired in ways he hadn't known he could feel tired—an ache of fear and exhaustion that went down to his soul. "Let's make a promise to each other, all right? I'll sleep if you'll sleep."

"You drive a hard bargain." She shifted under him to take on more of his weight and switched her lantern to her outside hand. "I'm from a city called Matis. It's south of here. You're Kondalani, right? Is that where you came from, before you were here? Or were you in Usbaran?"

She was trying to take his mind off of his foot, and Eshu found he was grateful for it. "I was in Ras Kir'uun," he answered as they made their way slowly down the stairs. "For a party." It sounded so stupid, now.

"So you went from Kondala, to Usbaran, to Ras Kir'uun. To here." She whistled, low. "You wizards get around."

"It helps to be able to walk through mirrors."

"It must. Do things usually try to eat you, when you're traveling that way?"

"This was a first," said Eshu with a bitter little laugh.

"I can come with you, when you go. If you like." Fern's voice was so matter-of-fact that at first he thought she was joking, but when he looked down to meet her eyes, Eshu saw that she was serious.

"To Kondala? Why would you want to go there?"

Fern shrugged. "I'm not particularly *trying* to go to Kondala, but it sounds like you had some trouble, so here I am. I want to help."

"It's just..." He struggled to find something to say that wasn't *People like you don't travel through mirrors*. "The Mirrorlands aren't like any country you've ever seen. They change based on your will and your imagination. It's easy to get lost there, if you don't know how to navigate them."

Fern grinned. It was a grim, tight little phantom grin, but she looked like she meant it. "Well, lucky for you, I'm a cartographer. I'm pretty good at learning to navigate."

Eshu rubbed his eyes. "We can decide this after we've slept. Speaking purely for myself, I'm in no position to make good arguments at this moment."

With Fern's help, Eshu reached the bottom of the tower eventually, and she introduced him to a tall, powerfully built old woman named Shell. As Fern explained how she'd found him, Shell raked her eyes over him, from his lost shoe to his wrecked cosmetics, and she looked as though she was formulating questions. At last, though, she shook her head and said only, "I'll fetch a blanket."

She came back with a blanket and a bowl of water—clean-smelling, Eshu thought, which he hoped meant it had come from a tank rather than the sea. "Lie down," she said as she set down the bowl. "I'll clean your foot."

"I think there's sand in the cut."

"Probably," said Shell. "Wouldn't be the first time I washed sand out of a wound. Just lie back and close your eyes. Stings more if you watch." Once Eshu lay down, she knelt at his feet and started to wash them by lantern light.

It burned even after he closed his eyes. Shell's raw-knuckled hands were surprisingly deft, but she couldn't wipe the sand clear without pressing into the wound. He gritted his teeth and tried not to twitch or struggle. Shell was trying to help. He had to remember that.

If there had been wizards here, they would've been able to weave the flesh closed and soothe the pain away—but the wizards had fucked off to only Njo knew where, and there was no one here to help him but an old sailor woman.

And a cartographer. Eshu cracked open his eyes to look for Fern and found her huddled under a pillar, wrapped in what looked like a camping blanket. Her curls fell into her face, and her hands were clenched into loose fists near her head. If he hadn't seen how her eyes glittered in the lamp light, Eshu would've thought she was sleeping.

"Done," said Shell, tying off a few strips of cotton over his feet. "Should probably stitch them, but we don't have stitches for people. Stay off your foot; keep it out of shoes. Wash the bandages now and then in boiled water. Should be all right in a week or so."

He wanted to ask what would happen if it wasn't all right, but Shell's answer was probably the same as his: *Fuck if I know.* "Thank you," he said instead.

When Shell went back to her post by the door, Eshu unfolded the blanket she'd found him and tried to make himself comfortable on the hard mosaic floor. He could feel every knob of bone through his skin, and he couldn't make himself care because at least it wasn't the Mirrorlands. His eyes burned with exhaustion. Sleep claimed him swift and dreamless, and he didn't wake until well after sunrise.

CHAPTER 3: THE CROWTAKER

Rukha woke around sunrise, which meant she must've fallen asleep at some point. A young woman sat up on watch with a harpoon over her shoulder, a teacup half-empty beside her. "There's more down in the kitchen," she said, when she saw Rukha looking.

"Thanks," said Rukha. She stumbled down to the kitchen, rubbing the sleep from her eyes with her knuckles. There, she found not only tea but also some cracked wheat porridge with apricots stewing over the fire, and a boy of about ten tending it. "You're the chef today?" she asked, giving him a little smile.

"Someone's gotta," he said. "Pa put me in charge of inventory, too. Look, I've got a list."

He shoved a weathered logbook across the table at her. The page on the left was marked with weather and soundings and navigational headings, all inked in a steady, clear hand; on the right, supplies were listed in heavy pencil. Skimming the list, Rukha saw that the boy had crossed out and updated quantities for the tea and porridge, and they were down to HONEY (2 JARS), DRIED FRUITS (7 JARS), WHEAT (10 SACKS). "You're doing a good job," she said, passing back the logbook.

He nodded seriously. "Pa's a ship's captain," he said. "He says I have to be in charge while he's gone."

"Where did he go?"

"Up to Lalani," the boy said. "To tell the prince what happened."

Lalani—it was the principality's capital, the biggest city in the region. (The part of Rukha that wasn't yet fully awake must have thought she was at university again and studying for a geography test, because it helpfully supplied: major exports, textiles, lumber, and fish; major imports, fresh fruit and grain.) Probably a week's journey away by foot, but only a few days by boat and just hours by airship.

And minutes, if you went by mirror. Rukha stirred slightly crunchy honey into her tea, watching the crystals settle on the bottom and melt. *Maybe that's where the wizards went.* "Thanks for the food," she said, scooping up her cup and bowl to take upstairs.

"You have to bring the dishes back," said the boy, with a threatening wave of his spoon. "Or we'll get rats."

They'd probably get rats anyway, with the bodies along the shore, but Rukha didn't begrudge him for wanting to bring a little order to his world. When everything else had fallen apart, at least he could keep the dishes sorted. "Promise," she said.

More people were awake when she made it upstairs, but not the wizard who'd come out of the mirror. He was still snoring gently under a quilt patterned with roses, his head pillowed on his arm. He had a strange, fanciful look to him, even for a wizard—the edges of his face were bright with feathers and iridescent scales, and there was a sheen like burnished gold to the hollows of his eyes. The gold had rubbed off on his sleeve, so it was probably eye paint; she wasn't sure about the feathers or scales.

She hadn't meant to offer to take him to Kondala City. It was clear on the other side of the continent. But if they went by mirror, it would be a detour of less than a day. Even if she'd never traveled by mirror before, she was used to making long journeys, and it only scared her a little to be that far from home. Anyway, she was a lot more confident in her own ability to get home than in Eshu's.

When she'd finished her tea and porridge, Rukha gave her cup and bowl to an old man headed down to the kitchens and struck out from the tower along the water.

By sunset, it had been grisly enough, but in the crisp new light of day, the scene on the beach defied description. Rukha tried to name what she was seeing, but her brain shied away from the task. She saw the bodies at the high tide mark, and she catalogued them practically: red cotton trousers on a leg. Skull, most of the flesh gone; black mat of hair clinging to a patch of rotting scalp. Hand, silver rings, crab picking at the fingers.

If she wanted to be here and not go mad, she couldn't even start to think of these as people. She had to think of them as things, scraps and objects that had used to belong to someone, or she'd start screaming.

Survivors combed the shoreline, gathering up remains and laying them out in long, long rows in the streets. She caught sight of Gull a few streets away, driving off stray dogs with a stick. When she looked out into the water, she saw a raft tethered to a buoy. There, divers went plunging into the sea one by one, only to surface minutes later with pieces of their old lives in their arms.

While Rukha watched, Shell broke the surface and flung a net full of something shiny onto the raft. Jewelry, Rukha thought, or money—things the drowned didn't need anymore. Shell hung onto the edge for a while, shoulders heaving with each breath, then climbed up on the raft and dove again.

Rukha made her way over to Gull and asked, "Can I help?"

He looked up and said, "If you see anyone, drag them in. I'm looking for people we knew."

Anyone. There was that unthinkable thought again—that every waterlogged hand or foot here had been someone's hand or foot; that those rotting mouths had laughed, once, and those gnawed legs had danced. Rukha blinked away tears and nodded, then went to the water's edge to see what she could find.

By noon, the sun was high, and the stench was unbelievable. Saltwater had shriveled Rukha's hands. She'd hauled in parts for what she thought was probably twenty people, but they didn't all match, so it might've been more. She got used to picking seaweed off of decaying faces, pulling aside shirts and gowns to show recognizable tattoos.

At noon, the divers came in with their hauls, and everyone helped carry the bodies up to a deep pit far away from the tower. There, they said their goodbyes and burned their dead.

Even after drying in the sun, the dead were still soaked through with salt water. They took a long time to burn.

Shell fed wood to the fire long after almost everyone had headed back to the tower, and Rukha stayed to keep her company. There was something absent in her eyes, as though in her heart she was scanning a distant horizon in search of a sail. "I dove down to her house today," she said as she watched the flames. Rukha knew that she was talking about her daughter, the one with the green glass ring. "Went in through the kitchen window. I thought for sure I'd find her there in her kitchen, with the fish nipping at her toes. But I looked in every room, and she wasn't there."

"Maybe she sailed," offered Rukha. "Before the earthquake. Gull said—"

"No, she's down there," said Shell firmly. "Just got to keep looking until I find her."

They made their way back to the tower, where a woman with grey streaks in her hair was measuring a crack in the tower wall. "About another finger's width since yesterday," she pronounced when she saw Shell coming. "It's going to come down sooner or later."

Shell stuck her thumbs in the waist of her trousers and leaned back to consider the crack. "Was hoping it'd be later. How long do we have?"

"Might be as much as a week, if the weather holds. If we

get more storms, though, might be sooner." The woman started winding her tailor's tape around her hand. "What do you think—comb the wizards' rooms and see what we can salvage, or leave them?"

"Salvage," Shell decided. "Get everyone out, bed them down somewhere else, and see what we can haul out before the tower falls. Just the necessities. Food, money, medicines if we can find any. Things that we can chuck on a cart and haul away."

"We should take the mirror," said Rukha. "We might be able to use it."

"Maybe." Shell looked doubtful. "Food and money first, though. Gull!"

It took a moment for her son to look up; he wasn't any more used to the name than Rukha was to hers. When he realized he was being called, though, he jogged over. "What's the news?"

"Rain here says we need to start making plans to leave the tower. Why don't you gather up some people to scout the countryside. See if there's any good caves, or anyone who will let us camp in their barn."

He nodded, but he was frowning in a way that made Rukha think he'd been contemplating this issue for some time. "I'll get some people together. But we can't keep doing this, Ma. When An—when our friends get back from Lalani, we need to start thinking about where we're going to go."

Shell's face might as well have been made of stone. "I'm not leaving until I find her."

"That's fine," he said, and the ache in his voice hurt to hear. "I just—there's too many bodies in that ocean. The kids can't wait here with all this death while you look for her."

It felt wrong to listen in on this conversation. While the three of them debated leaving, Rukha sidled away and into the tower, where she found that most of the children had spent the day salvaging from nearby buildings. They'd sorted their findings in three piles, and the boy from the kitchen was taking inventory with a couple of others who looked like they might be family.

The wizard sat to one side, reading a book that looked like it had been taken from the library. Same blued leather binding with gold accents. As he read, he picked scales off his face and set them down to one side. Most came off clean, but he hissed as one of them came off with skin attached.

"Hey. Eshu." He looked up, then slid a feather into the book to mark his place. "Um, should you be doing that?"

"Doing—"

"The scales."

"Oh." He laughed, a touch wryly. "They're not mine. Or I suppose they *are* mine, but they're only for decoration. Glued on." He offered one for her examination; it glittered and flashed in the light, violet to blue to pale sunset orange. "I don't usually leave them this long. They're meant to be taken off after a few hours."

"They look nice," said Rukha; it felt like the sort of thing she was supposed to say.

It was hard to know what you were supposed to say when you'd spent all morning carrying bodies through the streets, and being around living people again made it hard to forget that those people you were carrying had also been alive not that long ago. She'd thrown people's hands into the pit like they were kindling. *Don't think about it*, she told herself. Her chest was tight.

After a moment, Eshu said, "Thank you," and Rukha snapped back to the rotunda again.

She forced her tone brisk and upbeat. "We're going to have to get out of the tower soon. So I thought we should either try to go through the mirror, or carry the mirror out. *Can* you carry a mirror out, if you want to travel through it? Because it felt like the floor mosaic was kind of a cosmic map, so I thought maybe it was part of the magic, but I don't know anything about magic. So." She shrugged.

"You can carry it out," said Eshu. "You have to install it before you can use it again, but my—someone I used to know built mirrors. I remember the songs."

He rose slowly to his feet, putting a hand out to the wall to steady himself. Rukha came over to offer her shoulder, but Eshu waved her away. "I'm already feeling much better," he said, which Rukha could tell was a lie. "I just need to get used to walking on it."

"I heard what Shell told you last night about staying off your foot," Rukha countered. "You don't want me pulling down the mirror without you. You think I'll break it."

"No," said Eshu, with a look that said *Yes*. "I just. I want to be there. To make sure it's done properly."

"Right now? Unsteady as you are? You're more of a danger to that mirror than I am." Folding her arms, Rukha pulled herself up to her full height. Even with her boots on, with Eshu bent over in obvious pain, she only came up to his armpits. *Stubborn beanpole wizard.* "If there's anything special that needs to be done, tell me. I'll do it. I can follow directions."

He looked away, to where a little girl stood apart from the other children. She was sucking on the end of her messy black braid— Rukha had used to do that, too, when she was nervous. *I wonder if any of her family is here. I wonder who's taking care of her.*

At last, Eshu sighed and met Rukha's eyes again. "A traveling mirror has to travel covered. It's a practical concern, not a superstition. A covered mirror isn't available in the Mirrorlands. No one can pass through it. If someone tries to use the mirror while you're carrying it, one or both of you could be hurt."

"To say nothing of the mirror."

"The mirror, too," Eshu agreed. "But mirrors can be remade. People can't—at least, not without more powerful songs than I know."

Don't even let yourself start to wonder if he could've stitched together those people you burned. He can't. He just said as much. "Got it. Cover the mirror." Rukha made a little soldier's salute, fist to heart, then headed for the stairs.

Along the way, she scavenged a few blankets that hadn't already been stripped from the bedrooms. She hesitated over one of the offices, which had a gorgeous map of the continent on the wall. *They say the tower's going to fall anyway*, she told herself, then pulled down the picture frame and pried the map free of its matting. When she'd done that, she saw that it wasn't painted on paper, but on incredibly soft leather. Rukha let herself wonder for a moment what kind of creature had a hide that big and that smooth, then rolled up the map and stowed it with her blankets. She took the etching tools and pocket watch, too, for good measure.

Then she climbed to the mirror room again. Sunlight streamed through the windows and struck fire from every line of gold; it shone on the amber chips and kindled them to embers.

It was a little sad that something this beautiful was going to break into smithereens on the streets below. She wished more people had gotten a chance to see it.

By daylight, she could see the intricate frame around the mirror, all worked with cascading stars and moons fading from crescent to full. With that metal frame, the mirror was heavier than she'd thought, and she had to lower it gently onto a nest of blankets to be sure she'd be able to lug it downstairs. Once she'd gotten it horizontal, she wrapped it up so that not a sliver of light could touch the surface. Then she bundled up the ends of the blankets and dragged the mirror carefully down the long stair.

She found Eshu waiting for her at the bottom, looking worried to distraction at the muffled bump and clatter of the frame on the stairs. "Look, it's fine," she said, unwrapping the mirror to show him. And it was fine, too—not a single crack in the glass, not a single shooting star out of place.

He unclenched his hands from his robe and gave her a haunted little smile. "Thank you. I know it's stupid to worry about a mirror like this, when there are people here. I just—this is my best way home."

"Well, if this won't get you home, there's always walking."

Eshu wrinkled his nose. "I try not to do that."

"Not to *walk*?"

"I'm a scholar," he said, sounding very put-upon. "A long walk means detouring to the teashop on the way home from the library."

"I'm a scholar, too," Rukha pointed out. After the last few days, it almost felt good to be annoyed at someone just for being high-handed and arrogant. "Maybe I can't walk through mirrors, but I studied mathematics and navigation and geography and the natural sciences. I have a degree. And maybe it's different for wizards, but speaking as a geographer, I *walk*."

For a moment, Eshu looked as though he might try to defend himself. But eventually, he slid his hands into his pockets and let his shoulders drop. "I'm sorry. I've been a prick."

"A little bit. It's been stressful."

"I'll try to do better."

Rukha was still trying to figure out how you answered something like that—just *Thank you*, or maybe a firm *See that you do?*—when the boy with the logbook came over to rescue her. "How do you spell 'mirror'?" he asked. "I have to put it in the inventory. And how many blankets is that?"

Then the lunch hour was over, and the band of survivors dispersed again. Some went back to the water to pull out more bodies, and others struck out inland to search for shelter.

Rukha wanted to go with the scouts, but in the end, she stayed behind to keep an eye on the children. They passed the time finishing up the inventory, and when that was done, they started hauling food up to the rotunda so that it would be easier to carry out. Rukha took charge of the big sacks of grain and beans, while the younger folks made a chain to pass up onions and garlic and jars of honey and pickled pears.

All the while, Eshu sat leafing through his book, singing softly beneath the chatter of the children and the rhythmic thump of supplies hitting the tile. Rukha felt the deep rumble of his voice in her chest, like the purr of a cat or an airship engine. It wove through her nerves like a shining thread, leaving calm in its wake—real calm, not just locking her feelings in a drawer while she got on with things.

Between trips to the pantry, Rukha saw Eshu unwrap his foot. She almost set down her bag of barley to tell him off, but then his pale sole flashed in his ebony hands, and she thought that the wound didn't look half as bad as she'd thought it would. After a moment of looking, she left him alone.

By the time the scouts and the salvage crews came back, Rukha was starting to teach the older kids trigonometry, and Eshu's foot had healed without so much as a scar.

"There's nowhere close by that can take all of us," said Gull over dinner (fish and rice soup, tart with curls of preserved lime rind). "A few farms can take five or ten of us, if we're bringing our own food and we're willing to work, but there's nowhere set up for forty-three." It was the first time Rukha had heard someone put a number to the survivors, and it hit her like a blow—out of a city of thousands, there were only forty-three left.

Only forty-three who stayed, she told herself. *There are also the people who went by ship to Lalani. And they said there were others who scattered up and down the shore. It's not as bad as it sounds.*

It was still bad enough.

"We'll get the children out, at least," Shell decided. "They'll be safer on the farms. But someone has to keep watch for ships. I'll stay."

"I want to stay," said the girl who'd been sucking her braid earlier. The wet, pointed tip made a dark patch on her shirt. "I don't want to go to a farm."

"There will be rabbits and ducks on the farm," Gull said, light and singsong. "Don't you want to see the rabbits and ducks?"

If there was a right thing to say, that wasn't it. A black rage passed across the girl's face. She screamed, high and sharp and righteous, "I don't want ducks! *I want my mama!*" Then she burst into sobs and fled, shoving through the half-open tower door and into the gathering darkness.

For a second, everyone sat stunned, and then some of the other children started crying in that lost, helpless way that couldn't be soothed. Before the room could break into total chaos, Rukha sprang from her seat on the floor and snatched up a lantern. "I'll find her," she promised. Then she went pelting into the street.

She scanned quickly for the girl, listening for sobs or screams or pattering feet. The cries of seabirds and the incessant roar of waves made it hard to make anything out, but Rukha thought she caught a choked little hiccup from a ruined alleyway.

It wouldn't help to charge in after her. Rukha slowed her steps, calling ahead as she went, "It's me, Fern. You helped carry things with me today, remember? I saw you were sad, and I wanted to make sure my friend was all right. Can you tell me if you're all right?"

She couldn't remember what the girl had said to call her. Something innocuous and forgettable, Water or Cloud or Flower; someone had taught her not to give her name to strangers when she was afraid. But it meant Rukha didn't know what to call out to her now to make sure she was actually following a child and not a bird with a hiccupping cry.

"I'm going to come around the corner now," she said aloud. "Don't be afraid, all right? It's just me. You can be sad all you want, but you don't have to be afraid." She came around the corner lantern first. This close to the fissure, huge pieces of shell brick wall lay scattered across the paving stones, and they cast long shadows that made it hard to look for shapes. Rukha kept her eyes on the ground, scanning for a flash of yellow trousers or the long tail of a braid.

She found the girl curled up in the dark hole of a doorway, arms around her dirty knees. "Hey," said Rukha, coming to sit beside her and setting the lantern between them. She hooked her arms over her knees and looked down. The girl didn't meet her eyes. "We were worried about you."

"Where's my mama?" the girl asked. "No one will tell me where she is."

"Maybe they don't know," said Rukha.

"Well, they *should*!" Her voice was small, but it had a force of determination in it that Rukha respected.

"They don't know where a lot of people are, and it scares them, too. And sometimes, when people are scared, they try to pretend they aren't by acting like they know things they don't. And sometimes that just makes other people feel worse." Rukha leaned back, putting her hands down on the edge of the doorstep and stretching out her legs.

Slowly, the girl uncurled a little. She sniffled and wiped her nose on her shirt. "They don't want me to make a fuss, but I just want to cry and cry."

"It's all right if you cry on me. I won't tell anyone."

Then with a gulping sob, the girl threw herself at Rukha's chest and wept.

They sat like that for a long while, Rukha stroking the girl's hair and watching the alleyway. After a few minutes, Shell came around the corner with another lamp, but when she saw them, she just nodded and ducked away again. *She's a mother*, Rukha thought. *She's probably done this a thousand times. Maybe never at the end of the world, but she's held a child who can't stop crying and tried not to let herself cry, too.*

Not that this was the end of the world.

Slowly, the lamp burned down, and the girl's tears faded and dried. Her breathing slowed and became even, until gradually Rukha realized that she had fallen asleep.

She hitched the girl up on her hip and lifted the guttering lamp in her free hand. That was apparently all the jostling it needed, though, because the flame promptly died in a bath of oil.

By now, the stars and the half-moon were out, and they shed enough light to help Rukha navigate the maze of fallen masonry. She hummed to the girl as she walked, one of the old capstan shanties that her mother had sung to her in the cradle, and tried to focus on putting her feet right.

Something made Rukha falter. She couldn't have said what it was—not a stray-dog growl, not a flicker of movement out of the corner of her eye. Just the sudden feeling that the space behind her wasn't empty anymore.

She turned, and there was someone standing there.

In the darkness, it was impossible to make anything out except the person's outline: tall, cowled, with lank black hair spilling from beneath the hood. The stranger was a woman, Rukha thought, but she wasn't sure why. "Hello," Rukha tried. "Is this your place?"

It felt like the stranger smiled. "It is now. What's your name?"

Rukha Masreen was on her tongue. She'd spent her whole life answering to that name. But then she looked down at the scattered stones, and she remembered. "You can call me Fern," she said.

"Fern." The stranger seemed to savor that name for a moment. In her mouth, it sounded dry and harsh as a crow's cry. She tilted her head, and Rukha glimpsed a mask beneath the cowl: white and eyeless, like porcelain or bone.

Rukha's blood went cold. She knew who walked the night in a white-bone mask, stealing over battlefields and villages harrowed by fire. She knew who asked strangers their names in a voice like a crow's.

With a yell, Rukha swung the lamp hard at the Crowtaker's face, then took off sprinting for the wizards' tower before she could register whether she'd connected.

"Fern, what happened?" the girl asked, squirming in Rukha's arm.

Rukha just gripped her tighter and kept running. "Tell you later!" Her boot nails rang on the paving stones, and dogs began to bark from the alleyways as she passed. She ignored stealth, ignored caution, and poured on every bit of speed she could muster.

The door to the tower slammed open, and there was Gull with a harpoon and a lamp; Rukha barreled straight past him and into the rotunda, where people were just settling down to sleep. "Close the door!" she yelled.

"What happened?" This time, it was Shell.

"I saw the Crowtaker," Rukha said. She set the girl down and went to shove her shoulder against the door.

"Close the fucking door!" said Shell, and between her, Gull, and Rukha, they got it closed and bolted.

With the door shut at last, Rukha sank to the floor and sucked in a deep breath. White spots swam before her vision. She realized she was still holding the ring handle of the lantern, but when she held it up to examine, she saw that the glass was shattered. The edges were black with something that looked like soot. Part of her wanted to touch it. The rest of her knew better.

"You saw the Crowtaker," said Eshu, blinking. He was the only one in the room who looked more confused than afraid. "What, exactly, is the Crowtaker?"

"She's Death," said Shell.

"Not—not exactly Death," said Rukha, coughing. Her throat was still tight and raw. "Not just ordinary death, like everybody gets. She comes when things are bad. Plagues. Battles. Earthquakes." *Whatever happened here.*

"Ships fated to sink," Shell agreed. "You see her on the shore when you set sail, and you know you aren't coming back."

Slowly, Eshu nodded. "I'd heard children's stories, back in Usbaran. The locals sometimes called themselves different names when the weather changed. They said they didn't want to draw the storm's attention."

"Not sure it helps anything," said Shell. "They say the Crowtaker knows who she wants, and you can't hide from her if she has her eye on you. But until our luck changes, no sense calling her down on us."

It helped a little, talking about the Crowtaker like she was a story instead of someone that Rukha had just hit with a lamp. But the broken lamp was still in her hand, and she had forty-four people who were afraid and needed comfort as much as she did. "I don't think she's coming for us. I think she's just here. Like a scavenger."

"We should go tonight," said the woman who'd been measuring the cracks earlier. Rain, she'd called herself. "This place is unstable. Maybe what you saw was a warning. We've already got everything upstairs; we should go."

"I don't want to go back outside," said the girl Rukha had carried. She was chewing on the end of her braid again, and her eyes were big with fear.

"I'm going to keep you safe," Rukha promised. "I hit her with the lamp, see? She's not going to get you."

The girl didn't look reassured. "What if she takes you?"

"I'm not the only one who can drive her off. See that man there?" Rukha pointed to Eshu, who looked alarmed at being singled out. "He's a wizard, and he's going to sing songs to keep you safe."

"We're all going to keep each other safe," Shell agreed. "But Rain is right. Better to treat this as a warning. Get ourselves out with everything we can carry, tonight. Gull, Cloud, get the cart. Everyone else, get ready to carry."

They loaded up the cart by lantern-light, throwing on sacks of grain and boxes full of jars of preserves and clarified butter. Shell's salvaged jewelry and cash went into baskets, padded with children's dolls and blankets to keep them from jingling. Last of all came the mirror, swaddled in quilts for travel, although Shell gave it a dark look as Rukha and Eshu eased it into the cart.

The man who went by Cloud had been keeping a few horses fed on leftover hay, and while the rest of them loaded supplies into the cart, he took a lamp into the darkness. He came back leading two horses to hitch between the traces. "I let the rest go," he said. "They'll make their way somehow."

Then they left, a long procession of lanterns under the moonlight.

Eshu, who walked close by Rukha, looked weary and anxious but not in pain. He leaned in as they passed out of the city limits, and she shifted her lantern to her other hand to let him closer. "Do you actually want me to cast some kind of warding spell?" he asked, low.

"Couldn't hurt," she answered. "Everyone's afraid, you know? Even if there's nothing to be afraid of, it helps to have something between you and the darkness. That's why we closed the door, back in the tower."

"I was wondering," he said. "It didn't seem like a door would keep Death out, if she wanted to be in."

"But it made us feel better."

"I suppose it did." He looked thoughtful for a long moment, his steps measured and his face lightly creased with a frown. Then, slowly at first and then with gathering force, he began to sing.

He sang a song of silver armor, of high fortress walls that had never been conquered and cliffs that defied the sea. He sang of shield and dragonscale, of shell and stone and steel. He sang of rooftops shedding rain and hot tea driving off the chill of winter, and of fevers breaking in a blanket's warm embrace.

Rukha wasn't sure what Eshu's songs would do, if something came after them in the darkness. She wasn't sure if there was any magic at all in his words, or if he was just weaving nonsense into the shape of a spell because she'd asked him to. But it made her feel better to hear him singing, and she supposed that was what mattered.

The walk from Sharis to the farmlands was longer than Rukha had remembered, and everyone was already exhausted. Rukha let a few children ride on her back when their legs got tired, but mostly, everyone walked in silence. Every now and then, Rukha heard a bird calling in the darkness: the harsh laugh of a ruddy nightcatcher, the minor-key trill of a gossamer dove. Other birds that she'd forgotten the names of, or never learned.

In that quiet, it was easy to hear the crack behind them and the loud crash that followed. Everyone paused, straining to see what had happened through the long darkness. "No good," Shell muttered at last. "We'll take a look in the morning."

As they started walking again, though, Rukha couldn't help imagining the tower fallen, and the mosaic cosmos crushed on the streets below.

CHAPTER 4: THROUGH THE MIRROR

Eshu woke in a heap of straw, with a yellow-eyed barn cat casually washing her front paw on his chest. He groaned and stretched, which startled the cat enough to make her dig her rear claws into his stomach and then bolt into the shadows.

"Ow," he said to no one in particular. Picking straw from his robes, Eshu found a clear patch of planking to kneel on, then began the dawn prayer. *Njo, Far-Traveler, she who knows the way, be my guide and compass on my journey.* His calf muscles burned with the strain of last night's walk, and his back felt as though someone had welded all of his vertebrae together. His eyes ached down to the nerves at their roots.

When the prayer was over, he crawled over to the ladder and down from the loft. A pair of kittens looked up from a play-fight as he hobbled past, and a spotted pig whuffed amiably at him from a stout bamboo pen.

Down to the pump, to get enough tepid water to wash his face. There wasn't any soap, let alone hair cream or lotion. No one in the north part of Nanjeer seemed to worry about getting ashy. *At least there was soap, back in Sharis. I wonder if we remembered to take any with us.*

When he felt something vaguely approaching awake, Eshu chased down the scent of smoke until he found the morning's campsite. The others had set up some distance from the barn, in a fallow clearing close to the road. "Tea's up," said Rain, passing him a cup as he sauntered into the circle around the fire.

"Thank you. Did the tower fall? Do we know?" he asked.

"Hard to be sure from this far away, but I think so," she said. "Shell and a few others are going back today to wait for our ship. And to dive again. They'll know more when they get back."

He sat down heavily beside her on a felled tree, sipping his tea. "Rain isn't your name, is it."

"No," she answered. "But it's what I'm called."

"What did you do, before your city fell?"

Rain smiled. He noticed that she had a little notch in one of her front teeth. "Tailor. I did piecework when I was younger, but my wife and I saved up and opened our own shop for fancy custom work. I put the clothes together and do repairs, and she does the embroidery and beading. Well. Did." Her gaze fell to the dirt, and her fingertips stroked the handle on her cup. "All under the water now, of course. Maybe with what everyone's salvaged, we'll be able to start fresh somewhere else."

"Where's your wife now?" he asked. He'd learned to be delicate with such questions—so few people knew the answer, and fewer wanted to offer it—but her grief didn't seem to be a widow's grief.

"She was on a silk-buying trip to Kulmeni when the city fell," said Rain. "She's probably on the road home already. Sweet Sisters, I wish she had something better to come home to."

Eshu didn't know much about the Sisters, but he understood the impulse to prayer. "Do you know why this happened?" he asked.

"I don't know anything. Shell thought it must be the wizards, but they've never been anything but kind to me when they came to my shop. Never so much as a harsh word when the work was late." She laughed, faintly self-mocking. "Not to say that it means anything, that they were kind to me. That's the ugly truth, isn't it? You never really know a person until they hurt you."

Eshu drained his cup. "Not everything that's ugly is true."

"I suppose not." Rain stood and held out a hand for his cup. He passed it over. "Anyway. Thank you for your song, last night. For keeping us safe."

Then she put the cups into a bucket with the other dirty dishes and took the lot of them to the pump to wash clean. *I should go help her*, thought Eshu at first, but then he thought better of it. She'd taken the dishes because she wanted a reason to end the conversation, and she wouldn't thank him for following her.

Alone now, Eshu went to the cart to start hauling the mirror down. It was massive and ungainly, and even through the quilts, he could feel that some of the stars decorating the edges had bent a little during the journey. But the mirror's surface didn't feel cracked, which he supposed was the main thing.

Something large fell from a nearby tree, and Eshu nearly leapt out of his skin before he realized it was Fern. He let go of the mirror, which clanked back down into the bed of the cart. "Fucking—fuck!"

"You're a lot less poetic when you're startled," she observed. Her hair stood up in irregular curls and waves, with leaves tangled into the denser snarls.

"Did you just go to sleep in that tree? Like a cat?"

"I had a hammock," she said. "And a rescue line. Do people not go camping in Usbaran?"

"Not in the trees."

"They're missing out." After examining the cart a moment, Fern clambered nimbly up over the side and into the cart bed. "All right! Let's get this thing set up." She heaved up the back end of the mirror, waiting for Eshu to take his end again.

Between the two of them, they managed to get the mirror onto the ground, then they stood it up beside the cart. The earth here was uneven, carved by horses' hooves and scattered with loose stone and clods of earth, so they drove the mirror's elegant claw feet deep into the dirt to keep it upright. Eshu couldn't help clicking his tongue at it, the way his mother used to do at unripe fruit in merchants' displays. "This is not an ideal place to install a mirror," he said. "They should really be set up on a foundation of stone, out of the wind and rain."

"We could put it in the barn," Fern offered. "Dirt foundation, but at least there's a roof overhead."

"I suppose. For now. Until we find literally anywhere else."

They carried the mirror to the barn, each with a hand cupped under the bottom edge and Eshu steadying the top. Once they'd got it set upright, Eshu began easing the bent stars straight again. It kept his hands occupied while he tried to remember what Tuuri had showed him about how to turn a mirror into a traveling mirror.

First, you have to tell the mirror where it stands in the universe. Tuuri had preferred to work with runes, painting interlocking circles in shining ink and scribing them with words from a dying language. Eshu had once seen him pour molten gold into channels carved in stone, slowly shaping metal into meaning. That was Tuuri's habit, to speak in ways that couldn't be argued or taken back.

It didn't help anything to think about him. If he hadn't walked into that party, calm as you please, Eshu wouldn't be thinking about him now.

He began to sing the scent of hay, the smell of pig shit close and foul. He sang the gaps between the boards; he sang shafts of sunlight through them, and dust dancing in golden motes. He sang the kittens with their sharp blue eyes, the black-dappled barn cat with her back claws like thorns, the bamboo ladder and the rakes and stakes and rope. *Remember this,* he told the mirror. *Remember where the door of you opens.*

The mirror's face shone, the way a lover's face shone with a longing to be kissed. Eshu spread his hand over the surface, watching the light trickle between his fingers in streams of silver.

Then he let his hand pass through, and into the cold desert

beyond.

This was the hard part. The Mirrorlands were Nowhere, and right now, the other side of the mirror only opened onto nowhere. If he wanted to be able to find this mirror again, he had to create a landscape on the other side where he could find it.

He put aside Tuuri and his snide, certain runes. Instead, he thought of Mnoro, whom he'd always admired as a storyteller. Mnoro, who crafted hundreds of little mayfly worlds from adjective and metaphor, from glass and moss and butterfly wings. *She'd tell me to anchor the world on an image. Something that I wouldn't forget. A spill of red flowers, a cliff, a wall of thorns.*

Eshu stepped through the mirror, singing as he did of the farm beside the road to Sharis. He sang the barn from its corner posts to its rafters, from the ladder to the loft strewn with straw. He sang a silver pump streaming with clean, fresh water, and a tree with Fern's lantern hanging from one bough. He sang the cracks where the lamp had struck the Crowtaker's face, and he mended them with light until they shone.

At last, as the shapes of bean rows raveled out into the distance, he took a deep breath of the Mirrorlands air. It still tasted sharp, like ice and lightning—but here, in the place he'd built, there was the scent of straw, too. There was a faint aroma of pig shit that he'd brought into the Mirrorlands like a talisman to ward off the darkness.

Now, to find out if it had worked.

When he turned around, the mirror stood in the frame of the barn door, a bright panel of light in the gloom. He dipped his fingers through the surface as though through clear water—and as soon as he did, someone seized his hand and pulled him the rest of the way through.

"Don't scare me like that again!" said Fern fiercely, pulling him into a crushing hug. Her arms were powerful, for such a small woman, and they were at exactly the right height to make his ribs constrict. "I thought I'd lost you—I told you I'd go with you, and I had no idea how to follow you—"

He patted her shoulder awkwardly. "I just had to prepare the mirror's housing on the other side. I'd never done this before, and—"

"You've never *done* this before? I thought you were an expert!"

"My lover was an expert," he snapped, "and apparently I'm just an expert at dating assholes."

"Oh," she said, and let him go. "Well."

"Now, let's go through the mirror and never talk about him again," said Eshu.

"Are you sure you don't want to—"

"Completely fucking sure."

"Got it." She glanced out through the barn door. "How long do you think this will take? Maybe we should tell Shell we're planning to poke around in there."

Eshu shrugged. "With the mirror-ways broken, I genuinely don't know. Maybe as little as an hour. Maybe as much as a millennium. Somewhere in that range."

"Right, so I should definitely tell them not to worry if they don't see us for a while." She stepped out of the barn for a few minutes.

When she came back, she had her pack and her map case slung over her shoulders. "You were joking about being trapped behind the mirror for a thousand years, right?" she asked.

"You don't *have* to come with me."

"No, I'm going to." Fern squared herself up to the mirror as though she meant to punch it. This part was hard, too, if you'd never traveled by mirror before: looking at your own reflection and seeing the mirror first as a window, then as a curtain, and then as a door.

"Sometimes, it helps to close your eyes," Eshu offered. "Don't look at the mirror at all. Just trust that it will work, then put your hand out until it goes through."

"Will it feel any different?" Fern laid her hand on the surface of the mirror, studying the gap between her palm and the silver behind the glass. "When it goes through, I mean."

"You'll be able to feel the air on the other side. It will be colder and drier. You might feel wind on one side but not the other, and your body will know something's wrong. You might freeze, but if you do, it's important not to open your eyes. If you let yourself forget for even a moment that you can pass through the mirror, the magic will fail."

"So it's based on faith." Her lips quirked. She met his gaze in the mirror, then ran her hands through her hair to comb out the leaves. "You're Njowa, right? When you pray in the morning, you pray to the Far Traveler?"

"I don't pray *to* her, as though I'm posting a letter. But yes, I pray."

"Do you think she was real? Or just a story?"

A part of him wanted to give the wizards' answer: that all real things were only stories cloaked in the mantle of truth. That *real* was a matter not of fact, but of belief. But he'd been Njowa longer than he'd been a wizard, and with Fern looking up at him with that earnest curiosity in her eyes, the Njowa answer felt more true. "Njo isn't a story—she's the anvil on which the story bends. We're the story. And we're real."

"I like that," she said. Fern smiled, for what felt like the first time since the whole world had gone to blazes. Still smiling, she slid her palms through the mirror and stepped into the world beyond. Then there was nothing to do but follow her.

When Eshu emerged in the shadow of a barn he'd built, he found that Fern had unrolled an enormous map painted on soft leather, and she was examining it by the lantern's light. "It looks like the closest cities big enough to have wizards are Lalani and Ranit. If you go further out, there are more—"

"Geography doesn't work quite like that, here. It's based on familiarity, you could say. Impressions." *The cognitive locus*, his teachers would have called it. The seed idea of a place around which the pearl of memory was built. Not that it would help Fern to use wizards' words. "You know when you're on a long airship journey and you have a stopover in an unfamiliar city? And you get down from the landing and step into the marketplace, and something about the smell of onions frying strikes you. Or maybe the way they tile their fountains, or the sound of someone practicing scales on a flute like you've never heard before. And when you leave, whenever you hear that city's name again, it's all onions and tiles and scales."

"I know what you mean," said Fern thoughtfully. "In geography, we study something like that. Whether there's something meaningfully distinct about a place that's recognizable, that's separate from the accident of all its people coming together in that particular place at that particular time. Something like the character of the place? I'm not explaining it very well. Hard to talk about these things without too much jargon."

"No, that's exactly it. Something like the character of the place. If you want to go somewhere in particular through a mirror, you have to know the place's character."

Fern began rolling up her map again. Once that was done, she slid it into a scroll case at her side. "Well, how about Kondala City, then? You must know that place pretty well. Tell me about it. Help me to find it."

"Kondala City." *Home.* A wave of longing welled up in his chest until he was dizzy with it. He remembered his mother's house again, the herbs in the rafters and the faded rugs and the way her warm, moist flatbread felt in his hands. The smell of her morning coffee, brewed with cinnamon and ndua berries. He could almost taste it.

He shook his head to clear it. Fern watched him expectantly, with her arms folded and her chin high. She was counting on him to be their navigator in this strange land, and he couldn't fail her now. *It must be hard for her. She's probably used to being the one who knows the way, or the one who finds or makes it.*

So he sang her Kondala, the city in the mountains, with its steep winding roads and flowers climbing its white walls. At first, his voice trembled and cracked, but he sang her the great gardens at the city's heart until he found his strength again. He sang the trees with boughs like fans, pouring tufted blossoms in early spring; he sang the plums and pomegranates and the ndua bushes with their leathery leaves. The Hall of Ways curtained in green, the high bell towers of Njo's Rest, the coffee houses humming with conversation; the way the day's last light struck the new copper roofs on the houses lining the mountainsides, so bright that it was nearly blinding. He sang until tears tracked down his cheeks, until the refrain of his song was only *Asha, Kiga, Sunba, Mother*.

Beyond the light of their lamp, the empty desert stretched to infinity.

Eshu wiped his eyes. "Kondala City doesn't want to be found," he said at last. "They might have shuttered their mirrors, or—it's possible that the city has changed enough that it doesn't recognize itself in my song. That's not to—it's not a person. It doesn't think. It doesn't *want* things. It's just—"

"I know," said Fern. "They're the best words you have to explain it."

"Right." His chest was tight, but he forced himself to breathe down to his belly. It didn't help, really. "If—if it had worked, we would have seen a panel of light. Like our mirror. One of the mirrors in the Hall of Ways."

"Oh." Fern scanned the horizon, where the faintly brighter blue suggested a sunrise that would never come. "Is there a way of finding a nonspecific mirror?"

"Yes, but I don't know it. Usually, you can see mirrors on every hillside. If I wanted to go wandering, I could walk through any door I cared to. We used to—it doesn't matter." Another deep breath. He swallowed down the memory of walking arm in arm with Tuuri under strange skies. "This emptiness is new."

"Hmm." Fern looked around once again, then swung her pack off of her back and started pulling out a hammer and several sharp metal stakes.

Eshu blinked. "What are you—"

"Climbing," she answered, and started hammering a stake into the trunk of the tree he'd just built.

"Climbing," he repeated. "Why?"

"I think—" and the hammer came down "—if I can get high enough—" and again "—I might be able to see the terrain better."

"I already told you that the geography here is meaningless. It's a landscape of impressions, not—"

"You did, but unless you have a better idea, I'm working with what I know." Using the stakes like a ladder, Fern scrambled up into the tree's lowest boughs and was quickly lost to view. Now and then, he heard her hammering another stake into the tree trunk, presumably where the going had become tricky.

Without her there, the Mirrorlands felt colder and emptier. A gust of wind stirred the white sand into dancing whorls and sent it pattering against the walls of the barn.

Eshu watched the darkness beyond the lamplight, searching for that shimmer of not-quite-shadow until his eyes ached.

After what felt like a long, long time, he heard a creak of branches and a rustling of leaves. A few minutes later, Fern dropped to the ground a little way from him. "There's a mirror, way over there," she said, and she pointed in a direction that looked the same as any other. "It's in the bottom of an arroyo, but you can see it from the top of the tree. A sort of oval of light."

Eshu wasn't sure what an arroyo was, but Fern seemed to know, and he believed her.

They set out together over the sands, Fern enthusiastically speculating on the minerals that composed the black ridges and the way the silver trees might have spread and sustained themselves. "It's obvious that there's a spring somewhere in the mountains, or possibly several springs," she said. "My guess is that this black rock is just porous enough to let water drain through, and there's a major aquifer somewhere below our feet—"

"It's a dreamscape," said Eshu. He wished he didn't sound quite so desperate. "You can't just apply science to it."

"Then explain the arroyos. They're all more or less perpendicular to the mountains. I wonder what the rain is like here."

"It never rains here. The sun never rises. It's a void beyond time and space."

"It's hydrologically interesting."

Despite himself, Eshu took some relief in the bickering. The cold and darkness of the desert seemed much less terrible when Fern was darting ahead to collect rock and leaf samples or pausing to correct the scale on a hand-drawn map. She seemed to love the eccentricities of the Mirrorlands, and not to be unsettled by them. She made them seem like a place that could be known.

After what felt like an hour or two of walking, the faint gully they were following opened into a valley of black gravel and low stands of silver trees. There was water here, just a trickle almost too small to call a stream, and Fern stoppered a little in a glass vial. "I might find a microscope eventually," she said, when Eshu gave her a look. "I want to see if there are tiny creatures in it."

At the end of the valley, on a stone that jutted up from the gravel bed, there hung a mirror that shone with a cool, silvery light. Eshu's heart leapt at the sight of it. "There's no cognitive locus," he said, more to himself than to Fern. "No way of knowing where this leads."

"Well, then we'll just have to walk through."

"Is walking how geographers solve all of their problems?"

"Anything we can't solve with trigonometry!" she said brightly. Then, visibly nerving herself up, she stepped through the oval of light and into the world beyond.

A hungry wind hissed through the boughs of the silver trees. Eshu cast an anxious look around at the valley—the arroyo—and then followed Fern through.

He emerged into a crystal-lined cavern, so cramped that he had to stoop to keep from hitting his head on the rocks hanging down from the ceiling. The mirrorlight shone on massive gemstones that erupted from every surface in cracked cubes and angles, all of them swirled with violet and blue and deep, translucent green. *Amethyst?* he thought. *No—fluorite.* He could dimly remember attending a guest lecture once on the magical properties of crystals, but in Usbaran, his cohort had regarded that sort of thing as superstitious quackery. He'd never bothered to learn whether fluorite had any uses.

"Eshu?" said Fern. She pointed to a square on one wall where the crystals glowed with a strange, bright light. "I think that used to be a window."

And as soon as she said it, the topography of the cavern snapped into focus—the ledge of a writing table piled with books, the striations of shelves lining the walls, the narrow passageway that must have been an open door. An armchair, so crusted with crystals that it had fused to the wall behind it. A small rise not far from the exit, about the size of a human lying down.

This had been someone's study, once. Probably a wizard's study. Eshu might've spoken to the person under the crystal, once; they might've crossed paths at a party, argued some trivial point of rhetoric or technique, and forgotten each other immediately after they'd reached an understanding.

A crashing sound roused him from his troubled thoughts. Fern had taken out her hammer and stakes again and started smashing through the crystals blocking the window. They were only loosely fused together, and she cleared them quickly. A breeze swept through, warm and tinged with the salt smell of the sea. "No glass in the windows," she said, unrolling a blanket and laying it over the broken crystal. "And it's hot outside. Probably somewhere to the north. Come on—I want to figure out where we are."

She slid out with the blanket to protect her skin. The crunch of her boots on the other side said she'd landed on more crystals.

Eshu knelt beside the wizard encased in a crystalline tomb. *Just a mannequin of meat*, he'd called the human body only a few nights ago. It felt so stupid, now—an arrogant rhetorical flourish, meant to prove that he had the luxury of not caring. Now, as he passed his eyes over the bend of a knee or a smooth curve that suggested a skull, he was conscious that something had once inhabited this flesh, and that it was lost beyond recovery.

He bent down to kiss the shining rock. "Peace at your journey's end. Brother. Sister. Whoever you were. I hope you've gone on to somewhere better." Then he climbed to his feet again and scrambled out the window after Fern.

As soon as he got halfway through the gap, the heat hit him like a wall. Ras Kir'uun had drowsed at the beginning of orange season, and even on a cloudy day, Sharis had felt like a city that never grew cold. But here, the sun climbed toward high noon with a righteous fury, and the crystals encasing the city only reflected it back in a blaze of light and heat.

All around him, towering spires of fluorite and fool's gold clawed toward the sky. Downhill, where switchback streets led inexorably to the sea, shards of quartz gleamed like knives from every roof and balcony. Blood-brown garnets lay beneath the ruins of merchants' awnings, which hung in shreds over heaps of broken stones. Temples wept icicles of some thick, green stone swirled with black.

Whatever this city had been before, now it was a wasteland of glittering rock.

"Where are we?" he asked. *There are people somewhere under there*, he thought. *I wonder if anyone survived.*

Fern pulled out her enormous map and spread it out on the ground, using a few chunks of broken fluorite to weigh down the edges. "Hmm," she said, consulting her compass. "Probably somewhere on the north coast. Unless this is Lake Sura to the north of us; that's a salt lake. But I don't think it is. These mountains are too high."

While Fern talked herself through it, Eshu began to hum under his breath, seeking the tune for a song of finding.

"Does time pass differently in the Mirrorlands?" Fern asked. "Or is it just that we've traveled a long way?"

"A little of both, I think," said Eshu. "We walked a long time, behind the mirror."

"Right. That's going to make it harder." After a moment, she picked up Eshu's song and hummed along, slightly off-key. "If we assume that time passes only a little differently, and I know that's a big assumption, then my best guess is that we're in Zumera. It's the capital of the principality of Lidh. Exports, fruit and grain. Well, they used to be, anyway."

"Still in Nanjeer," Eshu hazarded.

"Oh, definitely still in Nanjeer. You can sort of see the architecture under all of this." She waved at the gem-studded streets around them. Eshu could just barely make out those now-familiar Nanjeeri verandas and arcades through sheets and clusters of crystal.

He began undoing his outer robe, then slid it off of his shoulders. Beneath the robe, his own body smelled foul to him; he'd never gone so long without washing. To her credit, Fern didn't so much as wrinkle her nose at the smell. "We're a long way from Sharis, though," Eshu said, after a moment. "How far?"

Fern pointed to a labeled dot at the tip of a bay on the western coast. "Here's Sharis. Or where Sharis used to be. And here," she swept her finger over to the northern coast, "is Zumera. It's about as far from Sharis as Kondala City is from Usbaran. Probably two days by airship—there's an idea." Tilting her head, she turned to survey the peaks to the east and west.

Eshu soon saw what she was looking for. A broad white stair wound up the western slopes to an airship landing, like a broad circular plaza carved into the mountainside. At least from here, it looked as though the platform had escaped whatever had happened to the city.

Maybe the airships were still running, and they could get a ride to Kondala City. If nothing else, they'd have a good view of the entire city from above. If there were any people here, they'd see them.

Fern was quiet while they walked. Sometimes, she'd pause and throw a hand out in front of Eshu, and they'd stop and listen to the sound of the wind or the faint creak of houses settling. Then, always, she set out again with a pensive look on her face.

As they reached the outskirts of the city, the encrustation eased a bit. Rose bushes still bloomed under a dusting of peridot-like raindrops; cats sunned themselves on the flat faces of massive pieces of quartz. Fountains still sang in courtyards and gardens, even with sapphires choking the basins. But there were no people in the houses here, although Fern knocked on doors and called out hopeful greetings.

Once, they passed a man rotting on a spike of tourmaline. His swollen flesh buzzed with flies. A coin purse lay beneath his hand, untouched. "We—we shouldn't leave him like that," said Fern softly. "What an awful way to die. We can't leave him here."

She swallowed hard, then heaved the man off of the spike in a rain of writhing maggots. Eshu had to turn and lean his head against a door frame until he stopped feeling like he was going to pass out.

He thought Fern carried the man into a house. Maybe she laid him on a bed, shrouded him in a blanket, said whatever words Nanjeeri people said for their dead. Eventually, though, he felt her hand on his elbow. "There's a fountain over there," she said. "Maybe wash your face."

"Right." Eshu lurched over to the fountain she'd pointed out, which lay at the heart of someone's orchid garden. He washed his hands and face, then sat for a long time with his eyes closed on a dark wooden bench and let the sun soak into his bare skin.

When he opened his eyes, he found Fern was sitting on the edge of the fountain with her boots off, washing her feet.

"How do you stand this?" Eshu asked. Fern looked up and over her shoulder. "How do you keep caring about hydrology, taking samples of rocks, when the whole world's coming apart?"

It was the first time either of them had said it, but he thought they'd both been thinking it for days. This wasn't one disaster. It wasn't even a series of disasters. Whatever had happened, it was happening everywhere at once, which had to mean that there was some kind of mind behind it.

Fern rubbed her feet with the hem of her shirt to dry them. "Even if the world's coming apart, it's still the world. And I really love the world, and I want to know more about it. That's all, I guess."

"You love people," said Eshu.

"People, rocks, plants, rivers, the sky—I love it all so much that it hurts sometimes. It's beautiful," she said. "But not exactly beautiful. It isn't just that I like looking at the world. I like that it keeps ticking on, like some enormous engine. I like how all the pieces fit together and move each other. And I like that I'm one of those pieces, looking for where I fit."

Eshu looked down and laughed. No mirth in it; just an attempt to dislodge the knot in his throat. "It's hard to love that machine. How it grinds away at you, being a part of it. It's easy to love individual people, maybe. I love my mother and my sisters. My friends Mnoro and Usamkartha—I worry about them. Where they are. Whether they're all right. But I don't actually like people very much. Or I thought I didn't, until I saw what the world looked like without them."

"It's funny. Or not funny, really. But I'm not worried about my parents at all. They're merchant sailors, so I grew up never really sure where they'd be. Or where I would look for them, if something went wrong." She lay back on the edge of the fountain, pillowing her head on her crossed hands. "I guess I always had to trust that they'd be all right, wherever they were."

Although she'd said she wasn't worried, the line between her brows suggested otherwise. "Do you really believe they're all right?"

"I want to believe it. It's nearly the same thing."

Not to a wizard, it isn't. It seemed cruel to say, though, so Eshu just stood and rolled his shoulders until his back cracked. "Should we go?" he asked.

"Let's go," Fern agreed. "Just let me get my boots back on."

They made their way to the stairs, which were made of cement that had slowly cracked over time and grown over with broad carpets of flowering vines. "Njo have mercy, I hate stairs," Eshu muttered, peering up at the distant airship landing. The stairs had looked a lot shorter from a distance.

"Don't you have some sort of song you could sing that would take you right to the top?"

"It's not that easy," said Eshu. "I could summon a wind and fly. I could build these vines into a drake and ride it to the top. I could even make the stones themselves carry me, if I wanted to."

Fern raised both brows. "That sounds pretty easy to me."

He rubbed his temples. "Whatever happened here, it was *magical.* Someone performed a really enormous, powerful working in this place. I don't know how to put it. This place's understanding of itself has changed forever. If you're right, and it is Zumera, then what it means for it to *be* Zumera is something different now. It's—fuck, let's just dive all the way into personification. This magic has made the city gullible. It wants someone to tell it what it is, and it will believe them. So if I tell it that the vines can shape themselves into drakes, or that the stones can move on their own, it might believe they can do that *all the time*. Do you understand this really shitty metaphor I'm trying to put together?"

"Not really," Fern admitted. "But I understand that you know what you're talking about, and you seem really worked up about it, so I'm not going to tease you any more about the stairs."

"Good enough." Then, with Fern leading the way, they began to climb.

It took the better part of an hour, but they didn't have anywhere else to be. *Except lecture*, Eshu thought, but he supposed his professors would forgive him for missing lecture if it was the end of the world. He and Fern stopped at landings, where there were benches and drinking fountains and well-manicured flower beds only just starting to grow over with weeds.

If he didn't think about it too much, it felt like going on holiday. It was a pity he couldn't stop thinking about it.

At long last, they reached the landing. Eshu hadn't traveled by airship since he started at the university, but even he could recognize that this was a major throughport, with glass-roofed shelters for waiting passengers and pallets of cargo waiting to be loaded. Gantries rose alongside the gondolas of gas-powered airships and the broader hulls of magical vessels, all of them dull and inert. Here, the smells of oil and ozone mingled with a sharp, heady scent of heated metal. Above it all rose the sound of tools, hammers almost drowning out a murmur of voices. "Hey!" someone called from the top of a gantry. "Stay where you are!" She was speaking Nanjeeri, so Fern was probably right about where they'd ended up.

Fern immediately raised both of her hands, slung her pack to one side, and sat on the ground, so Eshu set his coat aside and followed suit. Soon, a man and a woman in airship livery came to stand over them with swords out.

No one had ever pointed a sword at Eshu before. He'd always believed that someone with a sword was a poor match for a wizard in a duel—but now that he was staring down the sharp, glinting edge of a blade, he was all too aware of how quickly these two could silence his songs forever.

"Where did you come from?" the woman demanded. She was the taller of the two, and she wore her hair in a long braid that looked as though she hadn't unbraided it for days. "What do you want with us?"

"We came from Sharis," said Fern. She looked very calm, and Eshu almost wished she didn't. If she were panicking, he'd feel as though he were allowed to panic, too.

"You're a long way from home, then."

"Sharis isn't home," Fern said. "It's complicated. We came through a mirror—in a wizard's house, I think?"

"Are you wizards?" asked the woman with the sword. "You don't look like a wizard. Him, maybe."

"I'm a wizard, yes," Eshu confirmed. "But I didn't have anything to do with whatever happened in the city."

"We'll see about that." Without breaking eye contact with Eshu, she shouted back to the man in the gantry, "Send someone for Chief Alique."

A long, uncomfortable silence followed. If Eshu so much as twitched, the woman's sword twitched with him. *She'd really kill me*, he thought. *This is going to be how I die.* He tried to remember a song of warding that would take less than a second to cast, but they kept getting muddled with songs for finding and traveling and making deserts bloom. And even if he could find a song to help him, his throat was too tight to sing.

"You're scaring him," said Fern sharply.

"Good," the woman answered.

Fern rose to her knees. "Stop it! He's just trying to get home!"

Both swords pointed toward her. "Stay down," the man said. "I don't want to have to hurt you, but I will."

"You don't *have* to do anything," said Fern, but she sat again, muttering furiously under her breath.

The sound of a wooden hatch slamming open made them all jump. From one of the nearby airship hulls emerged a massive, sunburnt woman with a corona of coppery hair, spectacles sliding down her snub nose. Both of the people with swords snapped to attention, saluting.

"Well," she called in a booming voice, rolling with the accents of Cheresse in the far north. "This is an interesting conundrum, and no mistake. Stand down, my darlings. Fetch us a coffee. I'd like to speak with our intruders."

Eshu and Fern exchanged a baffled glance; a few steps away, their captors did the same. But, with every evidence of reluctance, they sheathed their swords and stepped back.

The towering woman strode toward them, her thumbs in the straps of her overalls. "My name is Erisse a'Degarre isman Alique, and I'm the Chief of Operations at this platform," she said. "And who might you be, my fine young trespassers?"

Fern audibly swallowed. "Fern. Just Fern."

"Ah, you poor dear." She shifted her considerable weight to one foot, turning her head to regard Eshu. "And you?"

"Kondala m'Barata Eshusikinde," he answered. "Most people call me Eshu."

"Kondala m'Barata Eshusikinde!" Chief Alique grinned so broadly that Eshu could see the gold canines at every corner of her smile. "Ah, the Kondalani understand how to build a proper name. Place, matronym, personal name; every bit of it functional. It's an honor, my dear, really an honor. How's the coffee coming?" she bellowed over her shoulder. "Apologies, apologies. Stores running low, you know, and the company coffee was never quite so good as the stuff they grow here in Zumera. But that's ruined, of course."

So it is Zumera, thought Eshu. *Fern was right.*

"Anyway! Stand up, my lovelies. They tell me you've come all the way from Sharis, and whether or not that's true, it's a very long way for you to travel. Let's get you to a proper table, shall we?"

She sat them down at one of the tables in the passengers' shelter. After a few moments, a young man with his tight curls tied under a kerchief came to bring them coffee. He didn't wear livery, so he probably wasn't airship landing staff, but he kept his eyes down deferentially all the same. "We're down to powder, Chief," he said apologetically. "If you let me nip down to the city, I know a good coffee shop; I could see if any of their stores survived—"

"And break my teeth on a diamond in the grounds? No, thank you. Leave it be for now." The man saluted and left them to their drinks, taking a cup for himself. "No butter for the coffee, but there never is; no one south of the equator is bold enough to try it with butter. But there is a bit of cane sugar, if you like that sort of thing." Her lips twisted in theatrical disdain.

Fern helped herself to the sugar, and Eshu sipped his coffee black. It was, as promised, absolutely abysmal coffee; he imagined that licking the underside of an airship's propellers would taste only slightly worse.

Only after everyone had had a sip did Chief Alique say, "Excellent! Now, let's do this thing properly. My measurements say we're outside of the zone of susceptibility, so we should be safe enough." She reached for her tool belt and drew what looked at first like another spanner—but now that it was in her hand, Eshu saw the intricate runes coiling over the surface amid bands of precious metals and tiny chips of gems. *A wand*, he thought. *So she's a wizard.*

Alique sketched a few quick sigils in the air, where they hung in glittering whorls. Then she hooked her wand on one as though it were a stubborn nut and gave it a twist. The whole design shifted, letters turning and interlocking, fracturing and reduplicating like images reflected in a kaleidoscope. "There," she said, with a low sound of satisfaction. "A charm of truth. So, my new friends, please explain to me what you're doing here in Zumera."

Eshu looked to Fern, who shrugged. Turning back to Alique, he began to tell their story, with Fern chiming in now and then to clarify something about the Sharisi disaster. Alique sat listening, chin propped on her hands, taking a sip of coffee every now and then until he had reached the street outside the wizard's house. Then, downing the last of her drink, Alique leaned back until her chair tipped back on two legs. She dispelled the charm with a flick of her wand.

"Hmm," she said. "Yes, indeed, my chicks: an interesting conundrum. I'd thought the Mirrorlands were lost entirely. I've been trying to contact headquarters for days, but no joy." She patted a breast pocket, in which Eshu could just barely make out the outline of a little oval mirror. "Scrubbed all flight plans as soon as we saw the lights in the sky, of course—"

"Lights in the sky?" Fern interrupted. "I saw lights in the sky over Sharis just before the earthquake."

"We thought it was a spot of tempest at first, but then—mm, well, you've seen the city. It was like watching a frost come over a meadow. All flash and glitter in the moonlight." Alique took out her mirror, peered into it, and then slid it back into her breast pocket. "Poor young Sparrow went to see what had happened. That's the dear boy with hair like springs. Not one of mine, but he's a dear, game little creature, isn't he? He found that the pulley system on the lift was nonfunctional, and so of course I told him to make it function again; he's an engineer, isn't he. Couldn't, he said. Rope was gummed up with emeralds, he said, which was when we started to understand the nature of the problem. Of course, I tried to report it to headquarters, but the mirror had gone dark."

"Where is headquarters?" asked Fern. "What city?"

"Tisaris," said Alique. "But it's no matter where it is; it could be on the moon, and we still ought to be able to use the mirrors to have a chat. There should always be someone on the other end, you see? That's what headquarters is for. Day or night, rain or fog, they're always there to tell us about the conditions in any destination. Why, if there were a war on, headquarters would just set up in an underground shelter and keep taking reports. We'd need them then more than ever."

"Do you think this is a war?" Eshu asked.

Something in his voice or expression must have betrayed the deep unease he felt, because Alique eased her chair back down and straightened. She seemed smaller, somehow, as though she'd put a shade over her bluster to dim it. "I'm prepared for the possibility," she answered. "That's why we have armed guards. That's why we post a watch. These airships are an asset, and we're ready to defend them if we can and destroy them if we must. But I don't think it will come to that."

"What about the people from the edge of town? We came through there, and it wasn't too bad, but the houses were still empty. Where are they? Did they take an airship?" Fern asked.

A cup rattled against a table. Alique heaved herself back from the table and stood. Contempt rolled from her in waves. "They're probably in the diamond districts, scraping their due from their friends' bodies. There are always profiteers, my dear lost doves. Always profiteers, and they'll always get their due. As will any of my folk who join them. Now, if you'll excuse me, maintenance waits for no one." Then, sliding her wand back into her tool belt, Alique strode off to the airship that she'd been servicing. The hatch closed behind her.

The man she'd called Sparrow was still sitting close by, not looking at them in the studious way that Eshu knew meant he was very interested indeed in their conversation. Although he'd been taking sips of his powder coffee the entire time, Eshu estimated that the cup had run dry at least half an hour ago. "If you'd like some entertainment with your coffee, we could start talking again," he called over. "Or does it spoil the effect if we know we're being watched?"

Sparrow ran a hand over his kerchief and hair with a self-conscious little smile. He had a nice smile; there was a gap between his front teeth that Eshu found endearing. "Sorry to eavesdrop," he said. "We just haven't had word from outside since it happened. The chief tries not to show it, but she's as jumpy as the rest of us. Airship folk like to know what's ahead. Before everything went wrong, we never had three hours together without reporting in to headquarters. Every bell, on the bell, it was weather and wind speed, then a round of departures and arrivals. Even aboard ship, regular as clockwork. This silence is an eerie thing."

"Like watching all of the mirrors in the Mirrorlands go dark. I know how that feels." Eshu rose from his chair and slid into one at Sparrow's table. "Chief Alique said you weren't one of hers. Are you from Zumera? Do you have family in the city?"

"Oh, no, I'm just passing through, although I won't deny it's been a long stopover. Crew on the cargo ship *Crest of the Wave*. We were bound for Lalani, but she snapped her runelines in a storm, and we limped into port here in Zumera about two months ago. More of a crash, really. Damage was so bad, we had to transfer all our cargo and careen her for repairs. Chief Alique and our skymaster had been retooling the runelines, but—well." He looked out over the city, which shone like the ocean in the high afternoon sun. "The skymaster was abed when the lights came. They probably didn't feel a thing."

Eshu reached for his hand, and Sparrow let it be taken. His palm had unfamiliar calluses, shaped to rope and tools and holystone. He was very warm to the touch. "It was lucky you were up here, then."

Sparrow shook his head. "Luck, nothing. I was here because I was making ready to sail. We were going to fly at first light. If we'd been done a day sooner, we'd be in Lalani now."

"And then whatever disaster befell Lalani, you'd be there instead of here."

"You think something's happened there, too?" After what felt like a long time, Sparrow turned back to look Eshu in the eyes. His eyes were a deep, warm brown flecked with gold. "No, you don't just think it. You dread it. You saw what happened here and in Sharis, and it eats you up not knowing why or how to stop it."

Eshu looked down at their hands. "Am I really that transparent?"

"It's not a bad thing to be." Sparrow pressed his hand, then stood and scooped up their cups. "Best be going. There's always work to do on an airship."

"And if I want to find you again?"

Sparrow paused, thumb hooked through the handles of three mugs. He looked a little lost—as though he wasn't used to being flirted with, or perhaps only as though it surprised him that people were still flirting after the world had fallen to bits. But he smiled all the same, a little flickering smile that reached his eyes. "Well, you just might be able to, if you look."

Only a moment later, Fern dropped herself into the seat that Sparrow had just vacated. Her lips had a just-bitten look; she licked away a drop of blood. "Could we talk?" she asked.

"I'd been under the impression that we were already talking," said Eshu.

When it had been just him and Sparrow, it had felt like an intimate conversation; with no one left in the passenger shelter but him and Fern, it felt uncomfortably like a conspiracy. Eshu was very aware of the guards pacing the edges of the platform.

Fern, too, seemed very aware of listening ears. She leaned in close and said, "I noticed that Chief Alique stopped casting the truth spell when it was her turn to speak. Did that seem strange to you?"

It hadn't, at the time. He'd been so anxious about the guards, and so grateful to be treated with civility, that he'd just been glad to have a chance to tell his story and be believed. But now that he had the luxury of remembering the interview, that choice struck the same sour note with him that it seemed to have with Fern. "It does seem unusual," he agreed. "But not necessarily suspicious, given the type of magic she practices."

"She doesn't sing her spells. Is that because she's Cheressian?"

"It's a style of magic called rhabdomancy. Wand-casting," Eshu answered. "It used to be very popular, back in the days when dueling was in fashion; a rhabdomancer could sling spells like weapons. But wands are easy to break and expensive to replace, and spells cast with a wand tend to fire quickly and dissipate just as quickly. No, I've always thought wands were a tool for hotheaded, impatient ruffians with no appreciation for nuance. It's very rare to see them used now, at least in Nanjeer and Kondala. Maybe it's different in Cheresse."

"Maybe." Fern rested her chin on her hands. "Do you think Chief Alique was telling the truth when she said that the people from the edges of town were collecting diamonds?"

He remembered the way she'd sneered at the mention of the people from Zumera, and—although he hadn't paid attention at the time—how Sparrow's cup had rattled on the table. As though his hands had been shaking with a feeling he couldn't give voice.

"I don't know," said Eshu. "But I suppose we could go find out."

CHAPTER 5: THINGS OF VALUE

Absolutely not. No one enters or leaves the platform without strict orders from Chief Alique." The woman folded her arms. Her livery and her saber said she'd probably been a guard before the disaster, the sort of genteel mercenary that airship companies hired to defend against rare pirate raids. Her frazzled braid said she hadn't slept in too long. Rukha made sure to keep her hands where the guard could see them and not to move too suddenly.

"But that has nothing to do with us. We're not airship crew. We're not even passengers," said Rukha. "We need to get back to Sharis and tell them what we've found here. They're expecting us."

"I'm afraid it's a matter of security," said the guard. "You're not cleared to—"

"Let them go, Anisha," her partner said wearily. He had enormous dark circles under his eyes; one of them looked like the yellowing edge of a bruise. "You saw how the chief treated them. If she didn't trust them, they'd be in the brig by now."

"We don't have a brig," snapped Anisha. "Sisters, am I the only fucking person on this platform who cares about protocol? Get Chief Alique to clear you, or go sit in the canteen. Those are your options."

When they approached Chief Alique, she was polite and apologetic and called them *dears* several times, but in the end, she took Anisha's side. "The city proper is what we call a susceptible zone, my ducks. That means that it's highly responsive to any magic worked—bluntly—where the gems are. If you try to unlock a mirror, you may well unlock every reflective surface for three city blocks, and that would make a fine lace of the fabric of reality. *Anything* might spill through. But I take regular measurements of the residual forces, and I'll let you know the very instant I think it's safe to travel again."

The whole business struck Rukha as rather condescending, but she didn't know enough about magic to argue the chief's point, and Eshu didn't seem inclined to. He kept stealing curious glances at that young engineer from the *Crest of the Wave*, as though he was a cipher that Eshu was eager to decrypt.

Rukha led them into the little canteen on the edge of the platform, where an older woman in faded airship livery sold them a bit of dry biscuit and a jar of jam. "It seems ridiculous to be paying for things, when everything's been turned upside down," said Rukha as they sat down to eat in the passenger shelter. "What will we do when the money runs out? What will we do when the *things* run out? Are people still going to farm and harvest and trade things at market? Would they even want to? There's no industry left in Sharis or Zumera. There's nothing to trade for. And how would they even regulate the value of currency, anyway, when their entire city's covered in gems—"

"They're trying to keep order here," said Eshu. "You asked me to sing a song of protection so that people would feel less afraid. Here, money is their song of protection. It's a ritual of exchange— just a way of saying that the old ways aren't lost."

"It's a little soon to be calling them the old ways."

Eshu rolled his eyes. "It was a rhetorical flourish."

"Anyway." She scanned the platform, mapping the paths that the guards walked and the movements of engineers and what looked like stranded passengers. There was Chief Alique, perched atop a gantry, examining a network of shining gossamer threads with an eye lens. *The runelines*, thought Rukha. She'd seen them a few times before on airship voyages, flickering in and out of view at the corners of her eyes; where Alique touched them, though, they became solid and gleamed with power.

She looked busy. Good.

Rukha leaned in to rest her head on Eshu's shoulder. "Act like this is a normal thing I do sometimes."

"But it isn't. Are you flirting? Because I'm entirely unprepared for you to be flirting."

Rukha sighed. "I'm definitely not flirting. I'm not interested in romance at all. I just want to talk quietly and not draw attention."

"All right." Then Eshu leaned his head against hers. His long locs tickled her ear. "I assume you have some kind of scheme."

Anisha crossed in front of the long white stair. Alique slowly began to untangle the runelines in her hands; sparks flew from her fingers like a shower of stars. "I was hoping you could make an illusion of us still being here, and we could go investigate the city while no one's watching."

"Tricky," muttered Eshu. "They'd hear my songs, and Alique, at least, would recognize what they were."

"Do you know any other way of working magic? Like—" she cast about for the word "—wand magic. Whatever you called it."

"Rhabdomancy."

"That. Or something less flashy."

"There's rune magic," he said, pressing his lips together as though the idea made him uncomfortable. "I took a class or two, but it's not my specialty. I'm not nearly as good at it as—I've mostly just watched it done."

"What about rocks? Are they magical somehow?" She offered a handful of stone samples from her hip pouch.

Eshu turned to her with a withering look. "No one reputable has thought rocks were magical in a hundred years."

"Says the man who fell out of a mirror." Rukha shrugged and started sorting the rocks in her hands. All of the new ones from the Mirrorlands and Zumera were still unlabeled, but she was running out of vials and pouches to keep them in, so they'd just have to stay unlabeled until she could find more.

Still, the thought haunted her: *Will anyone care about whether I label these, when the economy collapses? When the world's come apart and people are starving, will a handful of rocks matter to anyone?*

She closed her fist around a chunk of rough black rock and held it until her palm ached. *They matter to me. If the world's broken, someone needs to know where the parts are.*

"I think I've got it," said Eshu. Rukha looked up and nearly bashed her skull against his forehead. He'd bent low, examining the rocks over her shoulder. "Apart from my own limitations, the main problem with rune magic is that it's not very portable. I could cast an illusion that we were here, but that wouldn't solve the problem of concealing us when we leave. Rocks aren't themselves magical, but you can write runes on them—and rocks *are* portable."

"I'm just glad you finally found something good to say about rocks." Rukha passed him a couple of irrelevant hunks of raw sapphire. A week ago, these would have paid her rent for years; today, the best thing you could say about them was that they were portable. "Do you have anything to write with?"

"You're the mapmaker."

"*You're* the wizard. I've got pencils and a little watercolor kit that's almost used up. Nothing that would bind to that. You'd be better off writing with jam."

"It doesn't have to bind, so long as we're careful not to wipe it off." He examined the jam jar morosely. "Runework shouldn't be *sticky*."

"Wait," said Rukha abruptly. "Maybe I have something. I think I stowed it in here..." She upended her scroll case, shaking free her bundle of drafts and the huge map of the continent. Underneath, tucked safely away, were the etching tools and the fine gold pocket watch she'd stolen back at the wizards' tower. The watch could do with winding. "There you go. Carve all the runes you like."

Eshu took the etching tools, but he set them aside and started practicing with the jam and crackers. While Eshu worked, Rukha unrolled the big map on the windswept surface of the platform. She had the idea of recopying it and amending it, but the wind caught at the edges of the leather, even in the relative calm of the passenger shelter. It would certainly blow her looseleaf paper away. Instead, she took some time to pencil in corrections where a coastline had receded or a new town had sprung up.

Destroyed, she wrote beneath Sharis and Zumera. It made her feel guilty, as though she'd obliterated them with her own hands.

When she'd finished updating the map, though, Eshu still looked like he was a long way from done with his work, and Rukha had nothing left to distract her from her thoughts. She'd been trying not to think too much since they'd crawled out the window and into Zumera. She'd tried just to observe without making inferences, as though that was something the human brain could do. Because if she let herself start connecting her observations, if she really thought about what it meant that Sharis had fallen into the sea and the Mirrorlands had gone dark and Zumera had been crushed under a sea of gemstones, then she would be able to draw only one conclusion. Eshu had been the first to say it, but she thought she'd been dreading it as long as he had.

Whatever was happening, it was happening all over the country. Maybe all over the world. And that meant that it had probably happened to Matis, too.

Rukha traced her fingertips over the ink spot labeled *Matis*. She'd been trying very hard not to think about her home. The teashop with the indigo tiles, where all of the servers knew her by name and always gave her exactly enough honey and milk. Her parents' drawing room, the furniture covered in dust sheets during their long voyages. Her drafting table at the mapmakers' shop; old Heza and her son Kufa coming over to swipe her black ink and bickering as they always did over calculation of longitude. The moss roses in her window box, slowly unfurling their petals as the sun crept higher in the sky. The way her sheets smelled after she'd washed them and let them dry on the line, like soap but also somehow like sunlight. The little white cat on her walk home that sometimes rolled onto his side and begged for pets.

She made herself imagine her mother and father, buried under a sheet of diamonds or washed up on the rocky shore. She made herself see how dogs would eat Heza's body and how Kufa would rot in the sun. She thought about it until her eyes stung and her throat closed up like a clogged drain. Then she shut those thoughts like a book and sat back on her heels.

Before the earthquake, she hadn't understood the old superstition about giving a fake name to keep the Crowtaker from overhearing. But right now, the last thing she wanted was to be Rukha Masreen. Rukha had a family and friends and a city that were probably dead. At least Fern didn't have anyone but Eshu, and even he was a hard maybe at best. If she let herself be Rukha, that grief would swallow her up. It was better to be Fern.

Eventually, the shadow of the mountains fell across the platform, and the daylight began to fade. Eshu put away the crackers and knelt for his sunset prayer. Fern rolled the map back up as the airship folk began to file into the passenger shelter with supper from the canteen. Thin soup and flatbread, Fern noticed; their stores must've been getting low, too. "It looks like there's a little meat in it, at least," she offered. "Might help us get our strength up. I could grab us a couple of bowls."

"Njowa don't eat meat," Eshu answered. "But I'll take some bread, if you can spare the money. I'll find out where we can sleep for the night, since they seem adamant about keeping us here."

"Suit yourself." She shrugged on her pack and shouldered her scroll case, then started toward the canteen.

As soon as she left the passenger shelter, someone grabbed her by the arm. She threw a wild elbow and connected with something solid—then her captor slipped a hunk of stone into her hand, and she understood.

Oh, she thought. *I guess he figured out the runes.*

The air shimmered slightly, the way it did where the heat rose in waves from concrete of the platform. She couldn't see anything there, exactly, but suddenly she could see where something *wasn't*. It was like noticing a gap in an orderly bookshelf, or a dark patch of sky where a familiar star had been.

Eshu let her go, and she watched a copy of herself sit down outside the passenger shelter and begin to eat a piece of flatbread. She could smell the yeasty aroma of fresh bread; she could even hear the crisp, delicate sound of the blackened bits crackling in her hands. Her double dipped the bread into the bowl of broth, then tore off a big hunk with her teeth and swallowed almost without chewing.

"You're going to make yourself sick, my little starling," said Chief Alique, wiping her brow with a grease-stained cloth as she strolled up to the shelter.

Fern's mouth went dry. *She's a wizard*, she thought wildly. *She'll know it's only an illusion. She'll know we're here. She'll find us—*

"Thanks," said Fern's double, with a sheepish look. "It's just been a while since I've eaten. The jam and crackers helped a little."

To Fern's horror, Chief Alique reached down and fluffed her hair fondly. "If you need to borrow money for meals, you have only to ask. It would break my heart if you starved yourself on my watch."

"We're all right," said the double. "Really, thank you. And maybe, if you see him, don't touch Eshu's hair."

"As you like, dear." Then Chief Alique continued into the shelter, humming a rollicking Cheressian air. For the first time in a solid minute, Fern let herself breathe.

Eshu's hand found hers, and he pulled her toward the stairs. Fern knew, logically, that there was no way they should be crossing the platform without drawing some sort of attention. The woman sitting sentinel in the gantry should have seen them making for the stairs and called a halt; the guards should have heard the clanking of Fern's pan against something in her pack. Fern could hear it. As anxious as she was, the sound seemed as loud as a temple bell.

No one heard, and no one stopped them. They started down the stairs, and Fern let Eshu have the side with the railing. On her side, the mountain crags dropped away, every bush and vine gilded with the light of the setting sun. Below, empty houses shone red as carbuncles on the rim of the sea.

It felt a bit like she imagined being a ghost must feel. "How long—"

"Ssh," whispered Eshu, and he squeezed her hand.

By the time they reached the city, the sun had set, and the streets were growing dark. *No lamplighters anymore,* Fern thought. *But no candles, either? No wall lamps? Is no one left?* Then, down by the docks, she began to see red pinprick lights. *Torches. So* someone's *still here.*

Eshu finally stopped walking in a city street that looked just like all the others, except for that a blanket lay over the sill of an open window. "I forgot I'd left that there," said Fern.

"I'm glad you did, or I'm not sure how I'd have found this place again. I don't have your gift for directions." He tugged her toward the window, then let her go. She followed him through, shoving her pack through the window first and then crawling across the sill.

Once they were on the far side, Fern heard Eshu set down his stone on something. He tucked the blanket over the curtain rod and then sang a light into his hand. Abruptly, he was visible again, with his mismatched shoes and his outer robe thrown over his arm. He looked at the mirror with a despairing expression, then at the floor below it; Fern noticed that a sheet lay at the foot of it in a tumble of fluorite. *It must've fallen under the weight,* she thought.

"So, how long were you, um, not actually with me?" she asked.

"Not very long," he answered. "I managed the local illusion within the first hour, and that seemed to cover the etching work well enough. But the etching itself took longer than I expected. I'm not used to working with my hands."

Fern generously didn't comment on that. "Did you get a chance to look around at all?"

"A bit. Could you put your rock down? It's a bit disconcerting, talking to a diffuse void in my perception."

Fern set the sapphire aside, and Eshu seemed to relax slightly. "What did you see?"

"It's more what I heard. The stranded passengers aren't happy, which I expected. Most have been staying in their berths in the airships, which seems to pacify them a bit, but they don't understand why they can't leave. They have at least a vague notion of what happened to Zumera, and it upsets them. They seem to believe that everyone in the city is dead."

"But we know they aren't," said Fern. "Chief Alique said so. And we've seen the lights."

"I listened to her, too." Eshu set his robe down on an armchair, then sat. "And I got a look at her mirror."

"We both agree that that's incredibly dangerous, right?"

"It isn't as though I picked her pocket," he said, indignant. "I looked over her shoulder when she took it out."

"That's not much better."

"I am *trying* to tell you what I saw. Or rather—to show you." He closed his eyes and let the light drift from his hand. Fern held her hand out, and it alighted in her palm like a tiny golden star.

Then Eshu began to sing, his voice deep and rich and rumbling. For a moment, he hummed a melancholy tune, as though seeking the shape of the spell he meant to cast. That low melody caught in Fern's ribs; it vibrated in her lungs, set the pace of her heart, sank into her marrow. It ached like an old wound.

The wizard's mirror flickered into view in her hand as he fitted words to melody. An image played behind the glass, as though Fern was looking through a window into a darkened room. She wasn't sure what she expected. A body, possibly. The person in Tisaris who took and gave airship weather reports, slumped over a desk with a mask of flies. Or possibly just blackness; Chief Alique had said that the mirror had gone dark.

She didn't expect to see a map.

There were people on the other side, too, but she registered them only as an afterthought. Behind them was a map of Nanjeer drawn in chalk on an enormous hunk of slate, every principality swarming with annotations. She couldn't read a word of them— she supposed Eshu hadn't been able to make them out—but there were dotted lines and colored hashes, and erasures and crossings-out. There was Kondala on the far eastern horn of the continent, slashed across with worrying blue; there was her hometown of Matis, with little triangles drawn in green off the coast. When she tried to look for familiar landmarks and smaller cities, her vision swam, but it went very sharp when she looked at the places where the two of them had been.

Usbaran was crossed with red *X*s, from the mountains all the way down to the distant sea.

"I'm sorry," said Fern softly. "I—"

"Someone must have survived." When Eshu spoke, the spell faded, and the mirror grew dark again. "The wizards in Sharis did. My university had mirrors. They'd have evacuated, if they knew it was coming. As for Kondala, there's no way to know what those markings meant."

Before she'd met Eshu, Fern had always thought wizards were annoyingly smug. They'd always sounded certain about everything, even things they couldn't possibly know. Now, though, Fern was beginning to understand that their certainty was also a kind of attempted magic. They had to make themselves believe before they could bend the world around that belief. She put a hand on Eshu's shoulder and said, "We'll find out what happened to them."

"Could you tell what uniform they were wearing?" Eshu asked. "The soldiers in the image."

"The—oh." Until he said it, she hadn't realized that the people behind the mirror had been wearing uniforms, but now she remembered flashes of armor. Brigandine coats studded with nails; the glint of a sword at someone's side. "I don't really know the difference between different countries' armor. Maybe if there had been a flag or a crest or some bright colors, I could have guessed, but it was too murky. Or not murky, but—like trying to look at a pattern of dots, and if you look too long, you start seeing dots between the dots."

"An optical illusion."

"That." Fern rubbed her eyes. "But whoever's soldiers they are, they didn't look like they were using the mirror to communicate. They were just going about their business, updating the map. Talking, I think. But to each other, not to Chief Alique."

"I only got a quick look before she put it back in her pocket. I'm sorry it's not more detailed."

"You got the important things." She hesitated. "Thank you for looking for Matis. I hadn't—I hadn't thought you'd remember the name."

Eshu smiled, just a ghostly flash of teeth. With the light still held low in Fern's hand, he looked ghoulish and hollowed out; she imagined she must look the same. "You can say you're not worried about your parents, and I might even believe you, but I can't believe that you're not worried about your home."

She swallowed against the rising knot of grief. "I'm not," she said. Maybe if she kept saying it, it would start feeling true. "What should we do? Go see what those lights were by the docks, or go back to the landing? They'll probably be missing us by now. We've been gone a long time."

"We need to go to Tisaris to find out what's happening," said Eshu. "Maybe if we can learn about it, we can stop it."

"What, just the two of us? There's an army in Tisaris!"

"There are soldiers in Tisaris. We don't know how many. And we don't know whose they are." Eshu stood from his chair and began to pace. "Sparrow was right. It consumes me, not knowing why this is happening or how to stop it. I have to know, Fern. If they're our enemies, I'll cut through them like a blade of ice. If I have to, I'll storm the city in a whirlwind and wring answers from their commanders. I'll—"

"There are *people* in Tisaris, you arrogant fuck! How dare you threaten them, after all the shit they've been through? After all the shit *we've* been through!" Fern put herself in front of him, and it felt like staring down a mudslide as it raced down a gully. His eyes were shining golden; his voice still echoed in the bone arch of her ribs. He was a force of nature, and she braced herself to be crushed.

The light dimmed in his eyes. "I'm sorry," he said. "That was overzealous. A bit."

Fern sighed and shook the globe of light free of her hand. It floated up to the ceiling like a soap bubble. "I understand that you want answers. So do I! Everything's changed, and it's going to keep changing, and I'm afraid of what it's going to be. I've seen the bodies, same as you. I've helped carry and burn them, and I'm afraid of how many more there are going to be before this is over. I'm afraid it will *never* be over. But we aren't in some fucking hero story. We aren't just going to march up to the evil emperor's fortress and cast back the gates and defeat him in single combat in a pit of skulls."

"That was alarmingly specific."

"I've read a lot of hero stories," said Fern. "Anyway. I want answers, too. But I also want to know what's left. And I want to help the people who are left."

"You're right about that. But I'm not sure you're right about the rest." Eshu reached up to pluck the light bubble from the ceiling.

"It feels like absconding our responsibility to throw up our hands and say, 'This is beyond our reach.'"

"Do you really believe that you can take on something that can drop a city into the sea? Or crush people under a million diamonds? Or whatever horrible things they've done to Usbaran and Lalani?" Fern shivered. She remembered the Crowtaker's masked face, so tranquil before the lamp hit. "This isn't even a wizards kind of problem. This is a gods kind of problem."

"Then we enlist the gods! Shout for them at every shrine and temple, every sacred stone on every hallowed mountain! We can't just do nothing. If we're too small to fix it on our own, then we won't do it alone. We'll find someone who can help us." His voice broke. "Njo, there must be *someone* who can help us."

"Let's go to the people on the docks," said Fern. "Maybe they can't fix the world, but they might know more than we do. It's somewhere to start."

"It's fascinating how, after all of that, we end up doing what you wanted," groused Eshu, but he gestured her toward the window. "Out the window again, then. Don't forget your runestone."

Fern looked at the sapphire nervously. "Is it safe to use that here? You and Chief Alique were so anxious about doing magic in the zone of susceptibility."

Eshu rubbed his temples. "It's rune magic. Of course it's safe. You might as well ask why it's safe to drink a glass of water in a city and not to break open a dam."

"Just asking," muttered Fern. "I don't know anything about magic."

"Well, I don't know nearly as much as I'd like. Before we leave Zumera, remind me to crack open the rock on these bookshelves. There are probably some useful spells trapped under all that fluorite."

Fern pulled down the blanket curtain, and Eshu dimmed his little light. By now, the moon had risen over the mountains—it was still shy of full, which was a relief; they'd definitely been behind the mirror less than a day. "Why do you think Chief Alique didn't tell us about what she really saw in the mirror?" asked Fern, as Eshu unfolded himself on the outside of the wizard's house.

"That really depends on whose soldiers were on the other side," said Eshu. "Maybe she's a collaborator. Maybe she's acting under orders. Maybe she's trying to prevent a panic. There's no way of knowing without asking her, and I don't think I have to explain the logistical problems with *that*."

"What, you don't want to come up on her like a blade of ice or a whirlwind? Maybe some other kind of weather event?" Eshu made a show of tying up his hair and ignoring her, so she gripped her runestone and made herself easy to ignore.

They slowly found their way to the docks, letting the gentle slopes of the streets guide them under crystalline balconies and hanging ferns frosted in diamonds. For the most part, they stuck to the main roads; no one could see them, so there was no reason not to. Soon, the houses and shops gave way to warehouses, banks, forges, dry docks with half-built ships blasted with garnets.

Ahead, voices. Light spilled through the doorway of what must've once been a public house, before Zumera fell. The windows were still crusted over with some stone a deeper green than emeralds, and the light that filtered through them had a queer, deep-sea hue. Gripping Eshu's wrist, Fern eased through the door and into a corner of the room.

A group of people sat around the hearth, peeling garlic and onions and slicing up okra and little white eggplants. "Might be our last fresh vegetables for a while," said one old man, who shucked garlic with practiced hands. Just one press of the flat of his knife, then he slid a thumbnail under the papery skin and whisked it away. "If that boy can't get us out of here soon—"

"Then we'll walk," said a fat, pretty woman with a basket of dried beans in her lap. Fern saw that she was sorting out beans from stones, occasionally breaking the beans free and feeling their outsides with her fingers before dropping them in another basket at her feet. "It'll be like a tour of the countryside. Maybe we'll find a safe place to settle and take up farming. It'll be good for us."

"Nothing good about this," the old man muttered, but after that, he kept his silence.

"Have you ever farmed before?" asked an older woman. Her hands were gnarled, her knuckles swollen, but she held herself with a queenly dignity. "I used to garden, before my joints got bad. I could tell you everything about compost, worms, pruning.... I used to be up with the sun every day, kneeling in my little garden patch to plant seedlings one at a time. Those were good days. Now I'm not sure I'll be any use. Best leave me behind with the other fossils."

"Don't say that. We'll need what you know, wherever we go," said the woman with the beans. "Anyone can learn to farm. Not everyone can teach it."

"I'll just slow you down."

"Then we'll carry you." A bean plinked into the basket at the woman's feet. "Even if you didn't know a thing about gardening, you're our neighbor. We don't just abandon people. Did Mindha leave Kindara behind in the serpent's cave?"

"Kindara's knees probably worked a little better than mine," the old woman said wryly. "We can't all be as spry as the Sisters."

"We're not leaving you behind, and that's final."

Fern glanced at Eshu, but there was nothing there to look at but the gem-studded wall. She didn't have anyone to help her second-guess her thoughts, so she had no choice but to think them. *These don't seem like opportunists hungry for money*, she thought. *They seem like the people back in Sharis—just refugees who are doing their best.*

Her fingers tightened on the sapphire. She wanted to set it down and greet these people and ask them to tell their stories, but it would probably just make them more anxious to see her appear out of nowhere. Better to come in as though from outside, like a traveler who happened to be drawn in by the light and the sound of conversation. She gave Eshu's wrist a tug and led him back toward the door.

As they were about to pass through, though, the light caught on someone's pocket watch outside. Fern flattened herself against the inside wall, letting go of Eshu.

If he could talk right now, he'd tell her that it was ridiculous to hide when she was holding her sapphire. He'd tell her that his magic was much more reliable than the dubious concealment of an open room. But it made her feel better to hide, and he couldn't tell her not to, so she did.

Someone stepped through the door and immediately pulled off his hood. His tight, glossy curls shone in the firelight. "Good news for you," said Sparrow, grinning at the gathered people. "If you can be ready to go, we're ready to fly."

CHAPTER 6: BREAKING LAWS

As Sparrow stepped into the light, Eshu froze. He was keenly aware of how close they stood; he could smell Sparrow's hair lotion, the sour scent of his sweat, the engine grease on his hands. Eshu's heart beat loudly in his ears. Only a thin veil of magic stood between them; a touch or a word could tear it open. Part of him craved that revelation.

"Took you long enough," said the old man peeling garlic. "Where should we go? When should we be there?"

"The plan is to dip down by the docks a little after midnight. Already told the folks outside; they'll be waiting."

"Where are we going?" asked the gardener. She gathered up her skirts and stood, her back straight and regal despite her swollen knuckles and elbows. "Oh, I hadn't expected it to be tonight—I won't have time to get home and pack a shawl if we're going somewhere cold—"

"We'll try Cheresse first," Sparrow answered. "The north winds are gentle, this time of year, and the Kirami's swarming with storms. But if they turn us away in Cheresse, we'll replenish our supplies and try Ras Kir'uun when the weather turns. Our skymaster has some friends there who can help you get settled."

He told us that his skymaster was dead, thought Eshu, but his indignation warmed almost immediately into admiration. *No—he told us that his skymaster had been abed, and probably hadn't felt a thing.*

He let us infer the rest. This fucking asshole.

"Is it cold in Cheresse?"

Sparrow shook his head. "In winter, it gets a bit cold and rainy, but the summers are hot and mostly dry. I've only heard of snow there once or twice, when the wind came out of the wrong quarter. It'll be good for your joints there. Promise."

"I've heard they have beautiful gardens there," said the fat woman. She stood, too, and swept her long hair back from her shoulders. The beads on her golden earrings chimed. "And orange and lemon trees in Ras Kir'uun. Cherries, too, in some places. Flowers like white clouds in springtime."

"If nothing's happened to them," said the old man darkly, but everyone turned on him, and he put up his hands in mock-surrender. "I'm only saying! If you're right, and this has happened everywhere, no reason to think it's just Nanjeer. Could be Ras Kir'uun, too. Cheresse. Everywhere."

"Just because you're afraid doesn't mean the rest of us have to be," the fat woman replied. She folded her arms, staring him down until he looked away. "What good does it do to speculate about what might have happened in Ras Kir'uun or Cheresse? If we stay here, we're going to starve. *That's* a certainty."

"Easy enough for you to say," he muttered. "You're a doctor; you'll find a place wherever we go. No call for a sour old bastard in a fancy place like Cheresse."

"We can worry about finding you a place after we're in the air," said Sparrow. "I need to get back. Told the chief I was just nipping down to get her some real coffee, so she'll be expecting me soon with a sack of beans. But you listen for the bells up on the platform. When you hear us chime midnight, be ready to move."

"Sisters smile on you," said the older woman, hobbling across the diopside-covered floor to kiss both of his cheeks.

"And on you." With that, Sparrow slid his hood back up and stepped back into the night.

"If that chief of theirs doesn't blow us out of the sky with a lightning bolt," muttered the old man. He returned to his garlic, shaking his head as gravely as though he'd spoken a prophecy.

He's not wrong, Eshu thought. Chief Alique might not blow them out of the sky, but she'd worked the runelines herself; she knew every link, every carefully forged argument that kept the ship aloft despite the hungry pull of gravity. It would be trivial for her to take those arguments apart.

Eshu knew that he should find Fern's hand again and creep back to the wizard's house, retrieve their things and steal back to the airship landing before they were missed. These weren't their people. This wasn't their fight. But as he watched Sparrow go, he wanted it to be.

Before he could talk himself out of it, he began to run.

Sparrow whirled when Eshu touched his shoulder; Eshu glimpsed a wood-handled knife in his hand. "Who's there?" Sparrow asked. There was steel in his voice that hadn't been there on the platform. "Show yourself, Crowtaker. I'm ready for a fight tonight."

"I've come to help you," said Eshu.

At the sound of his voice, Sparrow turned to face him. His gaze very nearly met Eshu's—he'd almost remembered the difference between their heights—and then slid away along the glassy surface of Eshu's spell. "You're not doing too well so far."

Eshu slipped the runestone into his pocket. Earlier, he'd seen Fern snap suddenly into focus, like letters becoming a word. As though he'd always been able to see her, but he hadn't quite been able to make out that she was what he was seeing. It had been unsettling, and Eshu had been expecting it.

As Eshu faded into view, Sparrow's eyes narrowed, but at least he sheathed his knife. "How long have you been following me?" he asked.

"Only since the public house," said Eshu. "You were the last person I was expecting to walk through that door. I swear it."

"Never did trust a man who swore easily." Sparrow gave a crooked smile. "Eshusikinde, isn't it? 'Flowing like a river.' My father's name is Ogawende."

Another Kondalani name. "Maybe someday you'll tell me yours."

"Maybe someday you'll give me a reason to. But as you may've gathered while you were eavesdropping, I'm on a schedule. Coffee to fetch, rescues to plan. If you aren't going to turn me in, you'd best stay out of my way." He stepped back and made a little bow, Kondalani-style, hands out to his sides.

If he didn't speak now, if he didn't find the words that Sparrow wanted to hear, Eshu knew that the *Crest of the Wave* would take her chances at midnight without him. *You're a fucking wizard,* he thought desperately. *If you can't find the words to make someone listen, then what good are all your songs and incantations?*

His teachers had taught him that magic had many tools, but the truth would always be his keenest blade. "I think what your crew is doing is the bravest, most righteous thing I've seen since the world came apart," said Eshu. "I want you to succeed. Tell me if there's anything I can do to help you."

Sparrow hesitated, on the edge of turning away. His gold-flecked eyes were wide and dark in the moonlight. "Thras Nadi—that's our skymaster—they can manage the runelines," he said finally. "But we have to pick them up in the city. Takes a lot out of them to make the ship fly at that distance. If the chief decides we shouldn't leave, Nadi can't do that and hold her off. We could use another wizard."

"I'm yours," Eshu promised.

"Bit early for that kind of vow," said Sparrow. A smile touched his eyes. "Go on. Fetch your mapmaker friend, then get back to the platform and talk your way aboard the *Crest of the Wave.* I'll find you there. Remember—midnight bell is the signal to go. All the crew knows it. There won't be any other sign, so be ready."

"I will."

Sparrow was almost a block away before Fern faded into view at Eshu's side. "That was really awkward to watch," she said.

"You didn't have to watch," said Eshu.

Fern brushed back her hair with one hand. "What was I supposed to do? Just lurk around the public house watching them argue over what to pack? You're the only person in Zumera I know at all, and I've only known you for a couple of days."

"It feels as though it's been longer."

"It does," said Fern. "I don't know how to put it, exactly. Maybe it's just the kind of friendship that people make sometimes when things are shitty and they need someone to cling to."

There was a word for that in Kondalani—imbe'ingana, pressure-bonding. The way clay fused to clay when the potter crushed two pieces together, until it was impossible to tell where one ended and the other began. It had sounded sexier in stories.

"You don't have any moral compunctions about stealing an airship?" Eshu asked. "Or the terrifying fall to our deaths that we might face if this goes horribly wrong?"

Fern shook her head. "The only thing that worries me is not being able to get back to Sharis. Is there any way we could steal the mirror we came through?"

"What's one more theft?" said Eshu. "The person who lived there won't need it anymore."

The mirror didn't fit through the window, so they (or rather, Fern) had to smash out the crystals blocking the door. Then it was back down to the docks to stash the mirror near the public house. This mirror was lighter than the one they'd salvaged in Sharis, but by the time they set it down, Eshu's arms shook with exertion.

He tried not to think about how many pillars of crystal they'd passed on the streets. If he looked at them too long, he thought he could make out the shadows of people trapped inside.

They returned to the platform to find their doubles curled up against the glass wall of the passenger shelter, snoring on each other's shoulders. When Eshu knelt to obliterate the runes he'd carved into the cement, he saw a brief shimmer that he thought was Fern sinking into her double's place and releasing her runestone.

She was just barely smaller than the replica that Eshu had crafted; she was so strong and capable that sometimes he forgot how small she was. He wondered why she'd named herself after something as frail as a fern. Maybe someday she'd feel safe enough to tell him.

When he'd scratched out the runes on the platform, he curled up in the shape of his own sleeping body and arranged his clothes around him—shoes off beside him, outer robe blanketing his lap. The brisk wind off the sea was a balm, after the day's heat. He closed his eyes and pocketed his runestone, then let himself shiver awake.

He opened his eyes to find Chief Alique standing over them. She stood with her fists on her hips, her back arched and her expression unreadable. The blood drained out of his face. *Shit*, he thought. *She knows where we've been. She knows what we're going to do.* "Can we help you, Chief?" he asked, rubbing his eyes as though they were sand-gummed. He tried not to let his voice shake.

Then she stretched her hands over her head, and her back gave a series of tectonic cracks that made his spine ache in sympathy. "Help me! I'm here because I want to help *you*, my chickadees," she said. "Will you step into my office? My young friend Sparrow has brought up a sack of fresh coffee from the city. I'll brew you each a cup."

Fern shot him a wary look. Her eyes were wide, but she didn't seem afraid. *It's probably a trap*, that look seemed to say. *Should we go anyway?*

He nodded. "It's a bit late for coffee."

"Never too late for coffee," said Chief Alique. "In Cheresse, we took it after dinner, then sat up until after midnight talking. They said the lights never went out in Degarre, and at every hour, the streets rang with music. But you must forgive the Cheressian love for exaggeration. There were dark nights like this one, even in my dear Degarre." She twisted up her hair into a loose bun, then stuck some sort of metal rod through it to hold it in place. It wasn't the wand, Eshu noticed. She still wore that on her tool belt.

The airship offices lay against the mountain slope. Chips of sand in the white concrete walls sparkled in the moonlight. Snores drifted through the open windows—Chief Alique's people, he supposed, bedded down in their offices so that they didn't have to go back into the city.

At the end of the row of offices was a room without windows. Chief Alique drew out a silver key from one of the pockets on her tool belt and unlocked the door. She put the key back and took out her wand.

Eshu tensed. A song to summon a tempest was brewing in his chest, eager to be spoken.

Chief Alique set three spheres of golden light circling the ceiling, then hung her tool belt on a peg by the door and swept a pile of papers off of the low wooden bench along one wall. Then she collapsed into the chair behind her desk—he heard more papers crunch under her great weight—and rolled her neck until it crackled. "Be a love and close the door, would you?" she asked.

Fern eased the door shut. At the sound of the latch, Chief Alique seemed to relax slightly. She poured coffee beans from a cloth sack into a mortar and began to crush them. "In the morning, I'll send some of my folk down to fetch the mirror you came through, and we'll see it installed here on the platform. You'll be free to return to Sharis, or wherever your travels take you."

"That's very kind of you," said Fern. "But—I'm sorry, I know this is rude—why can't the passengers on the platform leave? You're running out of food up here. And people are getting anxious."

"I have to keep them safe," answered Chief Alique. "What do you think would happen, if they learned about Sharis? They'd lose their heads, maybe even riot. And then we'd be in a fine mess."

Fern sat on the bench; her feet didn't quite touch the ground. "They might riot anyway," she said. "At least if you told them, they might see that you're on their side. You're all figuring out what to do together."

"Have you ever traveled by airship, my dear?" Chief Alique asked. Fern nodded. "Often? Always safely? No disasters?"

"Not so far," said Fern.

"Not so far. Yes, it's probably best to say that—not so far." Chief Alique clicked her tongue. "I've had a few disasters, in my day. On a gearship, once, when there was an engine fire; twice aboard a runeship, when the runelines snapped. They used to break so easily, in the early days. Experimental runecrafting. Ah, but the fire is the one that I remember the best."

When the beans had been ground down, Chief Alique dumped them out of the mortar into a little sieve, then poured water over it from a silver jug. The water began to boil as it struck the grounds. The scent of coffee rose on a cloud of steam, and against his better judgment, Eshu's mouth began to water.

"The fire," said Chief Alique again. "I was the junior engineer aboard. Our ship was the *Lady of Andoumaire.* Such a fine, proud ship she was! Gasbag of emerald silks, and fine cherry wood furnishings inside; gold brocade on every sweat-soaked airman's back. Two engines, excellently maintained. We were over the water—the sea they call the South Sea in Cheresse, although of course you call it the North Sea in Nanjeer and Kondala. I was off duty, taking in a meal in the dining room with the passengers, and I hear a well-dressed fellow laugh that he smells smoke. Smoke!" She laughed, soft and bitter. "What a fine little joke. And soon everyone is remarking on the smoke, and I can see it beginning to cloud up the dining room. We were near the engine room, you see. A very common airship design in Cheresse. So I do as I've been trained to do. I leave my food and I run."

Chief Alique was not weaving a spell, but she was a wizard all the same; when she spoke, the steam over the coffee jug began to curl into thick black smoke, and the smell of coffee darkened into soot and ash.

"I won't tell you how we doused the fire, or how we landed here in Zumera on one engine and the gods' goodwill. If you knew more about airships, you'd appreciate the story. But no matter. That isn't the story I meant to tell you. My dear young mirror-travelers—I watched three dozen people who were a hairsbreadth from death, laughing as they waited like lambs for the butcher's knife." She poured them each a cup of coffee. "This is the lesson I learned, my doves: people are simply not made for disaster. Even when they see it, they don't understand it. So those who have been trained for it are obliged to protect them, to give them order, and to keep them from knowing things that would distress them."

Chief Alique set the cups out on the edge of the desk. She drank her own coffee hot and black.

As Eshu reached for a cup, Fern asked, "What about the people in Zumera? Don't you have an obligation to protect them?"

"These airships are spoken for," said Chief Alique. "The people aboard need it as much as anyone does, and they've paid for their passage. I can't just *give* the Zumerani a ship. That isn't how any of this works."

But the entire fucking city is covered in gemstones, thought Eshu. His anger was a hot knife in his gut. *Money is meaningless here. Is the ritual of exchange so important that you'd let people suffer to keep it?*

It was a vestige of order. It was all Chief Alique had left.

He left the cup untouched on the edge of the desk. "That makes sense," he lied. "I'm sorry to turn down your hospitality, but I'm afraid it really is too late for coffee. Fern and I should sleep."

"Suit yourself, dear," said Chief Alique, and she drained his cup, too.

With a little light in his palm to guide them, Eshu and Fern searched out the *Crest of the Wave*. It lay berthed near the northern edge of the platform, with lanterns at stern and prow. A figurehead loomed over them in the shape of a dragon rampant, its wings folded back against the hull and its carven teeth raised to the sky.

Magical airships could take any shape, of course, and Eshu had seen illustrations of fanciful ones in books—vessels shaped like swans and minnows, gazebos with intricate canework lattices, spheres of glass held together with witching iron. But commercial airships looked much like the sailing ships that had come before them, and but for the ghostly runelines extending out from her rearing figurehead, the *Crest of the Wave* would not have been out of place on the water.

It hurt to look at those runelines. Runecrafting took the lightning-wild magic of poetry and gentled it, fixed it in measured words without inflection—but the runelines that held an airship up were another thing entirely. A skilled runecrafter could create runes of sunlight or shape the lightning into words of power.

A master runecrafter could write her will on reality itself. When Eshu glimpsed the runelines from the corner of his eye, he saw steel cables holding back a yawning abyss.

A few of the airship crew were playing cards on the main deck, betting for one-zil pieces in the desultory way of people who were used to holding onto each other's money. They jumped to their feet a little too fast when Fern climbed aboard, though, and they were better-armed than any other airship crew Eshu had seen on the platform. "You can't be up here," said one, a woman with copper bangles on her bare arms. "This is a private vessel—"

"If it's a wizard and a mapmaker, I invited them," said a voice from beneath a blanket. A moment later, Sparrow struggled free of the blanket and climbed to his feet. "The captain knows. It's fine. They're fine."

"You should've told us, since we were on watch," the woman snapped. She kept her voice low, but Eshu could hear the fire in it. "Things are tense enough without throwing a couple of strangers in at the last minute. What were you thinking—"

"They want to help. They might actually be *able* to help. That's rare enough that I wasn't going to spit on the offer," said Sparrow.

"We can talk later," said another one of the crew, a burly man with a well-groomed beard and a shaven head. "It's nearly midnight."

Realizing it made Eshu's blood grow cold. Sparrow and his crewmates shared a look that said they understood what they were about to do. Below his feet, Eshu heard the sigh of timbers as people paced the lower decks. He thought he heard someone praying, the familiar dawn prayer that travelers spoke before a voyage: *Njo, Far-Traveler, she who knows the way, be my guide and compass on my journey.*

He remembered the doctor sorting beans, the gardener with her gnarled hands worrying whether she'd have time to pack a shawl. He wondered if they were praying, too.

The stair amidships creaked, then Eshu heard slow, regular footsteps. A Kondalani woman with a crown of greying braids climbed to the upper decks. She was tall—nearly as tall as Eshu—and her uniform was trim and fitted her sparse frame like a sheath for a blade. He didn't have to be told that this was the captain of the *Crest of the Wave.*

"What's o'clock?" she asked in a clear, carrying voice. Eshu recognized it as the voice that he'd heard in prayer.

"Near midnight," the bald man answered.

"Is all well?" Somewhere else on the platform, a bell began to toll.

The bald man saluted. "All's well."

The captain folded her hands behind her back. The moonlight threw her hollow cheeks into deep shadow. "Permission to cast off. Steady as she goes."

At both sides of the vessel, crew drew axes and hacked through the hawsers that bound the airship to the platform. Below, someone yelled, "*Hey!*" but the runelines were already beginning to hum with gathered power. Eshu heard a whisper on the air like wind, like blood, like crashing waves: *up and up and up the sun calls the moon calls the swift wind will bear you.*

Light chased down the runelines in prismatic streaks of fire, broke into a thousand threads of color and wove itself into the deep warp of reality. Every loose hair on Eshu's arms and neck stood on end. With a great groaning of timbers, the *Crest of the Wave* rose into the air.

The platform dropped away slowly, at first. A shining hook caught on the rail, a rope going taut behind. Someone hacked it free. Another hook clattered against the hull and fell away. Eshu gripped the rail with both hands, unable to look away as the guards below drew bows, nocked arrows. *The moon calls*, he thought. *The wind will bear us.*

Fern grabbed him by the arm and forced him down below the rail; an arrow seared past where he'd been standing and stuck deep in the mast. "They almost shot you!" she cried. Her eyes were so wide that he could see the whites all around.

They almost shot me, he thought, briefly dumbstruck. He couldn't push himself to understand what that meant. They'd almost shot him, and in his mind there was only *Up and up and up; the wind is a sea, and its waves will bear you.*

"Hit me," he told Fern.

"What the *fuck*—"

"Hit me!" She did, hard enough to make his head spin, and the world snapped back into focus.

Think. The skymaster must be trying to access the runelines, channeling their power through Eshu to make up for the distance. Maybe Thras Nadi hadn't meant to do it; maybe they'd meant to reach out for the captain and didn't even know Eshu was here—but he was here, and the spell coursed through him as though he was a copper pipe. His head rang with it. "All right," he said, and Fern looked at him with concern. "Fuck. All right."

"Do you need me to hit you again?"

"No, I need—"

Before he could figure out what he needed, a voice boomed from below, "*Crest of the Wave*, descend and surrender."

It was Chief Alique's voice. Eshu peered over the rail and saw her, alight with power, red hair crackling with lightning and wand out in her heavy right hand.

It didn't look like a weapon. She didn't look like a duelist. She was an engineer, the wand was a tool, and the *Crest of the Wave* was a mechanical problem she meant to solve.

"Descend and surrender, and no harm will come to you," said Chief Alique. "You have my word."

At the helm, the captain kept her eyes fixed ahead. "Tender no response," she said tightly. "As we approach the clock tower, lower a line. On my signal."

Then there came a keening sound like wire drawn over wire, and the airship fell from the sky.

Eshu grasped for the runelines, and they burned like ice and slipped from his hands. He tried to push his will into those gossamer strands and felt like his skin was turning inside out.

For a weightless moment, he thought, *I'm going to die.* He opened his mouth to sing, and the wind whipped his voice away. He grasped for arguments, for images, for *feelings* that he could use, and he found nothing but the rush of air and the certainty of death approaching.

If he died, he'd never know why this was happening. He'd

never be able to stop it. If he died, he'd never see his mother or his sisters again.

In freefall, he sang a breeze beneath them to buoy them toward the sea; he sang them white-feathered wings and hollow bones. The wind snatched the words from his lips, but still he sang the clouds like foam lapping their hull as the white air churned in their wake.

The sun calls; the moon calls, something sang through him, and he recognized Thras Nadi's logic soaring over his like a descant. They were working the runelines as he couldn't, pushing their will through him like a current of lightning. *Forget the pull of the earth and rise, rise, rise.*

The hull grazed a gem-studded rooftop, knocking clay shingles free—then slowly began to rise. Eshu hit the deck hard and went rolling. He crashed against a mast, and the song broke along with what felt like three of his ribs.

He heaved himself to his feet. It hurt to breathe. He felt something jagged in his side and wasn't sure if it was bone or splinters, but it sent a jolt of pain through his chest with every inhalation.

Then Alique answered. She didn't sing, but he felt her magic like a song: the remorseless pull of gravity. The eager ground to which everyone in time returned. The laws of the universe, every fixed planet orbiting every spiraling star, all of them circling the vast devouring void. All obeyed a commandment older than language, older than life. It was right. It was righteous. The first thing any creature did was fall.

No, thought Eshu fiercely. *It isn't right. Law it may be, but that doesn't make it right.*

He steadied himself on the mast and pushed down the pain, and he sang the great glorious anarchy of the spheres. He sang moons swinging in retrograde, sang stars leashed to each other in twos and threes; he sang the wild whirl of wind that broke across the equator in untraceable curls and billows. With his hand bracing his cracked ribs, hot blood pulsing between his fingers, he raised his voice and sang the swelling tides—the oceans rising from their beds to follow the moon.

There is an order, too, to these, sang the magic quelling the runelines. *There is no mystery that does not grow from order's seed. It is right that there should be order. Look around you—the city will tear itself apart without it.*

They were too close to the ground. Whatever titanic magic had written itself in diamonds here, it strained up from the ruins of Zumera to answer his song. Houses broke free from their foundations and rose skyward, coruscating in the light of the stern lantern. Streets ripped themselves up stone by stone in a whirlwind of sapphire and quartz. Trees dragged themselves from the earth in a shower of dirt and circled the *Crest of the Wave* like tiny islands, emeralds glittering like leaves on their boughs.

He heard a deep rumbling ahead and the sound of crystal snapping. Cracks formed in the sheet of amethyst enclosing the clock tower; fragments of stone washed free in waves. A shard sliced across Eshu's cheek, and he let go of the mast to shield his eyes. Through his fingers, he watched the clock tower break free. It rose like a whale breaching, shedding stone that shone like spray in the moonlight.

See, said Chief Alique's magic, whispering in her voice along the humming runelines. *My darling, my dove, my lost chickadee, there must be order.*

Pain made Eshu gag. He saw motes of light, drifting like ash across the starry sky. *The order of the universe is not yours,* he answered with all the power in him.

His knees hit the deck, and still he sang herbs sprouting from marble floors, leaves spearing toward the sun; he sang roots tearing apart palaces and palisades, tender and remorseless as justice. He sang the high charity of Njo's Rest, the alchemy of loans becoming gifts; he sang the kindness of friends and strangers. He sang Fern's strong shoulder under his arm. He sang Shell washing his feet with a sailor's hands—a mother's hands—in the wreck of her city. He sang the doctor's promise that wherever she fled, no one would be left behind.

The clock tower loomed ahead, bearing down on them like an iceberg through southern waters. The hands on two faces still pointed to midnight. Someone had punched out the face on the far side from the airship landing; it looked like an empty eye socket. "Rope," called the captain. "It'll be tight. Be ready to push off if we cut it too close." Someone lowered a rope.

Still Eshu sang. Someone held him propped up. He smelled grease. He smelled sweet hair lotion, and coffee, and sweat.

Sparrow, he thought. He sang Sparrow, too, the rattle of cup on saucer when he heard a lie he could not brook. He sang the joy of delivering good news, the promise of Cheresse or Ras Kir'uun, of a steady hand on the wheel and a swift ship to a safe port. *It eats you up not knowing why or how to stop it*, Sparrow had said, and he'd said it because he knew how it felt to be consumed with not knowing.

The runelines shifted like harp strings stirred by a breeze. Eshu opened his eyes—when had he closed them?—and saw Fern helping a bird-boned androgyne aboard. They swept the deck with their eyes, until at last their gaze fell on Eshu. "You've done well with my ship," they said, almost fondly. "I'll take it from here, my boy."

Again, there came that faint shudder of wordless melody, and Eshu felt the ship steady itself and begin to descend. Floating crystals ticked against the hull like ice.

He sagged in Sparrow's arms. "I think," he opined to no one in particular, "I don't actually like dueling very much."

Then the darkness swallowed him up.

CHAPTER 7: WILD GODS

The *Crest of the Wave* slowly tracked the coast eastward, searching for somewhere flat enough to set down. After the fall, there were wounded to tend to, and the ship creaked alarmingly when all of Zumera's refugees were aboard. They crowded every deck, sleeping under the stars in shawls and uncomfortable-looking blankets crusted with gems.

Fern sat with her pack beside their stolen mirror and watched Eshu's eyes twitch as he slept. "They get like this sometimes, when they try to work runes like they're incantations," the skymaster had said calmly. "Runes resist improvisation. It's like trying to push your shoulder against a mountain—it wears you out. But he did his best, poor boy. He'll be all right after someone's had a look at his ribs."

It seemed like something the skymaster was saying to themself more than to Fern, so Fern just said, "Thank you."

She'd broken a rib once, when she'd been sick for three months and coughed until it cracked. She hadn't even been able to see it when she looked at her chest in the mirror; she'd only known it was broken by the way it hurt and the way it healed. Even in the dim light, Eshu's looked a lot worse than hers had. Still, his breathing was quiet and even. The doctor from the public house had come to give him a quick look, and she'd said he was probably going to be all right.

So he was probably going to be all right.

I should sleep, thought Fern. *It's been the longest day already, and it isn't over yet.* She burrowed against her pack and fluffed it around until the softest parts were on top, and she sat there with her back aching and her hands going cold until the sun started to rise.

She might've slept. She thought she had, anyway. When she opened her eyes again, the sky was tawny golden at the edges, and the mountains had given way to wooded hills.

"There's a valley ahead, captain," said someone in uniform. "Looks like cedars and some sturdy hardwoods further back from the shore. We could set down there."

"Handsomely, then," decided the captain. She still looked tired and grim, but at the sight of the valley, she smiled with faint triumph. "Skymaster, prepare for descent."

They set down gently beside a little stream, in a field of long grass and scruffy thorn trees. The impact was enough to startle Eshu awake, and from the sound he made, he immediately regretted it.

"Where are we?" he asked, probing at the dried blood on his side.

"Maybe don't touch that," said Fern. "We're somewhere east of Zumera; if you want to know, I can get out the map, but it's probably better if you don't get up to look right now. I'm going to get the doctor. She wanted to see you when you woke up. She said you were probably going to be all right."

"That's the least reassuring thing you could possibly have said. Ugh, it feels so much worse when I lie down—"

"It helps to lie down on the side that hurts. I know, it doesn't really make sense."

"Were any bones, ah, protruding?"

"No," said Fern, "but there were some big splinters."

"Of bone?" Eshu prompted.

Fern smiled. "Just wood."

"I've never broken a bone before," groused Eshu, carefully propping himself upright against the rail. "I'd expected the first time would be falling down the stairs or some other mundane thing."

"Can you sing your ribs better, the way you did your foot?"

"I have no fucking idea. There are all kinds of structures under the skin that might have ruptured. Bones, fat, muscle, veins—I'd have to sing them all back together, and I don't even know which are broken." He sighed, then winced. "I wish I'd had a chance to go through the wizard's library. There was probably a book on this."

"Ah, you're awake!" The doctor stood over them with a leather bag in her hand. She undid the catches and set it down beside Eshu, giving him a disarming smile as she squatted at his side. "You can call me Doctor Branch. If you're ready, I'd like to take a look at your ribs again. There may be some small splinters or fibers I missed in the dark, and I don't want them to give you an infection."

"Excellent, *another* variable to worry about," Eshu muttered, but he pulled his robe off of his shoulders and let it fall around his waist. "I'm ready. And thank you for looking me over. I'm sure I'm not the only person you've had to look at this morning."

"I'm just happy to be useful," said Doctor Branch.

As the doctor took out a pair of tweezers, Fern climbed to her feet. "I'm going to explore the area," she said. "Watch my pack, all right?"

"If anyone tries to steal your tree-climbing equipment, I'll look at them very sternly," Eshu promised.

The airship crew had lowered a ladder over the side, so Fern climbed down and made her way toward the stream. A few of the people from Zumera were washing clothes in it, or taking a piss further downstream, so she hiked upstream along the grassy bank. At first, she'd thought she might take a look at what kinds of rocks were in the area and see what she could figure out about the local drainage basins. As soon as she saw people washing, though, she wanted nothing more than to be clean.

The water wasn't deep or wide, but it smelled clean and looked clear, which was a relief after the foul tides of Sharis. Fern kept walking until she'd reached the shadow of the trees, and there, she stripped off her clothes and had her first real wash in days.

This early in the morning, the water was bracingly cool. No soap to be had, but she rubbed water under her arms and through her hair until she'd stopped itching with grease. She had some exciting new bruises from the fall last night, and some scratches that she thought were from the broken crystals on the window ledge, but otherwise, she thought she was in pretty solid shape.

After her body was clean, she scrubbed her clothes on a big, flat rock until the obvious stains were gone. Then she left them to dry on the bank and waded back into the water, trying to guess by the plants and animals whether any calamity had come through lately.

As far as the stream was concerned, life went on as usual. Iridescent, lacy-winged insects rested on grass stems overhanging the water. Turtles basked on exposed rocks, and dark spotted salamanders drifted in the eddies. Schools of tiny grey fish scattered in every direction when she moved toward them, startled by her splashing feet; once, a little rodent she didn't recognize came down to the water to drink, then rubbed wet paws over its tufted ears. When her shadow fell across it, it froze, then darted for a burrow on the bank. All around her, some unfamiliar species of bladderwort drifted beneath the water, its fronds a bright, healthy green.

Fern had spent the last few months tramping through streambeds just like this one. She'd never thought that it would be a relief to see so many salamanders.

She joined the turtles for about an hour while the sun climbed higher in the sky and the air grew warm and sultry. When at last her clothes were mostly dry, she dressed reluctantly, put on her boots, and bid the turtles farewell.

She knew that she should go back to the airship, but it looked like the engineers were still swarming over the hull, and the solitude of the trees was welcome after a few tense days of seeing death and dealing with other people. Instead, she followed the stream deeper into the wood.

The saplings and stunted thorn bushes at the edge of the wood quickly gave way to a forest of mixed cypresses and tall evergreens. The space under the trees smelled sharp and green, touched with the scent of sea salt and the clear, mineral smell of the stream. Overhead, glossy leaves clattered in the breeze. Some sort of bird or insect kept up a constant, rasping song like the whir of an old spinning wheel.

She wished she'd brought her pack. She'd never been to the north shore before, and there were all kinds of leaves and fungi and insects that she wanted to draw or bottle. *Maybe there will be time to come back later*, she thought. The prospect of waiting for the airship to be repaired wasn't appealing, and she imagined the other passengers were eager to see if Cheresse was doing any better than Nanjeer, but she did like the thought of a few days to hike and recover.

Fern was still planning how she'd organize her specimens when she noticed that she'd met up with a trail. The path led up from a well-worn dip in the bank, like a watering spot. At first, it looked as though it might be an animal track. It was only broad enough for one person to walk abreast, and the undergrowth didn't seem to have ever been cut back. But when Fern looked more closely, she saw that the trail continued on the far bank, as though whoever came this way crossed the water and kept walking. And she did think it was a person's trail, although she couldn't have said why.

There weren't any footprints in the mud near the stream, so she guessed that no one had been through recently. *There's probably something on each end*, she thought, *so I might as well pick a direction and start walking.*

One direction looked as good as the other. Since she was on the left bank, and she didn't want to get her boots wet by crossing the stream, she made her way east along the trail.

Immediately, the forest took on a different character. That creaking-wheel rasp of birds or insects quieted, and the light seemed different somehow—softer, and warmer, and greener. As though it was filtering through greenhouse glass.

She swiped her wrist over her eyes and shook her head. *It's incredible how people change their environments*, she thought. *I wouldn't have imagined that a little trail like this would make such a big difference to how the forest feels.*

The path wound between hills, among towering trees with raised roots almost as tall as Fern. She almost wanted to linger there—flowering vines and sharp-edged epiphytes had rooted in the nooks in the bark, and she wanted to see if she could classify them—but her curiosity about the trail got the better of her. She paused only long enough to peer at a creeping centipede with red spots like eyes at its hind end, then continued on.

Slowly, the trail began to climb. She found a sturdy fallen stick to use as a walking stick and traced the trail up the rocky slope of a mountain, through berry bushes humming with tiny lantern bees and over a bridge made of unmortared stone.

It was almost a relief to see the bridge. As she'd pushed deeper into the mountains, further away from the airship and its passengers, she'd begun to wonder if she was following a human trail after all. She felt like the last person left in the world.

At a bend in the trail, she found a little shrine of carved rock. Someone had placed offerings here: a polished jasper serpent, a string of copper one-zil coins, half a melon that some little animal had nibbled to the rind. A copper bowl full of mucky ash, as though something had been burned here.

It wasn't a shrine to the Sisters, and Fern had never been all that religious, anyway. But Fern's parents had raised her to be respectful of strangers' gods, so she laid a hunk of fluorite from her pocket on the altar stone and knelt a while in contemplation.

The breeze picked up, and the leaves clattered overhead. From somewhere far below, she heard the rush of the stream. The sun warmed the nape of her neck.

Her mother had a trick to making her mind peaceful. She'd talk about what was happening like it was a story: *You're sitting in this chair, and there's hot tea in your hand, and you can feel the warmth against your palm through the cup. Your feet are sore. They hurt right where the spur of the heel hits the ground.* She'd lose herself in the moment, until all of her worries seemed far away. That trick probably worked better when the world wasn't coming apart at the seams.

If she thought about her mother anymore, she was going to cry. She still had a long way to walk today, and she couldn't afford to wear herself out with tears.

She climbed to her feet again. It was almost noon, and the people back at the airship would probably be wondering where she was. They hadn't looked anywhere near ready to fly when she'd left them, but she didn't know how long it took to inspect an airship.

Maybe they were looking for her. Or maybe they'd already given up looking for her. *Would Eshu wait for me?* she wondered. *Or would he leave me here and fly off with that engineer he liked?* She wouldn't have blamed him if he'd left already. He'd only known her a few days, and he knew she was good at finding her way. If he had gone, she hoped he'd at least left her pack.

She picked up her stick again and gave it an experimental twirl. It had a good balance. It felt good in her hand. *Hardwoods*, the airship crew had called these leafy evergreens—good for repairing the less flexible parts of an airship. Maybe if she got a chance, she'd finish the wood one day and make a proper walking stick of it.

When she looked up from her stick, someone was watching her from further up the path.

It was hard to make out more than the shape of a person and the feeling of attention. When Fern tried to look closer, her mind shuddered away before she caught more than the rough shag of cypress bark, a skull with two long curling horns, fur and scale and chitin and leaves. The coils of a serpent, dappled with sun and shadow.

She knew she should be afraid. She had been, when she saw the Crowtaker on the streets of Sharis, and the Crowtaker had just looked like a woman in a mask and hood. But when she looked up at this stranger, for no reason at all, Fern felt at peace. "I'm sorry," she said. "I didn't realize this shrine was anybody's. I was just leaving."

The stranger gestured with arms like graceful branches, tipped with claws and needles. It wasn't any sign language Fern had ever seen, but she felt immediately that it *was* a language, and she yearned to understand it.

With her stick, she began to draw in the dirt—the course of the stream that she'd followed, the trail over the hills, the mountain and the shrine. When she was done, she pointed to the far side of the trail, the one that went west away from the stream. "What's here?" she asked. "Who comes from there?"

The thousand shapes of the stranger slowly spun into focus, as though Fern was watching through the whirling lenses of an eyeglass-seller displaying her wares. Her eyes watered. For a moment, the sunlight was too bright. Then, when she'd blinked the glare out of her eyes, she saw an old man standing before her. He leaned on a polished walking staff. One eye was clouded with cataracts, but the other was deep brown and very keen. His wrinkled brown skin had burned and roughened from long exposure to wind and sun.

"Did he leave these offerings?" She pointed to the melon, the coins, the jasper serpent.

The old man nodded.

"Is he still alive?"

A gesture that she couldn't read—something like sorrow or regret in his expression that made her think, *No.*

"I'm sorry," she said. "Was it when..." Fern grappled for a way to say it. She remembered the piled bodies in Sharis, the eerie emptiness of Zumera. The man impaled on a spear of tourmaline. How she'd tucked him into someone's bed, maggots and all, as though he was sleeping. The people gathered together in cracked towers and passenger shelters and public houses, counting beans and jars of honey to figure out how long they had until things got really, truly bad. All of that felt so far away, at this little secret shrine in the mountains.

Finally, she took her stick and swiped away her map in one violent gesture of erasure. When she looked up again, the god was watching her with eyes like stars seen through the swaying canopy. There was a gentleness in them that was almost like compassion. The god offered a hand, a taloned claw, a branch dripping with moss.

It was probably a bad idea to take it. She'd grown up hearing stories of strangers who offered kindness in order to lead children astray. Back in Matis, Heza had liked to read out the headlines from the morning's broadsheets while she worked, clicking her tongue at every tale of murder or kidnapping. And this far out in the woods, probably no one would ever find Fern's body.

If she didn't take it, she might never know what had happened.

She put her hand in the god's and felt it close. The warmth there wasn't anything like the warmth of human skin; it felt like the sun-struck rocks where the turtles stood basking. Fern tried to think of the god like that—not like a person, but like the whole forest, stream and cypresses and rocks and turtles and epiphytes and centipedes and fish scattering in the shallows.

The forest took her gently by the hand and led her up the mountain, across moss-covered bridges and spines of rock with rusted chains to help her keep her balance. Just shy of the mountain's crest, the forest led her toward a shallow pool sheltered beneath a rock overhang. Steam rose from it, along with a faint smell of sulfur. *A hot spring*, she thought. She'd known that the northern mountains were volcanic, and that they were dotted with hot springs and geysers, but this was the first time she'd ever seen one in person. It wasn't as impressive as the ones she'd read about in books, with rocks stained blue and red and yellow, but it felt private and sacred in a way that she couldn't quite put into words. The forest crept right up to the water, saplings and berry bushes and piebald birds bathing at the water's edge.

The old man must have come up here to ease his aching bones until he couldn't make the climb any longer. Fern wondered if there was another shrine nearby, decked with gifts left by a younger man.

"Thank you for showing me this place," Fern said. "It's clearly special. And very geologically interesting. I won't forget it."

The forest pressed her hand, and she felt the touch ripple through her entire body. *Look deeper*, it seemed to say. *This is the only answer I know how to give.*

She shed her boots and tied up her trousers at the knee, then she waded into the water. It was as warm as her skin—blood-warm, her mother used to say. Then warmer, as she walked deeper into the water. Her bare feet felt shaped stone beneath the fine layer of silt at the bottom of the pool, and then irregular indentations like letters.

When she bent down to brush the dirt away, she found runes carved into the stones.

She straightened, and soon, the water lay like a mirror all around her. She looked down at her own reflection, strange and squat in perspective, and then across the water to where the forest waited.

Reflected in the water was something so beautiful that her heart ached—neither man nor woman nor androgyne, but something strange and green and shining. A person like the most perfect summer day, like the drift of clouds and the smell of berries and the way the trees rustled like an ocean in the breeze. Tears tracked down Fern's cheeks, and she didn't want to look away long enough to wipe her eyes.

Look, mouthed the god, beckoning with both arms. *See what I see.*

When Fern looked down into the water, she seemed to see the diamond sands of the Mirrorlands rolling in white dunes to the mountains. Streams wound across the sands in shining ribbons, rising out of the dry washes to nourish silvery trees. *Somewhere,* Fern thought, *there must be a river at the end of these streams. And beyond that, a vast and quiet sea.* If she looked long enough, surely she would see something gleaming on the horizon—

Then a bird alighted with a flutter of wings, breaking the clear surface of the pool.

When Fern looked to the edge of the water, she found that she was alone.

...and so I came back here," said Fern. "It was a strange thing. Sort of—I don't know how to say it. Sad, and kind, but very confusing. I'm a little tempted to say that I dreamed it all."

"Wild gods are often like that," answered Eshu. He sat tending a fire on the beach, since Doctor Branch had said that he wasn't in any shape to help the skymaster with the repairs. "I've known a few gods who spend their time among people, and they're a lot like wizards—they know and sense things that others don't, but you can have a conversation with them about it. You might not be able to follow what they say, but they at least say it in *words*. But wild gods aren't really in the practice of having conversations. They forget how, or never bother to learn."

Fern picked at her teeth with a fish bone as she stared into the flames. "Do you think it understood my question? Do you think it was trying to answer?"

"I think so. But whatever answer it was trying to give, we'll find it on the far side of the mirror." He hummed a simple, melancholy scale, and the firelight shifted from golden to blue; a different scale, and it deepened to violet.

"Stop screwing around with the fire!" called someone from the makeshift lumber yard close by. "I'm not keen to saw off my own hand in the dark."

"My apologies," answered Eshu, and the fire went golden again.

"We should try to set up that mirror we took," said Fern. "I know you want to go to Kondala, and I want to help you get there, but we've been away from the Sharisi folks a long time. They're probably worried. And they might have heard by now what happened in Lalani."

"Something terrible, no doubt," muttered Eshu. "It will be difficult to install the mirror here. The terrain just isn't distinct enough. We'd have to build some kind of—let's call it a landmark. Something that's memorable enough to anchor the spell in space."

Fern considered that for a moment. The practice sounded a little like a very old form of mapmaking that she'd only heard about glancingly in her history classes. It wasn't based on faithfully rendering the topography of coasts and mountains, but on charting a kind of storyteller's dictionary of landforms and monuments. This style had fallen out of fashion at least five hundred years ago, and as far as she could tell, no one in her discipline missed it.

That was probably a rude thing to point out. "It just seems as though we could use coordinates instead," she said.

"Use...?"

"Coordinates." Eshu still looked baffled, so Fern added, "You know, longitude and latitude? The grid lines on a globe? You can use them to assign numerical values to a place, and then you can find it in relation to other places, even if you've never been to any of them. And if you've got an astrolabe and a good watch, you can calculate them pretty easily. It's very helpful. Especially on ships, where you can't always see landmarks. Hasn't anyone ever tried to do that for mirror travel?"

Eshu coughed, then winced. "Magic is a bit more. Ah. Intuitive, and poetic. Somewhat less mathematical. I'm not sure knowing which arbitrary numbers were assigned to a place would actually help me to find it."

Fern threw her fish bone into the fire. "Well, if you can wait until noon tomorrow, I can at least figure out what the coordinates *are*, and then we can do your intuitive, poetic thing. So we'll have something to fall back on. Meanwhile, I guess we build a landmark? What kind of landmark do you even need to find a mirror?"

"Something particular," said Eshu. "In Kondala City, the Hall of Ways was a circular hall of white marble, with tall pillars and green silk banners billowing between them. The kind of place that, once you'd seen it, was impossible to forget. Or—I could be misremembering, but I think there was some sort of mosaic in the wizards' tower in Sharis—"

"The stars," said Fern at once. That mosaic was so clearly etched into her memory that she could still trace the whorls of black tile in her mind's eye. "I don't think we have time to make something like that. And I don't want to make you climb a mountain when your ribs are broken, so I don't think the shrine in the woods is a good idea. But maybe we can make a little sculpture out of driftwood or something."

"That might work. Even the barn was particular enough, just because people had lived and worked there until it shaped itself around them. It doesn't have to be the Hall of Ways."

Look at that, Fern thought. *We're having a normal, technical conversation, just as though everything isn't falling apart.* She looked around at the people of Zumera gathered around their campfires. A couple of children had made a game of bringing the old gardener plants to identify from around the shore, and Doctor Branch was teaching a couple of younger folk how to splint a broken bone. They huddled over one of the sailors from the *Crest of the Wave,* checking his broken arm together.

On the airship deck, the runelines stretched out in all directions like a spider's web. When she'd traveled by airship before, Fern had thought they were just some kind of delicate magical rigging, but she was beginning to appreciate how much more they were than rope. They were like a contract the skymaster had made with the forces of the universe, explaining how gravity was supposed to come to bear on the airship and its passengers. Sparrow had said that the runelines had snapped in a storm a few months back, and Fern had thought it was just like losing a mast or a sail. Devastating, but a ship could limp along with oars and jury-rigged masts. Even haul an anchor out and creep along by kedging, if the waters were shallow enough and the anchor was light enough.

Snapping a runeline must have been like trying to sail on the moon. She wondered what kind of force could do that to an airship. *I hope I never find out,* she thought.

As Fern watched, the skymaster pulled off a pair of crystal magnifying glasses and tucked them into a pocket, then dabbed their brow with a handkerchief and sauntered over to the ladder. They slid down the way the sailors did, barely pausing to put their feet on the steps, and then sat down by the fire.

Even after a full day of working in the sun, after a sleepless night fleeing a shattered city, they looked very tidy and poised. They were Kiruuni, slightly built, with a clean-shaven head and delicate hands. Over their airship livery, they wore a long, intricately embroidered sleeveless vest that Fern thought was called an ilani. It looked like it had very deep pockets, and Fern was a little jealous.

"I thought I smelled fish cooking," said the skymaster. "From the sea, or the stream?"

"The sea," Fern answered.

"Excellent. I can eat that. Would you be so good as to find some fish for me? It pains me to say it, but now that I'm finally sitting down, I don't want to get up again."

"Of course." Fern rose from her seat. She did a circuit of the camp until she found someone who was still cooking fish, then she checked to make sure it was saltwater fish and brought back a skewer. The meat didn't look like it had been seasoned—Fern's hadn't been, either—but it was still steaming and smelled incredible.

Poor Eshu had made do with a garlic and seaweed soup prepared in Fern's little camping pan. He'd chewed through the leathery seaweed without once complaining about the texture, which was more fortitude than she'd seen from him so far.

The skymaster took the fish skewer with quiet thanks. "My name is Thras Nadi," they said. "But if it makes you feel better to call me something else, you can call me Sand."

"Nadi is fine. You can call me Fern. And this is Eshu, but I guess you two have met by now." She dug her toes into the loose pebbles of the shore. "Sorry about your ship."

"The runelines are sound, at least. Small mercies. The hull took significant strain in the fall, but that's what our engineers are for. The *Crest* will be ready to fly again in another day. Two, at the most. By then, you two should be well on your way back to Sharis, or Kondala, or wherever it is you're bound." Nadi picked meat from bone deftly, never letting the fish's juices drip to the ground. They cleared their skewer in under a minute and licked their fingers clean after, then they wiped their hands with their handkerchief, one finger after the other.

After they'd tucked the handkerchief away, Nadi pulled a little hand mirror from their pocket and looked into it. At first, Fern thought they were checking their face—some kind of lingering fastidiousness, like the kind that made them clean their hands just so—but then she remembered Chief Alique's speaking mirror. Fern leaned forward and asked, "Is that the mirror you use to speak to headquarters?"

"It is," said Nadi. "But there's nothing to see."

Eshu, who had been playing with the fire again, looked up from his meditations. "When I looked over Chief Alique's shoulder, I saw soldiers in it. A map with areas hatched in red and green."

"Well, yes, but that's only the idle message. Here. See for yourself." Nadi passed the mirror over to Eshu, who studied its surface for a long moment before handing it to Fern. By now, the metal of the frame was warm from their hands. It looked like pewter or tin, worked in a simple design like a twist of hempen rope. Her mother had had a hand mirror a lot like this one.

When she gazed into the mirror, though, she felt strange all over—as though she'd shaken just barely loose of her body, and now she was overlaying it like colored ink overflowing its linework. She saw a trim little desk with an empty chair behind it, and a map of Nanjeer colored with chalk lines in red and green and blue and grey. If she looked hard enough, she could read every single city's name. Soldiers moved through the background, consulting charts and instruments that she recognized as water and mercury barometers.

Through her mind echoed a litany in a gentle voice, smooth and sexless as glass: *The attendant is away from the desk and will return shortly. Please await the next scheduled check-in.*

Her throat felt tight. She swallowed, then handed the glass back to Nadi. "And it's been like that since the lights?"

"That, I can't tell you. I was asleep when it happened, tucked under my blanket. My bunkmate had been sick in the privy pot, and I had the sheets all the way over my head to try to cut the smell. She saved my life, I think." They tucked the mirror back into one of their deep pockets. "I woke to a great weight on me and thought it was sleep paralysis. The kind of nightmare that rides you so hard that you can't move when you wake up. But instead, I found that my blanket was covered in jewels."

"I came to find them not long after," said another voice; Fern jumped a little, then relaxed when she recognized Sparrow. He stood over them for a moment, stretching his arms, then sat down at Nadi's side. "It was nearly an hour past midnight by then. People were panicking in the city. We had a whole crowd of people storming the stairs to the platform, saying people were dead all through the city. Demanding that we evacuate them. Chief Alique didn't take it well. She tried to tell them off in that way she has, sort of reassuring and commanding at the same time, and that just made them more upset, so she conjured up a line of soldiers and told them to force everyone back. A couple of people got hurt."

Got hurt, Fern thought, *as though it just happened by accident.*

"Anyway." Sparrow licked his lips. "She said someone needed to go down and see what was happening, and since I had to go fetch the rest of the Crests anyway, I volunteered."

"And once I heard what had happened, we decided that we wanted to get these people out. Then there was nothing left to do but convince our captain and crew." Nadi gave a thin smile. "I told him to tell the chief that I was dead. That gave us a bit more leeway to organize our escape."

"No chance that we'd try to run without a skymaster," Sparrow agreed. "It was hard enough to manage without them aboard."

"You did as well as could be expected," said Nadi. From anyone else, that would have sounded like faint praise, but their voice had a simple sincerity that was immediately reassuring.

Fern inhaled. "So, anyway. The mirror's not dark, but it's not showing anything that's happening. At least, not what's happening right now. I guess Chief Alique was telling the truth about that."

"Having second thoughts about stealing an airship?" asked Eshu.

Leaning back on her hands, Fern considered the question.

*When I asked Chief Alique about the people in the city, she cared more
about who'd paid their fares than about who needed to evacuate. And she
tried to say that was order—and maybe she even thought it was. But it
wasn't any kind of order I wanted to be a part of.*

"No," said Fern firmly. "It doesn't matter whether Chief Alique
was telling the truth about what she saw in the mirror. If I didn't
help these people, I couldn't look myself in the eye again."

"I'd drink to that, if we had anything to drink," said Sparrow,
raising an imaginary glass to the gathering stars. "That should be
our first order of business, in Cheresse. Make sure the wineries are
all right."

"You have no idea how much I wish I were going with you,"
muttered Eshu. "Sadly, I have to make sure Kondala City hasn't
dissolved in acid or turned into a convocation of moths."

"I hear there's good wine in Kondala, too," said Sparrow.
"Maybe after this trip is over, I'll come find you there."

"See what absurd tragedy has befallen us, and descend from
the clouds like a drake-rider from an old story to rescue us. There's
a pleasing poetry in that." Eshu raised an imaginary glass, too, and
they clinked over the fire.

They sat up talking until the fires had burned to embers,
swapping stories of travel—of geometric gardens perfumed with
jasmine and catmint, of busy ports all along the Kirami, of red
brick palaces in the far north that only Nadi had seen. Since
Sparrow had brought it up, Eshu told him of valleys lined with
vines on frames and arches, where the grapes hung heavy and red.
He told of how they tasted when the sun had warmed their skin,
and the grapes nearly burst in your mouth with melting sweetness.
When he spoke, Fern could almost taste it, too.

It wasn't until Fern bedded down for the night that her mind
returned to that dim realm behind the mirror, where soldiers
consulted barometers at desks arranged just so. She realized what
it meant that the map in the mirror was just some old weather map,

and had nothing to do with the world falling apart.

She didn't know anymore whether Matis was all right.

Early the next morning, Fern went with a couple of people from Zumera to scour the shore for edible berries. The old gardener from the public house, who asked to be called Acacia, explained how to recognize sea plums a little way back from the high tide line. They just looked like scruffy thorn bushes to Fern, but the berries were fat and ripe and left purple stains on her hands, and soon she'd figured out the trick of stretching the snarled branches out so that the berries hung down to be plucked. They weren't really plums—they had seeds, and not stones—but they tasted tart and sweet and just a little like apricots. There was an aftertaste of salt that only made the sweetness seem richer.

By the time the sun was properly up and Eshu and the captain had finished their dawn prayer, Fern and the rest had returned with baskets full of dusky blue berries.

"Praise the Sisters," said Sparrow as he came to get a handful of berries. "At least it's not canteen food."

"And they'll ward off scurvy," said Acacia. Her smile deepened the gentle lines around her eyes. "Glad you like it."

Not long after, the airship crew went back to their repairs. In the light, Fern could see better what they'd done: reinforced the stem (the poor dragon figurehead was cracked across the hips), and worked loose a few of the splintered strakes and planks to replace them with new. *The fall must've been worse than I thought.*

All of the cargo had been moved out to a separate place on the beach, so Fern went looking there for the mirror with its blanket wrapping. It was easy enough to find; it was close to the edge of the area, and someone—probably Eshu—had made sure it wound up near the top of the stack. She eased it free, then tucked it under her arm and began to drag it across the beach.

She'd seen a rock formation while she was foraging that looked like a good place to build a landmark. There were some interesting basalt structures rising from the waves to the mountains, all tall hexagonal pillars climbing in steps to the cypresses above. Even if he didn't care about rocks the way she did, surely Eshu would be able to remember those.

Fern passed by people fishing in the shallows or digging for oysters along the sandier parts of the beach; she passed barnacle-rimmed tide pools teeming with crabs and sea stars and dark red-purple urchins. Everything was going well until she caught her boot on a basalt ridge, and the mirror went down on hard stone with a sickening *crack*.

Her stomach clenched up into a knot. "Shit," she said, and immediately began unwrapping the mirror. Even before she'd got the blanket all the way off, though, glass shards tinkled on the stone.

CHAPTER 8: THE LONG WAY AROUND

Eshu circled the broken glass, as though it looked any less terrible from any other angle. The mirror stood propped against the rocks with a spider's web of cracks spreading out from one corner. "I'm sorry," said Fern for what must have been the fiftieth time. She hovered near his elbow as he paced, peering around him at the glass with horror in her eyes. Her hands were still stained purple with berry juice from this morning, and she was twisting them in the hem of her vest as though she meant to dye it.

He couldn't really blame her. He had a lot of choice words for her right now, burning unspoken in his throat. It felt like holding down a bubble of acid.

"Well, it's completely fucked," he said at last.

"I'm so sorry," said Fern again. "Can you fix it?"

"What do I look like, a glazier?" He shook his head. "Magic mirrors are hard to make. They take a lot of time and patience and specialist materials. They cost a fortune. And despite all of that, when magic mirrors break, it's *still* less expensive to replace them outright than to try to repair them. So no, I can't fucking fix it."

Fern chewed her bottom lip. "I didn't realize it was so complicated. You said back in Sharis that mirrors could be replaced, so I thought it was easy. I'm sorry—I would've been more careful if I'd known—"

"Stop saying you're sorry!" he snapped. "I don't care whether you're sorry. That mirror was my best way of getting home."

Her lips formed an *I*, but at least she didn't say the words. She looked anxious and hurt, and he was just angry enough to think, *Good*. He turned back to the camp, pressing on his ribs to ease the pain. It didn't help, really.

Fern trailed a little way behind. "Do you think the skymaster can fix it? They're a wizard. They know runecrafting. Maybe there's something they can do." She sounded miserable.

"As I said, it's a specialist art. They're not likely to know it." Eshu took a deep breath, which his ribs didn't enjoy at all. He was being a cock to her, and he knew it, and he didn't like seeing it in himself. She deserved better from him. "We're going to have to walk if we want to get to Kondala," he said, "and that's easily the most depressing thing I've said in a long, depressing week."

"Maybe the captain would take us," Fern offered. "It's a little out of their way—"

"You've seen the map. It's at least as far to Kondala City as it is to Cheresse, and it's in almost the opposite direction."

"Not the opposite direction," said Fern. "It's only a few days out of their way. It would be weeks of travel for us."

"We can ask," he said. "But it's better for me if I resign myself to the idea of walking as early as possible. I'll have longer to make my peace with it."

"There's another option," said Fern slowly. "Between here and Kondala, it's mostly wilderness and villages, but there is one bigger city. It's called Kulmeni. It's a principality capital on the Anjali River. They might have wizards. Or might have had wizards."

"Past tense," Eshu agreed. He remembered hearing the city's name recently, but he couldn't remember where. Something Sparrow had mentioned? Or Shell? "I've heard of Kulmeni. It's a bit out of our way, if I'm remembering the geography right."

"It looks like that on a map, but that's because maps are flat. The land isn't. There are mountains the whole way from here to Kondala. It would be exhausting to climb them to travel in a straight line, so we'd probably be following the Anjali for part of the trip anyway." Fern sounded calmer now that she had a problem to figure out, and that made Eshu feel calmer, too. When the broken mirror had been an insurmountable barrier between him and home, it had felt like he could do nothing but immolate himself in anger until he burned to a cinder. Now that there was a route, with a finite length and planned stops along the way, the panic began to subside.

"I'm sorry I shouted at you," he said eventually.

"It wasn't great."

"I know."

Fern rolled her shoulders and looked away. "I know I fucked up. And I know that this is going to be a lot harder for us because of it. But I'm going to fuck up again, and so are you. I don't want to beat myself up over it, and I don't want you to beat me up over it, either. I'd rather think about what we can do to fix it and keep going."

"Then that's what we'll do. I warn you, though, I may continue to treat every slight inconvenience as a catastrophe."

One corner of Fern's mouth twitched up. "Well, we're in an actual catastrophe, so I don't mind so much. It's almost refreshing to have little problems."

It was reassuring, in a way that Eshu hadn't expected it to be, that Fern had never even seemed to consider leaving him to make his own way. "Exactly. Better to pitch a fit at annoyances than to panic when something genuinely awful happens."

They made their way slowly back across the stony shore. Now and then, Fern let him rest under the guise of showing him some feature of the local tide pools, and he appreciated the veneer of dignity that it afforded him. "This urchin is ground up to make a dye we call Equatorial Red, because they only live here in the tropics," she told him as she held up a spiky ball that might've been a plant or an animal. "But you can find this same species in the waters off Ras Kir'uun, and I hear they've even been found around these little volcanic islands in the middle of the Dollami—" He let her words wash over him, a gentle tide of facts and anecdotes, and was surprised to find that it calmed him.

Back at the *Crest of the Wave*, the captain saw things more or less the way Eshu had expected her to. "We have wounded, elderly, and children," she said. "And our supplies are limited. We have no way of knowing if these disasters are a coordinated attack on Nanjeer, and Kondala and Nanjeer are closely allied. If I have to choose between Kondala and Cheresse, I'll turn my prow toward Cheresse."

"You're Kondalani, too," said Fern. "Don't you want to go home?" Eshu could hear her desperation, and he knew it was on his behalf—Kondala City was on the opposite side of the continent from Matis. Every step toward his home took her further away from her own.

"I do," the captain answered. Her face betrayed no emotion. "For my passengers, though, Cheresse is the better choice. Now, if you'll excuse me, I have repairs to oversee."

Fern took her coordinate measurements at noon—although it didn't particularly matter, since they couldn't use them to navigate by the mirror now—and jotted them down on the map. "I might want to know them later," she said.

"I can't imagine why it would be important."

"It doesn't have to be important. I might want to know, so I'm writing them down," she said, and that was the end of the matter.

The ship was declared airworthy by noon, and all of the cargo had been loaded again and the passengers settled well before sunset. Then there was nothing left to do but say goodbye.

"Try not to lift anything heavy," warned Doctor Branch. "Rest when you need it. And if you can sleep sitting up, it might help."

"Thank you. I'll do my best," Eshu promised.

"Be careful, if you encounter another place like Zumera," said Nadi, who found him next. They pressed a black runestone into his hand and closed his fingers around it. "In a zone of susceptibility, incantation is the worst possible school of magic to practice. It's unstable. It relies on the world's responsiveness to your rhetoric. A susceptible zone will do whatever you ask it to, a thousand times over, and you won't always be able to make it stop."

Eshu opened his hand to study the runestone. It felt heavier than it should have been, as though the magic worked into it had made it dense or as though the universe had warped slightly around it. *Warding* was carved into its polished surface. "I couldn't take this from you," he said.

"If you and your cartographer friend really mean to walk to Kondala, you'll need it more than I will. It will protect your camp against natural predators—tigers, mosquitos, constrictor snakes."

"Njo have mercy, do *all* of those live in the woods? Thank you, that's horrifying."

"All those and more, I'm sorry to say. And if you encounter anything otherworldly, it won't be much use." They patted his hand. Their fingers were thin and smooth and cool. "Stay safe, Eshusikinde."

Behind them, Eshu saw Sparrow standing with his thumbs in the waistband of his trousers. He caught Eshu's eye and waved.

Nadi followed his gaze, then quirked a smile and muttered a quick goodbye. Sparrow stepped into the gap, close enough that Eshu could smell cedar and cypress on his clothes. "So," he said.

"This is goodbye, then," said Eshu. "I'm sorry. I'm not used to saying it."

"Say 'until later' then." Sparrow grinned. It lit him up from the inside. "Not sure when 'later' will be, or where. But someday, somewhere, I'll see you again."

He had no way of knowing that was true, but Eshu longed to believe him all the same. "Until later," said Eshu, and kissed

Sparrow's cheek in parting.

The memory of that kiss lingered even as Sparrow climbed up to the deck, waving his kerchief over the rail. Then the ladders came up, and the captain took the wheel. "Permission to embark, Skymaster Thras," she said. "Steady as she goes."

He felt the runelines humming with power even before he saw them flickering against the deep blue sky. Rainbows and shadows danced between invisible filaments; bright light flashed wherever two runelines crossed, piercing and sweet as a high, clear note of music.

The *Crest of the Wave* rose into the air and struck out north across the seas. He and Fern stood a long time on the shore, watching the white shape of it grow smaller. At length, Fern dug in one of her pockets and pulled out a little waxed-paper packet. "Here," she said, handing it over. "I traded some salt for this before they left."

Eshu gave the packet an experimental squeeze and found that it contained something flat and hard and oblong. He unfolded the waxed paper, and an incredible perfume of sandalwood and orris root drifted out. It was stupid to cry over a used bar of soap, but his eyes were wet all the same. "Thank you," he managed to say.

"I just thought maybe you wouldn't be such a prick if you could finally have a real bath," said Fern, with a crooked little smile. "I couldn't get anyone to trade me for lotion or hair oil. Sorry. I know you miss it. I miss it, too."

"I'm hardly in a position to complain. Did you at least get some soap for yourself?"

"It doesn't matter," she said. "I've walked through enough swamps by now that I'm used to it."

"We'll share it," he decided.

"It'll be gone twice as fast."

"That had occurred to me. You deserve to be clean, too."

"All right, then." Her smile uncrooked itself. "You can go ahead and wash in the stream. No reason to set out tonight—this is a pretty good campsite, and we'd just wind up looking for one in the dark if we started walking now."

Eshu nodded and began stripping off his robe and shoes. The underrobe was in worse shape than he'd realized, sweat-stained under the arms and ripped and bloodstained where he'd hit the mast. The fabric was printed with intricate whorls of gold across peacock blue and green, with thin gold chains adorning his bare shoulders. Now, the hem was getting ragged and a few of the chains were dangling limply.

He'd worn it to the party hoping that some burly stranger would help him take it off later that night. It was a robe for getting laid in, not for a cross-country hike.

To distract himself from the ruination of his best clothes, he said, "Speaking of walking. Thras Nadi had mentioned tigers in the woods. Are we likely to encounter any?"

"This far north? Probably not." Eshu barely had time to sigh in relief before she continued, "We're more likely to see tigers when we get closer to the Anjali. And we could run into spur cats from here all the way down to Sharis, if we were walking to Sharis."

"What the *shit*."

With slowly mounting glee, Fern added, "And there are all kinds of venomous bugs. Spiders. Wasps. Ants that can make your skin swell up like a paper lantern. I saw a centipede in the woods yesterday—"

"And you go walking in the forest to *relax*?"

"It's not so bad if you know what to watch out for. And it's not all tigers and centipedes. There are fruits and flowers, and trees with bark that you can make into a tea to ease any pain. And interesting ridges and caves. And ruins. And villages older than my maps where the people speak a different language."

"Then you'll have to teach me." He stepped down into the stream, and his skin prickled at the slight coolness to the water. After a long day under the tropical sun, the water eased and refreshed him. It almost made him forget that they were alone on a beach in the middle of nowhere, and that his robe was a disaster, and that there was an endless, screaming ache in his ribs.

"I will," Fern promised.

The second day of their hike through the mountains, it began to rain. Sheets of rain poured between the branches, relentless as a river, so thick that Eshu could barely breathe without sucking in mouthfuls of water. The stream they'd been following flooded with churning red mud, and they were forced to find higher ground to stay out of the torrent. "Just a little further," pleaded Fern. "I think I see a fallen tree ahead."

Eshu couldn't see anything, but he wasn't the tree expert, so he followed her grimly through the downpour. There was, as it turned out, a fallen tree. Fern hitched her hammock over it and made them a little lean-to to keep off the worst of the rain, but by then the ground was soaked through, and it didn't help much not to be rained on. The water still seeped through all around, slowly diluting the red earth to muck.

"What do you think is happening out there?" Fern asked as they huddled together. She held her pack in her lap, with her arms wrapped around it and her chin resting on the fabric. The pack seemed to have been waterproofed earlier in its lifetime, but the waterproofing was starting to give out at the seams; they were dark where the rain had soaked them.

"I wish I knew," said Eshu. "We could speculate all day about coordinated attacks or vengeful gods, but we just don't have enough evidence to make an argument."

Fern nodded. "Let's think about what we do know, then. Whatever it is, it seems like it's only happening in cities. The coast where we landed seemed fine. And not just in places where there are people—nothing happened to the farms outside Sharis. It has to be a lot of people in one place."

"That's true. And the point of origin seemed to be near the coast. The suburbs of Zumera and Sharis were relatively unscathed." Beyond the shelter of the tent, the undergrowth bent beneath the heavy rain. Water sent ripples through a carpet of huge, teardrop-shaped leaves with white flowers nestled near the stems.

"That's also where the most people would be. And the poorest people. Coastal cities are usually denser near the water." Fern's gaze was fixed on the shifting plants, the sudden streams carving through the dirt and leaves of the forest floor. She looked very alone. "Hey, did you know—"

"Does your family live near the water?" asked Eshu.

Fern didn't answer for a moment. "When they aren't traveling, they live in the suburbs," she said eventually. "But my place was near the water. And everyone else I cared about lived there."

"Do you want to talk about it?"

"Not really," she answered. "If I let myself think about it too closely, I'm just going to start crying, and then I won't be any use to anyone. I hate feeling useless. It's better to be doing something, even if it doesn't help."

She sniffled. Eshu passed her a handkerchief, and she blew her nose loudly. "You can keep it," he said, when she tried to hand it back. "I suspect we'll be living in each other's pockets for the foreseeable future. What's mine is yours, and so on."

"If you're sure."

They listened to the rain drumming on the hammock and the leaves. It seemed quieter, now, as though the storm was easing. Or perhaps Eshu was just getting used to the sound. After a moment, Fern asked, "Can you make us a fire to get us dry? I feel like we'd both think more clearly if we were dry."

"It's easier to manipulate a flame than to create one. Do you happen to have matches, or a tinderbox?"

"I think my matches are wet," she said, but she swiped her hand clean on something in her pack, then she fumbled through the pockets until she came up with a little pewter matchbox. A couple of drops of water glistened on the outside surface, but the matches and striking paper inside were still blessedly dry. Eshu tried not to think about how few matches there were in the box.

Fern struck a match, and Eshu sang its flame into a fire unquenchable. They fed it wet sticks until they dried enough to burn, and gradually, the fire grew into something warm and cheering. Once they had a fire, Fern cooked some dried beans in her cookpan until they were soft enough to eat. She and Eshu passed the metal spoon back and forth until they were scraping the bottom of the pan, and then he washed the pan and spoon in the rain.

Afterward, Fern curled up against the wall made by the upturned earth around the tree's roots. "Wake me up when the rain stops," she said. Not long after, he heard her soft, resonant snore. *Good*, he thought. *Neither of us has had much sleep lately.* While she napped, Eshu sat feeding the fire and studying the runestone that Thras Nadi had given him.

There were predators in the woods. He'd seen them, gleaming eyes and dappled scales in the darkness; Fern had pointed out their scratches in the trees and their spoor on the trails. But the long-taloned spur cats had melted back into the shadows again, and the snakes had lain quiet amid the undergrowth. Even the red-painted centipedes had skittered away at their approach. *These humans will not eat you*, Nadi's runework told the creatures of the dark wood, *and they are not good to eat.* The forest heard, and heeded.

He sat untangling the rhetoric of the runework until the rain ended, and then a little longer, until the churning waters of the stream began to slow and smooth out.

His whole body ached, and he was covered in mud that was beginning to dry on his clothes and skin. He hadn't slept in a proper bed for days.

At the same time, though, this was the closest Eshu had felt to calm since he'd left the party in Ras Kir'uun. He didn't want the moment to end.

When the sun rose through a grey curtain of cloud, they walked down along the valleys again. The rains followed them east for a few ugly days, and Eshu picked up a cough that he couldn't shake. His throat felt raw, his lungs full of thick fluid, and coughing never seemed to clear them. On top of that, every cough made his ribs hurt more.

They stopped more often, now. Fern sometimes left Eshu in a shallow cave or under the hammock while she scouted ahead for an easier route. Until the clouds cleared, she couldn't take readings of the sun or stars, and he could see it made her anxious not knowing where she was. While she picked her way east by compass and guesswork, he sat coughing and shivering and wondering how he could tell whether he had a fever.

There were songs for breaking fevers, but he'd never bothered to learn them, and now he regretted it.

He hated how being sick made him feel. It wasn't only the torpor that sapped his strength, or the cold sweats, or the way every breath felt like choking. His mind, too, felt like it was failing. His thoughts became difficult to hold for very long, as though they started to turn to vapor the moment he touched them. Songs slipped from his grasp, or parts of melodies cycled endlessly without resolving.

He found himself dwelling on images from his childhood, while he sat in his wet robes and waited for Fern to come back. Those thoughts were easiest to catch, and felt the most real when he held them. He remembered helping Kiga and Sunba make the High Summer hut of gold-flowering reeds, Kiga sneezing and laughing at the pollen. His father feeding him candied ginger and lemon rind, when he was four and felt like he was dying; it was the first time he could remember being sick. Sunba sucking on the ear of cotton-bellied Brother Lion. He'd given that lion to her when he was six and she was three, and she'd loved him to shreds faster than their father could repair him.

Eshu missed his father.

"I think I have a fever," he said, when Fern returned again. There were new, bright scratches across her face that looked like they'd come from a thorn branch, and there were green seeds hooked to her trousers. "You said there was tree bark that could ease any pain? Because I would give my left eye to have my pain eased right now."

"We can look," she said, a little uncertain, "but I don't know if that kind of tree grows this far north. There are a couple of other kinds of things that I think might break a fever, but I just don't know the plants up here as well as I do down south."

"I've resigned myself to that eventuality. It has to be better than this."

They crept through the woodland together, turning over loam to check the color of rootstocks, feeling the texture of leaves and bark. Fern kept up a steady commentary about tannins and petioles and palmate leaves, while Eshu coughed up gobs of yellow-white phlegm.

He remembered feeling very lucid, and little else besides that. The parade of leaves and bark and berries faded together into a bright streak of green and black. A resinous smell seeped through the mucus in his throat and clung to his hands and the soles of his shoes.

When his memory caught up with him again, there was the sharp taste of some sort of tea, red and black with fruit pulp. He saw leaves swimming in the surface of Fern's cookpan.

The taste disagreed with him. He drank anyway, until he

gagged on it.

Slowly, the fever broke. He woke at the edge of a hot spring, wrapped in Fern's blanket, with his outer robe rolled up under his head. Half of his face was unclogged, and the other half throbbed with pressure. He realized as he looked up that he could see the full moon through the canopy.

"You're awake," said Fern, who sat in steaming water up to her chin. Her hair was plastered to her skull and her cheeks.

"Unfortunately, yes." Eshu's voice sounded like a rasp scraped over ironwood.

"A bath might help."

"Ugh." His limbs felt leaden, but he made himself unfasten his underrobe and take off his shoes. His feet were wrinkled with moisture, but he couldn't dwell on that. He slid naked into the hot water and breathed deeply for the first time in days.

The fluids in his face redistributed themselves. He blew his nose several times over the side of the hot spring, and each time, he felt cleaner and lighter. The water felt glorious, after days of humid air and lukewarm rain that shaded to cold at night. The full moon shone through a gap in the trees and glistened on his hands and Fern's hair.

Eventually, he ducked his head under the water and worked it through his locs. He couldn't remember where he or Fern had put the soap, but being able to *wonder* about soap again was such a relief that he felt like weeping.

When he emerged and shook his hair out, he found Fern was grinning. "You look better," she said.

"I feel better," he answered. "Still horrendous, but better."

"This might cheer you up. I found a sock," she said, and picked it up with a stick to show him. It was old enough that moss was starting to grow on the heel, but it meant that people had been here, at some point. They were finally leaving the trackless wilderness.

He waved the sock away. "How far are we from civilization?"

She wrinkled her nose. "It's hard to tell. The mountains on my map are basically just icons. They don't match the actual slopes at all, so I don't know whether any of the scales are right, and I haven't really been able to correct the real distances with all this rain. But assuming that the distance from the shore to the river is basically right, I think we're a day out from the Anjali. We should rest tonight and get our things really dry, and hope we find somewhere that will let us rent a boat."

"Do you know how to handle a boat?"

"A little. I've been canoeing a couple of times, on smaller rivers. We'll be going with the current, though, and your runestone will protect us from crocodiles, so it can't be that hard, right?"

"You failed to mention crocodiles when we started this journey."

"I told you about the tigers and spur cats. I assumed crocodiles were implied."

"Crocodiles are *never* implied."

"It's just a thing! Like in the hero stories. When you think of the Anjali, you think crocodiles and fancy gold lattices and people murdering each other in silk dresses." Fern looked completely serious, and she did read a lot of hero stories, so Eshu didn't feel equipped to argue the point.

He sighed. "If they can keep from murdering each other long enough to sell me a new robe, I'll try not to complain about the bloodstains."

"There." She smiled again, teeth flashing white in the moonlight. "You're back."

They didn't reach the Anjali the next day, but Fern said when she climbed down from a tree that she could see the river carving a deep groove through the forest. "And smoke," she said as she knocked wet bark off of her hands and trousers. "I swear I saw smoke rising somewhere further down the river. I think there are people here."

"Remember when that wasn't surprising?"

"Hush, you. Let me be excited about something."

Eshu's throat still ached, but he wasn't coughing anymore, and he could breathe through his nose again. His ribs still occasionally felt like hot knives to the abdomen when he twisted his body just slightly too far in the wrong direction, but they'd been better since he started drinking Fern's leaf and berry tea. Something to do with inflammation, she guessed, when he mentioned it; most of the plants she'd studied had inflammation mentioned somewhere in their lists of properties.

Once they'd made camp, cooked stew and said prayers, he began to weave that rhetorical thread into a song. The body, burning white-hot where it ached; the flesh setting itself aflame to scour out sickness. He sang cool waters and balms of wax and oil, and earth settling over the campfire to quench it.

It wasn't yet a spell, but the exercise of crafting one felt like a miracle after so long with his face full of fluid. He hummed wandering melodies and tuneless scales, searching for the pattern of notes that would make his pain unfurl like a blossom.

Across the campfire, Fern lay on her stomach with her map spread in front of her on a broad, dry stone. She carefully scraped away the mountains inked on the leather and sketched their true shapes in pencil, drawing winding streams between them with a practiced hand.

In her own way, Fern was also reshaping the world. *A wizard tells the world a story about what it is*, a god had once told him, *and the world answers, Yes.* As Fern worked, Eshu saw the landscape becoming a story sure as stone.

Then her knuckles brushed Kulmeni, and he remembered. "Rain," he said.

Fern looked up at the sky. "Probably not tonight."

"No—Rain, back in Sharis. The one who said the tower was going to fall. Her wife was buying silk in Kulmeni." He shifted around the fire to look at the map more closely. There weren't any roads marked on it, but if he connected the gaps between mountain ranges and traced the paths of rivers, he could almost guess where Rain's wife's road might be. "I wonder if she's still there, or if she's on her way back by now."

"We can look, maybe," said Fern. "Kulmeni's supposed to be one of the biggest cities in Nanjeer, though. Even if there's anyone there, we might not find anyone who remembers her."

"Lots of hero stories set in Kulmeni?"

"Mostly not. City comedies, sure, but I don't really like city comedies."

"It's hard to be a hero in a city, I suppose. Pressures from all sides to become something inoffensive and pleasing. Or offensive in ways that others find pleasing, which is nearly the same thing."

"Yeah. I guess people who read hero stories don't really want to see the world as ugly, you know?" Fern set her pencil aside and began to roll up her map. "City comedies will show you cruelty that breaks your heart, but we're supposed to laugh because it doesn't matter, really, in the end. Things will turn out all right, and everyone will end up married. That's how you know things turned out all right. It was all just a big misunderstanding, and that's the best we can hope for, so why bother fixing it."

When he'd been new to Nanjeer and still learning the language, Eshu had read dozens of city comedies. Mnoro had been mad for them, and they'd traded volumes at parties and gossiped about who they'd hoped would fall in love. It hurt in a way that he hadn't expected, to hear Fern condemn them so roundly. "I like that about them, actually. That it's possible to forgive people, even when they hurt you without meaning to. It helps to believe that even after you've had a falling out, you can still come to understand each other, and that understanding *means* something."

"I don't know. It feels like that's true in real life, more than in comedies. It seems like comedies are more about the teasing and mocking and less about the forgiveness afterward. Or like getting married is supposed to stand in for forgiveness. But maybe I just don't like them, and I'm not seeing them at their best." She reached into one of her pouches and pulled out a handful of little leathery leaves, the kind that she chewed to make her mouth feel clean.

Eshu held out his hand, and she dropped a few leaves in. "Is it the marriages?" he asked. "You said once that you weren't interested in romance."

Fern chewed for a moment. Her breath smelled sharp and herbal. "I guess that's it, really. It just seems like those stories only end in marriage because everyone knows they're supposed to, but I don't really care about that. I don't care about all the flirting and scheming and cheating. I don't care about who's fucking who or whether it's true love or which girl or boy or androgyne the heroine chooses. None of that matters to me. I just want to know that something's different for them after everything's over. That they changed each other, and it stuck."

"And the marriage is admittedly a lazy, conventional way of telling the audience that it will stick."

"Yeah. Marriages don't always stick, you know?"

"My parents' certainly didn't," said Eshu wryly.

Fern choked on a leaf. She coughed hard, then spat to one side and wiped her mouth. "Um. Sorry. That was a rude thing to say."

"It's all right. You couldn't have known." He picked up the cookpan, still crusted with the root vegetables that Fern had made into a dull but filling stew. The pan needed to be washed, and washing dishes was an excellent excuse not to talk about things.

"Do you want to—" began Fern.

He was already starting down the hill to the stream. "I'd rather not."

"Sure. All right." After a pause, though, she asked, "Does it really work for you to just drop heavy things like that and walk away? Your parents aren't together, your ex was an asshole—it sounds like you kind of do want to talk?"

"I don't want to talk. I want to be *understood*. And it's a real limitation on us as human beings that for the most part, one can't be understood without talking."

Eshu stooped beside the water. The waning moon was riding high in the sky, and the surface of the stream reflected it back in a thousand slivers of light. Fern's shape was a sturdy shadow at his shoulder. He knew that she was waiting for him to go on, but he had no idea what he'd say. It felt stupid to still be cut up about his parents breaking up when bigger things were ending.

He dipped the cookpan and scrubbed it out with his hands, feeling the crusted roots loosen and drift free on the current. *There. At least that's clean.* "If you insist on hearing it, could we talk about it in the morning?"

Fern looked as though she was about to put a hand on his shoulder, then she let her hand fall. "Sure. We've got nothing but time."

They turned back to the fire, and there was someone sitting there. From behind, Eshu could only see that the person was hooded, with narrow shoulders and lank, dark hair that gleamed in the firelight. "Who's there?" he called, more loudly than he meant to. He stepped into the circle of light, and the stranger turned to him. Beneath the shadow of her hood, he saw a bone-white mask.

"Shit," said Fern, fervent as a prayer. She threw her hand out in front of Eshu and wrenched the cookpan from his nerveless fingers. "Come at me, Crowtaker! I'll fuck you up, I swear it."

The Crowtaker stood, and stood, and kept standing. She loomed over them, her hood brushing the lowest branches of the trees. "Come sit down beside me. You've come a long way," she said. Her lips twitched. Her teeth were sharp behind them.

Eshu's legs were weak as water. "We don't want trouble," he said.

She gave a rusted laugh. "Trouble has found you, it seems. What is your name?"

"Don't tell her," said Fern tightly. She raised the cookpan like a battle axe.

His hands shook. He felt like a leaf in a gale. *This is Death*, he thought. *Death is here for me.* But he'd thought that before in Zumera as the airship fell from the sky. He'd met death with a song on his lips, and he'd brought them through it alive.

He began to hum. The music resonated deep in his throat, below the knot he couldn't swallow. It sang in his bones and the hollow places between them, in the bellows of his lungs and his hammering heart and every sparking nerve strung through his body. *You are alive*, he sang to them, and they heeded. *You are alive, and Death cannot have you.*

All around him, the drowsing wood rose up in answer.

He sang life into each drooping flower, into every withered leaf; he sang seeds swelling in a riot of root and bloom. Ferns unfurled, and lotuses speared through the shallows of the stream. At the heart of every flower was a mote of golden light, bright and warm as an ember.

The light quickened beneath his skin. It streamed down every vein and artery and picked them out in molten gold, as though his skin was only a veil over an unquenchable radiance. *You are alive, and Death cannot have you.*

Underneath his song, though, he heard a drone like a hundred thousand flies, and his bright blood ran cold as the Crowtaker began to sing.

Her voice rose from deep in her throat, harsh and tuneless. Flowers withered and fell; ferns dried up, and the wind rattled through them. *All life tends to death*, she sang, and the green wood rotted around her.

Eshu bled heat. His blood cooled and congealed; every hard pulse of his heart wracked him like a blow. Every breath felt like dredging fluid from his lungs. Vertigo swept through him in rolling waves, and he recognized on some level that it was because his body was failing.

The cookpan fell from Fern's hand. He heard the muffled ring of it as though from far away.

He heaved back the red-edged darkness in a rising crescendo, shifting the Crowtaker's song to an exultant major key. He sang the *Crest of the Wave* rising from the wreck of Zumera, the unbowed children of Sharis; he sang the survivors who faced death and did not flinch away. He sang life smuggled to the hinterlands in jars of honey, bags of rice, soap and salt and sea plums fresh from the shore—the human spirit triumphant, even in the face of the world's end.

Then the Crowtaker sang in a voice of famine, and suffering was in her song. She sang flesh sunken over ribs, stomachs swollen and straining; she sang lethargy and racking hunger, hair dropping in hanks to the hard earth. Blowflies buzzed and settled, drank blood from cracked lips. In her tuneless melody was the deep, spiraling dizziness of the end approaching, and the circling of carrion birds overhead.

Although his voice was faltering, still Eshu sang the life in her decay—the blowfly and the maggot, the vultures nesting atop the towering trees. The rot that was life, mold and moss and mushroom; young trees reaching their roots into ancient bones and growing tall, tall, tall.

She turned to him with a cradle-song on her lips. Her fathomless gaze peered into him and through him, into the unguarded recesses of his heart, and she sang of cracked walls and timbers falling. She sang Sunba speared through with a rafter beam, crows eating her eyes. She sang Asha burning, burning; she sang the scent of scorched hair and the crackle of flesh, and his sister's dying screams. She sang Kiga buried beneath the rubble of their house, crying for help that never came.

Why return to Kondala City? her song seemed to ask, seductive as drowning. *Nothing you love remains.*

"Stop it!" Fern shouted, but she was far away, and Eshu was in Kondala City watching his sisters die.

His song failed. Prayers and blood tumbled from his lips. There came a single loud clang, so close that Eshu felt it in his teeth—then the world went dark.

CHAPTER 9: TAKING SHELTER

Fern woke beside the ash of her campfire with the worst headache she'd ever had. Her skull felt as though it had been split open like a melon. *Ugh, Sisters, how could I have left the fire to burn out like this?* She swayed up to her knees, and a bubble of nausea immediately rose in her throat. She dropped her hands and was sick in the fire pit. There was blood in her vomit. Not a lot, but even a little bit made her skin go cold with worry.

Her cookpan was close by, but one side was stoved in, and the whole thing was covered in thick, flaking rust like it had been underwater for a few decades. She reached out for it. Her palm closed on the handle, and suddenly she remembered fumbling it off the ground and swinging with all her failing strength. The impact had resonated down Fern's arms so powerfully that she'd thought her bones were broken.

The Crowtaker's mask had cracked like mud in a drought, and cold and darkness had bled out of it. Her song had gone silent. Then there had only been the wind, and the darkness of the wood, and the dying fire throwing sparks.

She thought she remembered Eshu praying. *Njo, Njo, have mercy.*

Fern crawled across their little clearing to where Eshu lay huddled on the mossy ground. His hands were gathered up by his face, his knees drawn up toward his navel. When she laid a hand on his shoulder, he flinched and knocked her hands away.

"Hey," she said. "It's Fern. We're alive. I think."

"Shit. Do we really have to be?"

"I think we do."

"Fuck." Eshu peered up over his elbow, then began to uncurl. When he tried to sit up, though, he winced and sank back onto the moss. "I've changed my mind. I'm not getting up."

"It's all right. Your ribs probably aren't feeling great right now."

"I've always admired your talent for understatement. There is no part of my body that doesn't feel as though it's been crushed to a fine pulp. Our blood was congealing in our bodies. We're probably going to die of brain clots any moment now."

Fern flopped down beside him and stared up at the trees. Their branches were bare, now. They looked grey and rough, and they rattled like dead things in the wind. "Maybe," she said. "But until that happens, I'd like to keep going."

Eshu groaned. "Can't we just stay here a little longer? Rest until we have our strength back?"

"I guess we could. Maybe not *here* here, since this place is probably a zone of susceptibility right now, but somewhere close by. But I definitely wrecked my pan last night, so I'm going to have to sand off the rust. And we should probably make a better shelter if we're planning to stay put." Her hammock was starting to lose its waterproofing where it had rubbed against tree bark and the edges of rocks, and she wasn't sure she trusted all of her pitons anymore after she'd wrenched them out of hardwood trees so many times.

Fern stretched her arms up over her head and twisted until her back crackled and her muscles felt looser. She knitted her fingers together and flexed them backward, to the very edge of pain. *I'm just going to lie here a little longer,* she thought. *Just a little longer, then I've got to get up.*

She counted breaths. Ten, then fifty. *At a hundred, I have to get up.*

At a hundred, she dragged herself to her feet and brushed moss off of her clothes. "Come on," she said, reaching down to offer Eshu her hand. "If we're going to camp for a while, we need to find food first."

"Ugh." Eshu looked up at her hand as though it was crawling with scorpions. "Can't you just leave me here to die of a clot to the brain."

"Sorry, I can't."

"Then I suppose I have to get up." He took her hand and let her pull him to his feet. *He must really be feeling awful*, she thought as they broke camp and packed their things. *He isn't stopping to pray. He isn't even brushing his clothes clean.*

The clearing where they'd spent the night was almost completely barren, except for the moss and a few carrion beetles trundling over a fallen log. The trees had dropped their leaves and died; the ferns had shriveled, and the flowers dried to husks. When Fern and Eshu reached the stream, they found dead fish caught against sticks mired in the streambed, and lotuses rotting in the eddies.

"Did the Crowtaker's song do this?" Fern asked, mostly because she couldn't bear the silence.

"Yes," said Eshu. Fern looked up at him and waited for him to go on, but he just shook his head. "What, do you want me to embellish it for you? There's nothing else to be said. Whatever was here, she killed it. It's dead now. She won."

"But we're alive. And I don't think it's because I hit her with my pan."

"No. It wasn't much of an argument."

"My dad always used to say that swords didn't win arguments," said Fern. "And my mother would say, 'But they do finish them.'"

"I'll bear that in mind next time I'm arguing with a sword."

They had to walk a ways before they found a part of the forest that wasn't dead or dying. Fern broke twigs from saplings and bushes every now and then, hoping that the under-bark would be flexible and green. Every time, the twigs came off with a dry, final snap.

Eventually, though, she saw a flash of movement. When she looked closer, she could just make out one of the round little rodents that lived near the water here. It crouched at the mouth of its burrow, cleaned its ears, and then darted back underground again. "I think we're almost at the edge of the dead part," she said. "Listen for buzzing sounds. If we find lantern bees, they'll probably lead us to something we can eat."

"What's a lantern bee?" Eshu asked.

"Like a regular bee, except they glow like little lanterns. You can see it better in morning or evening, but you can sort of make it out even in the afternoon, if you're close enough. And they drink berry juice and nectar, so their honey is kind of like jam. It looks awful when it's dripping from a nest. Like something got murdered in a tree."

"Got it. Listen for buzzing, look for signs of murder."

"And maybe if you don't see any murder, look for some of the plants we were eating on the way here."

Eshu eased himself under a huge, low-hanging leaf, and a beetle startled and flew away in a flurry of shining blue wings. "I can barely remember anything that happened between the shore and the hot springs. I certainly don't remember what those plants looked like."

"It's all right. If I find some, I'll teach you."

Deeper into the green wood, Fern found a tekusa tree heavy with green seedpods, and she shinnied up into the high branches to pick the ripest ones and throw them down. The papery tekusa bark almost made her slip a few times, but the seedpods were familiar and heavy and squashed satisfyingly in her hands.

They split open the tekusa pods and threw aside the huge black seeds, then scraped the purple fruit from the seedpods with their teeth. Even ripe, the fruit was sour as much as sweet, and Eshu's lips puckered like a drawstring bag at the taste. "I've seen these in markets, and I've always wondered what they tasted like," he said. "This is a disappointment."

Fern laughed. "It's better in a drink. You can use the seeds as a spice, too, but you have to remember to take them out, because they don't get soft no matter how long you cook them."

When they'd eaten their fill, Fern sat a while in the sunlight by the water and started weaving a basket of reeds and grasses. They'd need something to carry food in, since her pack was nearly full and Eshu still didn't have anything but his pockets. She hummed as she did, one of her mother's old capstan shanties that had been pressed into service as a cradle song.

Across the water, a spur cat came down to drink, and Fern's song trailed away into a squeak.

The cat was massive—at least three times Fern's size, with wickedly curved talons on her rear paws and a few healed scars on her flanks. There was blood on her muzzle, old enough to be drying brown, new enough to shine a little in the light. When she stepped into the sunlight by the water, her rough, spotted pelt gleamed golden.

Fern tried not to breathe or move. Her blood hammered hard in her hands, her ears, the hollow of her stomach. *We're safe*, she told herself. *We're safe; Thras Nadi gave us the runestone, so we're safe, we're safe.*

The cat's yellow eyes met Fern's. Her long tongue lapped at the water. Then, after an eternity of a moment, she turned from the water and vanished again into the forest.

Fern released a long, shaking breath. She'd been afraid when she'd seen the Crowtaker, but she'd been ready to fight, if she had to. Something about the spur cat's unhurried calm, though, had left her quaking. "Eshu?" she said. "You still have that runestone, right?"

"No, I gave it to the Crowtaker as a keepsake—of course I still have it," he answered. He reached into his pocket, and his hand came out empty.

He didn't have to say anything. They both knew that if he didn't remember most of their journey, he probably didn't remember where he'd last had it, or how long he'd been without it.

"So, shelter next," said Fern eventually. "Do you think you can climb a tree?"

Eshu looked off to the far shore, where the spur cat's footprints still marked the mud. "I'm a fast learner."

By the time Fern found a tree that looked like it would be good for a shelter, the sun was high, and the air was humid and oppressive. She scaled the tree with pitons and hung her climbing pulley from a bough, then fed a rope through it until both ends were on the ground.

"You're sure spur cats can't climb," said Eshu, when she dropped to the mossy ground again.

"Absolutely sure. I can't remember why not—something about the way their legs are jointed, maybe? But they can't. Tigers can, but it's usually too much work for them to climb trees when there are deer or wild pigs or something like that on the ground." She mopped her brow and surveyed the wood. The evergreens had given way to deciduous trees, but the big ones would be too much trouble to hack down, and the saplings didn't grow as straight as she would have liked. "I wish there were bamboo here. You can build just about anything with bamboo."

"Do you often build shelters in the woods?"

"Only when I'm planning on staying in one place a while. This one time, my boss Heza and I got hired to find a bunch of abandoned mineral claims, so we made a little treehouse and took the area in grids until we'd found them all." Fern smiled at the memory. Heza had complained constantly about missing her news and coffee, and she'd snored every night like a rusted saw on rough wood. But she'd made sure Fern understood how to tie a strong knot and hammer a piton in well enough to hold her weight, and she'd always called a halt when the weather got too bad. They'd huddled together under a roof of banana leaves, listening to the rain and talking through a proof Fern had been working for fun.

She hoped Heza and Kufa were all right. If they'd made it through the disaster, whatever it had been in Matis, they would probably be fine. Kufa was sort of absentminded and impractical, the kind of man who'd make himself late preparing a fancy lunch and then forget to eat it, but Heza had always been clear-eyed. She'd know how to find food, make shelter, get her family somewhere safe. She'd have all of the maps on display and in their workshop, so she'd be able to find her way. If they'd made it through the disaster, anyway.

Fern tried to put it out of her mind.

She tramped through the wood with Eshu in tow, searching for straight young trees that she could use to make them a sleeping platform. Eventually, they found a little grove of hardwoods springing up in the footprint of a huge fallen tree, where the sunlight spilled through the thick canopy. Shading her eyes against the sudden glare, Fern said, "These will work."

She knelt down beside one and began to saw at the wood with her knife, wishing she had a serrated blade. It was hard to get purchase on the dense woodgrain, and blisters started rising under the old calluses on her palm. She could almost feel her knife's edge blunting.

"Isn't there any magic you can do?" she asked, when she'd hacked through less than a finger's breadth of the sapling. Her hands were aching and slick with sweat, and the knife was green where the bark had rubbed off. "Sing a bow saw out of wind or something?"

Eshu had been staring, unfocused, into the distance; at Fern's voice, though, he snapped to attention. "I hadn't actually realized you wanted my help with this," he said. "In retrospect, that was a stupid assumption." He folded his arms and studied the grove as though with new eyes, muttering under his breath as he examined the gash Fern had made in the tree.

He sang something that felt shivery and cold, like the wind off the freezing southern current that curled up Ras Kir'uun's eastern shore. The hairs on Fern's arms stood on end as he sang steel and ice and stone, frost overtaking the fields, swords gleaming in moonlight on a snow-silvered night.

That icy wind slashed through the grove like a scythe through grass. For a moment, the young trees teetered, then they toppled to earth with a tremendous crash of leaves.

Fern stretched her hands over her head, then cracked her knuckles. "Great. Now we need to strip the twigs off and carry these back."

They pared down the saplings to bare poles, then carried them back to the tree and hauled them up into the branches with the rope and pulley. Fern tied them down with vines across two level boughs, making a platform broad enough for the both of them to sleep. That work took her well into the afternoon, while Eshu sat scouring the rust from the cookpan at the foot of the tree.

"Hey," she called down to Eshu, when she'd got the poles situated where she wanted them. "Can you make some vines carry you up here? Because I don't think I'm heavy enough to haul you up, and it's kind of a tricky climb if you're not used to it."

"Why don't you just put all of my boasts to the test," said Eshu, but he was smiling when he said it, so she was pretty sure he wasn't offended.

He sang green vines into a throne, then sent them straining up into the branches above Fern's head. Those surging creepers coiled around and around, seeking something to grasp and hold. When their tendrils caught in the high branches, they grew thick and powerful as cables, and Eshu rose upon them until his seat was level with Fern's platform.

Fern grinned as she hooked him in and helped him onto the bed of saplings. "Now that I know you can do that, I'm going to have to put you to work again. We could use some railings and reinforcements."

"You mean this isn't safe?" Eshu walked across the platform— four steps from the outside edge to the Fern-sized gap where the branches spread out from the trunk; six from bough to supporting bough. He gave an experimental bounce on the balls of his feet. Fern's knots held.

Sitting, Fern dangled her legs over the edge. "It's fine if we just want to sit up here, but not if we want to sleep on it. I was planning to do the railings with more poles, but vines will work, too."

"If you insist." Again, Eshu sang that root and tendril song, that green-leaf song that sent vines tumbling in green curtains all around them. His voice was rough at the edges, and he cupped a hand at his broken ribs, but still he sang the vines into knots and loops and whorls. They descended to grasp the edges of Fern's platform and bind it fast to the tree, then looped under and around until they'd shaped a lattice of rails.

At last, Eshu lowered himself to his knees and sat with his head leaning against a leafy vine. Some magic must still have been singing through it, because a little branch unwound over his shoulder and burst into white and purple flowers.

"Are you feeling all right?" Fern asked. "A week ago, it seemed like you were always looking for a reason to work some magic. You'd be singing all the time, trying to solve problems with spells and runes. Now, it's like you're not here, you know?"

Eshu raised a brow. "I broke three ribs, came down with some hideous illness, and walked across an untold amount of jungle, then fought a wild goddess and lost. And out there, where we can't see it, the world's still ending. And there's nothing I can do about it. So no, I'm not feeling all right."

"Hey. A little over a week ago, you were ready to storm Tisaris all by yourself."

"A little over a week ago, I was an idiot."

"Never an idiot—"

"I didn't appreciate the scope of what I was facing. You were right. This is the gods' business, not a wizard's." Eshu didn't meet Fern's eyes, and the bitterness in his voice sounded like shame.

Fern pulled a tekusa pod out of her pocket and tossed it into his lap. "Well, there's plenty of wizard business left in the world," she said. "And when you're feeling better, we're going to go find it."

With that, Fern slid down to her first piton and scrambled down to the forest floor. Her pack was there, and the mostly-scoured pan; she'd want to haul the pack up, at least. She might be able to scare up something worth cooking in the woods or the stream, if she used the last of the daylight. She hadn't heard any monkeys in this region, so she probably didn't have to worry about the pan getting carried off in the night.

Near the water, she found a few edible greens and dug up some lotus roots, which would probably fry up well if she could find any oil or grease. By now, the shadows were long, and she could make out the lantern bees drifting slowly between the trees. She followed them to a patch of berry bushes, where parasols of tiny blue-black berries drooped under their own weight. Snapping the stems, she gathered a few clusters like a bouquet and carried them all back to the tree.

High above her, golden light filtered through the woven vines. That warm light reminded her of the lighthouse on the north coast of Matis, where a sharp spur of stone extended out into the sea. She couldn't even remember how many times her father had put a hand on her shoulder and pointed to the lighthouse through darkness or fog, telling her, *Look, Rukha. We're almost home.*

She wiped her eyes. There was no use in thinking about that. She needed a way to carry the food up to the treehouse. Taking off her vest, she gathered all the corners up and tied them together around the plants to make a bundle. Then she looped her rope through it and through her pack straps and climbed up into the tree.

There, Eshu was singing to himself. He sat cross-legged, eyes closed, with his back against a thick wall of vines. A spark of light pulsed between his long fingers, shining dully on his dark, dark skin.

"Hey, Eshu," she said as she started to haul up the pack and the bundle. "Are you busy?"

"Not exactly," he said. He didn't open his eyes.

"Are you not-busy enough for dinner? I got some things. They're probably edible. I think."

"Encouraging." He released the light, which drifted up to the place where the vines met high overhead.

"I don't know the plants up north as well as I'd like. The berries are definitely edible. I think this—" and she indicated a bundle of greens "—is basically the same thing as kanan back home, but the leaves are a little pointier."

Fern hadn't realized how tense Eshu looked until his face relaxed. "Oh, it *is* a real food. I used to have kanan stir-fried with garlic and vinegar back in Usbaran."

"In Matis, we'd mostly cook it with green onions, peppers, and a little lemon," said Fern. "Shaved lamb, too, if you could afford it. There was a food cart close to my shop where they'd wrap it in flatbread so you could take it with you."

"Ugh, why would you tell me this," said Eshu mournfully, picking up a handful of raw probably-kanan and taking a bite. "I miss bread."

"I miss oil," Fern said, like agreement. "Maybe there will be something in Kulmeni. If not people, we might be able to find what's left of a general store."

"I do love that our hopes have been reduced to petty theft."

Fern popped a berry into her mouth. It was more seed than fruit, but it tasted like sweet tea. "It's not theft. It's salvage."

"As you like."

They ate in silence for a while, until there was nothing left but the lotus roots. Fern pushed those to one side, then wrapped herself up in her hammock and stretched out on the platform. "Eshu? Do you want to talk about your family now?"

He sighed and settled back into his spot against the vines. A tiny mote of light formed at his fingertips, and he rolled it over his knuckles like a coin. "I don't. I really don't. But I should, so here it is."

"You don't have to—"

"I should." He folded his hands together over his stomach and let his head fall back. "My mother is a lawmaker. The family moved to Kondala City just after I was born so that she could get to work more easily. The work took more from her than I think she meant it to. So my father raised us—me and my three sisters. He made our meals, led us in prayers, bandaged our scrapes. He used to sing all the time. Even when he didn't have words yet, he'd just—sing, little nonsense sounds, and he'd pick my sisters up and dance them across the floor."

Fern offered him a tentative smile. "No wonder you sing so much."

His breath hitched. The mote gleamed through the gaps between his fingers. "One day, he told my mother that he wanted to go back to their village. He said he missed the old temple and the gold grass hills, and his parents' house at the edge of the forest. He said he wanted his children to grow up in the open air."

"She said no," Fern guessed.

Eshu shook his head. "She asked us what we wanted," he answered. "I think if we'd said yes, she would have gone with him. She loved him so much. She felt guilty for spending so much time away from home. But I wanted to stay in the city with my friends. Sunba didn't want to leave her school. Kiga and Asha were too young to know what was happening, but Kiga didn't want to leave us. So my parents had their marriage sundered, and we stayed in the city, while he went back to the hills alone."

"That's a heavy thing to put on a kid," said Fern. "You shouldn't blame yourself for what happened. It's not your fault that your parents split up."

"It's not that," said Eshu softly. "I miss my father, but it's not that. Ever since last night, I keep thinking that if I'd only chosen differently, maybe they wouldn't have been in the city when the lights came. Maybe whatever happened to them is my fault."

Fern reached out and laid a hand on Eshu's knee. "We don't know that anything happened to them. We're going to go there and find out, and it doesn't help to think the worst until we know more. But even if something happened, it wouldn't be your fault. Promise."

"I don't think you can promise that," said Eshu, but he took her hand anyway and gripped it tight.

Fern fell asleep to the soft rustle of wind in the leaves, like an endless dark ocean heaving around her.

Fern walked barefoot across the sand, and the inky night swallowed her. *One foot in front of the other*, she told herself, but her voice echoed strangely in her mind. It sounded like someone else's.

To her right, the sea crashed and heaved. It licked up over her ankles and washed the sand away beneath her. The water was cold.

She looked up. There were no constellations she knew in that sky. There were no constellations at all.

I'm in the Mirrorlands, she thought. Diamond sand washed over her feet and out into that endless, hungry sea. "Eshu? Eshu, are you here?"

No one answered.

A knot rose in her throat that she couldn't swallow down. *There has to be a mirror somewhere.* She'd figure out what to do when she found it. She just needed to get up high to see more of the terrain.

Far along the shore, she saw a crumbling tower. Dark vines wrapped around it like a scaffolding, bricks and vines holding each other up. Looking at it made her skin feel tight and hot, as though she wasn't supposed to be seeing it.

The cold sea lapped at her feet. A cold wind sliced through her clothes. She kept walking.

Her heel came down on something that squelched and cracked. She didn't want to look down and see what it was. She already knew, the way she knew that the tower ahead was wrong.

Fern bent down anyway and picked up the rotting hand. The flesh was cold and slippery in her fingers. It sloughed easily off of the bone. On one finger, there was a little ring with a glass bead. Fern knew somehow that it was green.

She felt sick. Her guts knotted up, and her heart clenched like a fist. "I'm sorry, Shell," she whispered. "I think I found your daughter." She slid the ring off and tucked it in her pocket. Then she knelt at the shore and dug down until she had a hole big enough for a burial.

The tower was closer, now. The vines rustled in that cold sea wind, like and not like the surge of the waves. She didn't want to go to it. If she didn't, though, she might never find a way home.

The stench of rot overpowered the salt smell of the sea. The shore was littered with bodies. Headless corpses draped in deep blue silk, tattooed arms separating at the joints, dog-gnawed feet and faces and hanks of hair washing in the shallows like some hideous weeds.

Something was wrong here. Those rotting fingers reached and flexed. Corpses staggered to their feet, reaching out for her. "Please," hissed a head with the eyes rotted out. "Bury us—"

"I have to go!" shouted Fern. She began to run. Water and sand sprayed out behind her with each footfall. The tower loomed over her until it blotted out the horizon, but it never seemed to get closer. Skeletal hands reached for her, clutching her hair and the fluttering ends of her shirt, catching her ankles and wrists. She twisted out of their grips and kept running.

Her hands caught on the vines. They burned as though she'd touched lightning, then ripped free of the tower walls.

Beneath the stains of centuries, she could still faintly read the black letters painted there: *SHELTER. ALL WELCOME.*

Fern snapped awake with a scream.

"What the fuck?" yelled Eshu. He shoved himself upright and cast a light in each hand, looking around wildly.

"Just a dream," said Fern. She gasped for air. Her heart was throbbing so hard that she was afraid it would burst.

Eshu huffed and leaned back into his nest of vines. The lights flickered, then faded. "I thought you were being murdered."

"Just a bad dream." Fern wrapped her hammock back over her shoulders and tried to settle down on her side again. There weren't any bodies out here. The ocean was a long way away, and Sharis even farther. They didn't even have a mirror, so she couldn't have gone to the Mirrorlands.

Something dug into her hip. *Probably missed part of a twig when I was trimming the poles*, she thought, and she slid back a little on the platform. The sharpness followed her. She rolled over and patted her vest down, searching for a burr or a wood chip.

Instead, she found a ring in her pocket, with a smooth bead set in the band. When she held it up to her face, she smelled salt and rot.

A week passed. Fern finished scouring her pan, and she dug up some green nuts that made enough oil for her to season it. She caught a snake and bashed its head in with a rock, then she fried it up with the last of the nut oil and some lotus roots. It wasn't very good, but she felt better after she'd eaten it.

Fern's monthly cycle didn't come, which she'd half-expected after the stress of the last month. No doubt it would pick back up again someday or another, but until then, it was one less problem to worry about.

She dug a privy pit nice and far away from everything they cared about. It still attracted curious flies and beetles, no matter how much dirt she threw in.

In the early mornings, she made them a shed roof of broad leaves, pressed between sticks to keep them straight and overlapped to keep the rain out. When the midday sun broke through the canopy and made the high boughs oven-hot, Fern and Eshu napped under the shelter of their roof until late afternoon.

She made Eshu help her weave a reed basket for gathering. He seemed willing to hold green twigs in place while she tied off reeds and looped long withes between them, but he didn't offer to help. Maybe he wasn't sure that he *could* help. "There," she said when they'd finished. "That's something to be proud of."

"If you say so," he muttered.

At first, Eshu only made the climb down from the platform twice a day so that he could empty his bowels and search for fruit. As the days passed and his ribs healed, though, he began to venture further afield, returning with their basket full of kanan and tekusa and the fruits they'd taken to calling umbrella berries. He brought other plants he found, too, asking Fern if this root or that fruit was edible. One of them turned out to be ginger, and that night they ate kanan and lotus root so spicy that they cried with joy. They weathered a rainstorm that made their tree sway like a dancer, and their knots and vines held.

One morning partway into the second week, Fern sat with her legs dangling over the side of the platform and said, "We should probably get back on the road. I mean. Not that there is a road."

"Can't we just wait a little longer?" asked Eshu. "We can keep going when we're well."

"Sure. I just thought—you're sleeping on your back now," she said. "And you're not wincing all the time. You carried a whole basket of lotus roots the other day. If you aren't all the way well yet, you're getting there."

"I don't feel well." He hummed a low, familiar melody, and the vines obligingly bloomed for him. He picked the sprig of flowers and tucked it behind his ear. "I know this is stasis, and I hate that I'm keeping us here. I hate that I'm not stronger. But I'm not."

Fern crawled across the platform and sat beside him, cross-legged. "Sometimes, you don't feel better because there's something else wrong. I've noticed you haven't been praying lately."

"I know." Eshu looked away. "I keep meaning to. I just haven't."

"And you haven't shaved your beard off."

"I don't have a razor."

"You could borrow my knife."

"I don't have a mirror."

"I think you're depressed," said Fern.

"And what? You're just going to cheer me up again?"

"No, probably not. I don't know a lot about depression, but I don't think it works like that." She leaned on his shoulder. "But I do think you can be depressed just as easily in Kulmeni as you can here."

"I hate how much I've been relying on you," Eshu said under his breath. "You look at this forest and see what you can do with it, and I just see this undifferentiated mass of green and rot and teeth. I feel so stupid and useless here. Nothing I've ever studied has prepared me for this, and it just makes me feel—helpless."

"Well, now you know how to find food and make a shelter. And probably how to weave a basket. If you want, I can teach you the other stuff. Like seasoning a pan, or finding your way by the stars." She sat back and stretched. "I didn't know how to do all this at first, either. No one does. You learn, or you figure it out."

Eshu licked his lips. "Just one more night," he said. "Then we can go."

"One more night," Fern agreed. "Want me to give you a shave? I think we've got a little bit of soap left."

For a moment, Eshu looked like he was going to refuse. His face was hollow and tired, deeply shadowed under the eyes. But then something shifted in his expression, like a light coming on in a window far away. "All right," he said at last.

They scraped away two weeks of beard by the stream, and then they dug up some lotus roots and ginger for the road.

When the sun set, Fern knelt with her back to it and watched her shadow stretch out before her. She didn't know how to say Njowa prayers, and she didn't understand the faith of the Far Traveler, but she understood that Njo was important to Eshu, so she sat back on her heels and listened to the forest. After a while, Eshu sank down beside her and began to speak the sunset prayer.

CHAPTER 10: ROADS TO NOWHERE

They fetched up in a fishing village two days down the Anjali, where old men and women sat mending nets on the docks and pedal boats drifted on the deep, smooth waters. It was the first time in weeks that Eshu had seen people who weren't Fern, and he nearly kissed the first stranger he met.

After the wrecks of Sharis and Zumera, it felt bizarre to see a village where life continued more or less as usual. Smokehouses prepared fish and bacon; weavers made baskets; children chased each other through narrow alleys until their parents shouted them home. People swept their doorsteps and hung flowers in baskets by their windows.

They traded lotus roots and ginger for hot, spicy soup, and the man who served them introduced himself as Malun Esara. "What's a Malun?" Eshu asked under his breath as they ate.

"It isn't anything. It's just a name," said Fern. Her eyes were wet and her nose running from the spice, but she grinned anyway, and he grinned back because she seemed to want him to.

This place didn't fear the Crowtaker. After hearing people name themselves Rain and Shell and Branch, that calm felt alien— almost naïve. A quiet part of him watched the villagers going about their day and whispered in that rasping, rusted voice, *What are any of you but meat?*

There were crocodiles in the Anjali, just as Fern had promised, and they sunned themselves on the village's outskirts like lazy, malevolent dragons.

Eshu and Fern traded a few of their sapphires to a couple of fishers to take them up to Kulmeni. Both were cheerful and heavyset, tattooed to the elbows with fish scales. "Half-brother and sister," said the woman proudly, when she caught Eshu looking. "But they used to call us the twins, 'cause we were always copying each other. I'd lay down my life for that muddle-headed fool."

"She knows I'm the brains of the operation," her brother laughed as they pedaled. The two of them matched rhythm easily, and the paddlewheels churned them down the river.

"Do you go to Kulmeni often?" Fern asked. She perched on the boat's railing, near the back where the fish lay in a heap.

"About once a week," the woman answered. "Have to warn you, things are a bit strange these days."

"Strange how?" asked Eshu.

"The mist, for one," said the man.

"The roads don't always go where you think they do," his sister added.

"You hear things, if you're walking alone. See things, sometimes."

"And then the business with the prince, but we don't get involved with city politics," she finished. "One prince is as good as another, that's what I say. We'll pay our taxes either way."

Fern and Eshu exchanged a look. More than surprise, Eshu saw pain in her eyes—she had resigned herself to Matis falling like every other city had; for the first time since Zumera, she was wondering whether she'd been wrong. *Whether she'd been wrong to go with me.* Eventually, though, she ventured, "But it's still there. The city's still standing. And people are alive."

The woman laughed. "Bless your heart, child! Takes more than a spot of bad weather to take down us Anjali folks!"

"Why would you want to go to Kulmeni if you didn't think it

was still there?" the man asked, as though it was a joke. His broad, cheerful face looked so free of care that Eshu wanted to break it a little.

"Let me tell you about Sharis and Zumera," he began.

Over the next few hours, as the paddlewheels turned and the riverbanks slid by, Fern and Eshu unraveled their story. Every now and then, one of the fishers asked a question—*How did you know everyone was dead, if you didn't see the bodies* or *Whole streets paved with gems, and no one picking them up; I never*—but Eshu could only answer, "I don't know what to tell you. It was true."

"Well, tall tales or no, you've clearly had a hard time," said the woman, whose name was Palam. Her brother was Kartan, *like in the hero stories*, which meant something to Fern and fuck all to Eshu. "What's in Kulmeni for you? Work? Family?"

"Wizards, we hope," Fern answered. "We can walk the rest of the way to Kondala City if we have to, but if we can get there by mirror, it'd be faster. An airship would be good, too, but even an onion cart would be better than bushwhacking through the mountains for two more weeks."

"You could've gone along the shore," said Kartan. "Longer way around, but easier going, probably. Gentler on your feet."

"Not much water, though," said Palam. "Got to remember, seas are salty."

Kartan reached across the boat to shove her shoulder. "Well, shit, good thing you're here to keep me in line. Seas are salty, of all the—would you listen to this woman, she's some kind of wilderness survival expert. Seas are salty, no shit. Tell 'em what color the sky is next."

They were rounding a bend in the river, and as the boat rocked and righted itself, the deep green trees slid past like a curtain. Ahead, a valley opened up between two gently sloping hills, with the river coursing smooth as glass between them. More than that, Eshu couldn't say, because a thick mist lay over the land and water alike. He glimpsed lamps flickering at the edges of the deep grey fog, and heard the shouts of dockworkers and the doleful toll of buoy bells. Every sound was muffled, as though his ears were full of cotton wool.

A moment ago, the sky had been a high sapphire blue with lacy clouds drifting in wisps across eastern horizon. As they eased into the valley, though, the sky dulled to grey and then was lost to view entirely.

As they drew close to the docks, Palam and Kartan abandoned the pedal wells and instead guided the boat with a pair of stout poles. Lights cut through the fog, some with green lenses and some with red. "Do the colors mean anything?" Fern asked.

"That was the new prince's idea," Palam explained. "Shows which docks are available to rent. We want a dock with one green light. That's a small dock. More lights, bigger docks. Three's for a cargo barge—think that's as big as they get."

"It seems like a complicated system," said Eshu.

"Try figuring out the docks in this mist without it," said Kartan with a snort. He dipped his pole deep into the water, then levered them past a huge stone structure that loomed out of the fog. Eshu glimpsed mossy rocks, nesting birds, the suggestion of shaped stone or concrete vanishing into the invisible sky. *A bridge*, he guessed. There must be more of the city on the far shore.

"What happened with the old prince?" Fern asked. Her voice was so quiet that Eshu could barely hear it over the sounds of the docks and the water lapping against the hull. "Did he die, or…"

"He died a few weeks back," said Palam, and for the first time since they'd met her, she had nothing further to say.

They pulled into an open docking space, and Fern and Eshu said their goodbyes while Palam and Kartan paid their docking fee. The moment the dockhand had the money, she pulled a little chain that changed the lens in the lamp from green to red. She didn't even have to look up to find the chain—it was already an automatic movement. *This new prince moves fast*, Eshu thought almost admiringly. *I suppose he must have had to, after whatever happened to Kulmeni.*

All around them were people, splicing ropes and hauling fish and joking to each other about some recent kingdom drama on the low theater circuit—bargemen smoking stemweed; tattooed women with their collars turned down, playing cards on a barrel; merchants in saffron and turquoise jackets choosing fish at auction. There were children with baskets full of vibrant jungle flowers, crying *Orchids, jasmines, lilies of all colors!* A pair of girls with long braids stopped to buy each other flowers, threading their fingers together over a bouquet of bell-shaped lilies and kissing each other's cheeks.

Amidst the busy press of people, Eshu felt like a wild creature— some fox or feral dog slinking between market stalls in the late hours, sniffing about for scraps. He was keenly aware of his filthy clothes and unkempt hair, the ashy skin on his elbows and between his fingers.

"Where to?" Fern asked. "Just ask around until we find someone who knows where the wizards are? Look for a map to Kondala City?"

Even as Eshu opened his mouth to answer, the Crowtaker's voice was in his ear: *Why return to Kondala City? Nothing you love remains.* He shuddered. "Not yet," he said. "I, for one, would very much like to buy shoes that match and a robe that no one's thrown up on. And then I'd like a long bath with soap, some lotion and eye paint, and someone to fuck me blind. And then whatever's left of me can look for a decent meal."

"All right," said Fern. "Then we should find a place to stay first, so that we can find each other later. I have some gems left; we can probably find somewhere to sell them. Do you have any money?"

"Not much," Eshu admitted. "Probably not enough for a new set of shoes."

"So that's the first thing we have to do. Change our gems for money."

They made their way along the wharf, past tackle shops and pawn shops and fruit stands full of ripening oranges and tekusa pods. Here, even the alleyways were marked with street signs in Nanjeeri and Kondalani. Most looked freshly painted. *Bonecut Alley*, said one near a butcher's shop; *Hookers' Way*, read another.

They turned onto Wire Street, where the air was thick with the smell of smoke and hot metal. There, amid silversmiths and tinkerers, Fern found a jeweler's shop with a glass storefront. The wizened old woman behind the counter looked at Fern's gemstones under a lens, tutted about inclusions and impurities, and made them an offer that Fern immediately refused.

Eshu listened with only half an ear as they haggled. Outside the shop, the mist curled across the street in fingers and furls, shifting and reshaping in a way that even Eshu could tell had nothing to do with the wind. *Is this another zone of susceptibility?* he wondered. *If I work a spell here, will the city rise up in answer?*

Something unseen moved through the mist, trailing streamers of shadow in its wake. A cold sensation pricked at the back of Eshu's neck. "Wait for me," he told Fern. "There's something I have to do."

"Wait, what? Where are you going? We don't even have a room yet; that's not how this works—" she said, but he was already halfway out the door. The bell jingled dully behind him as the door swung shut.

He stood on the paving stones of Wire Street, listening. The mist muffled the nearby ring of hammers and shop door bells, the murmur of conversation and the cries of water birds perched on the peaked rooftops all around him. Eshu ignored them. He wasn't sure what he was listening for—something that made his skin crawl. Something that made him want to run the other way.

He began to hum a searching song just as the door burst open behind him. "Eshu, what was that?"

The song slipped. He lost his place, and the threads of magic that he'd been spinning unraveled into nothingness. "Fuck me," he muttered. "Sorry," he said, louder. "I thought I saw something."

"Something?"

"One of the things from the Mirrorlands. A hungry ghost."

"Oh. Shit." Fern scanned the streets, but she must not have seen anything, because she put her hands in her pockets and looked back at Eshu. "You could've told me that before you walked off."

"I didn't want to frighten the jeweler," he said, but if he was honest with himself, the jeweler hadn't even crossed his mind. He'd seen the trace of the creature in the mist, and he'd been drawn to it like a compass's needle to true north.

If you've developed a death wish, Eshusikinde, then it really is all over for you. He shook his head, which did nothing at all to clear it. "Anyway. I'm clearly hallucinating from malnutrition. Did you make a good trade?"

"Decent. She wanted me to throw in the diamond dust from the etching set, so probably no more etching gems for us." Fern dug around in her pocket and took a couple of leather thongs with coins threaded over them. They looked a lot like the one- and five-zil pieces the moneychangers had given him when he'd come to Nanjeer, squares of varying sizes with circular holes cut through the center, but Eshu could tell by the numbers stamped in the metal that he was holding a lot more money than he'd ever had in Usbaran.

"You didn't give her the runestones?"

Fern rolled her eyes. "No, I didn't even put them on the table. I thought we might still want them—maybe even more, now that we're in a city. And I didn't offer my Mirrorland samples, either. I'm hoping I can rent a microscope somewhere and take a look at them while we're here."

"With this kind of money, you could probably buy a microscope."

"But then I'd have to carry it and take care of it. Unless you're planning to stay here and watch my microscope." She gave a lopsided smile. "I don't know. I think we should find a room to rent before we start thinking about moving in."

"If you insist," said Eshu. "While you're on the hunt for a microscope, could you also inquire about wizards and mirrors? I'd like to look a bit more like myself before I have to face my peers again."

"Sure. Take as much time as you need." She led them back down Wire Street, past the same silversmiths' signs and open blacksmiths' forges that they'd passed on the way up. When they reached the place where the street should have intersected with the wharf, though, there was only a circular plaza with a fountain quietly bubbling. A middle-aged woman with flour on her forearms sat at the fountain's edge, smoking a long-stemmed pipe and gazing into the water. Eshu could just make out the flash of fish beneath the water's surface, white and black and orange-golden.

"Excuse me, mistress," he said. "Where is the wharf from here?"

The baker looked him over, taking in his torn clothes and ragged hair and mismatched shoes with an expression that was as pointed as a comment. "You must be new here," she said.

"Yes," Fern agreed. "We just got here today."

The woman took a long drag on her pipe, then blew out a cloud of bluish vapor. At length, she said, "Listen for the birds screaming. They're loud over the water, begging for fish and bread. And listen for the way the boats creak when the water rocks them up against the docks. Look for the new dock lights and ships' masts over the rooftops. They'll be hard to make out through the mist, but just keep your eye out. You'll see them eventually."

"What street should we look for?" asked Fern.

"Don't worry about streets. That only helps if you've lived here a long time. Listen for the birds; they'll steer you right."

"Thank you so much," said Fern. When they were out of earshot, though, she muttered, "That wasn't very helpful."

"It sounded like how you'd give directions through the Mirrorlands," Eshu answered. "Impressions. The feeling of a place, more than the absolute location of it."

"But we aren't behind a mirror."

"No, but it's possible that whatever happened here, it follows mirror-logic now. It's worth looking into, at least."

Eshu closed his eyes and listened to the city around him. There was a low, continuous hum of activity wherever he turned his attention—cart wheels on paving stones, fishmongers crying the day's catch, forge hammers and corner buskers and laughter and cups clicking on tables. He let those sounds pass through him as though they were water and he a streambed; as though he were a flute and they a flautist's breath.

He listened for the cries of birds and the lapping of water against boats' hulls. Slowly, he began to hear the birds' calls through the clamoring dark, and he took Fern by the hand and pointed. "There. The wharf is there," he said. It didn't feel as though he'd picked a set of sounds out of a cacophony. It felt as though he'd listened them into being.

Fern pulled him by the hand down what felt like a long street, and as they walked, he began to smell fish and wet wood and unwashed bodies. "Huh," said Fern. "I guess it does work like the Mirrorlands."

He opened his eyes on the red and green lights of the wharf, and he couldn't help smiling. *At least all that university training is worth something at the world's end.* "Do you see any inns?" he asked.

"Sort of. There's a sign that says *Rooms for Let*." Fern pointed to a printer's shop with a second story that extended slightly over the street. When Eshu peered through the mist and the yellowish grime on the window, he could just make out the sign on a bit of curling cardstock.

They met with the printer, a reed-thin young man with nervous hands and a weak chin. He asked whether they were married, how long they meant to stay, and whether they could pay in advance, and he let them know that the master printer kept a sober household. "If you mean to go drinking, you'd best not return drunk. They'll toss you out and keep your money," he confided. "Lost the last tenants that way."

This suited Eshu well enough; he meant to go out drinking, but if the night went well, he'd be spending the night in someone else's bed anyway. "That seems fair," he said, and slipped three of the thick twenty-zil coins off of the leather thong. The lotus flowers stamped on them had almost worn smooth.

Fern gave him an uneasy look, but pulled a few coins free. "Baths in the rooms, or in the city?" she asked.

"In the city," he answered. "But Kulmeni is famous for its bathhouses. I can promise you won't be disappointed."

"How will we find them? If the city is..." she gave a helpless, all-encompassing gesture.

"Ah, not to worry! We've got a guidebook we print for newcomers. Just a bit of frivolity, back in the old days, but since the change, the prince has asked us to do full-color print runs, so now they're quite smart and helpful." He took a couple of loosely sewn pamphlets down from a wire rack and passed them across the counter.

When Eshu opened one up, he found them full of handsome etchings printed with vibrant colors: *Heron's Bridge*, read one etching, showing a grey stone bridge rising out of low mists into a pristine blue sky. Another was labeled *The Garden of Sighs*, and showed women in red and blue wrap gowns walking through cascades of flowers and bowers agleam with lanterns. Flipping through, he found the bathhouses illustrated with marbled pillars and delicate traceries of steam rising from the green water. A man was stepping out of the bath with his arms raised to towel dry his hair, all of his muscles hatched in loving detail.

Eshu's skin warmed. "I'd like a copy of this," he said. "To help me find my way."

The printer's expression said he knew precisely why Eshu wanted this book, and likewise knew that it was none of his business. He named his price, and Eshu gladly paid.

"You mentioned the change," Fern pressed. "What happened? Were there lights in the sky?"

The printer nodded. "That's what they've been saying. I was asleep when it happened, so as far as I knew, it was just a bad fog. There were some disappearances—something bad; they could barely recognize the bodies when they found them—then a bit of rioting and looting. The riots weren't so bad, really. I've seen worse when the university lets out for the Heron's Feast. A few people tipped over carts and burned them, but it was in the middle of a plaza, and nothing else caught fire. A couple of windows got smashed. But then there were the curfews, and—actually, I've got some back issues. Not much use for them but kindling, so if you want to read them, they're yours." He went to the wood rack by the cold fireplace and pulled out a stack of newspapers, sorting through them and muttering dates to himself. When he'd separated out four issues, he passed them over to Fern, who rolled them up and stuck them in her pack.

Eshu and Fern were led up to their rooms—little more than closets with beds, but there *were* beds, which was already a vast improvement over the last few weeks.

"I'm out to make myself human again," Eshu announced at the curtain that separated their rooms. "You're welcome to join me."

"No, you go on," Fern said. She was turning up the wick on her lamp; a newspaper lay open on the bedspread. "I want to read these first, and then I'm going to update my map. Maybe I'll run into you later?"

"Not if I've done it right. Leave those on my bed when you've finished?"

"Sure thing. Stay safe, all right? You've had some bad luck lately, and I don't want you to get eaten by a mirror ghost." She hesitated, rocking back and forth on the balls of her feet, then leaned in to give Eshu a one-armed hug. *On my good side*, he thought as her pointy chin dug into his ribs. *Still so careful of hurting me. My sisters were never this careful—but I don't think I've ever let them see me really hurt.*

He wrapped his arm around her shoulders. "I'll be careful. Promise."

Then they parted ways, and Eshu descended the stairs to the mist-wrapped city of Kulmeni. He took out his guidebook and flipped through it until he reached the illustration of an open-air marketplace. Crosshatched merchants lined the streets, peddling mangos and tekusa and oranges and orchids and parakeets and lamps with delicate dangling beads in a dozen hues. *The Covered Market of Prince Hezina III*, read the caption, and Eshu could just barely make out suggestions of intricately worked archways and a mosaic-tiled ceiling in the background.

As he walked, Eshu began to sing the marketplace: the vendors' cries, the songbirds caroling in their cages, the sharp-scented oranges piled in pyramids. He sang the stink of people crammed too close together, the begging dogs and pickpockets and the perfumes of far-off Cheresse. The versification felt workmanlike to his own ears—dull, literal imagery, without the spark of insight to kindle poetry from unlikely similes and straining metaphors. But it was enough to carry him forward, and he supposed that was what mattered.

The way was lined with trees at the height of their bloom, and long strands of white flowers hung from every bough. They gave off a scent like honey and musk, sweet and heady as the meads of Usbaran. Eshu passed a polished rail of wood and brass that overlooked the long slope down to the river; he'd had no sensation of climbing. He picked his way between the towering tenements of

some working district, where washing hung across every alleyway
and beggars sat on doorsteps with bowls in hand.

He slipped a single coin into an old man's bowl. "Sisters keep
you," the man muttered at the click of metal on wood, but he didn't
look up, and Eshu moved on with his song still on his lips.

Then, out of the mist, he saw lamps through the archways of
the covered market, and a smile wiped the song away.

He bought himself a satchel and two pairs of new shoes, a thick-
soled leather pair for the wilderness and a set of sandals for the city.
Then a sleeveless robe in hues of shifting violet, embroidered with
delicate white traceries of leaf and vine. Traveling clothes like Fern
wore, with pockets and boots and trousers that tied at the knee. *I
ought to get myself a compass*, he thought, but then he came across a
Kondalani food stall, and the taste of familiar flatbread and spiced
lentils pushed the thought out of his mind. He stood chatting a while
with the merchant in Kondalani, trying to see if they knew anyone
in common and learning a bit too much about her innumerable
nieces and nephews. She recommended him three different places to
get his locs tidied and tightened, and another that dealt in cosmetics.
At the end of the conversation, she told him that he needed to eat
more and gave him a paper sack of candied ginger for a treat, and he
had to turn away before his wet eyes betrayed him.

Next, the bathhouse. Stepping out of the marketplace, he sang
pillars of steam, waters gilded with rippling lamplight, and a warm
bath submerging his ankles and thighs and hips. He sang bath oils
perfumed with ambergris and sweet creamy lotions and the scrape
of a razor over his skin; he sang sweet-smelling soaps until he
ached with the itch of his own filth.

At last, Eshu caught sight of a copper dome green with patina.
The mists unfurled around the bathhouse, revealing marble walls
worked with intricate carvings. Nude youths sported and splashed
in woodland pools, their fleshy bodies so lovingly rendered that
Eshu was half-convinced that their skin would dimple if he touched

it. A mother nursed her infant as a young man dressed her hair with combs. An old man reclined in a mountain hot spring with his eyes closed, letting attractive young men and women fawn on him as engraved steam rose from the water.

As soon as Eshu opened the doors, the thick scent of perfumes threatened to overwhelm him. He smelled flowers and herbs and musky resins, sharp citrus and heady vanilla; for a moment, he steadied himself on the doorframe. He hadn't realized how much he'd grown used to the smell of leaf mould and unwashed clothes, acrid body odor and rot.

When he'd collected himself, he rented a private bath for two hours and bought soaps and lotions and a sharp new razor. The room to which he was led was small, but the bath was deep and beautifully tiled in blue, and the water was almost too hot. Right then, *too hot* was exactly what he wanted.

When Eshu finally emerged from the bath, worked lotion into his joints, and put on his new clothes and sandals, he almost felt like a person again. His shaven legs felt silk-soft, sensitive to every shift of the robe; his face was fresh and smooth to the touch. His locs spilled over his shoulders, still sparkling with droplets of water. He studied his reflection in the fogged mirror, wishing he had a little silver eye paint to complete the look.

"Can't be helped," he said. His voice still had a rough edge to it that he didn't like; there was a grimness and fatalism now in his intonation that made him feel like some dire prophet. "Can't be helped," he tried again, all false singsong flippancy.

It felt wrong. The whole thing felt wrong, like a mask he'd pulled over a corpse's flyblown face. He didn't belong in these fine clothes or this fine bathhouse with its perfumes and oils. Maybe it didn't belong in the world anymore, now that everything else lay in ruins. *Will I ever be able to feel like a person again?* he wondered, halfway to despair and closing on it fast. He prodded at his ribs on his bad side, where a little echo of pain remained. The pain didn't have any answers, but liquor and a thick cock might make him forget why he wanted them.

"Where can I find drinks and smart company in Kulmeni?" he asked the attendant on duty, a willowy young woman with her hair in two plaits over her shoulders. "I'm willing to round down to lively company, but the drinks are non-negotiable."

"There's a place my friends go sometimes, called the Vine on the Trellis," she offered. "I've never been, but they say it's very nice. There are drinks and food there, and sometimes music. But, ah, I don't think the company's for hire there. If that's what you're asking."

"It isn't. I appreciate the information—thank you." Eshu tipped her a five-zil coin engraved with fives and fish and jasmine flowers, then stepped back onto the dim, clammy streets.

By now, it was evening, and lamplighters were making their rounds. He'd missed the sunset prayer again, but by now he'd missed so many prayers that it hardly seemed to matter. No one else but Fern cared whether he spoke the prayers or kept the fasts, and she only cared because it mattered to him. *Does it still matter to me?* he wondered. It had been so easy to say that Njo was his anvil when he'd been bent around his faith. But the last few weeks had started hammering him into a new shape. He wasn't sure he liked it.

With the name of the Vine on the Trellis on his lips, Eshu strode into the shifting vapors. Even before he began to weave his song, though, he could feel that something had changed as the dark drew down. The tropical heat had almost bled out of Kulmeni, and the coolness that remained felt like more than the absence of heat. He shivered and wished he'd brought his outer robe—but that was filthy, and he'd left it at the foot of his rented bed.

It wouldn't help, anyway. This wasn't an ordinary evening's coolness, with warmth still radiating from the sunstruck paving stones and brisk winds that smelled of the streets and the river.

This was the cold of the Mirrorlands, and it tasted of sand and emptiness.

The streets were empty, and the houses were dark. *But they're not houses*, Eshu thought. *They're just the memories of houses. Cognitive anchors to lead people to a locus.* This wasn't a city, exactly—or not just a city. Not anymore.

Eshu began to hum a warding song, the kind that drew an unseen circle around him and wove it into a lattice of steel. Ever since he'd fallen to the Crowtaker, a part of him had wondered if it wasn't better just to give up and leave his body for the beasts—but as the mists parted to welcome him, he was filled with a desire to live so intense that it made him feel faint and sick.

Something was out there, just beyond his sight. He felt it watching him, pacing him like a spur cat shadowing its prey, stalking slowly down the other side of the thoroughfare. If he thought about it too long, he could almost make out the shape of it through the mist: heavy paws and long bony spines along its back; burning eyes in a too-human face. Lips rotting back from sharp, leonine teeth. If he ran, it would catch him. There was no mirror here for him to flee through.

Eshu stilled and felt the creature still, too. His whole body was weak and cold with fear. He remembered Fern standing defiant before the Crowtaker, between him and an unfathomable eldritch monster, and his own cowardice shamed him. "Come at me!" he called into the gathering shadows. "Let's see how you dance."

Across the way, the mist began to shift and curl. Streamers of fog raveled out from something caught at the center, like water weeds wrapping the drowned. It hurt to look at it. Not a piercing pain, like looking at the sun, but a queasy ache like trying to look at the back of his own skull.

The ghost stepped onto the street. The silence of its claws clicking on stone ached in Eshu's ears. *Fill that silence*, he told himself. *Drive it out, until nothing remains but your voice.*

Eshu pressed his attack in a blazing falsetto, chasing down a high, sweet note to pierce the shadows. He sang a maze of blades, keen as grief, sharp as sorrow—he sang sunlight striking fire from the edges, skin carved asunder beneath folded steel. The mist around him shuddered apart as he sang. He strode light-footed into the street to meet his foe, and his blades were a tempest around him.

Then the creature dragged a taloned hand through the blades, and they parted like water beneath its touch. Through the gap, he saw its face: the rot-slick skin sloughing off of its cheeks, the lank hair peeling back from its skull. The penetrating eyes that saw and knew him.

He sank down into his chest voice to sing a warding song. *Be armor; be granite walls; be the tortoise shell and the urchin's spines. Be the waves that guard the island and the air that guards the globe.* Wind wrapped him in a whirling sphere that stirred his robes and lifted his heavy hair. Eshu's heart thundered in his ears. He raised his voice until he could barely hear what he was singing—until he could hear nothing but the deep earthquake rumble of his voice.

The creature didn't drop its hand. The wind skimmed across its knuckles and ground them bloody. He looked into the creature's eyes, searching for fear or hesitation or fucking *curiosity*, for Njo's sake. He saw only hunger.

With a glissando like a scream, he shaped the barrier into a single strand of wire and sent it shredding through the ghost's decaying viscera. He heard someone shout, and then there was a light bobbing through the darkness as the ghost hissed and lunged. Eshu caught it by the jaws as its guts slopped out across the paving stones; teeth clashed together, scraping the edges of his fingers. Hot breath steamed out of the creature's reeking gullet with a smell like rot and saltwater.

A heavy *crack* echoed through the street. Eshu glimpsed a flash of something gleaming white-golden, of iron studs and polished wood—then the creature collapsed in on itself like a paper flower dissolving in the rain.

He looked down at his new robes, expecting to find ichor and intestines, and instead found them clean. Then he looked up at the stranger who'd come to his rescue, and his breath caught.

The man was very nearly Eshu's height, but built like a mountain. His heavy shoulders and arms were smooth with fat, but when he shifted his grip on that huge studded club of his, Eshu could see muscles rippling beneath. All the exposed skin beneath his neck had been worked with tattoos; vines traced his clavicles, and blackwork rings encircled his forearms like bracers. Even if he hadn't just saved Eshu's life, Eshu would've wanted to fuck him.

The stranger raised his lantern and gave a smile that reached his dark eyes. "Sorry for stealing your kill, friend."

"For rescuing me? I'm not sure that needs forgiveness."

"Heh, you looked like you had it. You some kind of wizard, then?" His thumb traced one of the gleaming marks on his club. They were runes, Eshu realized, as the fear began to leach out of him. They were carved in the same style that Tuuri preferred, graven in an all-but-dead language.

But Eshu had gone several weeks without thinking of Tuuri, and he had no inclination to start now. "Was it the magic that gave it away, or the immaculate fashion sense? My name is Eshusikinde, but you can call me Eshu."

"Beejan Acala," the man answered. "You're new around here, right? But not new to these things." He made a gesture that took in where the ghost had been.

Whatever had been there, whatever knot of malice and possibility had begun to coalesce into a creature at Eshu's attention, it was gone now. Eshu tried not to think of its eyes and teeth. "I met one once in the Mirrorlands. It thought I looked delicious."

"Can't say I disagree." Grinning, Beejan shifted his grip on the club and gave it an experimental swing. "Feel like hunting a few more?"

"Is that what you're out here to do? Hunt hungry ghosts through the streets?"

Beejan laughed. "You ask that like you aren't out here doing the same thing."

"*I* was looking for somewhere to get drunk. The ghost was purely a chance encounter."

"Well, if you like, we can still do that when my shift's up."

Eshu tilted his head. "This is a job, then? I'm sorry; it just seems sudden for such a niche industry to have sprung up here. I can't imagine there's a tradesman's guild for it yet."

"I report directly to the prince. After these things started eating people, she got very interested in seeing them cleared out." That heavy club made another arc, its dull studs gleaming in the light of Beejan's lamp. "You never answered me, Eshu. You want in on this? There'll be pay at the end of it."

"I'd have said yes even without the money." But that wasn't quite a *yes*, either. Eshu looked Beejan in the eyes, tied back his hair, and said, "Yes, then. Let's go fuck their shit up."

They set out into the darkness with Beejan leading the way. He seemed to know every back alley and garden path, every canal and gutter; he was a fixed point in Kulmeni, and his memory anchored the streets.

"What did you do before you started hunting ghosts?" Eshu asked.

"Heh, I was a runner," said Beejan. "Got things where they needed to be. Paid the right people, cracked the wrong people's heads."

So he'd been some kind of criminal—normally that would've given Eshu pause, but after what had happened back in Zumera, he wasn't so charitably inclined toward the law. "Was there much actual running, in that line of work?"

"You'd be surprised. Some cops can't be bought, and cracking their heads has consequences. Still got a fair turn of speed, when I care to run."

Looking at Beejan move, Eshu believed it. He had a self-assured grace that Eshu envied; for all his bulk, he had a light tread, and every step had a coiled power to it that made Eshu long to see him really *fight*.

"What about you? Where do you come from?" Beejan asked.

"Fuck me, I don't even know how to answer that question anymore. Kondala City's where my family lives. I go to school in Usbaran, or I will, if there's still an Usbaran. A friend and I walked here from outside Zumera, on the north coast."

Beejan whistled. "Zumera! That's a long way. We sent a ship out to Zumera after Granny took over, but it hasn't come back yet. What's the news from there?"

Took over what? Eshu wondered. "Bad," he said aloud. "Almost the whole city is gone. Buried under a thousand princes' ransoms in jewels."

"Shit! What a way to go, though. Hope they bring us back something."

It hurt to hear Beejan so detached. Eshu reminded himself that he hadn't seen the corpses buried under carpets of fluorite, the bodies impaled on spears of tourmaline; he hadn't met Sparrow and Nadi, lying their asses off to get refugees out of the city. He hadn't met the refugees. "And Sharis fell into the sea," he said. "I was there. It was surprising, to see that Kulmeni was still standing. I'd expected to be picking over rubble."

"Don't sound so disappointed," Beejan laughed. "It's not the end of the world! Not for us. Not yet. We're still here, and there's still a lot of work to do. Everything's changed. The mighty brought low, the criminals made good; money flowing out of the prince's coffers and into our pockets. And, sure, we've got hungry ghosts to hunt down, but that's just job security."

"Until they eat someone."

"Until they eat someone," agreed Beejan. "Best to keep them from eating someone, if you can."

They ducked into a trellised avenue fragrant with bean flowers and late-blooming clematis. Flowers hung in curtains and coils, red and white and yellow blossoms swaying in the light breeze. His feet crunched on the delicate shell of the pathway as the wind picked up, making the trellises creak and groan. *The Garden of Sighs?* Eshu wondered. It looked like a good place to get lost in, if you had a lover and a little time to waste.

Beejan paused at a stone arched bridge. Beneath its gentle arc, a stream sang through the gardens, plashing down tiny waterfalls and laughing over smooth stones green with moss. His lantern turned the water to molten gold; it gleamed golden on the smooth curve of his cheek. In that spellbound moment, with the perfume of the gardens heavy on the air, Eshu suddenly wanted very much to fit his hand to that curve and see how Beejan's lips tasted. "Something's here," Beejan said.

Eshu froze. The garden was quiet around him, except for the creaking of the trellises and the soft rustle of leaves. He cast about in all directions, but Beejan's lantern illuminated nothing but drifting mist.

And water. Eshu's gaze fell to the stream. The lamplight turned it into a series of glistening mirrors, broken in places by shallow waterfalls. In the surface of that water, he saw something like black smoke reflected. His heartbeat throbbed in his ears.

"Let yourself be afraid of it," Beejan said, low. "Whatever you're afraid it is, *just let yourself see it*. You can't kill it unless you can see it."

Beejan shifted, putting his back to Eshu's back. His skin radiated warmth in the clammy air. "What do you see, when you see these things?" Eshu asked.

"Long spider legs," said Beejan. "Or—not spider legs, exactly. Sort of the way a spider moves. Still, so still you almost miss it at first, then all of a sudden it goes skittering like—" He shivered. "And eyes. Glowing out in the mists. Almost man-height, but not exactly. Like it's hunched over, watching you. Waiting."

"Something more than animal cunning in its eyes. It recognizes you."

"Yeah." Beejan breathed in through his nose. "I think there's more than one of them out there. They're circling. Trying to flank us."

Eshu peered into the curling mist. Tree limbs slid in and out of view, ghostly shadows against the distant glow of the streetlamps. He couldn't see anything moving, but he felt what Beejan meant: something prowling in slow circles, just beyond the lantern's reach. It was watching them with glowing white eyes in a face as much like a hound's as a man's. He could almost see the long limbs tucked up like a spider's, almost hear them clicking over the damp earth and gravel.

Flame danced over his fingers in gouts and flickers, unstable without a song to anchor it. It felt as though a sudden breeze would flay him open. He forced himself to breathe. *Let yourself be afraid. Let yourself see what you've been trying not to see.*

He shut out the whisper of Beejan's breath and the warmth of his body and the soft scrape of his soles against the bridge. He closed his eyes against the mist and the bridge and the gilded stream. His eyes wouldn't help him find the creatures. His fear knew where they were.

Eshu felt them moving in, and he raised his voice in a tempest. He sang a gale that whipped the mists away—a clean cold wind like a blade of ice. The air smelled of ice and lightning, like a spring storm sweeping up over the frigid southern lakes.

When he opened his eyes, the ghosts were all around them. Some crept from the mist on long jackal legs, and their faces had too many eyes in them. Others looked almost like people, or like things that had been people once. Their long arms hung limply from their shoulders as though the tendons had been cut; their lank, dark hair curtained their faces. One looked up at him with gleaming eyes, and her smile was knife-bright.

"You'd better—" Beejan said, but Eshu never heard what he'd better do, because the creatures all came at them at once. The lantern fell in the first frantic defense. The creatures funneled in along both sides of the bridge, cutting off any retreat; they leapt across the water, and Eshu flung them back with gust after gust of wind. At his back, Beejan roared a challenge and swept his club through the mass of ghosts. Eshu felt the breeze of it, heard it strike flesh and bone and something that was neither.

His chest swelled with the gale song. He called down hailstones like fists; he sang the lightning in searing filaments, jagged white-hot columns slicing from earth to sky. He sang storm-wracked ships, sail-shredded; he sang the cyclones that carved through Ras Kir'uun in high summer. The whirlwind screamed around them as Beejan's club came down again and again, breaking jaws and crushing skulls. Once, something with claws got to him, and Eshu smelled his blood hot and coppery on the air.

Then there came a long howl from somewhere beyond the bridge. The ghosts looked up as one; heads cocked, heeding. Then they fled, limping and skittering back into the mists.

Beejan got in one last swipe that made a rotten-limbed shadow hiss and shudder into vapor. The runes on his club were shining with a bright white light. "Fuck off!" he shouted into the darkness. "And don't come back!—they'll be back," he confided to Eshu. "Can't be helped. Seems like there's more every night."

"Job security, I believe you called it."

Beejan bent to pick up his lantern. It had gone out when it fell. He struck a match, then lit the wick again. "You put up a good fight back there. I'd love to spar sometime, if you'd be up for it."

Eshu grinned. "I'll have to decline, I'm afraid. I'm still healing from a few broken ribs, and your club would absolutely demolish my delicate bones."

"I'd be gentle with you."

Eshu's skin went hot. "Oh, I wouldn't say I want *that*."

"Are we flirting, then?" Beejan asked. He set his lamp to one side and sat back on the rail of the bridge. There were deep gashes down his biceps, but he didn't seem to notice them. With the lantern light gleaming from his sweat-sheened skin, picking out his thick muscles and the smooth swell of his gut, he looked beautiful and vast and invincible.

"I thought we'd been flirting since you said I looked delicious," said Eshu.

He stepped into the gap between Beejan's knees to kiss him, and Beejan drank him down. He curled one arm around Eshu's shoulders and tangled a hand in his hair, wrapping locs around his fingers and pulling until Eshu's skin prickled with the sweet ache of it. Beejan's lips parted; his teeth dragged over Eshu's lower lip, and that pressure was too much and not nearly enough after weeks without a touch. Eshu crowded in closer, chasing the kiss as deep as he could take it.

When they broke, Beejan kept him close with that hand in his hair. Their noses brushed; Beejan's long eyelashes grazed Eshu's cheeks. In the Mirrorlands chill of the garden, Beejan was a furnace, and Eshu couldn't get close enough to the heat of him. His breath came shallow and quick. "What if we skipped the drinks," he said, "and instead you took me home and did whatever you liked with me."

Beejan laughed, just a faint gust of breath against Eshu's mouth. "When someone asks you to do whatever you like to them, they've usually got something in mind."

"You get that request a lot?"

"It's come up."

"I'm not surprised." And Beejan was right, but it was hard to articulate what he wanted. It felt like asking for some kind of emotional restoration that a hookup couldn't possibly be prepared to give: *I want you to give me pain with structure so that the world doesn't feel so harrowing and random. I want you to make me feel strong by giving me something I want to endure.*

Eshu straightened, scanning the mist beyond Beejan's shoulder. Searching for the dull glow of eyes from the darkness or the sudden, fluid movement of too many limbs.

He saw nothing. The mist had already begun to roll back into the gaps that his whirlwind had cleared. But as he peered up from the shadowed ground, he saw that the quality of the light had changed. A faint blue-violet glow filtered through the mist, as though somewhere the sun had pulled itself up from the cradling mountains. Dawn was fast approaching; he'd barely felt the night slipping away.

"I want you to leave me marks to remember you by," said Eshu at last. "In case I can't find you again—did that sound ridiculous? It felt as though it was a bit ridiculous."

"No, it sounds good." Laughing, Beejan heaved himself up from the rail and picked up his lantern. "I'll teach you how to find me. Your name was Eshusikinde, right?"

Almost no one in Kondala used the full name; no one in Nanjeer did. It felt astonishingly intimate to hear it in Beejan's voice. Eshu swallowed. "You can call me Eshu, if that's a mouthful."

Beejan grinned. "I don't mind a mouthful. Eshusikinde, then. Let's go home."

CHAPTER 11: HIGH PLACES

G inger root and onions! Garlic and peppers!"
"Coffee here! Get your hot coffee here! Spiced or plain!"
"Fish! Mussels! Snails in their shells!"

Fern drifted awake in a nest of newspapers, her shoes and clothes still on and her face mashed against the back of her hand. The room was hazy with sunlight; it filtered through the thick mists as though through a gauzy curtain. She reached over to the little table beside the bed and fumbled around until she found her pocket watch. For a few seconds, she just lay still and felt it tick in her palm while she listened to the merchants' cries coming through her window. It took a moment for her to register that it was just shy of nine o'clock.

Just like that, Fern came all the way awake. She sat and hastily uncrumpled the newspapers, rubbing them flat against the windowsill until they mostly didn't look like someone had slept on them. Then she gathered them up, put them in order, and went to lay them on Eshu's bed. It didn't look slept in, so either he'd found someone else's bed to spend the night in or he'd gotten lost in the city. *Or a hungry ghost found him.* She squashed down that thought. He was all right; he was probably just hungover and enjoying being in a bed again.

There wasn't a bath, but there was a washstand with a mirror. Fern studied her face a moment, examining how much sharper her cheekbones had gotten and how many knots there were in her hair. There were little bits of stick and vine twisted up in there, just barely poking out of the mats.

No point in trying to unsnarl all that without a comb. Instead, she got out her knife and sliced through the worst of the tangles. It came out uneven—she should've waited until she had scissors—but she felt so much better and lighter that she was half-tempted to shave her head just to have the whole mess gone.

When she'd mostly evened out the edges, she splashed her face and neck with water to clear off the hair scraps. Then she stripped off her shirt and scrubbed under her arms with a damp cloth and a soap cake. She wondered if Kulmeni knew how lucky they were to have soap cakes. Probably not.

"All right," she told herself. "First things first. Find the wizards. See if they have mirrors. See if they can get us to Kondala City. Then find Eshu. Then..."

She licked her lips. Her tongue found a rough place where the skin was dry, and before she had time to think about it, she was worrying that little patch of skin with her teeth until it tore. A drop of blood beaded up on her lip. She licked it away, but it welled up again. *I've got to stop doing that.*

After she found Eshu, they'd figure things out.

Fern stepped out onto the paving stones with her map case slung over her shoulder and her watch held before her. She still wasn't sure how to navigate a place like the Mirrorlands, but she knew how to find her way around a new place without a map: learn the logic of the terrain. Get a sense for how the city changed as she got closer to the river or higher into the hills. Learn the differences between the east and west banks. Figure out what she was looking for. Ideally, get up high enough that she could see the whole thing spread out.

It was nearly half past nine. She'd heard a clock tower chime the half-hour last night as she pored over the newspapers. As she stood beneath the print shop's awning, she closed her eyes and tried to fix the guidebook illustration of the clock tower in her mind. The smooth white cylinder of it; the clock face worked with intricate brass leaves and curlicues. The copper dome faded to green, with the Sisters standing back to back on top. Mindha held the magic feather aloft, and Kindara stood with her flute held to her lips. Still meditating on the graceful angles of their arms, she listened for the half-hour's melody.

After what felt like long minutes, Fern heard the distant song of bells. Their music rose bright and deep and golden, cutting through the ragged cries of coffee sellers and fishmongers, and Fern opened her eyes and followed it.

As she walked, she tried to notice everything she could about Kulmeni. The winding, narrow alleys closer to the river; the broad, straight roads slicing across them with gutters and grates down the sides. The arrangement of tenements and shantytowns close to the river, and the smokestacks feeding white clouds into the mists. The way some houses had verandas and rooftop gardens, and others had fences of brass. The coffee sellers with their thick eye paint and their blue glass rings, raking cups across boiling-hot sand; the woman with the waist-length braid and the golden lip ring, who flirted shyly with Fern when she bought a cup of cold mint tea and some sweet rolls in syrup.

The taste of the syrup: cinnamon and orange peel and a touch of anise. *Trade goods*, Fern thought. Probably from closer to Zumera, where the orange groves covered the hillsides. She wondered if anyone here had heard about Zumera, but she couldn't bring herself to ask the woman at the tea stand. Kulmeni had its own troubles. It felt cruel to throw more at them.

By the time she'd finished her tea, the hour was approaching ten. She brought her cup and bowl back and then stood a moment beneath a nodding mimosa tree, licking her fingers clean. Again, she listened for the tower's chime.

When it came, the song rolled over her from directly overhead. She gazed up and up and up, until her neck hurt from craning it. There, breaching the drifting mists, stood the clock tower with its high copper dome fading into the grey-blue sky. Wiping her hands on her trousers, Fern went to the door at the tower's base. It wasn't locked, so she opened it and stepped inside.

Inside was a shrine to the Sisters, with a slender young man in a green waist wrap sweeping the tiles and whistling a hymn to himself. Fern recognized the song—something about the trials Kindara set for her suitors—but she couldn't remember the words. "Is the tower open to the public?" Fern asked. "I was hoping to get up to the top and draw a map."

"Oh! Are you working with Prince Teyam?" the man asked.

Fern blinked. "I don't think so. I was just hoping to make a map for myself, but I'm happy to share my work with the prince, if she needs mapmakers."

"You should look into it. She'd probably pay well—Prince Teyam's been throwing money at every problem she can. But the Sisters are always happy for more donations," he said, with a meaningful glance at the offering well near the doorway. Back in Matis, offering wells were usually laughing fountains with water pouring from the Sisters' hands; here, though, there was just a shallow silver basin lined with shining coins.

Fern got the feeling that her access to the clock tower depended on whether she put money in the well, so she worked a few smaller one-zil coins loose of their string and tossed them into the water.

The man dipped his chin. "Stairs are at the back. Careful coming down; there's no railing."

Like so many other ornamental pieces of architecture in Kulmeni, the clock tower stairway was worked of shining bronze. Each step was an intricate lattice of curlicues and flourishes, so delicately wrought that Fern was half afraid they wouldn't bear her weight. But the stairs were solid beneath her feet, and she kept one hand to the central pillar as she followed them up. As the man downstairs had said, there weren't any railings to catch her if her foot slipped on that polished metal.

Seventy-two steps. Even after all her weeks hiking through the woods, all those treetop camps she'd made, the climb left her breathing harder than usual. As she reached the central chamber, where the great brass mechanism of the clock hung suspended like an idol, she paused to catch her breath.

Here, gears whirled over her head, their great teeth catching and interlocking, ticking off the seconds in a steady rhythm. She watched them until her heartbeat kept time with the tick of the clock and her breath came slow and easy. It reminded her a little of the stellar mosaic at the top of the wizards' tower back in Sharis; it was the kind of distinct, unforgettable place that Eshu would call a *cognitive locus*.

The clock faces were some sort of translucent material, like porcelain or white glass, and the sunlight filtered through them as though through a lamp shade. High above, higher even than the clockwork mechanisms, pigeons sat tranquilly preening their storm-grey feathers. The floor was painted white with their thick, chalky droppings.

Below each of the four faces of the clock, there was a narrow window paned with glass. There was nowhere clean to kneel down, so Fern resigned herself to pigeon shit and stooped to peer through the window.

All around her lay the drifting mists like a great white ocean. The surface rippled and flowed in the breeze, breaking around domes and spires and towering amsara trees. She could just barely make out the shape of the bridge that linked the city's two halves, a long arcing span that rose from the thick mist over the river.

Fern took a sheet of blank paper from her map case and spread it out on the floor. She began to sketch the outlines of the city, working quickly to estimate relative distances and positions. There was a new copper dome, still gleaming reddish in the afternoon light; it was possibly a public building of some kind, possibly a temple. She'd have to check the guidebook later. That stand of trees was probably in a park or a garden—no one back in Matis would've let an amsara tree get that tall close to where anyone lived. They were beautiful, but their roots went shallow, and their wood wasn't all that flexible. A bad wind could send them crashing down.

She turned back to where she'd seen a set of four spires piercing through the veil of mist. It had looked like a good candidate for a wizards' tower or a university, and she was eager to get it on her map. When she looked again, though, a row of tall tenement buildings shouldered above the neighboring rooftops. Rust stains poured down the bare cement face beneath every window, and the rooftop garden was crowded with washing lines and tables covered in gleaming glass bottles. Then the mist swallowed it up again. Fern blinked and scrubbed a fist across her eyes.

To her left, she glimpsed those four spires rising up toward the high blue sky. *Maybe I just remembered wrong*, she thought, but that was only a reflex. She understood on some level that the spires had been exactly where she remembered them being, and that now they were somewhere else, because that was just the way Kulmeni worked now.

"Like the Mirrorlands," said Fern to herself. But that didn't mean pure chaos that you had to be a wizard to navigate. The Mirrorlands had an underlying geological structure that had nothing to do with the pathways people had built across it. Even if she didn't really understand that structure yet, she knew in her bones that it *could* be understood.

She sat up there for a long time, watching buildings flow in and out of view as the sun passed across the sky. The clock tower grew warmer as the day burned on, but after the weird, dull clamminess of the city streets, Fern didn't mind so much. Even the pigeons weren't so bad, after a while. She liked their murmuring squabbles, the rustle of their wings and the way the sun flashed emerald and amethyst on their feathers.

Eventually, she climbed back down again. The man in the waist wrap was gone, and a heavyset woman with a faint, wispy beard was counting coins from the offering well. Fern nodded as she passed by, then stepped out into the streets.

She tried to hold the image of those spires in her mind—the tiny balconies ringing every window, the vines that crept up the sheer white stone walls. How the sunlight glittered on the many-colored tiles of their rooftops. But as the spires came into focus in her mind's eye, she couldn't help imagining the wizards' tower from Sharis, with the crack up its side and the mosaic floor hidden at the top of the tower.

She couldn't help remembering the way the crumbling tower had loomed on that grey Mirrorlands shore. Her mind kept drifting back to the vines wrapping its broken stones, and the smell of human rot all around her.

Fern's hand went to her pocket, and her finger slid into the circle of the green glass ring. It fit perfectly over her index finger. The metal was warm from being held close to her skin.

The spires, she told herself firmly. Rooftops of red and turquoise and indigo blue, with white tiles dividing them into intricate patterns like the scales of a cone seed. White walls sparkling in the sunlight.

She passed through a street lined with second-story balconies, some adorned with little iron tables and others with red hibiscus bushes in clay pots. Elegant young men leaned on the railings, wrapped in their own thoughts as they smoked something that smelled of nutmeg and pitch.

Then through a street full of laughing children chasing black and white chickens; past a laundry thick with steam and a sharp scent of soap and lye. Through an alley where every window was barred and broken glass crackled underfoot, and into a garden drifting with thick clouds of purple blooms.

A part of her wanted to stop and ask someone about what the city had looked like before the lights in the sky. Whether there had always been a garden by that alley, and if not, whether people who lived in that alley ever found themselves in the garden. Heza had never been much for social geography, but Kufa always liked asking people questions about their shortcuts and back ways.

She wished he was here. Heza knew how to map a city, and Fern knew how to map a wilderness—but for all his absent-minded ridiculousness, Kufa had been the only one of them who could map a people.

The spires, she thought. *The spires, and the wizards, and maybe Kondala City after.*

A bank of mist rolled back, and she found herself before a palace with an indigo-tiled roof and four towers rising from its expansive wings. Amsara trees in full bloom lined the approach. Their bark peeled away in long strips, revealing the rainbow of layered copper-reds and blue-greens and browns that lay beneath the golden outer skin. Fallen blossoms covered the flagstones beneath them in crimson heaps.

Oh, thought Fern, as she stood before the open gates and listened to the wind rustling in the amsara leaves. *So it's not a university. It's the prince's palace.*

The newspapers from before the coup had called Teyam Acala a mercenary, a bandit—sometimes a river pirate, sometimes a coarse highway robber. They said she brandished a pistol at children to make their parents surrender their valuables. The threat she posed to the city was nigh-incalculable; her supporters were a mob of criminals who chafed at reasonable curfews.

The newspapers from after the coup wrote with excitement of Prince Teyam's many initiatives. The back funds paid to contractors, the lamps at the docks, the fresh street signs. The hired enchanters who would fix the mirror-ways. The peacekeepers who patrolled the streets at night to beat back the nightmares.

It was facile to say that the truth lay somewhere between these two stories. Truth wasn't a matter of middle grounds and averages. She'd have to go see for herself.

Up the long approach to the polished brass gate. She could almost see the places where guards ought to be; it was as though generations of stolid sentries had impressed their shadows on the walls that separated the boulevard from the palace gardens. But today, the gates stood wide open, and no one watched them.

"Is the prince in?" she asked a couple of well-dressed strangers coming the other way down the garden path, but they were too caught up in their argument to notice her.

"—price of sugar will go up if we don't hear back from the east soon—"

"As if we haven't noticed there's been no mail service for weeks!"

"She *says* they're investigating the issue." The androgyne in the green silk ilani rolled their eyes. "Ships to Zumera and Xhonai, drakes to Tisaris and Kondala City. But they should've been back by now."

"If you'd ever made the passage to Xhonai by water, you wouldn't say that. But the drakes, I grant you. The drakes ought to have been back by now."

What came next, Fern couldn't make out. She wanted to run after them and ask what Kulmeni had heard about the rest of the continent—whether they'd glimpsed something in a mirror or had an airship come in with grim tidings. But those two didn't know anything, or they wouldn't be so anxious right now.

The prince would have answers. Or the prince would *want* answers that Fern had. *You aren't just here to ask a favor with the mirrors,* she reminded herself. *You've seen things that maybe no one*

in Kulmeni has. That's valuable. You can trade it, if you have to. Fern
wasn't sure she liked how much of her life had become selling and
trading, now that she was back in a city.

At the other side of the gardens, there was an imposing door
that stood partway open. This one was guarded, but the guards
weren't uniformed; one stood picking her fingernails with a
pocketknife, and the other was eating a fluffy flatbread wrapped
around what looked like shaved mutton and persimmon jam.

"I'd like to see the prince," Fern said. "I've just arrived from
Zumera. I have news about what happened there."

Knife glanced over at Mutton Wrap. They had a similar shape
to their faces, as though they were sisters or cousins. Same high
cheekbones and prominent chins; same broad bridge and regal
arch to their noses. Probably the same glossy dark curls, too, except
Knife had shaved hers off. "Zumera, eh?" Knife said eventually.
"How'd you get here?"

"Walked," said Fern. "Overland. It took a long time."

Mutton Wrap swallowed a big bite. "You don't sound
Zumerani. Your a's are all wrong."

"I'm not. I was just there before I came here. Please—I need to
tell the prince what happened in Zumera."

Polishing off her lunch, Mutton Wrap straightened. "What do
you think, Lali? Let her through?"

"Granny will probably want to hear what she has to say. For a
laugh, if nothing else. If it's bullshit, we can always cut her loose."

"Fair enough. I'll hold the door. You take her in."

Lali folded her knife up, stuck it in a pocket, and gestured Fern
in ahead of her. Her grin was feral, like she was the type of cat
who played with her food. The thought of that woman where she
couldn't see her made Fern's skin itch, but she swallowed down the
anxiety and stepped through the doorway.

The palace still bore scars from the coup. The plaster walls
were gouged and scored; bloodstains still darkened the white grout

between intricately glazed porcelain tiles. Doors still hung off their hinges, or the jambs had splintered.

Fern couldn't let herself forget that Prince Teyam had come to the palace with a mob at her back. She just wished she had any idea what to do with that information.

The hall went long and straight to a second door, this one shut. Lali knocked and called, "Granny!" Without waiting for an answer, she took the handle and pushed it open. A strong smell of herbal smoke wafted out, heavy and spicy and sweet.

The room had been a throne room once, with tall stained-glass windows streaming sunlight onto a high-backed throne. But the throne was empty, and it looked like the back of the room was being used for storage. Fern could make out rolled rugs and furniture piled haphazardly around the foot of the throne, along with some gorgeous ceremonial sets of armor and swords with gemstones in their hilts.

At the front of the throne room, though, stood a desk strewn with papers, and behind it sat an old woman who could only be Prince Teyam Acala.

She was slim and lean-faced, with heavy lines carved from nose to jaw and hooded eyes that gleamed with obvious intelligence. Her white hair was tied back from her face, and old blue tattoos stood out on the dark skin of her upper arms. She wore a long sleeveless shirt belted with a cloth-of-gold sash, and her trousers were tied up at the knee over tall, sturdy boots. Fern could tell because the prince had her boots up on the desk, right next to an ivory-handled pistol.

The prince took a long drag from her pipe, then slid her feet down. "Thought I told you to close up shop after those spice merchants."

Lali leaned against the doorframe and gave Fern a little push into the room. "She says she's come from Zumera. Figured you'd want to hear it."

"Zumera. Hmph." Prince Teyam tapped her pipe stem against her lower lip. "Well, go on. Hope you don't mind if I smoke, because I don't plan to stop."

So Fern told her the story that she'd been accumulating since that night in the woods a few days out of Sharis. She'd half-expected Prince Teyam to interrupt, but mostly, she didn't—she just waited for a pause in the flow of Fern's tale to ask a few clarifying questions. The rest of the time, she smoked her pipe and took notes left-handed on a scrap of paper. Her grip on the pen was steady and sure.

"You don't actually have word on what happened to Tisaris, then," Prince Teyam observed, when Fern told her about the idle message on the airships' mirrors.

"No. Just that they weren't answering. And that seemed to worry people."

Prince Teyam pushed back her pen and refilled her pipe. "Worries me, too. Do me a favor, and keep what you saw in Zumera close to your chest for a while—I've got a team there, and once they see what you saw, they'll do a proper survey. No sense panicking people until we know more. As to the mirrors, I've got enchanters trying to fix them. Not just the travel mirrors, but also the little speaking mirrors. So far, no joy, but I would like you to tell them what you've told me. And if your wizard friend can help them out, there's a position for him in my service."

Fern was pretty sure that was outside of Eshu's area of expertise, but she just nodded and said, "I'll tell him."

Pursing her lips, Prince Teyam blew a smoke ring across the table. It wreathed her face in a corona of dim, herbal blue. "And you want a position, too, eh? That's why you came here with a story for me, is it?"

"I just want to get my friend home to Kondala City, however that happens," she answered. "I heard you sent drakes there, and obviously we aren't drake riders, but—"

"There's no news back yet from Kondala City," said Prince Teyam. "And no point speculating about how to get you there if we don't have a good guess as to what we'll find. I promise you this, Fern, the papers will hear about it as soon as I do. Now, do you have any skills I can use? Kulmeni's in need of people with skills, and I'm not too particular about where I get them."

"I can make and read maps," said Fern. "And I know a bit about soil quality and drainage. I can help for a little while, if you need any of that, but I'm not planning to stay here long."

"A geographer." Prince Teyam tapped her pipe stem against her lower lip. "Yes, we might have a use for you." She tamped down the smoldering stemweed, then rose from her chair. "But first, the enchanters. Lali, show her the way. She doesn't know what she's looking for."

"And where are you going?" Lali asked. Reaching into a pouch hidden by her sash, Prince Teyam pulled out a little metal ball and a bit of fabric. Fern had grown up on merchant ships; she knew what those were for. Her blood went cold.

"Got a noon meeting with the mayor and the city council," the prince said placidly as she tipped a bit of black powder into her pistol. She followed it with the fabric and the ball, then shoved them down the barrel with an elegant brass ramrod. "Think we've finally come to an agreement on the sewers, but never hurts to make sure we're all on the same page."

Lali grinned. "Fair enough. No one wants to wade through shit."

"That's the problem with this job, my girl. If you aren't ready to wade through shit, you've got no business wearing the crown." Then Prince Teyam holstered her pistol, kissed Lali's cheeks, and strode out. Her bootheels rang on the tiled floor.

Fern let herself breathe again. Her heart was beating like a hummingbird's wings. She unclenched jaw and fingers, muscle by muscle.

"So, guess I need to take you to the university," said Lali. Either she couldn't tell that Fern was trembling all over, or she was pretending she hadn't noticed.

"Sure," said Fern faintly.

She followed Lali out of the palace and into the veiling mist. Up a curving cart path that hugged the side of a hill. Down a narrow footbridge, across a culvert choked with algae and wine bottles. Into a packed fabric market, where merchants auctioned breathweight silk for dizzying prices and homemakers picked over discount piecework scraps. Coins clicked onto strings; scissors sheared through fabric; old men with tailors' notches in their teeth had loud opinions in the middle of the street.

Through an alleyway piled with empty orange crates, Fern could just barely make out something rising from the thick riverside mist. As the fog parted, though, she thought, *Ah*. Suddenly she understood the winding way they'd taken. Lali had been seeking the bridge across the Anjali.

From the river, Fern had glimpsed the ambitious span of it, with mammoth pylons of stone and cement and an archway tall enough to let sailing ships pass beneath. But as she followed Lali up the rising slope, it felt less like crossing a bridge than climbing a mountain. *Bet the people here think of directions in terms of the river*, she thought to herself. *Bet it matters to them which side of the water you grew up on*. For a moment, she thought of asking Lali about it—but then she remembered who Lali was, and she kept her mouth shut.

At the highest point on the bridge, the mist burned away at last. For the second time since she'd come to Kulmeni, Fern glimpsed a high blue sky crossed with feathery clouds like flycatchers' tails. She wondered if the sky up there had anything to do with Kulmeni's weather anymore. Whether the rain swept over the city as though the streets still lined up the way they had before the word broke apart, so that it fell in patches no bigger than a city block.

The bridge eventually sloped down again, to the east side of

Kulmeni. The west bank of the Anjali had smelled of fish and smoke, but the smell of smoke was lesser here on the rocky eastern bank. If she let her imagination fill in the gaps, Fern could make out sprawling houses with walled gardens and potted plants nodding on the verandas. As they stepped off of the bridge and onto the broad streets, she saw shadowy carriages drift by with their silken curtains fluttering. Their wheels hissed across the smooth stone tiles. *Oh*, Fern thought. *So this is where the people with money live.*

Lali spat in the street, then wiped her mouth and moved on.

They passed through a long archway dripping with flowers, then into a grassy courtyard, past teashops and optometrists' offices with intricate glasses on display. In places, Fern thought she saw the trace of gentrification—shops with signs so new that the weather hadn't worn the paint. There were apartments crafted from what must once have been a temple to the Sisters; she could still faintly see the Sisters' shadows where their figures had protected the bricks. There must have been a half-dozen places advertising rooms and empty shops for let.

She told herself firmly that she wasn't here to map Kulmeni. Even if she were, she'd be no help with this social geography stuff. Still, she wished she had someone she could talk to about it.

At long last, they reached a pillared colonnade that looked out over a sunken garden. Tall acacia trees rustled in the breeze, shedding their white petals over banks of laurel and hibiscus. People sat together on long, low benches or on the grass, books or teacups spread between them—some people laughing and chatting, others simply sharing their silence.

It had been a few years, but Fern still knew a university cloister when she saw one. Her heart leapt at the sight. She wanted to go up to the nearest cluster of people and sit down on the grass with them, drink in their arguments and learn about third-dynasty Kiruuni philosophy or the art of the far eastern islands. She didn't want to be a part of their conversation, exactly; she didn't even want them to say hello. She didn't know what she'd say to them if they did. If she could just sit with them and watch life going on the way it had before the world had broken, she thought that would be enough.

Lali laid a heavy hand on her shoulder, and Fern had to keep herself from flinching at the unexpected touch. "Those three over there are the wizards. The big northerner and the other two." She gave Fern a little push toward the garden. "Shoo. Play nice with the other kids."

"You aren't staying?" Fern asked. She'd half expected to be supervised. *No*, she thought, *what I expected was for the wizards to be some kind of prisoners*. It had rattled her, seeing Prince Teyam load a gun like it was a normal thing to do before a meeting. It had made her wonder what other weapons there might be in this new government, wielded openly or concealed.

Lali, though, only gave a rolling shrug. "I've got places to be. You need someone to take you home, find a carriage for hire and see if they're feeling charitable. See you around, Fern."

As Lali sloped off into the mists, Fern turned back to the cloister. She drew in a fortifying breath, then stepped lightly down the shallow steps and crossed the grass to where the wizards sat.

There were three of them: a heavyset man with a long queue of hair pale as millet. A plump, dark-skinned woman with her lips and eyes painted in blues and indigos, who sat with her legs folded and a book open across her lap. And a third man, whose eyes bloomed with roses and whose mouth was a keyhole and whom the wind plucked like a harp hung from a hillside tree.

Fern blinked and shook her head, and there stood a stringy middle-aged man, beginning to bald at the temples. He saw her approaching and tucked his thumbs into the embroidered flaps of his pockets. He didn't say anything, but his sour expression made her feel like she was interrupting something important. "Excuse me," she said. "I just got here from Zumera—"

"Good for you," said the sour-faced man. "I don't see what that has to do with us."

"No need to be rude," the other man cut in. His smile put Fern immediately at her ease; his green eyes were clear and sharp, but they gleamed with good humor. "My name is Tuuri Vilara, and these are my friends, Usamkartha and Mnoronenga."

"Just Mnoro," said the woman. She closed her book, with her finger tucked in to mark her place. "Did you need something?"

"You can call me Fern." It came easily to her lips now. Maybe she didn't have to use that name here in Kulmeni, but she didn't feel like tempting the Crowtaker today. "The prince said you were working on fixing the mirrors. She said I should tell you what I told her, about the speaking mirrors that the airships use to speak to Tisaris—"

"You've heard from Tisaris?" Usamkartha had been slouching; now, he unbent. His eyes were avid, as though he were a hawk that had just sighted a fieldmouse. "Well! What do you think of that, Tuuri Vilara? What do you think of *that?*"

"We didn't hear from them, exactly," said Fern. "There's—I think they called it an idle message? Like a magic-lantern show playing on a loop, saying that the attendant was away from the desk."

"Still, that's interesting in itself," said Mnoro. Her accent was a little more pronounced than Eshu's, but her voice was warm and musical. "It tells us that the mirror network *is* still functional. Whatever spellwork bound the idle message into the airship mirrors, it hasn't been broken, which it would be, if the imagined framework had fallen apart."

"You're confusing *imagined* with *notional,*" said Tuuri Vilara. He sounded as though he'd already had this argument several times, and didn't relish having it another. "A failure of the imagined framework might not have affected the runework in the mirrors themselves, which are notional and can function without imagination. Rune magic is highly stable."

"Say what you like about rune magic, the cognitive structure of the mirror-ways *has* collapsed," snapped Usamkartha. "And I would much rather understand why than split hairs about vocabulary."

"For the imagined framework of the mirror-ways to collapse in the way you're describing, either the world would have to have been reshaped to the point of being unrecognizable, or practicing wizards would have had to die in the thousands—in the *tens* of thousands," said Mnoro.

Usamkartha nodded. "As you say. And while I have no inclination to be optimistic about the state of the world, I am not yet ready to presume that all of my colleagues are either dead or suffering some sort of global collective amnesia."

"Everywhere we've been, the wizards have been dead or gone," said Fern softly. All of them turned to her at once, and her shoulders went up. "I'm sorry. It's just—in Sharis, their tower survived the earthquake, but no one could find them. They thought they must've gone out through the mirror. And in Zumera, when we came out in a wizard's study—"

"You've traveled the mirror-ways," Tuuri Vilara interrupted. "After the event."

"I was traveling with a wizard," said Fern. "His name is Eshu. Eshusikinde."

Mnoro dropped her book and whooped, "Eshu! He's alive! Njo, I *told* you he was alive!"

"You know him!"

"Of course we know him—how do *you* know him?" Mnoro rose to her feet and kissed Fern soundly on both cheeks. She smelled of rose perfume and old paper, and her eyes were bright with welling tears. "Eshu! Is he here?"

"Yes, he's here," said Fern. Her cheeks felt as though they would split from smiling. "He came out of the mirror in Sharis a few days after the earthquake, and I've been trying to help him get home since then."

"You've come a long way, if you met in Sharis," said Usamkartha. His teeth were cowrie shells; his blood was a swollen river rushing whitewater through his veins.

Fern blinked, and Usamkartha was frowning at her again. "Sorry—this is a lot," she said.

"Sit down," said Tuuri Vilara, gesturing her to a patch of grass. "We're going to have a lot of questions for each other, and it will help to ask them in a sensible order rather than slapdash, as they occur to us."

They spoke until the midday rest was over and the cloister had emptied. As Tuuri Vilara had promised, the wizards had many questions about the mirror-ways that Fern had walked and what she had seen there. When a woman with a corona of soft, tightly curled hair came to chivvy the wizards back to work, it still felt as though there was much more to be said. Fern parted from them with a promise to return the next day and to bring Eshu, if she could roust him.

Ordinarily, Fern would have enjoyed an afternoon walk home, but she still didn't know Kulmeni well enough to walk its shifting streets. So she hailed an open trap carriage with a pretty yellow awning and paid the driver to take her across the river.

The city looked different from a carriage, and not in the way that Fern was used to them being different. The fog was as opaque as marble. A few times, she heard people laughing, the heavy footfalls of horses, or the chime of shop bells, but she only once saw another person on the road. The air was colder than she had expected it to be; she found herself shivering a little against the carriage wall.

At the peak of the high arched bridge, she looked out over Kulmeni, and she saw nothing but curls of mist sloping off into an endless field of white.

CHAPTER 12: FALLING OUT

For the first time in weeks, Eshu woke in a bed. The warm length of Beejan's body fit against him, chest against his back; his hand lay in the hollow under Eshu's ribs, and it was so comfortably, casually possessive that Eshu immediately felt at ease.

He hadn't realized until then that he'd become used to waking up afraid.

"Hey," Beejan said, kissing Eshu's shoulder. "Was wondering how long you planned to sleep."

"Forever." Eshu dragged Beejan's arm down around his waist and nestled back against his chest. "Until the stars fall and the moon splits asunder. Maybe by then I'll have caught up on all the sleep I've lost."

Beejan grinned against Eshu's neck. "My work schedule runs on a less astronomical timescale, so I'm going to have to get up before that," he said. "But I wouldn't say no to having you in my bed a while longer, if you feel like staying."

The temptation was greater than Eshu had imagined. Beejan's bed felt warm and clean and safe, with crisp cotton sheets thrown over their legs and gauzy mosquito netting curtaining off the outside world. The grey light from the window softened the world's edges, blurring the lines between waking and dreaming. If he could lie here just a little longer, and pretend there was no world outside of Beejan's arms, Eshu thought he would be content.

He sighed and turned to kiss Beejan's lips. "No, you're right. You've got work, and the woman I've been traveling with will be wondering where I—"

"Bee!" someone yelled from the hall. There was a heavy knock at the door, then the sound of a key turning in the lock. "Put some pants on, I've brought breakfast!"

Eshu sat up just as the door swung open. Through the mosquito netting, he saw a heavyset woman with a shaved head, a market basket slung over one powerful arm. She eyed him up and down, then set her basket aside and said, "Bee, you've got to start putting a scarf on the door handle or something. Not sure I brought enough for three."

Beejan nudged open the netting enough to grab his trousers from where he'd flung them last night. "Do you really want to know how often I have company over?" he asked as he buttoned himself up. "This is Eshu. Eshu, this is my sister Lali, who has a key and no manners."

"Hush, you; I brought you breakfast. I don't need manners. Pleasure to meet you, Eshu."

"I hadn't realized I'd be meeting your family so soon," said Eshu. "I'd have worn clothes."

Lali snorted. "Oh, don't go to any trouble on my account. After a day of herding petitioners, I could use someone easy on the eyes."

While Eshu got dressed, Beejan and Lali laid out breakfast. Lali set out fresh curd cheese and three kinds of pickled vegetables in serving bowls, while Beejan warmed flatbreads in a pan on his little iron stove. "Could you chop these for me?" he asked, tilting his head toward a basket of root vegetables—garlic, kicha, sweet mannari with its wrinkled peel.

"You're Njowa, right?" said Lali, while Eshu set to peeling the mannari. She reached into her basket and held up a parcel wrapped in waxed paper. "Is it just meat you can't have, or meat and dairy?"

"Only meat," Eshu answered; Lali put the parcel back. "I'd give anything for a little Kondalani goat cheese right now."

"We can do that," said Lali, laughing. "Our granny's the prince. Stick around, and we'll get you just about anything you want."

Eshu was so startled that he nearly sliced his finger open. He looked up at Beejan, not sure whether to feel fond or suspicious. "So when you said you reported directly to the prince..."

"Well, it's true. And it sounds better than saying I report directly to my granny, doesn't it?"

Lali laid a lion's-paw hand on Eshu's shoulder. Her grin was relentless. "Look at it this way," she said. "Now you can tell people you've fucked a prince's heir. You'll drink on that story for years."

Despite himself, Eshu smiled. "Me and half of Kulmeni, by the sound of it."

"So you'll have that in common!" With a great rolling laugh, Lali took Beejan's other knife and gave the garlic a whack to break it open. She chopped it with practiced efficiency, then started peeling and slicing the kicha root. Her hands were as deft on the knife as Beejan's had been on his heavy club, and Eshu found himself wondering if they'd been runners together before the disaster had elevated their family to royalty.

Once the vegetables had been stewed and tossed with ginger and red pepper oil, once the flatbread was steaming gently on a serving plate, the three of them sat around Beejan's table and ate. Between bites of pickled yellow beans, Lali and Beejan traded reminders—an aunt unvisited, a friend's party coming up; the oil looked low in Beejan's kitchen, and Lali knew a trader selling pure sunflower oil for cheap.

It made Eshu miss Sunba so much that his chest ached. He'd probably never speak with her like this again, and the knowledge was a hard knot beneath his ribs.

He pushed back from the table and stood, and both Lali and Beejan trailed off. "Everything all right?" Beejan asked.

"I'm fine," said Eshu, and he did his best to try to mean it. "I just realized how late it was getting. My friend will be wondering where I am."

"Right, sorry, you mentioned her," said Beejan. He stood, too, arms open, and let Eshu walk into his embrace. If he felt how Eshu's heart was racing, or how he gripped Beejan just a bit too tightly, he had the grace not to mention it. "It was a pleasure meeting you, Eshusikinde. Feel free to drop by any time. Just—knock, all right? I might have company."

"I look forward to it," said Eshu, and kissed Beejan one last time. His lips were still spice-warm, and they lingered on Eshu's for a long, sweet moment. Then, gathering up his things, Eshu took his leave.

Eshu came back to the printer's shop to find it bustling with activity—he could hear the steady thump of the presses from well down the street. When he stepped inside, the door to the back room was open; someone on the other side was shouting over the drumbeat of plate on paper and the creak of the slicing arm, but he couldn't make out a word of it. Through the opening, Eshu glimpsed ink-stained typesetters snatching up letters from wooden cases and a pair of burly printers turning the crank on the paper roll. "What's the news?" he asked the printer at the front desk, raising his voice to be heard over the cacophony.

"Big windstorm overnight. Carved right through the Garden of Sighs and tore the roofs off a couple of houses," the man answered. "First big weather we've had since the change."

A chill went through Eshu's body as he remembered that bladed wind slicing shadow-creatures to ribbons. His gorge rose, choking; he swallowed it down. *That was my doing,* he thought. *My magic. This is a susceptible zone after all.* "Anything else?" he asked.

The printer answered with a shrug. "Nothing exciting. Prince Teyam and the city council reached an accord on the sewer systems. They're going to do some kind of flow-tracing exercise with colored corks before they commit to rebuilding. Kind of boring and technical, but people like to hear about the prince's projects."

It sounded like exactly the kind of boring, technical mapping problem that Fern would love. With a few parting words to the printer, Eshu went up to his and Fern's rented rooms.

He found Fern sprawled out on her bed with a map spread before her and a pencil tucked behind her ear. Her hair was shorter, uneven around the edges but glossy and clean; she wore a new set of clothes and fresh stockings.

This must have been how she'd looked in Matis—calm, collected, well put together. If Eshu had met her on the street, he wouldn't have doubted for a moment that she was as much a scholar as he was.

He knocked on the doorframe beside Fern's curtain. "I'm back," he said, and she jumped at his voice.

"Eshu! I was afraid you'd gotten lost. You look so much better now!" She slid off the bed, picking up her map and holding it open for him. "The good news is, even if the wizards don't get the mirrors working, we can get to Kondala City from here! I bought a local map, and there's a good trade road to the east. It'll be a week or so if we walk, but there are villages and waystations all along the road. They might be just fine. And even if they aren't, they'll be a place to stop."

"The wizards," Eshu repeated, already feeling a bit overwhelmed. "So you did find wizards here?"

Fern's eyes went wide. "Shit, I should have started with that! There are wizards here, and they're your friends. Usamkartha, and Tuuri Vilara, and—"

"*He is not my friend.*"

Fern went still, and Eshu immediately regretted the fury in

his voice. "They said they knew you," she said, her expression quizzical. "They were so glad to hear you were alive."

Eshu's blood was pounding in his ears. His fear felt too big for his skin; he wanted to do something rash, like set a fire or flee. When he spoke, his voice shook, and there was nothing he could do to steady it. "I would rather walk a hundred thousand years than step through another mirror for Tuuri Vilara."

"That's fine," said Fern. "We can go by foot. We don't have to go by mirror. We can go right now, if you want. I can get us some traveling rations and—"

"Will you *please* stop trying to fix everything! Njo, maybe I don't *want* to go right fucking now!"

Fern stepped back a pace, her eyes narrowing. "You're being a real asshole. I get that maybe you and Tuuri Vilara have some kind of a past—"

"There is no 'maybe' about it."

"—but that doesn't give you the right to take it out on me." Her hands fell to her sides. "I know this trip has been hard, but you don't get to scream at me just because it's hard."

"I'm *not* screaming." Eshu sat down on the edge of the bed, head in his hands. His thumbs pressed against his temples like the jaws of a vise. "I just had half a normal day. Half a day! And that was nearly too much for me. I've spent weeks waking up afraid and hungry, watching people die and rot all around me, and this morning I woke up in a bed! I ate some fucking *cheese*! Someone kissed me goodbye and told me to drop by any time, like he expected the world to keep going from one minute to the next! I *miss* that, Fern. I miss believing that the world will keep going."

"But it will," she said. "Maybe not the way we remember it, or the way we want it to, but it will keep going."

Why return to Kondala City? Nothing you love remains.

Eshu shook his head. "Do you actually believe that? Or is it just something you tell yourself so that *you* can keep going?"

She sat down beside him, cross-legged, and folded her hands in her lap. Eshu had the sense that she was trying to catch his eye, but he couldn't make himself look up to meet her gaze. "I believe it," said Fern at last. "Remember the first time you took me through the mirror? You told me that Njo wasn't a story—we were the story, and we were real. And in the story I'm telling, we keep going. You, me, the rest of the world. One foot in front of the other."

Eshu couldn't remember the last time he'd knelt for prayers. Some dawn or dusk back in the jungle, he supposed, with Fern sitting vigil over him. Being Njowa had mattered so much to him back in Usbaran, when he and Mnoro had been the only Njowa at the university; they'd kept the feasts and fasts together, knelt for prayers together, warned each other which street vendors fried their vegetables in pork or duck fat. When their exam period meant they couldn't make it home for High Summer, they'd built a holiday hut out of blankets instead of reeds and hidden in its shelter, trading city comedies. Faith had been a kite string linking him home—to Kondala, to his family, to the centuries of far travelers who had come before him.

Now, though, it felt as if that string had been cut. "There's a difference between telling a story and lying to yourself," he said, and hated himself for it.

"What's wrong with you?" Fern demanded. "Don't tell me it was just a day eating cheese. You haven't wanted to go home for a while now. Ever since Zumera. When I first met you, you were in such a hurry to get back, you couldn't wait to go through the mirrors. But after we got out of Zumera, something changed."

"Well, you broke our mirror," said Eshu.

The map crumpled in Fern's hand. "I said I was sorry—"

"I don't care if you're sorry!" Eshu snapped. After weeks of putting his anger aside, the rage rising in his throat felt dire and glorious. "I would've been home by now without your *help*. To you, Kondala City's just a place on a map, but my *family* is there.

Why do you think I wanted to go there, for the sheer fucking fun of it? I wanted to go because if the mirror-ways were broken and so was Sharis, my sisters might be in trouble. They might *need me*. It had already been, what, four days? And if they were trapped somewhere, maybe screaming for help..." The Crowtaker's cradle-song rang in his ears. Again, he saw Sunba's dead eyes, Asha wreathed in flames, Kiga crying until she had no voice left to cry. "That's what you took from me when you dropped that mirror. You took whatever chance I had of saving them."

"Stop talking like that!" Fern rose to her feet, her eyes blazing. "Maybe they are dead. Maybe they're not. What *good* does it do to assume the worst? Maybe my parents and my friends are dead. Maybe Matis is just—just a crater, and everything I love is gone. But I'm not going to give up hope until I see for myself." Tears streaked down her cheeks, but she gritted her teeth and wiped them away.

"Maybe you should go back to Matis," said Eshu. "Let me be. I'll go back to Kondala City on my own, when I'm ready."

"Don't push me away now. Not after everything we've been through."

Eshu took a deep breath. It felt like he'd swallowed a knife. "We aren't *friends*," he said, as much to himself as to her. "We're just people who got caught in the same tempest of shit. And I'm grateful to you for helping me out of it. But now we're out of it. We don't need each other anymore."

Fern's eyes were red around the edges, but she stood straight-backed, her hands clenched at her sides until her knuckles showed through. "I thought we were friends. But you're really not treating me like a friend right now."

"I'm not. I'm sorry."

"You're not sorry." Fern scooped up the map and folded it into crooked quarters, then pressed it hard against Eshu's chest. "Fine. We're not friends. Go get over yourself somewhere else." She drew the curtain shut over her room, and Eshu was left there in the little hallway with a map cradled to his chest and his bag still over one shoulder. He hadn't even had a chance to set it down.

Beejan answered the door around six o'clock in the evening, yawning, sleep-tousled and bare-chested. When his gaze fell on Eshu, he broke into a grin. "Back for more?" he asked.

"If you'll have me," Eshu answered. He tried to grin in answer, but the smile felt like a mask. "And I know this is short notice, but—would it be all right if I stayed for a few days?"

CHAPTER 13: OVER, UNDER, AND THROUGH

Fern pressed her fists against her eyes until the crying had mostly stopped, then scrubbed away the last of her tears with the back of her hand. She hated crying in front of people; she hated how they treated her when they saw her crying, as though she'd somehow made things worse by bringing her feelings into it. As though they were the reasonable ones just because they weren't leaking from the eyes.

We don't need each other anymore.

"Fuck you, too, Eshu," she muttered, and curled up on the bed feeling miserable.

She tried to nap a little, but the noise of the printers' shop rattled her nerves—the press itself wasn't so bad, but every time the printers shouted at each other or the newspaper boys, she froze like a mouse in a snake's shadow. After an hour or so, the yelling put her so on edge that she laced up her boots and went out into the city again just to be away from it. She stepped onto the still-unfamiliar streets, picked a direction, and started walking.

Part of her wanted to find Eshu. Part of her hoped she'd never run into him again. The rest of her was just so tired of thinking about him all the time.

Maybe he was right—maybe she should've gone back to Matis when she had the chance. Now she was on the other side of the country, with no way to get home except a long, long walk.

At least there was a trade route that would take her to Sharis, eventually. Local maps called it the Queen's Highway, probably because it went through Tisaris before it went anywhere else, but everyone she knew back home had always called it the Long East Road. If anyone was still trading in Nanjeer, it would be along that road. She might be able to hitch a ride on a cart, if she was lucky. Rent a horse. Maybe by the time she was partway home, the airships would be running again, and she could fly the rest of the way.

Or she could just stay here in Kulmeni for a while and see if the wizards could figure out how to get the mirrors working, and then she could be home in a few hours. It didn't do any good to think about the worst that could happen. Better to dwell on what she could do right now.

Fern put her hands into her pockets, and her fingertips brushed Shell's daughter's ring. *Eshu said there was someone here from Sharis,* she thought to herself. *Rain's wife. A dressmaker. She'd want to know that her wife was all right.*

She turned her thoughts toward that cloth market she'd passed through yesterday—the smells of fresh, clean silk and cotton, and the sound of shears. The ill-tempered old tailors arguing about thread-of-gold and embroidered appliques.

The ring slipped onto Fern's index finger, and she absently pushed it on all the way.

She passed through a tea garden, its doors curtained with beads; the scents of clove and candied orange peel hung heavy on the air. From there, she walked along a limestone wall curling with vines, their red-throated flowers bursting in a spray of stamens and pistils. Then she found herself outside a barber's shop, where a pair of old ladies wove a bridegroom's hair into an intricate tracery of braids.

Then, at last, the market, with its piles of cotton prints in madder red and indigo, kicha-yellow bolts swirled with whorls of purple and black. Fern took in the racks of thread and boxes of beads; the silk dyed and undyed, thick enough to make into armor and thin enough to show every freckle of the wearer's skin. And everywhere, from the scrap bins to the auctioneers' platforms, were people arguing over price.

Fern squared her shoulders, then stepped up to the nearest silk merchant who didn't seem to be helping anyone. "I'm looking for a woman from Sharis," she said. "A dressmaker. She came to buy fabric maybe a month or so ago? Before the lights in the sky?"

"I think I remember her," said the merchant. "Tall woman, tattoos on her arms and neck?"

"Maybe. I've never actually met her," Fern admitted. "But if she's still in Kulmeni, I have a message from her wife."

The merchant glanced over Fern's shoulder at a customer eyeing the silks, and she sighed. "Look, I wish I could help you, but I've got to run a business. If anyone knows where to find her, it'll be Kurosh Hura. He keeps a hostel at the end of the street— look for the Warp and Weft. It's even odds she took a room there, and if not, he'll know where else you can look."

"Thank you so much," said Fern. The merchant looked as though she was still expecting something, so Fern pulled a five-zil coin loose and set it down on the counter, which seemed to satisfy her. With that, Fern turned and wove her way through the crowd toward the hostel at the end of the street.

The moment she stepped through the door, the noise and bustle of the fabric market seemed to fade away. The hostel was the sort of sober establishment where her father liked to stay when he was traveling for work—all warm tinted glass and pierced-copper lanterns, dark tooled wood and booths screened off with lattices. At a few occupied tables, older folk had hushed conversations over patterns and contracts, and a fresh-faced serving-man topped up their glasses with cold mint tea whenever they looked low. Condensation beaded on the glasses and slid down into puddles on the tabletops.

"Excuse me," Fern said to the man behind the main counter, who wore his hair in long, glossy ringlets and his beard braided with black and gold ribbons. He looked every bit the Kulmeni rake—charming and dangerous, with mirth glittering in his deep-set, painted eyes. "I'm looking for Kurosh Hura."

"Then you've found him," the man answered, grinning. "Welcome to the Warp and Weft. How can I help you today, young mistress? A room? A cup of tea?"

"I was actually hoping you could help me find someone. There was a woman who came from Sharis maybe a month or two ago to buy fabric—"

"Ah, yes, Mistress Fanaz," said Kurosh at once. "She comes to Kulmeni every year for silks. Our farthest traveler; may Njo smile on her steps."

Hope rose beneath Fern's breastbone. "Is she still here? I have a message from her wife—or not a message, exactly, but something her wife wants her to know."

Kurosh shook his head, making a clicking sound with his tongue. "I wish I could say that she was, but Mistress Fanaz cut her stay short after the change. She's probably halfway home to Sharis by now, if the weather is kind and the roads are clear. Whatever message her wife has for her, she'll have to deliver it in person."

He must have seen how the news made Fern droop, because he reached behind him for a dewy pitcher of cold tea and poured her a glass full. "You must have come a long way, yourself, to have a message from Sharis," said Kurosh. "Take a cup of tea. Rest a while. This is an Njowa household, and caring for travelers is my work."

"Thank you," she said, cupping the glass in both hands. The warmth bled out of her palms, and with it, the anxiety and grief of the morning. She sat down in one of those latticed booths and sipped her tea, listening to the low rumble of voices all around her.

Most were talking trade—ships held at the docks, waiting for clearance that never came. The silk moths had laid fewer eggs last summer than in recent years, and fewer still fertile. The price of cotton was going down, the price of dye on the rise. There had been no goods from Zumera or Tisaris or Kondala City since the change; everyone's stores were stretched thin, thin.

"I only wish we knew what was happening," said a Cheressian woman with hair like polished rosewood. "The airships do not fly, the mirrors are black—I only want to be home, with my dear babies."

"The prince has her best people working on it," her tablemate answered, and patted her hand. "They're scouting all the major cities. There are wizards trying to fix the mirrors—"

"And what has come of that?" the Cheressian snapped. "All I hear is that the prince is busy, busy, busy. Green lights at the docks! Hired blades hunting for nightmares! Corks in the sewers! But I have seen a cup-and-ball conwoman working the streets, my friend; I know how the hand distracts the eye. She is working some crime against us, and we will not see it until she has our silver in her purse."

"Her and every other prince," said a warm, rumbling voice that Fern recognized as Kurosh's. "The last one was a criminal in his own way, as much as she is. Better to depend on each other than on the whims of princes."

"Don't be a fool, Kurosh. It does a thinking person no good to despair that all princes are bad, and thus we can expect no better than we have."

"Never accuse me of despair, dear heart!" laughed Kurosh, filling the Cheressian's cup. "The prince isn't the only person in Kulmeni who's busy. I'll bend the ears of a few riverboat captains and see if any of them have a mind to sail north to Cheresse. It'll be slower than an airship, true, but faster than waiting for the prince's best people."

"As if I could afford to charter a ship," the Cheressian scoffed.

"You'd be surprised what people will give, when it's for a mother trying to get home to her babies."

"I don't expect to be surprised at all." However, some of the hard lines of her face had softened, and when her tablemate turned the conversation to other matters, she let herself be led.

The room was quiet after that, but for the rustle of paper and the click of cup on table. Fern lingered there as long as her drink lasted, but when she'd drained it to the soft tea leaves at the bottom, she could think of no further excuse to stay. "Here," she said, putting a patina-stained ten-zil piece on Kurosh's counter. "Thank you."

"The tea was my treat," he said, reaching out as though to push it back.

Fern shook her head. She couldn't think of how to say thanks for what the drink had given her—for the first moment of true peace she'd had since she'd walked with a wild god in the forests east of Zumera. She hadn't realized how much she needed the reminder that not everyone who had survived had done so with a gun in their hands. Instead, she said only, "This is for the next traveler. In case they're thirsty, too."

Fern knew she ought to go back to the wizards—she'd promised them she would—but the more she told herself she should, the less she wanted to. She didn't want to be responsible for telling them what had happened with Eshu, or for explaining why he wouldn't be coming. Even listening to them muse on arcane technicalities would've felt too much like listening to him talk.

So instead she went down to the riverside, hoping she could learn something about the night that everyone here called the change. In every other city she'd been to, which admittedly was only two cities so far, the destruction had been worst at the water's edge.

Tying up her trousers to the knee, Fern made her way to the docks again. Past the ghostly sailing ships and the pedalboats laden with fish and bananas; past the sailors lingering on the piers, passing time amid the empty crates and barrels. The prince had promised them pay while she held their ships at harbor, or so the newspapers said, but these sailors looked as though it had been a while since they'd had a good meal. They passed around a twist of stemweed, smoking it down to their fingers before tossing the end in the river.

Fern kept walking, past where the red and green lights faded into the mist behind her. A thin, rocky shore stretched ahead, with a retaining wall on one side and the grey Anjali on the other. Crab fishers knelt in the shallows, pulling up traps with long sticks with hooks on the end. Most were empty; an old woman muttered to herself and spat as she lowered the trap back down again.

"Excuse me," said Fern. "Have there not been crabs lately?"

"Not enough," the woman answered. Her face was so heavily lined that it looked like a river basin in the dry season; she was missing most of her front teeth, and the gaps gave her voice a gentle whistling sound. "It's those ships not setting out. Scares the crabs, listening to the timbers groaning." She tramped down the shoreline, giving a baby crocodile a prod with her trap-lifting stick. It scuttled away into the water with a powerful thrash of its tail. "You one of the prince's folk?"

"Um. No." Fern followed behind, suddenly very alert for more crocodiles. She could just about make out some dark shapes below the surface of the water, but she couldn't tell if they were crocodiles or big fish or possibly just ominous logs. "Is the prince asking people about crabs?"

"Mm. Not as far as I know. Just figured, a girl like you doesn't come here to ask an old lady questions unless someone's paying her to do it." The woman lifted another trap, then made a satisfied sound and hauled it in to put a single large crab in her bucket. "Here's an interesting thing. Take a look."

When Fern peered into the bucket, she saw that the crab inside was split perfectly down the middle—half an opalescent blue, half a dark brownish green. She'd heard about butterflies split down the middle, with male wing patterns on one side and female on the other, but she'd never seen a specimen like this before. She reached out to touch the line that divided left from right, but pulled her hand back when the crab waved its claws at her. "This is really rare," she said. She couldn't keep her eyes off it as it scrabbled at the side of the bucket. "I don't know how rare, exactly, but I bet naturalists would want to study it. Important people would want to have it on display."

"If you meet any of them, you can tell them to find Sedge on the docks. I'm selling, if they're buying." Shuffling the cage around again so that the netting lay correctly in the frame, Sedge levered the trap back out into the river until it sank to the bottom.

Sedge, thought Fern. *So some people here are afraid of the Crowtaker, after all.* "Do you mind if I ask you a few more questions? I'll try not to take too much of your time."

"If you're going to stay and talk, you can pick up some snails," said Sedge. She plunged her hand into the water and pulled up a river snail with a long, conical shell. "These are good to eat. See the ridges on the shell? You're looking for these. You find any other kinds, put them back."

"Anything else to look out for?"

"If a crocodile comes up wanting a meal, just give 'em a whack with a stick." Stepping out to a rock a little deeper in the water, Sedge hooked another trap and pulled it dripping from the river. It must've disappointed her, because soon Fern heard the splash of the trap sinking down again.

Fern squatted down at the water's edge and searched for snails like the one Sedge had shown her—those elongated black shells with the ridges that even her unpracticed hands could recognize. She found them at first one at a time, clinging to sticks and river grass; soon that taught her to recognize their shapes amid the mud and stone along the shore. The water was cooler than she'd expected. "What was the night of the change like?" Fern asked, dropping a handful of snails into the bucket.

"Hmm." Sedge sucked at her teeth. "What was it like? Warm night. Clear sky. I was having a cup of beer with—mm, shit, let's just say with a friend. Out on the docks. You know, you can see more stars on the river than you can in the city. It's on account of the smoke." She hooked another trap, but dropped it the second she'd got the netting above the water. "This is someone else's. Can't be seen stealing his crabs. Not that he has any, poor bastard."

Another handful of snails clattered into the bucket. "Then what happened?"

"I'm getting to it, I'm getting to it. Anyway, my friend—can't tell you her name; you understand—my friend says, 'Look at the sky.' And the sky's cracked open. Like an eggshell, but with light coming out of the cracks. And suddenly the air gets cold, and we both hear thunder. She thought it was ball lightning; you hear about that sometimes. Do you know about ball lightning? It doesn't just vanish like normal lightning; it sort of rolls through the air in a big ball." Sedge gestured with her stick. "Stupid, I thought. But she wanted to stay out and watch. She'd never seen ball lightning before."

The next trap had a crab in it, and Sedge was distracted a moment in untangling it from the netting. She looked the crab over once she'd pulled it free, then tossed it into the bucket. "Nothing special about this one. Just a river crab. Anyway. Then the sky got dark. You couldn't even see the stars, it was so dark. And this mist started rising out of the water. Just thin curls. The kind where old people sometimes say, 'The Sisters are dancing in their silk skirts and veils.' Hah! I guess I'm an old person, too." She shook her head, laughing. "I told my friend I was going in. It was too cold out for me to be sitting on the docks at my time of life. I'd catch a chill. I heard later there were some ugly things on the streets. Maybe so. I didn't see them, but I know Crowtaker business when I hear it. So that's all I can tell you about the night of the change."

As she spoke, Fern watched as thin bars of mist drifted and unfurled across the surface of the water. Just like silk veils, she thought at first—but the longer she watched them, the more entranced she was by how they intersected and interwove, radiating out from some unseen point in gauzy filaments. If she could see them from above, perhaps they'd look more like the strands in a spider's web. Or the cracks in the sky.

"Thank you for your time," said Fern, and she tossed a last double handful of snails into the bucket. The two crabs in it were like little islands in a sea of black shells—one green-brown and ordinary; the other sheared in half by some quirk of nature, its left side jewel-bright.

Fern frowned. There was an idea hovering on the edge of conscious thought, but she couldn't quite put it into words. It wasn't even about the crab, really. It was the way that looking at that split shell made her feel: like she'd just put her hand through the mirror. As though she was in two worlds at once.

She was thinking too much like a naturalist, wondering about bilateral gynandromorphs. She had to think about the change like a wizard.

The world had broken here in Kulmeni, but the broken places weren't empty. She had to stop thinking about them as breaks, as voids, and instead start thinking of them as a territory all their own.

"Just one more thing," said Fern. "If I keep going this way, will I find a storm drain outlet? Like a great big open pipe? Maybe with a grate over it?"

"Yeah, there's one with a big grate," said Sedge. "To keep the crocodiles out."

"Does it work?"

Sedge grinned wide and cavernous. "Mostly."

The top half of the storm grate swung open enough to let Fern climb over the bottom. She heaved herself up over the rusting iron lattice and dropped to the ground on the other side, checking her bag of canteens and sample bottles as soon as her boots hit the ground.

All there. *All right*, she told herself. *You can do this. One foot in front of the other.*

The storm drain was wide and dark. Concrete, probably; Fern trailed her hand along the curved wall of the pipe and felt particles of smooth stone embedded in it. The sound of the river echoed strangely down the pipe, a murmuring counterpoint to the distant peal of dripping water. There hadn't been rain since she'd arrived in Kulmeni. The water flowing along the bottom of the pipe was only a thin trickle. She should've brought some kind of lantern. If she was right, though, she wouldn't need one.

Eshu had said that this place worked like the Mirrorlands, and she was beginning to follow its logic—how Kulmeni had become a network of landmarks, which she could find if she only thought *ships* or *bridge* or *silk*. Unnumbered people had marked every part of the city with meaning, from the shoreline where Sedge trapped crabs to the university garden to the silk market at the city's heart. *Cognitive loci*, the wizards called them. Places you remembered.

But what if Kulmeni wasn't just *like* the Mirrorlands—what if, when everything had broken, the Mirrorlands had instead bled through the cracks? What if the Mirrorlands now lay like fog banks in the between-places that everyone passed through on their way to wherever they were going? If that was true, then she could step into the Mirrorlands as easily as she could walk down the street.

Just trust that it will work, Eshu had said, in that barn outside of Sharis. If she tried, she could still remember everything about that place: the shafts of light pouring through the boards in the walls, the scent of pig shit and the tiny kittens pouncing each other in the hay. *If you let yourself forget for even a moment that you can pass through the mirror, the magic will fail.*

Fern let herself drink in the sounds of the river, the smells of rust and old rot and city water. No crocodiles in here. No other people, as far as she could tell. She walked down the pipe until the outlet was only a tiny circle of light behind her, and the water beneath her feet gleamed like a braid of silver. She felt like one of the Sisters, crawling out of the womb of the earth.

Trust that it will work. Somehow, after every cruel thing Eshu had said today, that memory still filled her with a sense of peace.

She closed her eyes and kept walking. Dry sediment crunched under her heels, echoing up and down the pipe. She kept walking until the echo faded, and her boots dug deep into the sand.

When she opened her eyes again, the desert of the Mirrorlands rolled out in all directions around her. For a moment, she stood still amid the dunes and watched the shining sands shift in the wind. On one horizon lay a chain of low, black mountains; on the other, the desert faded into the starless indigo sky.

She spread her arms out wide and felt the wind on her palms. It blew down from the mountains, cold and dry and gentle as a sigh. She wondered whether there was a forest on the far side—whether strange trees of obsidian and silver formed a shadowing canopy, nourished by rains that never made it across the mountains.

She could go looking, she supposed. No one was stopping her. She could find landmarks in the desert and cache her canteens for later. It wouldn't be a single trip, but maybe she could get a little closer to the mountains every time. Over time, she could make herself a route for a long journey. But that was assuming she could get out again, and getting out was going to be the tricky part.

Before she did anything else, before she even let herself think about getting out, she knelt down and filled one of her sample bottles with sand. Once she'd corked the bottle, she put it in her vest pocket, where it would be safe if she had to drop her bag in a hurry. She'd lost some of her Mirrorlands samples somewhere between Zumera and Kulmeni, and now that she actually had a chance to analyze samples again, she didn't want to lose them if a hungry ghost came after her.

Next, she climbed up the dunes to walk the ridgeline. Each step she took carved deep into the sand; she had to walk slowly for fear of losing her balance. She'd hiked in deserts before, in the south marches of Ras Kir'uun, but they'd been all red stone ridges and gravel flats dotted with juniper scrub. It was beautiful countryside, but never gentle—not even after the summer monsoons had lashed the hillsides and left the slopes carpeted with purple flowers.

The desert in the Mirrorlands was like something out of a storybook. The soft white dunes seemed to go on forever, curling over themselves like waves in an ocean. There was no starlight or moonlight for them to reflect, but still they caught the faint twilight glow of the sky and magnified it a hundredfold.

At the crest of the dune, she held her breath, listening to the desert all around her. First of all she heard the steady rhythm of her heartbeat. She let out a breath and let her heart grow calm. In the darkness, she heard the soft hiss of sand over sand, and the rush of water.

She half-climbed, half-slid down into a valley, following the sound of water. At first the terrain was all fine, sugar-grain sand, but the longer she walked, the rockier the valley became. Soon, she was picking her way over a loose scattering of black stones. Amid them, she saw a few clear crystals of what was probably quartz. "Forms in geologically active areas when magma cools," she said to herself, squatting to pick up a big crystal. There was no real light to hold it up to, but she turned it over in her hands all the same. "Survives weathering well. Lots of color variants—I think due to inclusions? Most rock taxonomy is just cataloguing structure and inclusions."

She thought she heard something laugh, far out over the dunes, and she shivered. Shoving the hunk of quartz in her bag, she scurried deeper into the wash.

The sides grew steeper. Here, thick white thorn bushes bent in close together over a thread of water, and she stooped and reached through the thorns to dip a specimen bottle in the water. Her hands were shaking. She fumbled the cork, and she had to slam down her hand to catch it.

Her fingertips brushed the familiar, ridged cone of a snail shell. For a moment, she just knelt there with her hand in the stream, unable to parse what she was feeling. But it made sense. If the Mirrorlands could bleed into her world, of course her world could bleed back.

She corked the water sample, snatched up the snail, and put it into her pocket with the bottles. No time to think about it. No time to wonder about how to get to the mountains or what would happen if she walked the other way. If there was something out there with the luxury of laughing, she didn't want to meet it.

Fern pulled herself out of the thorn bushes and straightened, looking all along the ridges encircling the wash. Her whole body tensed, ready to flee the moment she knew where she was running.

The stream sang on behind her. The wind rattled the thorns and whispered over the tops of the dunes.

She heard footsteps on her left, and she bolted.

Stones turned underfoot as she sprinted across the bottom of the gully. Something shouted; she swallowed a scream and kept running, sand and black gravel spraying out behind her.

If she was right, anywhere could be a door back to Kulmeni.

The Mirrorlands answered travelers' wills. All she had to do was know where she was going and really *believe* she could get there. Eshu hadn't believed in her, but fuck Eshu.

She remembered the storm drain and the grey light pouring through the rusted grate. The braid of water running down the bottom of the pipe, and the way the concrete walls felt under her hand. Rot and sewage, wet stone and fish; she remembered Sedge moving like a heron through the shallows with her long stick and her bucket.

The gully ran straight ahead of her. The sides rounded and smoothed into a half-circle, then a horned crescent, until the sand closed together at last into a long pipe. Her toes dug into mud and found purchase on concrete. Before her was a light. She couldn't tell how far away it was. Maybe it didn't matter.

As the Mirrorlands faded around her, Fern chanced a glance back over her shoulder. Behind her, a pale figure stood at the mouth of the pipe, laughing and watching her run. Then she slammed into the grate of the storm drain, and the laughter faded away.

CHAPTER 14: EVEN MONEY

Y ou don't have to come, if you'd rather sleep," said Beejan. "Wouldn't blame you for wanting to keep daylight hours."

"I may distantly remember going to bed before midnight, but not with any real fondness," Eshu answered. "The rest of the world is upside down; why not my sleep schedule?"

Beejan laughed. "That's the kind of enthusiasm I like to hear. Come with me, then—there's a place that does strong spiced coffee. It will keep you up all night."

The coffee was sweet and hot and every bit as strong as Beejan had promised, with a grainy texture of ground beans and spices that reminded Eshu keenly of Kondalani coffee. The woman running the stall poured them three tiny cups each, and Eshu sat for a moment simply appreciating the aroma of the coffee and the intricate enamelwork on the porcelain.

Beejan downed his coffee one cup after another as though they were bitter medicine, then chased them with cold mint tea. "Having second thoughts?" he asked, eyeing Eshu's full cups.

Eshu glanced up, then tossed back a cup of coffee with a faint pang of shame. "No," he said. "No, it's just not something I appreciated properly before. Drinking from cups. Being able to go out for coffee whenever I like."

Beejan smiled, then reached out to lay a hand on Eshu's wrist. His thumb and forefinger were still warm from his last cup of coffee. "Take your time. Never let it be said that I denied a man his pleasure."

By the third cup, Eshu's blood felt laced with lightning; his hands shook faintly, as though at any moment they would break into moths and flutter away. As Beejan led him toward the prince's palace, Eshu kept catching glimpses of movement out of the corner of his eye, and he couldn't have said whether they were rats or hungry ghosts or creatures of his own imagination.

It was only the coffee, and possibly the paranoia that came with living alongside hungry ghosts and wild death gods. No doubt Eshu would get used to it, the way he'd become used to wearing shoes of two different sizes or sleeping in the same filthy clothes every day.

The lamplighters were just starting their rounds when Eshu and Beejan reached the palace's brass gate. Red petals drifted down from the trees ringing the plaza, briefly gleaming like jewels as the lamp light shone through them. Someone with a broom was shuffling the shed petals into a heap, and someone else was shoveling them from the heap into a wheelbarrow.

Through the gate and into a courtyard garden; their shadows stretched before them to the half-open door. A tall, rawboned woman was waiting there, watching them approach with her arms folded across her chest. "You're late, Bee," she said, when Beejan and Eshu drew close. "Who's this?"

Beejan curled his arm around Eshu's shoulders in a way that felt delightfully possessive. "This is Eshu. I'd like to have him with me on my patrol, if Granny clears it. And I'm not late; I'm just not early."

She didn't look impressed. "What's he got going for him, besides a pretty face?"

"He's a wizard," said Beejan.

The woman snorted. "Rather have him fixing the mirrors, then. Lot of good a wizard will be when a ghost makes a mince of his intestines."

"If you need me to duel you to prove my worth, or my combat prowess, or some other stupid thing, I'm more than happy to do that," said Eshu. "But it will make all of us late, and I'd rather not have to explain to the prince why your bones are made of driftwood and your blade won't hold an edge."

The woman glanced over at Beejan, then grinned until her gums showed. Her teeth were betel-nut dark at the edges. "I like this one. All right. It's not my business if a ghost has him for dinner. You get inside and introduce him to Mama."

Beejan kissed Eshu's brow, and together they went laughing into the main hall of the palace. There, the lamplight caught on chandeliers of buttery polished brass and fell warm and golden on the tiled floor. "Aunt Sheeram will take you up on that offer of a duel, if you see each other again," said Beejan. "You know how some people only fight because they have to? She's the other kind of person. She's looking for a reason, and if you don't give her one, she'll make one."

"Understood."

"I don't know if you do. She thinks you're funny, so she'll let you get yourself in trouble. Probably thinks it'll teach you a lesson if you dance a little too close to death. But she's a mean one."

The door to which Beejan led Eshu was hanging askew, the hinges torn free of the doorframe. "Well, that's alarming," said Eshu.

Beejan shrugged. "You want to tear down a prince, sometimes you have to tear down some doors."

"It's remarkable how pretty that sounds, considering how little it actually explains."

Letting his arm fall from Eshu's shoulders, Beejan drew up short at the door. His eyes were bright, as though some remembered flame still burned behind them. "What do you want me to say? We didn't come in here with flowers in our arms. It was a coup. We killed people."

Did you kill people? Eshu wondered, but he suspected he knew the answer. "I'm sorry."

"I'm not."

With that, Beejan turned away. He put on a smile and stepped into the room, where a half-dozen people lounged on mismatched chairs and wooden crates. Most sat up straighter as he entered, but one—an old woman with white hair and a stemweed pipe in her hand—only waved him in. "How's the night treating you so far?" Beejan asked, leaning on the back of a heavy chair lined with shining violet silk.

"Bad news," answered a fat woman with a thin scattering of beard across her chin. "But leave that 'til later. Who's this boy? He doesn't look like any cousin of yours."

Beejan made a little half-bow, holding his hands out palms-up to present Eshu to the others. "Aunt Maleh, Tir, Safi, Zaynam, Granny, this is Eshu. A wizard. Met him on patrol last night, and he held his own against a whole swarm of ghosts. With your leave, he'd like to give us a repeat performance."

The old woman rose to her feet. She was slim like an iron rod, and she carried herself with a calm self-assurance that Eshu recognized from his mother's many years in politics. Here was a woman who was used to being listened to and heeded. "I'd heard there was a new wizard in Kulmeni," she said. Her voice was dry and rough, her eyes bright and keen as a bird's. "If you're looking for work, there's plenty to be had in my service."

Eshu sank to his knees, his robes pooling around him. "Your highness."

Her lips quirked at one corner. "No need to stand on ceremony. Up, boy. Let me look at you."

As Eshu stood, the prince held his gaze. She seemed to be evaluating him, but for what, he couldn't say. Her expression gave nothing away. At length, she patted his cheek and stepped back. "Beejan might not have told you that his was a family line of work," she said. "And I don't blame you for not knowing what he didn't tell you. But there's plenty of other work outside of this room, and I'd rather put you where your skills can be best used."

With the mirrors, thought Eshu, and he fought down a fresh wave of panic. *With Tuuri.* "I don't really know anything about building mirrors," said Eshu. "My expertise is, ah. More to do with this world."

The prince tapped her pipe stem against her chin. "Disappointing. Still, we do what we can with the tools we have. Beejan!" Beejan folded his hands behind his back, squaring his shoulders. "Don't bring outsiders into family business again," said the prince. "Do this again, and you're out. I don't care if you're blood."

Beejan looked down. Eshu saw his fingers flex. "It won't happen again."

The prince caught him by the jaw and forced him to meet her eyes. "You'll take responsibility for this one. Are we clear? Prove to me that he can be trusted. Prove that he deserves a place at our table. If not, it's on your head."

"Clear," said Beejan, raising his chin out of her grip.

"Right. Now that that's settled, let's get down to business. Sheeram, stop skulking. Sit." At the prince's orders, Sheeram came inside with a couple of latecomers, and all of them took seats. There was nowhere left for Eshu to sit, so instead he stood awkwardly admiring the details worked in plaster around the high corners of the room: interlocking vines and whorls, painted red and turquoise and indigo.

The prince lounged against the arm of her chair, pipe hovering near her mouth, one knee up on the seat. She took a long drag from the pipe, then exhaled blue smoke. "News. Maleh, save yours for after the new blood clears out. Anyone else?"

"Some river traders are starting to get antsy. They want to leave, mirrors or no mirrors," said Sheeram. "The airship folks are keeping quiet, but I'm hearing complaints all along the docks. Couple of people were mentioning the curfews under Old Prince Shithead."

"They want to go, let them go," said the prince. "Let *them* pay their sailors. Let them waste their time moving their boats around. It'll give 'em something to do besides make trouble in my city."

"There might be trouble if what they say doesn't agree with what our scouts say, when they get back," said Maleh. "It'll be hard to catch that story once it gets legs under it."

"If you read the papers, a few weeks ago I was shooting babies in their cradles," the prince replied coolly. The hairs on the back of Eshu's neck rose. "A story's like anything else with legs. A well-placed pistol shot will stop it running."

"There's interest in your sewer mapping plan," said many-ringed Zaynam, in the pause after the prince spoke. Eshu admired how little it sounded like an interruption. "It was in the papers, and now the word is on the streets. A lot of people are curious about where the water's going now that the streets are all screwed up. Schoolchildren talking about watching your cartographers drop the corks or counting them when they come out the drains. You want my advice—let the city get involved. They're hungry for a project. You need their hands and eyes. Let them feel like they're helping you out."

The prince nodded, puffing on her pipe as Zaynam spoke. "A good idea. See if you can get that out to the papers tomorrow morning; with any luck, it'll make the evening's printing. Where are we on food?"

A slim cousin—Tir or Safi, Eshu wasn't sure which—leaned forward in their seat. "Local trade's still good," they said. "Fish and fruits and rice are still coming in. But we're low on grains, spices, sugar, soy beans, and citrus, and we're really, really low on salt. I'm sorry, Granny. We either need to send someone out to get more or start rationing."

"Fuck me if I'm going to get caught rationing salt," said the prince, letting her foot fall to the ground. Eshu jumped a little, but no one else did. "Where did we used to get salt from? Xhonai?"

Tir-or-Safi nodded. "Xhonai for sea salt. Tisaris for rock salt. As far as I know, there's nothing wrong with the trade road to Tisaris, unless Aunt Maleh's heard differently."

"We'll talk about that later," said Maleh grimly.

"It's just that people are complaining," said Safi-or-Tir, his voice tuned to a conciliatory pitch. "In the spice market. It isn't just for baking and seasoning. They want to pickle things, and they're running out of salt for brining."

"Hmph." The prince pressed her lips together. "It's what people do in the long, bad times—either they pretend everything's fine, or they get themselves ready for worse times. They can't do that, they lose their heads. We'll make salt a priority."

"Salt and money," said one of the newcomers, an older man with ropy muscles and blackwork tattoos down his arms. "We're coming to the end of the treasury."

"Already?" said Maleh. "Gods' teeth!"

"Most of what the old prince had isn't liquid. It's properties, movables—debts, too, near as I can tell." The man shrugged. "It's been three kinds of headache figuring out that crocodile fucker's accounts."

"Don't you worry about that," said the prince. "We're making a start on filling up the coffers again tonight. If all goes well, there will soon be enough coming in for us to make a tidy profit on top of the cost of running the city."

"So you keep saying, but I'm still on pieceworker's wages," muttered Sheeram.

The prince narrowed her eyes. "I don't want to hear it, Sheeram. You want to go back to pushing vhesha in the slums? Then go back. Lord it over the smoke-hounds for a month—maybe two, if you're lucky. See how you do when your supply runs out. For my money, running the city's a better bet."

She met Sheeram's eyes as though daring her to answer, but Sheeram only kept her eyes fixed on a point just beyond the prince's head and said nothing.

It must have been Beejan's turn, because he straightened in his chair. "There are more hungry ghosts every night," he said. "They've started hunting in packs, or something like it. A dozen or so of them jumped us in the gardens last night, all at once. Like they were coordinated. Just want to make sure we ask whether the wizards know anything about that."

"I'll take that back to them," said a woman whose name Eshu hadn't heard. She looked mixed Kondalani, but she had the Acala family cheekbones and dark, straight brows. "If nothing else, we can start arming the patrols better. More runework weapons, or—"

"No, I want to hear what our resident wizard has to say," the prince cut in, and Eshu nearly leapt out of his own bones as her sharp gaze fixed on him. "Well, Eshu? You have a theory?"

Eshu swallowed. He was keenly aware of all of the prince's clan turning to look at him, ready to pronounce judgment should he answer wrong. His professors had never fixed him with such a withering look of contempt as Sheeram did, nor such a pitying expression as Maleh's. His gut was churning, and the coffee didn't help.

He pushed down the fear and the coffee and the indignation and forced his voice level. "Based on my experience fighting these creatures—and I want to stress, my experience is limited—they become more material as we pay attention to them. Our thoughts give them shape and substance. While we can use that to our advantage in order to attack them with material weapons, there may be second-order effects that we haven't considered. Such as making it easier for them to manifest in our world on their own."

Slowly, by degrees, the room relaxed as he spoke. Sheeram sat back as though sensing that there was no blood to be had in this appraisal, and Beejan loosed his grip on the arm of his chair. The prince nodded thoughtfully. "Take that theory back to our wizards, too. See whether they think it's bullshit."

"Will do." The woman who seemed to speak for the wizards darted a glance at Maleh. "I'd also like to present my news after we've broken up, if that's all the same to you."

"Yes, yes," said the prince. "If that's all the news, let's do assignments. Zaynam, you're on the papers again. Tell 'em about the city-wide cork float. I don't care what the details are; you're smart. Make a plan that sounds good, and I'll back it. And put together an article or two wishing the trade ships good riddance. Get your brother to help you if you can't finish it all tonight. Safi, find someone you trust who can run a salt-mining expedition down toward Tisaris. I'm happy to invest in their equipment and wages, but I expect a percentage of the profits. Don't settle for less than thirty percent on top of repaying the investment."

The young man nodded. "Will you want me or Tirna to go with them?"

"If it were any other time, maybe, but right now I can't spare you. That's why I said, find someone you trust." The prince turned to Sheeram, who shifted in her chair. "Good news for you, my girl—Beejan's out of my good graces, so you're hunting ghosts tonight. Tell your people to pair up. I don't want anyone getting jumped alone. That includes you."

"Thanks, Mama." Sheeram's teeth glinted in the lamplight.

With a gesture, the prince dismissed her thanks. "Beejan, Eshu. We're selling one of the prince's properties to Lady Valikram. She's old money and a mercenary bitch besides, so she's good for it, but she's got a guard corps like a private army. Can't be sure she won't try to jump us when we go to make the exchange. A wizard would make a nice surprise, if she tries anything stupid."

"If you need some extra backup—" began Maleh, but the prince shook her head.

"Bring in too many of our people, and we look like we're spoiling for a fight. You know that every one of Kulmeni's aristocrats would love to black my eye. Even if they come out at a loss, all they've proven is that fighting is an option. There's more of them than there are of us. We'll lose that war in the long run."

"The people might back you, if it came to a fight," said Zaynam.

"Pah!" The prince spat on the tiles. "The people are sheep with the scent of a wolf in their noses. They don't love me. Half of 'em don't even like me. They'd follow anyone who looks like they know where they're going. Fuck the people. You can't depend on them."

She took out a little silver canister and refilled her pipe. The smell of stemweed was sharp on the air. "So. We send two—my best runner, and a wizard. Enough to hold their own if things go to shit. If Valikram's folks want to fight it out, beat them if you can; run if you can't. If we start a war, it'll be on our terms, not hers." The prince blew out a long stream of smoke. "Think you can handle that, Eshu?"

Eshu wanted to refuse. He'd stood here listening to the prince figure out how to run the city as though it was a criminal enterprise, and it had felt as though his soul was creeping out of his body. He didn't want to be here. He hadn't tagged along after Beejan to help him head off a territory war. But if he said no, he had no idea where he would be sleeping at the end of the night. If he said no, Beejan would have to go in alone.

He nodded. "I can handle it," he lied.

Beejan was quiet as they left the palace. He still carried himself with all the self-assurance and strength that had heated Eshu's blood last night, but there was something different in his eyes—a weariness or a wariness that made Eshu's skin prickle with unease.

"Does it usually go like that?" Eshu asked, when the silence had stretched too long.

"More or less," muttered Beejan. "Granny values loyalty above all else, so of course everyone wants to prove they're still on her good side."

"And no one's quite as loyal as family."

"Something like that." Beejan let his hand trail through the flowers on the shrubs that lined the garden walkway; a fine golden cloud of pollen rose behind him and caught the lamplight. "Some of us are better than others at working around her. Zaynam knows how to put her in a good mood; Uncle Farrakh and Basia can get her attention with numbers. But Granny makes the decisions, and she expects us to step into line."

When they reached the other side of the garden wall, Eshu's chest unlocked a little, and he took his first deep breath since he'd knelt for the prince. "On the off-chance you brought me there as a witness, may I just say—your family's a bit fucked up."

Beejan laughed, but there was no joy in it. "I said you could stay home."

"I didn't realize when you offered what you were trying to protect me from."

"There's still time to go back to my place, if you want out," said Beejan. "No judgment. I'd be happy to come home to you in the morning and kiss the breath out of you."

When Eshu met Beejan's eyes, he could see that he meant it. There was a gentleness in his gaze that was different from the heat of last night, but no less earnest and warm. Sighing, Eshu rose onto his toes to kiss Beejan's lips. "Tempting as it is to be your kept man, I'm not about to let you walk into this deal alone. My—the woman I was traveling with assured me that Kulmeni was a city of revenge and duels and crocodiles. So far, I've only seen crocodiles, but she's never been wrong about anything important."

"So when the two of you parted ways, should I assume you were in the wrong?"

He remembered Fern's eyes, red and wet with tears. How small her voice had been. *You're really not treating me like a friend right now.* "Yes," said Eshu, and it hurt like closing his hand on a thorn. "I was wrong."

Laying a hand on Eshu's shoulder, Beejan said, "She might want to hear that."

Eshu wasn't sure that it would help, but he pushed that anxiety down beneath all of the others. "Let's survive this first, shall we?" he said lightly. "What do you know about Lady Valikram?"

"Not much," Beejan admitted. "Never had any real use for nobility, before the change. But I hear she's got a hot temper and a wicked sword arm, and that's enough to make me cautious."

"Encouraging. And I suppose you don't know anything about the former prince's property, either."

A shrug. "A little more. The place that Valikram's buying is a bungalow on the river. East shore; south side of the bridge. The old prince used to take his mistresses there for a little privacy, back when he was young enough to get it up."

By now, they were approaching the bridge. Eshu felt the familiar burn of climbing in his shins, his thighs, the meat of his backside. "I take it he didn't have any legal heirs. No doubt your grandmother saw to that."

"It wasn't like that," said Beejan. "It wasn't a massacre. We seized his holdings after the run on the palace, sure, but they mostly went quietly. No heirs rising up in arms. No servants making desperate last stands. They just wanted to know that they'd have a place to go at the end of it."

"And what is that place?"

Beejan gave his club an anxious, absent twirl that sent the mist spiraling in thick whorls. "The old prince had a mulberry orchard, up north along the river. A big working estate. Fruit and silk and lumber. We shipped his household up there to live—told them it was for their protection."

And what happens when the treasury runs dry again, and you have to sell the estate to the north? Eshu wondered, because it was easier than wondering whether the old prince's household was even now nourishing the mulberry roots.

Ahead of them, the far shore of the river rose out of the mist. The east shore lay high over the water, buttressed by a retaining wall faced with marble and overgrown with cascades of papery red flowers. The houses stood proud from each other here, with velvety lawns and gardens thick with flowers and high fences in between. Down the medians of broad boulevards, flowering shade trees grew, all palmate leaves and sprays of perfumed blossoms in cream and peach and gold.

Fern would've known what those trees were called. She would've been able to explain the different colors of their flowers— different cultivars, maybe, or something to do with the acidity of the soil. Some small, comforting fact that he'd immediately forget, and recall again at the most inappropriate time.

We aren't friends.

"This is the place," said Beejan, pausing at an iron gate. He took out the key that the prince had given him and turned it in the lock. It came open with a low, dull click. "Could we have a light?"

"Of course," said Eshu, and sang a globe of sunlight into his palm. It floated free like a soap bubble, and he conjured another— then another, and another, until the old prince's bungalow was radiant with gently drifting lights.

Beejan hid a smile behind his hand. "Showoff."

"What good is being a wizard if you can't show off?" asked Eshu lightly. "And besides, if you want Lady Valikram to know you've brought a wizard, this is as polite a way as I can think of to do it."

"Besides telling her. With words."

"I suppose that's also an option."

While they waited, Eshu glanced around the property that they were here to dispose of. The house beyond the fence was a sprawling single story, with a broad veranda lined with hibiscus and kuana vines. Thick trees and flowering bushes lined the property in an artful tangle, obscuring the fences and creating the illusion of deeper woodlands just beyond. It was difficult not to feel as though the city was in another world, instead of directly at Eshu's back. Cities, he supposed, were no less built by the imagination than the Mirrorlands.

Then Beejan's fingertips brushed his elbow, and Eshu remembered himself. He turned to face the iron gate with a song waiting unsung beneath his breastbone.

Two figures stood there, framed in bars like spears. One was an older woman, her dark hair gone to grey at her right temple and tiny spectacles perched on the bridge of her nose. She scarcely came up to Eshu's chest, but she was trimly built and dressed well, clad in a pure white tunic draped in turquoise silks embroidered with magnolias. On her hip, she wore a slim sword with a jeweled hilt. Her palm rested just shy of her sheath, her many rings twinkling in the light of Eshu's globes.

Then the other woman stepped into the light, and Eshu forgot all about Lady Valikram and her spectacles and her blade.

Eshu and Beejan were tall, but she dwarfed them—a towering creature veiled in a waterfall of silks, clad in a coat of scale mail from a bygone age. The lights traced flowing patterns on her cool blue hands, as though they had passed through some subtle ripple across the surface of her skin. Other shapes moved there, beneath those sinuous threads of light and shadow, shimmering briefly across her knuckles and then dipping once more into the darkness below her wrist.

Eshu had been in the presence of gods before. He knew what she was. He knew what she could do.

"So," said Lady Valikram. Her voice was soft but clear. In the silence, it carried. "This is how the usurper greets a lady of Kulmeni. In the dead of night, with a ruffian and a petty conjurer."

"Be welcome, Lady Valikram," said Beejan. "Prince Teyam recognizes the worth of your offer, and how justly one of your birth deserves—"

"Spare your honeyed words for the wasps," said Lady Valikram. "The usurper cares nothing for my birth. She wants my money; that's the only worth she recognizes."

For the briefest of moments, Eshu saw Beejan calculating. Deciding whether he was being tested, and whether he cared to pass. *He still thinks Lady Valikram is the threat*, Eshu realized, and a chill went through him like a knife. *He doesn't understand what's at stake.* "Very well, my lady," said Beejan at last. "The fact of the matter is that the city is in crisis. If you won't open your coffers because Kulmeni needs you, we're happy to exchange this property for money instead."

Lady Valikram smiled, thin as a blade. The god at her side stood waiting, her veils flowing around her in every faint breeze. "So are all thieves happy to exchange their spoils for money."

"Will we make an exchange tonight, Lady?" Beejan asked. He couldn't possibly know what he faced, but he knew enough to be cautious; Eshu could almost feel him shifting his weight, readying himself to make a stand or to flee. "Or did you only come to trade pleasantries?"

"And what god do we have the pleasure of addressing?" asked Eshu, while Lady Valikram inhaled to speak. "I've met many gods in my travels, but I've never yet had the honor of your acquaintance."

Something shifted beneath the layered veils. It felt like a smile. "The wizard sees much," came a voice like the rush of floodwater over broken stone. "But seeing is not understanding."

"You and Teyam's brood see the city as something to be assessed like a pocket watch, then auctioned off for petty cash," said Lady Valikram, low and dangerous as a serpent's hiss. Her face was twisted with contempt. "Spoils of her greatest robbery—her greatest con. Convincing the people to let you sell their livelihood and their heritage out from under them, and then walking away whistling with your gains. You will not be permitted to profit from your crimes."

The god reached up to draw back her veil, and Eshu glimpsed slitted green crocodile eyes. He knew those eyes; he knew the hue of her skin and the shimmer of her fishscale mail. In the stillness between one heartbeat and the next, he understood how irretrievably fucked they were.

This was the Anjali River.

A song welled up in Eshu's throat—a desperate melody of life triumphant; seeds shuddering and cracking into riotous bloom. Beneath his feet, the garden answered. Roses unfurled their thorny talons; kuana vines burst from the manicured grass, straining and winding toward the sky.

Then a wall of water struck Eshu from behind, and the torrent filled his mouth and drowned out his song.

CHAPTER 15: THIN WALLS

In the early morning, Fern loaded all of her belongings back into her backpack, washed her face, and went downstairs to tell the printers she was moving out. "Are you sure?" asked the man at the counter. "You're paid up for the rest of the week, and the owners aren't likely to give you your money back."

"I'm sure," she said. "I didn't really expect them to give it back, anyway."

He leaned his elbow on the counter, chin propped on one hand. "Where are you headed, if you don't mind my asking? Not to pry—it's only that I heard they're letting cargo ships cast off again, and I wondered if you were taking the river out of Kulmeni."

For a moment, Fern let herself imagine it: taking a riverboat up to the coast, then boarding a swift packet ship that followed the clockwise currents around the north horn of Kondala. There would be long days at sea, watching seabirds and whales; she'd have stopovers at the white docks of Xhonai, the floating markets of Morra, and Pasaris at the far-south heel of Nanjeer. The silent speaking mirrors might have grounded the airships, but the packets were made of sterner stuff—they would be making their rounds until the stars burnt out and the seas ran dry.

She shook her head. "No, I still have a little more business in the city. I just wanted to go somewhere quieter."

"It is a bit loud when we're doing up to five editions a day," the printer admitted, laughing. "Well, best of luck to you with your business."

"And best of luck with yours," she said, and with that, she set off for the Warp and Weft.

The woman at the counter set her up with a room to herself, with a bed curtained off with mosquito netting and a window box spilling over with vines. After Fern had settled her pack, she came downstairs for a fine Kulmeni breakfast—hot lemon tea, kicha and goat meat in a creamy yogurt sauce, pistachio and mannari pastry swimming in spiced honey. After weeks of picking wild kanan and frying snake meat without oil or salt, it seemed an impossible luxury to have someone else bring her a hot meal.

When she'd filled her belly, though, she rose regretfully from the table and set out again into the bustle of the silk district. Merchants chatted about the likelihood of rain as they set up awnings over their wares; a few old men sat at a table on the Warp and Weft's patio, discussing some aristocrat's order of satin as they smoked stemweed and drank cold coffee. Fern passed them by, turning her steps toward the university.

By the time she reached the far side of the bridge, a gentle rain had begun. Little globes of light drifted over the rain-slick streets like a thousand, thousand lantern bees. When Fern reached up for one, it chased her hand in a lazy orbit before drifting away.

At this hour, with the rain lashing the laurel leaves and running in sheets down the roofs, the cloister was deserted. Fern sat a while in the colonnade, watching the rain drip from the shingles to the jasmine vines below.

Eventually, she made her way inside. In the shelter of the high-ceilinged hall, she caught snatches of lectures on polynomials, a lively discussion of Manira Yasri's *Ethics*, students dully reciting Kiruuni verb conjugations. It didn't feel like home, but it was close enough to make Fern's throat go tight.

She stopped to question a porter mucking out a gutter, who

pointed Fern in the direction of a dormitory on the far side of the cloister. There, at last, she found Mnoro and Usamkartha in a common room that smelled of candlewax and stale coffee.

Mnoro, who had been reading, immediately put her book aside. She wore white and indigo today, a pretty Kulmeni tunic and trousers with a gauzy wrap, and her eyes and lips were painted indigo to match. "Welcome back!" she said cheerfully. "I was afraid we'd scared you off last time. Where is Eshu?"

"Um." Fern swallowed. She didn't want to explain what had happened; these were Eshu's friends. Either they'd take his side, or she'd turn them against him, and she didn't want either of those things. She didn't want to be involved in their friendship at all. Instead, she only said, "Eshu isn't coming today."

Mnoro's face fell, but she quickly recovered. "Well, I'm not surprised he doesn't want to see Tuuri Vilara again. Sit down, let me make you some tea."

"It's all right. I had tea before I came," said Fern, but she did take a seat on the sagging couch across from them and started spreading out her notes from this morning's venture into the Mirrorlands. "Where is Tuuri Vilara, anyway?"

"They have him enchanting more weapons for the night watch," said Usamkartha without looking up. He dipped his pen and continued writing, and the words crawled up his arm in teeming palimpsests.

"Tuuri is the only one of us who has much experience with runecrafting," Mnoro said, like agreement. "I've been studying up since we got here, but he has at least six years on me."

"What do they need enchanted weapons for?" Fern asked.

Mnoro took a sip of her tea. "Have you ever heard of hungry ghosts?" Fern nodded. "The way Tuuri explained it, they're not all the way real. Just sort of a formless hunger. But they get more real the longer you look at them, and that means that by the time they've become something you can fight, they're right on top of you."

"And they're here, in Kulmeni, eating people," said Usamkartha grimly. "Don't omit that crucial detail."

"Right," Mnoro agreed. "So Tuuri's designed a rune to help stabilize the ghosts at the point of contact. It's not much of an advantage, but it can give the night watch a few extra seconds."

Usamkartha snorted. "And it looks flashy, which keeps people from questioning why there are armed enforcers roaming the streets. The prince likes her spectacle."

Mnoro glanced to the door with a frown furrowing her brows. "The prince also has ears," she said.

"She can do what she likes to me!" Usamkartha pronounced. "I'm already dying. A dying man is invincible."

"You're *not* dying," Mnoro snapped. "We're going to find a way to fix you."

"I'm dying," said Usamkartha, leaning in toward Fern with a conspiratorial look.

She leaned in, too. When she looked at him straight on, he was an ordinary man of her mother's generation: lean-faced, dolorous of eye, his hair greying and balding. The veins stood out like serpents on the backs of his hands.

When she let her mind wander for even a moment, he was a mass of shining scales and coils.

"What happened to you?" she asked quietly.

With his free hand, Usamkartha thumped his book. "I am writing a manuscript on my condition, if you care to know the details," he said. "The first true theoretical work on the aftereffects of traveling through a broken mirror—the condition has been called *fragmentation* by past scholars, but I believe it is more properly termed *abstraction*. If I'm going to die from this, at least my death advances the field of scholarship."

Mnoro rolled her eyes and finished her tea. "You're not going to die. Tuuri and I have a lot of promising options for fixing you."

"It's his fault I'm *in* this state, so you'll forgive me if I'm not interested in any 'options' he has to offer," said Usamkartha.

"I'm not going to defend him after all the shit he's pulled. But like I said, he's the expert runecrafter, and even if we weren't in a massive susceptible zone, this feels like a runecrafting problem."

"What did he do?" Fern asked. This, too, felt like an old argument, where the specifics had worn away until only a core of optimism and fatalism remained.

Mnoro and Usamkartha exchanged a glance with each other, then both looked uneasily at the door. "We'd been behind the mirror for a few days before we found this place," said Mnoro at last. "We were all tired. We'd fought off half a dozen hungry ghosts by then, and they just kept finding us. Or maybe our fear was creating them—it's hard to tell with the Mirrorlands. But when we found the mirrors that led to Kulmeni, the first thing Tuuri did was try to tip them face-down. He said he was trying to keep those things from following us out."

"Which is horse shit," interrupted Usamkartha. He was a ship splintered on a reef, a lightning-struck tree, a hornet's nest smashed on the ground. "But even *if* it had been true, I still would've been trapped on the far side of the mirror."

"Anyway," said Mnoro heavily. "When the mirrors hit the ground, they broke. And Usamkartha came through while they were breaking."

"Hence, abstraction." Usamkartha's gesture took in his concave chest, his thin arms, the blanket over his knees. "I'm becoming untethered from reality—soon I'll be nothing but a loose assemblage of metaphors with a migraine."

"We'll reel you in," said Mnoro, putting a hand on Usamkartha's shoulder. "Promise."

He grimaced, but didn't shake her off. "If you're finished making ridiculous declarations, I'd very much enjoy talking about something else."

Fern looked down at her hands. "Um. So I found a way into

the Mirrorlands yesterday."

Mnoro had been pouring herself another cup of tea; at Fern's news, though, she let the cup overflow. When the tea started pattering onto the floor, she quickly righted the kettle and found a cloth to mop up the spill. "I take it from your tone that you didn't go through a mirror," she said when she'd regained her composure.

"I. Um. No. I went through a storm drain." Fern winced at how stupid that sounded. "What I mean is, maybe it isn't that Kulmeni works like the Mirrorlands; maybe they're mixed up with each other now. Like the world cracked open, and the Mirrorlands bubbled up through the cracks."

She looked from Usamkartha's face to Mnoro's, waiting for them to laugh at her. But Usamkartha gazed into the middle distance as though in deep thought, and Mnoro pressed her indigo-painted lips together. "It's not beyond the realm of possibility," Mnoro said, "but Tuuri would have a lot of objections to the premise."

"Chiefly, that the Mirrorlands are not some kind of overcooked soup," Usamkartha muttered.

"I was thinking more like lava. Here, look. I took this sample there." Fern took a sample vial of sand out of her pocket and held it out for them to study. Mnoro took it, tipping it back and forth in her hand so that the sand slid along the glass, then handed it back. "The first time I went to the Mirrorlands, I saw a lot of things there that reminded me of our world. Not just—I mean, it wasn't just that it had a sky and a ground and some trees. There was a geography to it that made sense. Water flowed away from the mountains. Thorn bushes grew along the bottoms of the arroyos. It wasn't just a dreamscape; it was a desert."

"Well, you are a mapmaker," said Mnoro gently. "If the Mirrorlands are responsive to the imagination, they may have responded to your expectations of desert geography."

"Maybe," said Fern. "But when I went there yesterday, I found snails in one of the washes, and I've never found that species anywhere but in the Anjali River. And I definitely didn't expect that."

Mnoro's eyes went wide. "You found *snails*."

"Little river snails," said Fern. "The kind street vendors fry down by the docks."

A cascade of leaves spun through the air at the periphery of Fern's vision. "Did you find anything else on this adventure?" Usamkartha asked.

"I'm not sure yet," said Fern. "I did take some samples, but I'd need a microscope to examine them. I was hoping you could find one for me?"

Mnoro grinned. "Absolutely. I'll have it for you by tomorrow—I want to see what's in these bottles as much as you do."

"Now, explain to us how you managed to get into the Mirrorlands through a storm drain," said Usamkartha.

Fern took a deep breath, twisting the green glass ring around on her finger as she considered how to frame it. Just as she opened her mouth to speak, though, the door to the common room swung open, and Tuuri Vilara stepped through. He untied a leather apron and hung it on a peg by the door. "That's the runework done on the night watch's swords," he said, dusting off his hands. "Is there any tea left?"

As Mnoro poured him a cup, Tuuri Vilara's gaze fell on Fern. He looked at her curiously—not as though she was an unexpected guest, but as though she was a riddle he meant to unravel. "Fern," he said, enunciating the word in a way that made her hackles go up. "Our visitor from Zumera. I see you've returned to us."

"I promised I would," Fern answered.

Tuuri Vilara's warm smile never flickered, but something shifted in his expression that she didn't like at all. "Might I speak with you in private?"

When she'd been a child, her teachers had taken her aside sometimes to tell her to behave herself: to sit still, to pay attention, to keep her eyes on her work. For all Tuuri Vilara had asked politely, the request felt uncomfortably like being called out of the circle for a dressing-down.

Fern glanced from Mnoro's worried face to Usamkartha, who looked away. *Even he doesn't think I should go*, she thought.

"I guess," she said, and stood from the table.

Tuuri Vilara led her out of the common room and into a dormitory that contained two bunk beds, a bookshelf, and a worktable beneath a latticed window. She had only a moment to admire the room's clean design before Tuuri Vilara closed the door behind her.

Without Mnoro and Usamkartha there, he suddenly looked a lot less warm and kind.

"Is there anything you haven't told us about your time behind the mirror?" he asked, slowly circling her. She felt like a sheep being herded—or hunted. "Any piece of information you kept to yourself. You might not have even realized it. Something Eshusikinde told you, perhaps. Something that helped you locate the mirror in Zumera. Maybe a working mirror you didn't mention."

This morning, she had been on fire to tell him about how she'd found a way back into the Mirrorlands. She'd wanted to consult with him, an amateur seeking an expert's advice, and see what he made of her theories. When he looked at her with that cold, hungry expression, though, she only wanted to be somewhere far away. "I told you everything," she said, and started edging toward the door.

He laid his broad hand against the door, holding it shut. In that moment, he loomed over her like a thunderhead, infinitely tall and powerful. A cold wave of fear coursed through Fern's body. "We both know that's not true."

"I told you everything!" she said, louder, hoping that Mnoro and Usamkartha would hear her through the door. "I don't know about any more mirrors. Just the one we broke outside of Zumera, and the one from Sharis—"

"Then explain to me how you came to be walking through the Mirrorlands yesterday," he said. His smile was a wolf's, all gleaming bone teeth.

There came a knock at the door that startled both of them out of their standoff. "Tuuri," said an unfamiliar voice. "It's Basia. Something's come up."

His eyes still locked with Fern's, Tuuri dropped his hand to the doorknob. He hesitated for a long, excruciating moment, then swung the door open. "Basia," he said, turning to her with a mild expression and gesturing her in. "What news from the prince?"

Basia glanced down at Fern and frowned. She was an elegant woman of middling height, with a soft cloud of tight curls and broad golden hoops in her ears, and she seemed to hold Tuuri at bay with no more than the weight of her gaze. When she spoke, her voice was rich and deep. "I'm sorry to cut your visit short, but this matter is urgent and sensitive. You'll have to resume it another time."

"Another time," Tuuri agreed pleasantly. "Goodbye, Fern. I'm sure we'll see each other again."

Fern knew she was supposed to say *Goodbye* here, like this was a normal conversation. But the word felt like ashes on her tongue, and she couldn't make herself speak it. She hurried out of the room and shut the door behind her, then sank down almost immediately against the wall and buried her face in her hands.

He hadn't done anything to her. He hadn't even threatened her—not really; he'd just put his hand on the door so she couldn't leave, and somehow that had been as bad as watching the prince load her ivory-handled gun.

Her heart felt like it was going to beat straight through her skin. She thought Mnoro said something, but all Fern could hear was her heart hammering and the blood rushing in her ears. She drew in a long, shaky breath and held it as long as she could, then exhaled slowly. Her breath felt hot against her palms.

"... timetable has changed." Basia's voice. Fern could make out the drum of her fingernails on the worktable. "The prince has been very patient with your team so far. She understands that you're doing specialist work. But she cannot keep paying for failure. There are a dozen airships ready to go at a word, and eventually, the balance of the budget will tip in their favor."

"An airship launch is difficult to conceal," Tuuri countered, all unctuous self-assurance. "If she no longer wants to keep the fall of Tisaris a secret, that's her decision, of course, but until then, she is paying for our silence as well as our work. Factor *that* into your budget."

Fern's eyes snapped open. *They've heard back from Tisaris,* she realized, with a flash of betrayal that drowned out her fear. *And if they've heard back from Tisaris, they've heard from Kondala City, too; it's closer than Tisaris—*

"You say you've made progress," said Basia. "Fine. But we need a stable, reliable pathway between Kulmeni and Tisaris, and we need it *tonight*. This afternoon. Can you do that for us, or not?"

A pause that stretched just slightly too long. "I can do it," Tuuri said eventually.

"Good." Fern heard a chair scrape across the floor.

She didn't know what they'd do if they caught her eavesdropping. Scrambling to her feet, Fern darted across the room to Mnoro and Usamkartha and started gathering up her notes. "I have to go," she said. "I'm sorry, I know it's sudden—"

"What did he say to you?" Mnoro asked, casting a dark look at the dormitory door. "Did he do anything he shouldn't have?"

Fern swallowed. "He didn't want to let me leave," she said. "I'm sorry."

"You don't have anything to be sorry for," said Mnoro. She reached out for Fern, gently squeezing her shoulder. "I shouldn't have let him pull you aside. I'm sorry. I knew better."

"You didn't want to make a scene," said Fern, low. "You're stuck with him, aren't you?"

Mnoro seemed to be choosing her words carefully, as though she knew that at any moment Basia might step out again. "The prince is very interested in our progress," she said. "And he's the resident expert on mirrors."

Usamkartha made a disgusted sound. "We're stuck with him," he said bluntly, and then shattered into a thousand snow-white moths.

At the Warp and Weft, the dining room was so crowded that patrons had spilled out onto the patio. Fern was seated at an outdoor table with a pair of rice merchants, who were having a very involved conversation about pest management that she did her best to drown out.

She heard snatches of other conversations, too, at other tables. Someone had glimpsed a nightmare creature prowling the docks, weeping putrid flesh. A man claimed he'd seen the Crowtaker perched upon the clock tower in the Sisters' place. Sailors' pay had been delayed again, with no word on when more would be coming.

Rain drummed on the awning overhead. A slim server brought Fern a bowl of chicken and butter beans swimming in pepper sauce, with slivered almonds sprinkled on top and lentil wafers on the side. As Fern ate, she cracked open a book that Mnoro had lent her about the mirror travel.

From the table of contents, Fern could already tell that it was mostly about things she didn't care about. Several chapters devoted to the process of enchanting, installing, and reinstalling a mirror; two whole chapters on mirror repair. There was an introduction on the theory of mirror travel that looked promising, but it was so dense with jargon that Fern couldn't figure out if it actually had an argument or if the author was just trying to prove they knew the language of the discipline. She wished it had a glossary, but apparently real experts knew all the terminology already.

She could find nothing on the geography of the Mirrorlands. There was nothing about its history. There wasn't even any speculation about the dark mountains or the half-buried streams, or what nourished the white thorns and silver trees. The Mirrorlands in the book were a nullity—a void, something infinitely less than a fluid medium. As far as Fern could tell, more theoretical work had been done on air than on those endless dunes.

She twisted Shell's daughter's ring around her finger. The book had nothing to say about how she'd come across it. It shouldn't have been possible for her to fall into the Mirrorlands while she slept. The version of the Mirrorlands in the book was firm-edged, immiscible, accessible only through mirrors that had been appropriately enchanted and installed.

A natured object may be crafted from the unnatured space, the book said, *but it must be considered merely "natured" and not real, for it cannot survive removal from the notional framework of the mirror realm.* Tables followed of objects imagined into being: flowers, gold bars, songbirds in brass cages, a basket of ripe plums. Not one had made it out of the Mirrorlands.

Maybe I dreamed the ruined tower into being, the way Eshu dreamed the tree, Fern thought. *Maybe I even dreamed the bodies on the shore. But I shouldn't have been able to take the ring out of the Mirrorlands unless it was real.* Not that it helped, when this author and Eshu couldn't even agree on what "real" meant. Either this book was wrong, or something about the way the world had broken had changed the relationship between her world and the Mirrorlands.

"—still no word from Zumera," said the old woman across the table, and Fern's head shot up.

The prince had told Fern to keep news of Zumera close to her chest. But she was also keeping Tisaris a secret, and had been for the Sisters only knew how long. She'd promised that as soon as she knew about Kondala City, the papers would know, but that obviously wasn't true of any other city, so Fern had no reason to believe her.

Maybe it would start a panic if the news got out. Maybe it wouldn't. But it certainly hadn't eased anyone's hearts not to know.

"Actually," said Fern, "I just came from Zumera."

The rice merchants stared at her as though they'd just realized she was there. Fern's face burned. She immediately wished she hadn't said anything. "Well, go on," said the other merchant, a middle-aged androgyne with a delicate filigree nose ring. "What's happened?"

At that moment, Kurosh Hura came through with a silver pitcher full of fresh mint tea. As he topped them all up, Fern said, "Zumera's had a disaster. Tisaris, too. And the prince knows about it."

Kurosh Hura hesitated, pitcher poised over Fern's glass. "What's this?" he asked.

"I don't know about what happened in Tisaris, but I saw Zumera with my own eyes," said Fern. People at other tables were turning to look. She wished she could stop talking and melt into the ground. "It was some kind of magic. I don't know what kind. But the whole place was buried in gemstones."

"That doesn't sound like much of a disaster," began the old rice merchant, but Fern shook her head violently.

"It was bad. People got crushed. People got impaled. There was a wizard buried under the rock and you could just—you could see the shape of him, but that was it. I found a man in the street who was rotting in the sun, and I..."

The androgyne reached across the table and squeezed Fern's hand briefly. "Shh, dear. It's all right. You're here now."

"And the prince *knew*?" someone asked. Fern couldn't see who. There were too many people around, getting up from their chairs, getting into her space, and it only made her feel worse.

She swallowed down the rising anxiety and nodded. "I told her myself. And she told me not to tell anyone. She was afraid of causing a panic. And just today I found out that she knew about Tisaris, too."

"What happened to Tisaris?" asked someone else.

"I don't know," Fern said. "I just heard that it fell. And that the prince wanted it to stay a secret."

"Fucking Teyam Acala," said an older man with a braided beard, slamming his hand down on his table. Plates and cups rattled; his spoon fell to the floor with a clatter. "We always knew she was a crook—"

"What did you expect? Princes lie," said someone else. "You think old Prince Vahid was any better?"

"You realize what this means, though," the old rice merchant said. "Trade goods aren't coming. Half our fresh produce comes from Zumera. Most of our grain comes from Tisaris—spices and salt, too. There are lean times ahead."

"I don't know what her scheme is," said the man with the braided beard, "but mark my words, she'll suffer for it if we do."

The crowd was getting so loud that Fern could barely hear herself think. She wanted to cover her ears and duck under the table. She felt the pressure of dozens of eyes on her, judging her, doubting her, demanding answers.

Kurosh Hura raised his voice over the heightening roar of indignation. "Friends," he boomed, gesturing with the tea pitcher. "Your grievances are reasonable. I'm the last person to say they aren't. But this is a house of peace and rest. If you mean to launch a revolution, please settle your accounts with the house and take it to the streets."

The clamor of voices crested and broke. Diners went back to their seats, still muttering to each other darkly about trade goods and secrets and the prince's many crimes.

Fern finished her food as quickly as she could, then went to settle her bill. "Thank you," she said, while Kurosh Hura counted out change. "Maybe I shouldn't have said anything. I just—if it had been me, I would rather know than not know."

"You did a brave thing," said Kurosh Hura, pushing two one-zil coins across the counter. "Perhaps not a wise thing, but a brave one."

"If things do get bad—"

"Then the work before us is the same as it always was, and always will be." He gave her a reassuring smile. "We must take care of each other."

CHAPTER 16: WINDOWS AND DOORS

Crawling out of the mud on the bank of the Anjali, Eshu coughed up water until his lungs burned. He dragged himself hand over hand on clumps of reeds, knots of river grass that came apart under his fingers, until he lay on the rocky shore in a wet heap. A few yards down the strand, he heard Beejan swear, low and feeling.

He didn't know how far the river had carried them. He remembered the remorseless current, the drag of his feet against the river bed; he remembered breaking the surface, choking, screaming for air.

A heavy *crack* sounded across the shore, then Beejan shouted, "Get out of here!" Eshu raised his head in time to watch an enormous crocodile scuttle into the shallows and then vanish beneath the water.

Eshu hauled himself onto his elbows and knees, then climbed unsteadily to his feet. "Are you all right?" he asked, then coughed again. His throat felt raw. He pressed a hand against his broken ribs, half-afraid that they'd broken again, and winced at the dull ache under his palm. Dull was better than sharp, at least.

Beejan gave his club an experimental twirl that made the runes flare white and golden. He stretched his arms high over his head, then rolled his head around on his neck until his vertebrae cracked. "Wet, but mostly in one piece," he said at last. "No thanks to Lady

Valikram and her pet god."

Eshu glanced out over the river. In the light of the waning moon, it looked smooth as glass, broken at the shoreline by long reeds and a dappling of lotuses. But he remembered the torrent at the river's heart, and how it had felt to be pulled to the bottom. "If she'd wanted to kill us, we would be dead," he said. "The Anjali wanted us to survive. We still have a message to deliver."

"Shit." Beejan laid his club over the back of his neck, bracing his hands on either side of it. "I've never fought a god before."

"I have. I don't recommend it."

Beejan shook his head. His expression was far away, his eyes fixed on the distant lights of Kulmeni. "She's the city's god. If the Anjali is against us, we've fucked up somewhere."

Eshu wanted to say, *Maybe your grandmother's first mistake was trying to run the city like some kind of criminal racket.* But he was tired and sore, and his clothes were still heavy with river water, and he didn't have the energy for the conversation that would come next if he said it. Instead, he only wrung out the skirt of his robe and tied it up around his knees. "Come on," said Eshu gently. "We have a long walk ahead of us."

He missed Sparrow and his slapdash heroism. He missed feeling like he was doing something right.

It was nearly dawn by the time they made it back to the city. Somewhere on the horizon, the sun hung red and blazing, but the mists still lay over Kulmeni like a thick shroud.

Eshu's feet ached to his bones. He'd lost count of how many times he'd turned his ankle on a rock in the darkness, even with a bubble of light dancing on his palm to show the way. He wanted nothing more than to curl up in Beejan's bed, draw the mosquito netting closed, and let sleep claim him.

But then Beejan would be facing the prince by himself, and tired as he was, Eshu didn't want to leave Beejan alone. He was starting to see why Fern had stuck with him so long, even when he'd been an asshole to her—when all you could do was keep someone company, you held on with both hands.

They found Prince Teyam in her bedchamber. She came out at Beejan's knock, wrapped in a plain cotton robe with her hair in a scarf and a pistol in her hand. "You look like shit," she said, raking them up and down with her gaze, and opened the door wider to let them in.

As soon as he walked in, Eshu sank down onto a silk-upholstered divan and stretched his legs out in front of him. The prince gave him a look that seemed to assess exactly how much the mud on his clothes had reduced the value of her divan, but in an uncharacteristic act of mercy, she didn't comment. "Looks like the deal went badly," she said, setting aside her pistol to take up her pipe. "Did you win?"

"She had a god on her side," Beejan answered. "The Anjali River."

The prince paused, her pipe halfway to her mouth. "The river. You're sure about that."

"I've treated with gods before," said Eshu. "This was the Anjali, and if she kept us alive, it was so that we could bring back a declaration of war."

Tapping her pipe stem against her lower lip, Prince Teyam said, "Tell me everything."

Between the two of them, they unfolded the events of the night while the prince smoked and listened. She had few questions for them, but they were clear and pointed: "Do you still have the key?" and "Did they make any demands?"

Beejan still had the key. Lady Valikram had wanted nothing but to see Prince Teyam gone. Neither of these answers seemed to please her.

When her pipe was finished, the prince went behind a latticework screen and tossed her robe and her hair wrap over the top. A minute later, she emerged dressed in fitted trousers and a crisp cotton shirt with a high collar. She wore a sword slung low on one hip and a holster on the other. "You understand that this changes things," she said as she tugged her boots on. "Can't hold the city without the river."

"We can try another way," said Beejan. "Even gods can be persuaded. Offerings, maybe, or—"

"Say all the prayers you like," said the prince. "But the problem I sent you to solve still needs solving: this city needs money to run."

Beejan straightened. He was still standing, hands tucked behind his back, as though she was a commander and he, her soldier. He must have been as tired as Eshu, but he let none of it show on his face. "Tell me what you need me to do."

Prince Teyam dipped her head in acknowledgment. She checked her reflection, then tied up her hair and stabbed a couple of brass rods through it to keep it in place. "First, get some rest," she said. "Eat a meal. Wash. Get some sleep. You two did what I asked of you; I shouldn't have expected better." If he hadn't been looking for it, Eshu would barely have noticed how Beejan's shoulders tensed at that. The prince wasn't finished, though. She turned, resting a hand on her hip in a way that drew Eshu's eye to the hilt of her sword. "After you've slept, you're going through the mirror with a salvage crew. Basia says our wizard has just about found a working route, so no point in delaying any longer."

Our wizard—she could only mean Tuuri. Eshu's stomach went tight.

"What do you want us to salvage?" Beejan asked.

"Anything you can get your hands on," answered the prince. "Money, for preference. Gems. Movables. We want small and valuable, easy to fence; don't waste your time on some antique

Cheressian rug, or we'll have the same trouble we had with the old prince's shit. Don't get sentimental. You'll have a handcart, not an oxcart, so make everything count." She clicked her tongue. "Wish I could send you to Zumera. Apparently the streets are paved with jewels there. But that way isn't open yet, so Tisaris it is."

She fixed her gaze on Eshu, and despite himself, he sat up straighter on the divan. There was something in her eyes that he feared instinctively, the way a mouse feared a serpent or a hawk. Every nerve throbbed with an urgent yearning to live. He couldn't imagine how it must have been to grow up under her watch.

"Let me go with him," said Eshu. He desperately didn't want to go. If he went, it would only tangle him deeper in whatever war was brewing between her and Lady Valikram; if he went, he'd have to see Tuuri again, and he would rather swallow broken glass. "Please," he said anyway. "I need to know what happened in Tisaris. And you could use another wizard."

Prince Teyam snorted as though his plea amused her. "Fine," she said. "It'll save me finding one more. But mark me, boy—if you slow them down, my people will leave you behind."

Back at Beejan's place, they stripped out of their muddy clothes and washed each other clean. When the last of the mud had been scrubbed away, Beejan seized Eshu by the hair and took him hard and fast over the edge of the bed. It hurt almost enough to clear Eshu's head; he longed for a pain that was brighter and sharper, but he was too exhausted to ask for more.

Afterward, they curled up together, Eshu's head tucked against Beejan's shoulder, and fell asleep to the sound of a gentle rain lashing the roof.

The rain was pouring down in earnest when they woke. "Time to go," Beejan murmured against Eshu's hair. He nuzzled against the hollow of Eshu's cheek, then dropped a kiss as light as snowflakes on his lips. "If you've changed your mind, I won't blame you. This is more than any reasonable man could ask of a hookup."

"Unfortunately, I'm both stubborn and prideful, so I'm coming with you," Eshu replied. He slid out from under Beejan's arm and began to dress in a set of travel clothes: a jacket with pockets, hardwearing boots, trousers that he could tie at his knees. The long tunic that went with them was his sole concession to luxury, dyed a deep blue and embroidered in red and gold at the collar and sleeves. Fern would have been proud of him for making a sensible choice for once in his life. He wished she could see him.

Then, under the shelter of Beejan's umbrella, they crossed the bridge to the university.

Sheeram was waiting for them, idly tossing her knife. When she noticed Beejan, she caught it by the hilt and sheathed it. "Heard you got your ass handed to you last night," she said. She gave a feral grin, black-edged at the gums. "From what Mama said, it wasn't even a fight."

"You heard right," said Beejan. "And if you want to take a swing at the Anjali River, I'm happy to step out of your way."

Sheeram laughed. "I'm not as stupid as you think, Bee. I see you brought your wizard boy. What's he here to do, carry your balls for you?"

Whatever Beejan would've said, he was interrupted by the rumble of wheels on tile. Basia and Lali came around the corner, both of them rolling wheelbarrows, and Sheeram immediately found something new to complain about.

"What's this wheelbarrow shit?" she demanded, stalking down to meet them. "Mama said we'd have handcarts. We'll be lucky if we can fit a couple of good-sized goats in those."

"It has to fit through the mirror frame," said Basia calmly. "We tested this earlier. The wheelbarrows are as wide as we can go without stressing the frame."

"Anyway, we're not after goats. We're after money. Jewelry. Movables." Lali knocked her knuckles on the side of the wheelbarrow; it rang dully under the blow. "Unless you've had a score big enough to fill a handbag, you don't get to bitch about a wheelbarrow."

Sheeram rolled her eyes. "Fine. Are we going through a mirror, or are you all going to stand here ganging up on me for another hour?"

"We're just waiting on—ah, here he is!" Basia grinned, peering around Eshu and Beejan. "Everyone, this is Tuuri Vilara. He's our expert on mirrors."

A frisson of cold dread lanced down Eshu's spine. He'd expected this moment, but he wasn't ready for it. He didn't think he ever would be.

He turned around.

Tuuri was still as beautiful as he'd been when Eshu had loved him; that was the worst of it. He was dressed in the Kulmeni style, in a sleeveless white tunic that flattered his broad shoulders; his emerald sash cinched in his tapered waist. When Eshu looked into Tuuri's ice-green eyes, they still gleamed with wit.

It would have been easier if he could have looked at Tuuri and seen only a monster. Eshu had faced monsters, now, and he had survived them. But instead, he saw the face that he had once loved with his whole heart, and some frail, foolish part of Eshu still lit up with joy to see him.

Tuuri raised his brows, then schooled his features into a warm, companionable smile. He made a deep bow from the waist, his eyes never leaving Eshu's. "Eshusikinde—what an unexpected pleasure. These are strange times, indeed."

Eshu wanted to turn and flee. Every muscle and sinew ached with the effort of keeping still. But he forced a smile onto his face, tight and strained at the corners, and he dipped his head incrementally in acknowledgment. "The pleasure is all yours."

Tuuri laughed as though it had been a joke. "You wound me, darling."

"Cut the flirting," snapped Sheeram. "If I wanted to watch a pair of wizards fuck each other with their eyes, I'd go to the theater. You're the mirror expert. Get us to Tisaris."

Tuuri held Eshu's gaze a moment longer, as though to prove that he could, then turned back to Sheeram. "My colleague and I are trained in mirror travel, but I acknowledge we're short on time. These runestones will let you pass through the mirrors without special training." He passed out a collection of smooth river stones, etched deep and inked in gold.

Eshu caught a glimpse of Beejan's runestone before he pocketed it. Runecrafting wasn't Eshu's specialty, but even he could see that the runework was bullshit—just an elaborate prop to help new travelers believe they could do the impossible. Tuuri had never relished teaching people to have faith in themselves.

They crowded into the university's mirror room, with its midnight-blue walls mazed with interlocking geometric lattices worked in gold. One of the mirrors was broken; Eshu shot Tuuri a questioning look, but Tuuri ignored him.

"Fix this place in your memory," said Tuuri. "Unless you have a clear image of it in your mind, you may find it difficult to return."

"We live in Kulmeni," muttered Sheeram. "We know how this fucking works."

Get him, Sheeram, thought Eshu savagely.

Tuuri's smile never faltered. "Then perhaps you would care to go through first?"

Sheeram snorted, then gripped the handles of one of the wheelbarrows. She levered the front wheel up over the rim of the mirror, then rolled it on through until she vanished in a flash of brilliant light.

The rest went through one by one, until only Beejan and Eshu were left. As Beejan stepped up to the mirror, he hesitated, reaching back for Eshu's hand. "Hey," he said. "You all right? You're shaking like a leaf."

Eshu hadn't realized he was shaking. "I'm incredibly not all right," he said.

"What did he do to you?" Beejan asked. He traced his thumb over the back of Eshu's knuckles, so gentle and patient that Eshu nearly recoiled at the touch.

He broke my heart, he wanted to say. *He made me believe that I was worthless. He needled me in a thousand little ways until I felt like he was tattooed on my skin, and now I'll never be free of the marks he left.*

At length, Eshu said, "He is the worst thing that ever happened to me, and that includes the end of the world."

Beejan laced his fingers through Eshu's and gripped him tight. "I won't let him hurt you," he said, as though it were something he had any power to stop.

Hand in hand, they stepped into the eternal night of the Mirrorlands.

As soon as Beejan's feet touched the sand, Sheeram socked him hard in the shoulder. "Don't hold us up like that, Bee. We don't have time for this handholding shit."

"Leave him alone," said Lali. "This place is fucking creepy. Don't take it out on him."

Sheeram spat. "All the more reason to get out of it."

The going was hard. The wheelbarrows wallowed in the fine sugar sand, forcing their pace to a crawl; every time the slope collapsed underfoot, they lost long minutes digging the wheels out again. Eventually Eshu pointed them down into one of Fern's arroyos, where the rockier earth offered better footing, and Tuuri's eyes flashed with temper at the diversion.

"I've warned you before about straying from the path," said Tuuri, light and infuriating. "There are all sorts of dangerous creatures on these untested ways."

"Let me know when you find a path, then," Eshu said, which

at least shut him up.

They followed the serpentine path of the arroyo for almost an hour before Tuuri found whatever he was looking for. By then, Sheeram was muttering dire threats under her breath, and even the normally glacial Basia was starting to look uneasy. Eshu had sighted something dark moving over the dunes far away, drifting and diffuse like a thick swarm of flies, and he knew that if he'd seen it, Beejan had, too.

At a place that looked like any other, Tuuri raised his hand over the dunes, and the sand scattered back from a path of rough black stone. "The lost road to Tisaris," he announced, as grandly as though it had been a thousand years buried instead of a month. Lali and Sheeram gave a ragged cheer as they pushed the wheelbarrows onto the first solid ground they'd had since Kulmeni.

The path led them up a ridge line with a copse of stunted silver trees in the lee of it. As Eshu summited the hill, the wind pulled at his jacket and washed over his face, crisp and cool as meltwater.

Ahead of them lay a rectangle of pure light, more a window than a door. While Beejan and Basia moved back to help wrestle the wheelbarrows up the hill, Eshu made his way to the mirror and raised his hand as though to touch the glass.

He felt sunlight on his palms for the first time in days. Leaving the others behind, Eshu stepped through the mirror and into the Crossroads of Tisaris.

He'd passed through here before with Tuuri, both of them wine-drunk and half in each other's arms already. He remembered the white marble balconies open to the eight points of the compass rose, the high coffered dome of the ceiling, the sunset striking fire in the west. Now, that gilded dome lay cracked open to the high blue sky.

Something almost unbearably bright lay at his feet, rivaling the sun for warmth and brilliance. It had smashed the marble floor where it fell, leaving cracks that radiated out like spiderwebs.

He knew what stars were. He understood that they were far-distant suns, perhaps with other worlds and moons around them—Asha had been passionate for stars, regaling him with their taxonomies of heat and size and brightness. She had told him about stars caught in each other's orbits, spinning each other in a thousand-year dance that snared the whole of space in their wake. Eshu knew that the thing at his feet was not a star, and yet he could not shake the conviction that it was somehow what a star *was*.

The rattle of a wheelbarrow touching down pulled him out of his musings. Sheeram pushed through, huffing, with Beejan close behind her.

"Hmph," said Sheeram, clearly unimpressed with the Crossroads. She set the wheelbarrow down and put her hands on her hips, surveying the ravaged hall as though daring it to impress her. "Guess we got lucky. All the other mirrors are broken."

Looking around him, Eshu saw that she was right. All of the mirrors had been shattered, one way or another—some lay broken on their backs, and others looked as though something heavy had struck them.

Eshu frowned. He didn't have Fern's gift for geometry, but something seemed odd about the pattern of broken mirrors. If the star had fallen through the roof and punched a crater into the floor, then the damage ought to have radiated out from the point of impact like the petals of a flower.

Then Tuuri, Basia, and Lali came through the last mirror in a bickering knot, and Eshu put those thoughts aside. "If you know where a jeweler's shop used to be, you're welcome to go looking," Basia was saying. "But our best bet is to find the airship landing. A lot of money changes hands there. There will be vaults, cashboxes. Safes for passengers' valuables."

"I want to hit up a bank," declared Sheeram. "Always wanted to rob a bank. Come out like a scoundrel in a city comedy, big old sack on my shoulder, whistling 'Queen Kejah's Tits' all the way home."

"If you know where any *banks* used to be in Tisaris, feel free to whistle whatever you like," Basia said witheringly. "The airship landing is at least going to be easy to find. I also want to check the Petal Fern Quarter, while we're here. Think of it as Tisaris's east side. No guarantee of cash, but plenty of valuables. Heirloom jewelry, silver plate—"

"Sounds more interesting than an airship landing. Point me toward the Fern Thing." Sheeram wrapped a nut in a wad of betel leaves, then popped it in her mouth and picked up the handles of her wheelbarrow.

As though sensing that she was about to be overruled, Basia looked to Beejan for support. He just shrugged and said, "Don't see what harm it would do to split up. You and I can take Eshu to the airship landing; Lali, Sheeram, and Tuuri can try the Petal Fern Quarter. We'll work through the evening, then meet up here again when we're done. Camp through the morning, then head home tomorrow afternoon."

"That sounds reasonable," Basia agreed. "Lali, do you mind?"

Lali just laughed. "Someone's got to keep Aunt Sheeram in line. Come on, Tuuri; you're in for a master class in swearing."

Eshu had to admire how neatly Beejan had managed to separate them from Tuuri, all under the guise of keeping Sheeram and Basia happy. When Beejan had promised not to let Tuuri hurt him, Eshu had imagined him standing between them like a bulwark, and dreaded it. He knew how readily Tuuri could shift the battlefield to his liking. But Beejan had understood, the way only a man who'd lived through it could understand, that the only way to win was to walk away.

After Basia had given the other team their directions, she led Eshu and Beejan down the long, shallow steps of the Crossroads. By now, it was early evening, and the sun was in their eyes as they dragged the wheelbarrow west along a road lined with water gardens and mimosa trees. Curious fish followed them all the way down the water's edge, nearly leaping from the water in their eagerness to be fed. Dragonflies darted between the waterlilies, their wings glinting in the sunlight.

Ahead of them, a fallen star lay half-submerged in a pond. Even through the murky water, it shed a brilliant white light. The plants around it had burned yellow and brown, and the water was full of fish bones.

It wasn't the worst thing Eshu had seen. He had seen people rotting under the punishing sun of Zumera, raining maggots on the ground; he had seen the sunken wreckage of Sharis. But somehow, that dead water lingered in his mind as though it had been burned into the back of his eyelids.

Eventually, the road left the gardens behind and began to climb. The hill cast the three of them in shadow. Eshu recognized the shape of the structure as an airship landing—the artificial plateau ringed with outbuildings; the queer shimmer in the atmosphere that hung above a network of runelines.

There was a fence with a decorative brass gate barring the way. No one was there to stop them, so Beejan heaved the gate aside and let them through.

All around them, the grounded airships lay like beached whales. Some had burned; others had been abandoned; one runeship stood shuddering in a web of lightning, a star tangled up in its runelines. It made the hair stand up on Eshu's skin to watch the electricity pulse through it like a heartbeat.

"Spread out," said Basia. "Beejan, take the ships. Stay clear of anything that looks like it's going to collapse or explode. I'll take the east. Eshu, take the west."

Eshu did as he was told. The buildings along the western side had been hit hard on the night when the stars had fallen. Stars lay gleaming amid the rubble of barracks and office buildings, workshops and waystations, and Eshu didn't dare step inside for fear of bringing the ruins down on him.

At last, he found a building that seemed only superficially damaged. A star had crashed through the red terra cotta roof, but the walls still stood, and the telescope nosing out of an upper tower seemed to promise the sort of plunder that Teyam wanted. He tried the door and found it unlocked.

Eshu stepped over the threshold, into an entry hall with wilted plants in each corner. He sang a globe of light into his hand and let it drift along the ceiling, which had been plastered and painted with the Nanjeeri constellations. The plaster was cracked, now, and had peeled away in places, but still he recognized the six legs of the Fly, the long tail of the Dragon with Four Heads.

He crept through the archway at the end of the hall. Immediately, the rotten meat smell of the dead washed over him, and he gagged and pressed his hand over his mouth and nose to stifle it.

A star lay in the center of the room. By its light, he saw the trim little desk, the slate board chalked over with a map of Nanjeer.

Eshu's chest tightened. He knew this room. He had seen it last in Thras Nadi's mirror.

The prognosticators hadn't seen their doom coming. The soldiers in their fine brigandines had been no more able to defend themselves than the fish in the star-struck pond. Numbly, Eshu closed the door on an attendant who would never return.

The six of them returned to camp beneath the cracked dome of the Crossroads about an hour before dawn. Sheeram's wheelbarrow was heaped with gold candlesticks and silver plates, jewelry ripped from dead men's hair. It was at least twice as full as Basia's, which made Sheeram unbearably smug.

"We had to leave a load of houses, too," she said between bites of smoked mutton. "Too much trouble to unbury them. And there were half a dozen rugs that would fetch a thousand zil apiece at auction, but *someone*" she shot Lali an aggrieved look, "didn't want to carry them."

"It's just efficiency," Lali insisted. "Sure, you could get a thousand zil for a rug, but they're fucking heavy. Ten hundred-zil necklaces weigh less than a tenth as much."

"And then you're trying to find buyers for ten things instead of one thing. That takes time. Don't act like I'm stupid—I know there's more than one kind of efficient." Sheeram gave their smoldering campfire a savage poke that sent up a shower of sparks. Basia was roasting carp over the embers, and the heavy smell of fish made Eshu feel sick to his stomach.

Then Tuuri sat down at Eshu's side, and Eshu nearly leapt out of his skin. "Shh, it's only me," said Tuuri gently. His fingertips brushed Eshu's hand. In the dim light of the fire, his eyes were very bright. "I'd been hoping we'd have a chance to talk tonight."

On Eshu's other side, Beejan tensed.

Met with no rebuff, Tuuri closed his hand over Eshu's and leaned in until their shoulders touched. Pins and needles prickled down Eshu's arm; every nerve sang with terror. He felt frozen, like a fledgling bird in a serpent's jaws. "I feel awful about how we left things between us," Tuuri crooned against his ear. His breath was warm on Eshu's skin. "I wish we hadn't fallen out with each other."

With a great wrench of will, Eshu yanked his hand away. He didn't bother to hide the revulsion in his voice. "You forfeited your chance to talk to me long ago. We're done. There is nothing you could say to me that would change my mind."

"I don't want to change your mind," began Tuuri, but Eshu didn't let him finish.

"Bullshit," he snapped. "All you ever did was try to change my mind! I wasn't allowed to have a single opinion you didn't approve; I wasn't allowed to have friends who weren't your friends—I couldn't be *proud* of myself unless you decided I'd earned it. And

Njo forbid I tried to criticize you! You would spin me around until I thought whatever you'd done was my fault—"

"Eshusikinde," Tuuri said, offering his hands palm-up as though in supplication. "Please. You're shouting."

"*Of course I am shouting.*" Swaying up to his feet, Eshu rounded on Tuuri, who ducked back like he was the one being menaced. "Do you understand what you did to me? I was so fucking afraid of your disapproval. And I *worshipped* you, Tuuri. I wanted nothing more than to be worthy of you. But you made me feel like I was nothing."

"Eshu," said Basia in a tone of warning. "Now might not be the time."

"Let Eshu speak," said Beejan.

Tuuri let his hands fall to his knees. "If you felt that way, I'm sorry," he said, with the inflection of every man with a *but* in reserve.

"There is no 'if' about my feelings," said Eshu. He willed iron into his voice. "I told you how I felt. You've put an 'if' into them because even now, you'd rather I doubt myself than you take responsibility for any of the shit you put me through."

"I can't talk to you when you're like this," said Tuuri.

"Good," said Eshu. "I would genuinely rather set myself on fire than talk to you again." And with that, he turned on his heel and fled the Crossroads.

Eshu passed through the water gardens, unseeing. His skin crawled so badly that he wanted to rip it off. He took a left turn at random, then a right; he stalked down a boulevard and into an empty plaza. He hated that it was empty. He hated that he was here.

He threw himself down at last in the shadow of a statue honoring some hero astride a rearing drake. The hero's head and the drake's had been smashed by a falling star, and now lay in flinders on the stone of the plaza.

Eshu wished a star would strike him down. He had known better than to pick a fight with Tuuri. There was no justice to be had in telling him what he'd done; Tuuri wasn't interested in justice. He would never apologize to Eshu because he didn't believe he'd done anything wrong.

Thumping his head back against the statue's plinth, Eshu saw Beejan approaching in the clear light of the star.

Beejan didn't say anything. He just set his club aside and sat down next to Eshu, hands folded over his lap, and gazed out into the shadows at the edge of the plaza.

"I ought to say I'm sorry for making a scene," said Eshu eventually. "But I'm not sorry. I wish I'd made a scene sooner. I wish I'd called him to account in front of everyone who ever considered him a friend and let them see how he answered." Every word tasted bitter.

"It's easy to fight something with fangs and claws," said Beejan. "It's harder to fight something that tells you it loves you. Because you're also fighting the part of yourself that wants to be loved. Believe me, I know." Beejan freed a hand and laid it on Eshu's knee. His palm was warm and broad, and gentle in a way that felt worse than pressure. At least pressure would've given Eshu something to push against.

Eshu took Beejan's hand in his and clasped it hard. "We could leave tonight. Both of us. Leave your grandmother and all her machinations behind."

Beejan stiffened. "It's crossed my mind," he admitted. "More than once. But Kulmeni needs *something*, and fuck if anyone else has a plan."

Eshu gestured over the plaza, taking in the empty stones stretching on into darkness. "Is this what Kulmeni needs? The plunder of Nanjeer's ruined cities?"

"It needs someone to beat the nightmares back," said Beejan. "Not just the kind of work Aunt Sheeram and I do—you didn't see the city before we stormed the palace. People were afraid. Now, at least, they're starting to live their lives again."

"Your grandmother doesn't care about the people."

Beejan looked away. "She cares more than the last prince did, at least. More than Lady Valikram would."

"She explicitly said 'Fuck the people.'"

"Yeah. Yeah, she did." Sighing, Beejan climbed to his feet again and offered Eshu his hand. "Anyway. I know she's a piece of shit. Every choice is shit. But I'm staying. Not for her—for Kulmeni."

The star at Eshu's back shone on Beejan's outstretched hand, casting a long shadow across the plaza. "I just want you to understand," said Eshu. His longing for compassion ached like a void in his chest. "When your grandmother speaks, I hear Tuuri in her voice. She has that same ugly way of crushing you to nothing with a word. And I wouldn't put anything I treasured in Tuuri's hands—let alone a city."

Beejan swallowed. "I know. I hear it, too."

Eshu put his hand in Beejan's and let himself be pulled.

CHAPTER 17: SHARP EDGES

An anxious energy filled the dining room of the Warp and Weft when Fern came down for breakfast. Conversations rose, tangled, overlapped; now and then, strident voices tore through the murmur of discontent, and everyone glanced up in alarm. At one table, a pair of older men got to their feet as though they meant to come to blows, and Kurosh Hura himself sailed across the room like an arrow to urge the men back to their chairs. He topped up their coffee, and that seemed to pacify them.

Zumera and *Tisaris* were on everyone's lips. "They say Zumera's fallen," said a diner at the table beside Fern's, between bites of pickled beans. He apparently didn't know that Fern was the one who'd said it. "And the prince has known about it for weeks—"

"She's not the prince of Zumera," snapped the woman who shared his table, peeling an orange with her thumbnail. "She's had her eyes on Kulmeni, and I say, good for her."

"Where do you think your sugar comes from?" the man replied. "And those oranges you like so much, where do you think those come from?"

The woman huffed and shoved an orange segment into her mouth.

It was no better in the markets. People flocked around spice merchants' tables, demanding salt and sugar; as Fern watched, a lean old androgyne swiped away the price of salt and marked it up a full ten zil a sack. The crowd gave a cry of outraged betrayal.

"What are you doing?" someone shouted, her voice ratcheting high with alarm. "Put it back, you money-gouging pricks!"

"Sorry, love; it's the law of the marketplace," said a man behind the counter, who was weighing salt into sale bags. "The price will go back down when we're sure of our supply."

"There's no more salt coming," the woman answered sharply. "Tisaris is a crater. Everyone there is dead! And no one's heard from Xhonai in at least a month—"

"You must think I'm some wild god from a hero story, if you think I can make salt out of thin air." The man tied off a bag and set it behind the counter with the rest. "Try another shop if you don't like our prices."

"I'll take this to the prince, you see if I don't."

"Take it to the prince if you like. Take it all the way to the Anjali River if you think she can do better."

The woman stalked away, her market basket empty and her face purple with rage.

All the way to the university, Fern ran into knots of people talking about the fall of Tisaris. Some were squatting over torn bedsheets, painting protest banners and tying them to poles; others shared tips on which merchants still had sugar or coffee or lemons. Still others sipped sweetbush tea in opulent tea gardens and deliberated whether any of it was true.

On the east bank, she saw soldiers in aristocrats' livery patrolling the streets. If they meant to calm the growing panic, they had the opposite effect—every time they marched past in their bright scale armor, citizens paused to watch them with wide, wary eyes.

Outside the university, a pair of carriage drivers waiting for a fare gossiped mutinously. "We put her on that throne," one said. "We can take her off again."

"She should've known better," the other agreed. "Now she's given us a taste for beheading princes."

Fern hurried past. Her gut churned. She'd meant to start *something*, but it hadn't been this. She didn't know what she'd thought it would be, if not this. Suddenly it seemed naïve to have ever imagined it would be anything else.

Inside the wizards' dormitory, at least, the common room still smelled reassuringly of stale coffee. "Welcome back!" said Mnoro, fluttering across the room in her bright blue gown to kiss Fern's cheeks. "I found you a microscope. You've got your samples?"

"Right here," answered Fern, and patted her pockets.

They set up by the window in the bedroom, where the light was best. The microscope was a different design from the kind Fern had used back in Matis—it had only one ocular lens instead of two—but the stage setup was the same, and that was what she needed.

While she and Mnoro started preparing the plates, Usamkartha shuffled over to the work table, a blanket clasped around his shoulders like a cloak. Every time Fern's gaze wandered away from him, the shape of him shifted. He was a dark stream in a sun-dappled wood, a peacock with feathers of iridescent black, a loose coil of smoke on a wayward breeze. He was the sounding-song of an ice whale, vanishing into the inky depths of the southern seas.

He was a middle-aged man with a migraine, and he pulled down the shade on the latticed window as though the thin sunlight pained him.

"Um," said Fern. "Is there anything I can do for—"

"Not unless you know how to reassemble someone on the most basic conceptual level," Usamkartha grumbled. He took a deep draught of coffee and winced. "Just get on with it. If I'm dying, I'd rather die learning something."

His breath came in slow, rasping gasps. He was a wildfire; he was a snowfall at sea. He was a new and distant star, bursting into brightness and dimming from view. Tigers had torn his body apart and strung it like a necklace through the trees.

Fern looked away and started assembling her sample vials. She felt sick.

She dipped a dropper into the sample from the Mirrorlands stream, then caught a droplet between two glass plates. With a clean dropper, she measured out another plate's worth of water from the Anjali River. *You've done this a dozen times*, she told herself. *Just like checking the health of a watershed.* She slid the Anjali plate into the microscope and turned the magnification knob until the tiny creatures in the water came into focus.

A whole world of microscopic organisms lay pressed between plates of glass no thicker than fingernails. Unfamiliar diatoms drifted in green shoals across the backing light, some shaped like grains of rice and some like fish scales or fans; swift, single-celled creatures darted across the plate like soap bubbles on a breeze. Vast insect larvae squirmed and thrashed amid their smaller brethren like sea monsters in a hero story.

She'd seen a hundred samples like it at university, some under a microscope and others in books of micrography etchings. Someone at the university in Kulmeni could probably tell her exactly which insects she had trapped in her sample, and which instar they'd reached in their growth.

Her hands shook; she was half-certain a careless twitch would send her samples scattering across the floor. Bracing her wrists against the table to steady herself, she swapped in the sample from the Mirrorlands.

It was quieter than the water from the Anjali. No great worms twitched in the water, desperate to grow wings; no bits of river weed lay across the sample like panes of stained glass. But the swift single-celled creatures were there, and the diatoms were there: faint green specks that floated through the water of a land that knew no sunlight.

"It's not just the snails," she said under her breath. "It's the whole—I don't know what to call it. Diatoms and amoebae and things I don't know the names for. The water here and the water in the Mirrorlands flow into each other, and everything that lives in them goes with it. They're all mixed up with each other now."

"Is there a chance we can stabilize this place?" Mnoro asked. "This is a susceptible zone; it's responsive to ambient magic, and more so to directed magic. We may be able to force the boundaries back into place."

Usamkartha rested his hand on his chin. "It couldn't be done with pure incantation. We'd need a network of runelines that spanned the entire city, and even then, one bad earthquake would tear through them as though they were spider webs. If we had more wizards, I'd say it was just barely within the realm of possibility, but—" He shuddered, then broke into a murmuration of blackbirds that sang and wheeled and beat their wings against the ceiling. Then the birds faded to flame-edged ash and left Usamkartha doubled over at the workbench with his head cradled in his hands.

It hurt to watch him like that. It hurt more, knowing there was nothing Fern could do about it.

Usamkartha looked up at Fern and bared his teeth. Pain lined his brows. "Get on with what you were doing," he said. "Pay me no mind."

Hurriedly, Fern took out her sample vial of Mirrorlands sand and tipped a little bit onto a new glass plate. "Sometimes, sand can tell you about the geological history of a place," she said as she swapped plates in the microscope. Anything to distract them all while Usamkartha gathered up his dignity. "Like—did you know, the Parja Salt Flats used to be underwater? You can kind of guess from the sedimentation, but if you look at the sand under a microscope, it's actually all little shells and coral and things. So geologists think it must have been part of the ocean, hundreds of thousands of years ago. Or longer, maybe."

"The Mirrorlands don't have a geological history," groused Usamkartha. "They're an unstable, incoherent assemblage of dreams, continually recreated at the moment they're perceived."

"That's clearly not true," said Mnoro. "If it were, the Mirrorlands wouldn't be able to seep through the cracks in our reality. There clearly is something there when we aren't observing it, even if it's only water and air."

"Oh," said Fern, and sat back as another piece of information clicked into place. "That explains the mist. It's not magic, it's just physics. The warm, wet air in Kulmeni hits the cold, dry air from the Mirrorlands, and you get mist."

Mnoro gave Usamkartha a sidelong smirk. "See? It's physics."

"Physics is a squalid rookery of glorified theorems," said Usamkartha. Fern was pretty sure that meant he didn't have an actual argument.

She put her eye to the microscope again, rolling the focusing knob in painful increments. Grains of sand blurred across her vision—first large and diffuse, then slowly coming clear.

Here, a fragment of violet fluorite cloven into a perfect octahedron. There, a piece of sapphire, crystallized in radiant six-pointed stars. A hundred colors of quartz, clear and cloud-pink and citrine and amethyst. The tessellating triangles of diamonds, ground against each other until they'd become infinitely fine. For a long, horrifying moment, Fern glimpsed Zumera in microcosm, and she forgot to breathe.

"It's not just here," she said, and pushed back from the table so hard that the microscope rattled. "Shit. *Shit!* It's not just Kulmeni, it's everywhere. Zumera. Sharis. Probably Tisaris, too. The Mirrorlands are bleeding through everywhere."

"Your singular experience aside, traveling mirrors are *not* storm drains," said Usamkartha waspishly. "They don't *leak*. If what you're describing is plausible, there should be some kind of residual emission that we can trace from a mirror." He rose to his feet with a full-body crackle of bones, resettled his blanket cape, and strode off with an air of singular purpose.

"I don't think that's what Fern is saying," began Mnoro, but Usamkartha was already out the door, so she gave Fern a helpless shrug and followed him.

They passed through the empty cloister with Usamkartha at their head; he was a comet, a diving hawk, a ship sinking into a deep ocean trench. Fern and Mnoro crossed the threshold into the lecture hall with stardust in their hair and saltwater lines crusting their shoes.

He led them into a room with three mirrors in it, where the walls had been worked in dizzying geometric designs that shone with gold leaf. *A cognitive locus*, thought Fern. It still helped, in some indefinable way, to know the name of this place. "Here," said Usamkartha, and he immediately began sketching runes on the floor with a piece of chalk. "Mnoro, make yourself useful. This will be only half as annoying with two of us working. What was the argument for—"

Whatever rune he wanted, Fern never heard, because at that point someone in the corridor screamed.

The tiled floor rang under booted feet. Fern smothered a shout of alarm, pressing herself back against the wall in a fruitless attempt to hide. The soldiers found her anyway.

They entered the room like a pack of hunting wolves and moved to secure every corner. There were five of them, all dressed in shining scale mail, with a magnolia crest on their shoulders. Their blades were out; behind their armored masks, Fern glimpsed sneering lips, cruel eyes.

She knew that she was about to die. She could almost feel their swords slicing cold across her throat.

They drove Fern to stand with Mnoro and Usamkartha in the center of the room. Usamkartha shuddered and flickered like a guttering candle, now a cascade of leaves in a windstorm, now a tiger with eyes of flame.

"We are here on behalf of Lady Valikram and the Sovereign

Lords' Alliance," said one of the soldiers, who wore an extra strand of braid over her right shoulder. "If you cooperate, you will not be harmed."

"With what do you expect us to cooperate?" Usamkartha demanded.

The soldier gestured with her chin at the mirrors standing close around them. "These traveling mirrors and their keepers are now the property of the Sovereign Lords' Alliance."

"You can't simply declare us property," snapped Usamkartha, drawing himself to his full height. When he had been curled up over his book like a shrimp, he had been laughable; with his shoulders back and his blanket clutched against his breast, he had a dignity to rival that of kings. "I refuse. Take that back to Lady Valikram, whoever she is—I *refuse*."

The soldier raised her blade. "We are authorized to kill you. Don't be a fool, old man."

Usamkartha glanced at Mnoro. His eyes were stone and star and shadow, velvet and moss and bone. "Finish my manuscript," he said. "List yourself as an author if you must, but my name comes first on the byline. Do you understand that? *My name comes first*."

Then he smashed his fist through a mirror, and the world broke.

The walls melted into honey and blood. Roses ran riot between the mirrors, and their thorns were blades were teeth were tongues and then the room gave a long convulsive swallow. The gilded geometry of the room unfolded into an orrery, planets screaming down infinite rings of iron and flame.

The leader of the soldiers ran, and her people followed. All but two of them made it out the door before blistering black pitch rained down from the ceiling and the tiles dissolved into a maze of razor blades.

All around Fern and Mnoro fluttered a swarm of incandescent white moths, and within the compass of those wings, no harm came to them.

"Do you know what he did?" Fern asked, almost shouting to make her voice heard over the howl of wind and the euphoric clamor of bells.

"I don't know," Mnoro answered, and shook her head. Her face was streaked with tears.

Together they crossed the heaving sea of the floor to the doorway, where the water receded and left them on dry tile again. When Fern chanced a glance behind them, the three mirrors stood tall in a pristine room, and the interlocking gold-leaf polygons of the walls had shuddered back to true.

Fern's breath caught up with her like a blow to the chest. She sank against the corridor wall, panting, trying to gather the pieces of her brain together enough to make a plan.

Her hand found its way into her pocket and brushed against two familiar lumps of rock. *Eshu's runestones*, she thought. "Here, take this," she said, and offered one to Mnoro. "It might keep those soldiers from finding us."

Mnoro studied the runework a moment. Her expression softened, as though she recognized something about it—the handwriting, perhaps. The grammar of the arguments. Some tiny trace of Eshu that she knew as well as his face. "Thank you," Mnoro said, and closed her hand on the runestone.

Fern watched until her vision slid away, and Mnoro faded from view. Only then did she grip her runestone tight in her fist and let herself disappear.

In the empty corridor, Mnoro found Fern's hand and asked, "What now?"

Fern considered. They could try to sneak back into the dormitory to gather up Mnoro's belongings, but there were likely to be more soldiers there. The soldiers probably knew the east bank well, if it was where people with money lived; Fern hardly knew it at all, so there would be no advantage in hiding here.

Kurosh Hura was no friend to either Prince Teyam or Lady

Valikram. He might be persuaded to look the other way, if Fern came back from a riotous night with a friend looking for shelter. "If we can get across the river, we might be able to hide you on the other side," whispered Fern. "With the city the way it is, they'll have a hard time looking for you."

"I've gambled on worse plans," Mnoro answered, and gripped Fern's hand tighter.

They crept through the streets together under the red light of some distant villa burning. The air was thick with smoke and ash, the roads choked with townsfolk panicking; every now and then, a troop of soldiers came swarming down the street, and Fern and Mnoro tucked themselves into alleyways until the soldiers had passed.

It took them three aching hours to make it to the riverside. Every time Mnoro begged to sit down, Fern stood watch with her heart beating rabbit-quick, gripping her runestone until she thought her hand would bruise. Every time, the soldiers passed them by.

At long last, from a waterside pathway that tracked the Anjali River, Fern made out the arch of the Heron's Bridge. "We're almost there," said Fern under her breath. "Do you need to rest?"

"Just a few minutes," Mnoro said miserably. "It's been years since I did this much walking."

Fern heard Mnoro sink down onto the lime flagstones with a groan. She cast an anxious glance behind them, searching for the flash of moonlight on steel. There was nothing behind them but bougainvilleas, stirring gently in the breeze. They were right beneath the retaining wall here; if they were cornered, they'd have nowhere to go but the river.

When she looked ahead, someone stood in their path. She wore a tattered black hood and a white porcelain mask, and her eyeless gaze peeled away Eshu's runework as though it were paper.

Fern cast about for a weapon—a stick, a spar, a bit of broken concrete; all she had was her pocket knife, and she knew the

Crowtaker could take a blow from that and laugh. She pulled out her stupid little knife anyway and put herself between the Crowtaker and Mnoro, ready to give her life dearly if she had to.

Then a spear of driftwood and whitewater came down on the pathway, and a towering woman clad in fish scale mail emerged from the river.

"Go home, scavenger," the woman said in a voice like a flood current. She shed water in sheets. "You have no place here."

"I have a place everywhere," said the Crowtaker, with a rattling corpse fly laugh. "Do not think the Lady Valikram does not see my shadow behind her when she looks into the mirror."

"Kulmeni has survived a thousand years," snarled the woman from the river. "I have watched my city grow from the muck; I have fed her and sheltered her and brought her the world's bounty. She will last a thousand more, and she will never know despair."

Her spear flashed out, swift and keen—and passed through the Crowtaker's robe as though it were only vapor. Still laughing, the Crowtaker began to sing, and the bougainvilleas withered at her song.

Every heartbeat ached. It felt like Fern was trying to pump iron through her veins. There was no time to run—she found Mnoro's hand again and asked, "Do you trust me?"

"Yes," Mnoro answered.

"The river's a mirror—jump!"

If she was wrong, they'd drown with the Crowtaker's dirge in their ears. Fern closed her eyes, held her breath, and jumped.

They plunged beneath the surface of the river and fell, still dry, to the endless Mirrorlands sands.

Fern sat up with her hands on her knees, still half-certain that the Crowtaker was coming for them. But as the seconds shaded into minutes, she heard only the soft tick of sand on sand and the pounding of her own heart. "I think we're safe," she said, and let her runestone go. The broad, empty expanse of dunes seemed to swallow her voice. "Unless we run into Tuuri here, maybe."

"Don't give this place any ideas." Mnoro gathered herself up and began brushing sand off of her skirts. In the dim light, it was hard to make out her expression, but Fern thought she saw tears glittering in Mnoro's eyes.

Fern didn't blame her. They'd watched Usamkartha come apart at the seams, and there had been no time to grieve for him. There'd been no time for anything but running.

"I didn't know him the way you did," said Fern slowly. "But for what it's worth, I wish I had."

"He was such a headache of a man." Mnoro swiped the back of her hand over her eyes. "He had no patience for anyone. He didn't have time for optimism. He didn't trust it. Sometimes I wondered if the only things that were real to him were the ones that hurt. But he..." Her voice shook. "He loved learning and teaching more than anyone else I know. He could explain things in a way that cut to the bone of them. And fuck me, I'm going to miss him."

He sounded like a hard man to be friends with—but he had been Mnoro's friend, and that was what mattered. Fern got to her feet and paced across the sand to Mnoro, hesitating just out of arm's reach. "Would it help if I held you?" she asked.

"Not really," said Mnoro. "But hold me anyway."

So Fern gathered Mnoro up in her arms and held her, and Mnoro held her back. For a long moment, there was only the warmth and solidity of that embrace—the softness of Mnoro's stomach against Fern's ribs; the surprising strength of her arms around Fern's shoulders. The shudders that wracked her as she tried to pull herself back together.

Even if it didn't help, it felt like it meant something to be there with her in her grief.

Eventually, Mnoro let her go. "Fern," she said, and her voice was steady again. "While we're here, let's go to Kondala City."

"So you really don't know what happened to it?" Fern asked.

Mnoro shook her head. "They told us from the beginning what had happened to Tisaris. But Kondala City—they told us they didn't know yet, and we had no way of getting anything else out of them. We assumed that meant it was bad."

Fern remembered Eshu's songs of Kondala City, with its gardens full of pomegranates and its bright copper roofs and the Hall of Ways curtained in green, and her heart sank. After all the jungles she'd crossed, all the mirrors she'd walked through, she'd somehow managed to convince herself that if she could only *get* there, everything would be fine. "Let's go, then," she agreed, before she could talk herself out of it. "Let's go, right now."

They started off toward the mountains, across the glittering dunes. Fern led them down into a dry wash, where a scattering of black rocks seemed to make a path to guide their way. "Where are we going?" she asked. "I mean—where in Kondala City?"

Mnoro thought for a moment. "There's a shrine way up in the hills—Njowa Ya'lele. Njo's Rest. It's far enough away from the city center that it might still be standing."

"Eshu told me about it," said Fern. "It had a bell, right?"

"A big brass bell," Mnoro agreed. "It'd ring out prayers for the whole city, morning and evening. Always just a heartbeat ahead of every other temple. My mothers used to take me up there to hear the songs on holy days—you had to start walking while it was still dark if you wanted to catch the dawn prayers. There would be hundreds of us, all walking up that long switchback road in the dark, rubbing sleep out of our eyes and singing. Njo, I miss the singing."

"Could you sing one of those songs?" Fern asked, as gently as she could. "It might help us find our way."

For long moments, they walked together in silence. The Mirrorlands were quiet but for the crunch of their shoes on the rock and the slow rhythm of breath. Then, first softly and then with growing strength, Mnoro began to sing.

Her voice was nothing like Eshu's. His pealed out deep and resonant, starting low in the chest and ringing out like thunder; rage and triumph roughened his edges, and grief and joy sharpened them. His music was something shattering—something elemental and sublime.

Mnoro's voice, though, was clear as water, and every note rang true. She sang the long road, the oxcarts and the golden reeds in blossom; she sang aunties shushing babes and old men gossiping as they walked. She sang children still half-asleep in their fathers' arms, children running ahead up the long hill, children everywhere laughing and fighting and beating prayer drums as loud as they could. She sang the long black horizon touched at last with orange light, and the pealing of the bell, and families stopping where they stood to kneel in prayer.

The prayer song rolled out across the Mirrorlands in a lilting minor key, mourning for something that Fern had never lost and rejoicing in something that she had never had, and her heart ached with a longing to understand.

Ahead, the wash began to climb, and they climbed with it until the sun shone on their shoulders and the sky faded to blue overhead.

Before them lay a temple of elegant white spires and shining copper domes, with streamers of green silk blowing from their finials. A grove of cedar trees stood sentinel around it, perfuming the air with their warm, woody scent.

For a moment, relief passed through Fern in a wave. *It's still here*, she thought. *If nothing else—this place is still here.*

Then she looked out over the valley, and her breath hitched. Where the city had been, nothing remained but a perfect circle of black glass.

CHAPTER 18: PASSAGE OF ARMS

Eshu stepped out of the mirror and onto broken glass.

The mirror room rippled and shuddered around him as though it was breathing. Veins of gold pulsed in time with his heartbeat; flowers sprouted and blossomed and withered in the time it took to blink, then broke into riotous moth scales that flashed a thousand hues and burned to cinders. The kaleidoscope of reality turned, and Eshu turned within it. He tried to speak, but his words turned into golden carp and flitted away into a deep welter of river weeds.

At once, he understood that something unfathomable had happened here.

He stumbled over the bodies of two soldiers in Lady Valikram's colors. He couldn't tell if they were dead or alive. He wasn't sure he wanted to know. They were made of iron and ivory and ash, meat and melody; their blood stained his shoes red-black. He scrambled toward the door, into the reassuring sanity of the university hall.

From the outside, he could see only the mirror room with its intricate geometric tiles and its pierced-copper lanterns casting a warm, orange glow.

The rest of the expedition filed through after him, into the wild tangle of chaos and then into the hallway. "Shit," said Sheeram, wild-eyed, chin jerking from one side of the hall to the other as though she was seeing phantoms. "What was that?"

"A localized collapse in reality," Tuuri said. He looked far too calm for what he'd just seen.

Basia frowned. "Is this related to Usamkartha's—"

"Probably," said Tuuri shortly. "In any case, we should be much more concerned about the soldiers. Not yours, were they?"

Basia shook her head.

Tuuri smirked. "I didn't think so. Where there are two, there are probably more."

"And us with two barrowloads of treasure." Sheeram spat to one side. "Beejan. See if you can find us a way out."

"No promises," said Beejan, but he sloped off down the hall all the same.

Long, tense minutes passed. Lali trimmed her nails with her knife. Sheeram kept shifting her grip on her sword hilt as though her palms were sweating. Basia ventured back into the mirror room long enough to seize a sword from one of the soldiers, and came back with ice frosting her hair.

Finally, Beejan's silhouette filled up the far end of the hall, and Eshu breathed out. "There are soldiers all through the university," Beejan said. "I heard them say they were looking for the wizards."

"Wonderful," muttered Tuuri. "We're potential hostages."

"I'd call that an optimistic assumption." Beejan glanced at the wheelbarrows uneasily. "We need to hide these. See if we can get them across the river by boat—they'll be watching the bridge. It would be a good idea to split up, if we can."

"I've got one of these," said Sheeram, thumping her hand down on the side of a wheelbarrow. "Lali, you're a stone ox. You get the other one."

"Thanks," said Lali. She nudged her brother. "You want to come?"

"I'll worry about getting the wizards out," said Beejan. "Take the service doors. They're not watching those as closely. You might be able to shovel some dirt over the loot to hide the shine."

"Then I'll run interference," said Basia. "I know this area. I've got a few tricks." She sprinted light-footed down the corridor, and was lost to view.

Lali kissed Beejan's cheek. "Stay safe. See you on the west side." Then she and Sheeram set off together, pulling their heavy wheelbarrows into the waiting darkness.

"Well, come on," said Beejan, shooting Tuuri a dark look. "No sense hanging around here, waiting for someone to find us."

"Oh, I think not," Tuuri answered. An infuriating little smile played about his lips. "Much as I've enjoyed our reunion, I fear that matters of state are becoming rather fraught here in Kulmeni. It's past time I took my leave."

"What about Usamkartha?" Eshu demanded. "And Mnoro, if she's here—"

Tuuri shrugged. "I thought you'd rather set yourself on fire than talk to me. Do me a favor, will you? After I go, break the mirror behind me."

With a burst of song, Eshu flung up a wall of thorns over the door to the mirror room. He sang it dense and thick and curling, each barb sharp and wicked as heartache. "No. You don't get to say cryptic shit like that and then stroll off into oblivion while I puzzle it out. Why do you want me to break the mirror? Tell me something I'll believe, and I might even do it. Just be honest with me for one fucking time in your life."

Tuuri rolled his eyes as though saying a prayer for patience. "You know that I can lay down a rune to unravel your work."

Beejan brought his club down on his palm with a satisfying smack. "Not faster than I can unravel your skull, I'll wager."

"Excellent! Let your meathead boyfriend beat me to death." Tuuri threw up his hands in mock-surrender. "Very refined. Very dignified. You've come a long way, Eshusikinde—"

"You don't get to use that name with me." Eshu stepped forward until he was nearly chest to chest with Tuuri. The vines behind Tuuri were as green and as cruel as his eyes. "I just want an answer. Does it really cost you so much to give me that?"

Sighing, Tuuri lowered his hands to his sides. "Since you so *pointedly* insist. Take down your thorns, and you'll have an answer."

Eshu didn't trust him. He didn't think he'd ever trust Tuuri again. But if Tuuri needed one last surrender to make him spill his secrets, it was a small enough sacrifice. Eshu would never again lay anything he valued on the altar of Tuuri's pride. He stepped back a pace and sang the thorns down into the cracks between the stones.

Anyway, if it came down to a footrace, Beejan was faster.

Tuuri gave him a long, calculating look. "You know that the Mirrorlands have changed. You've seen the empty hills. Do you know why the mirror network has broken, Eshu?" The nickname grated in his mouth.

Eshu shook his head. "It has something to do with what's wrong with Kulmeni."

"This is true—but those are two separate effects of the same problem." Humming a tiny melody, Tuuri sketched a glistening slab of stone in the palm of his hand. At first, Eshu thought it was made of marble; as Tuuri's song picked out the details, though, he realized that it had been crafted of sand. "Have you ever built a sand castle?" Tuuri asked lightly.

Eshu thought of the High Summer huts, crafted of reeds and twigs and flowers. He thought of the blanket forts he'd built with Mnoro, two years and a lifetime ago. "No," he said, "but I get the idea."

"Imagine poking a finger through to make a window." Tuuri drove his finger through one of the castle's towers until Eshu could see his chest through the hole. "The sand is in tension with itself. If you're lucky, it will hold together. But the more holes you make, the greater the strain becomes." Suddenly, the towers were shot through with shafts of light; the castle walls were riddled with holes, as though they had weathered a cannonade.

Still, the castle stood. Tuuri tilted his head, evaluating the effect. "But eventually, inevitably, the castle will collapse. Perhaps you're *very* good at building sandcastles. Perhaps your castle is made of cement. But one day, a tide runs too high, or some idiot pokes a hole where it doesn't belong, and the whole thing falls in on itself." With a sweep of his hand, Tuuri dashed the image to nothingness, then delicately dusted off his palms. "Do you understand this metaphor, Eshu? Or should I put mirrors on either side of these holes to make it more explicit?"

Cold rage rose in Eshu's breast. "How long have you known this was going to happen?" he asked between clenched teeth. "Mirrors are your life's work. How long have you known?"

Tuuri raised his hands. "I wouldn't say anyone *knew*. It was a theory. In professional circles, it's been theorized for over a century. Almost as long as there have been traveling mirrors. Of course, no one expected it would happen for millennia. Certainly not in our lifetimes."

Eshu wanted to scream. All those times when Tuuri had taken him traveling behind the mirrors, whirling between Cheresse and Ras Kir'uun and Kondala in a day, he had *known* that they were crossing a collapsing bridge together. He'd known that when it fell, Sharis and Zumera and Tisaris would fall with it. He had known, and he had danced across that bridge anyway, because he had never met a problem that was his responsibility to fix.

The people who made mirrors had known for longer than either of them had been alive, and somehow they'd buried that information where other wizards hadn't even known to look for it.

"So it breaks first where the holes began," said Beejan eventually. "Cities with traveling mirrors."

Tuuri smirked. "Perhaps he's not as much a meathead as I thought. Yes, cities with traveling mirrors. Although I expect the effects will spread to other reflective surfaces, as well. Even water might be reflective enough to erode the Mirrorlands' boundaries."

Fern had said the effects seemed to be worst near the water. "And so you're just going to leave the whole world broken behind you and jaunt off into the Mirrorlands?" Eshu demanded. "Why should you get to—"

"Let him go," said Beejan.

Eshu flung an accusatory arm out toward Tuuri. "He needs to face justice for what he's done. For what he's allowed to happen. Give me one reason why we should let him go, after all of the shit he's kept from us."

Beejan shrugged. "Because then he'll be gone. I don't trust him in my city. I don't trust him with you. So let him go. Maybe he'll find a way out, or maybe a hungry ghost will make a lunch of him. Either way, he's not our problem anymore."

It was a good reason. Eshu's shoulders sagged. He looked over at Tuuri and shook his head wearily. "Fine. Get out."

"And you'll break the mirror behind me?"

Eshu glanced into the mirror room, with its deceptively clean lines. Shards of glass lay scattered on the floor. "Do you really think it will help?"

"Who knows?" Still smiling, Tuuri strode into the room and up to the unbroken mirror. He turned back one last time, made an extravagant bow, and said, "Goodbye, Eshusikinde."

And with that, he was gone.

Eshu clenched his fists until his nails dug into his palms. "Let's get out of here," he said.

"You sure you don't want to break the mirror?" asked Beejan.

"I don't want to break it. Because I know less than nothing about the mechanics of the mirror network, I'm basing my decision solely on how much of an asshole Tuuri was to me. The mirror stays."

"Harsh but fair." Beejan hooked his club to his belt and laced his fingers together behind his head. "So, where are we headed? Odds are, no one's looking for us specifically yet. We could probably just go home."

"There is no place I would rather be right now than in your bed," said Eshu. He stepped into Beejan's space and let his brow rest in the crook of Beejan's neck. "Take me home, please. Wreck me. I need to get his voice out of my head."

Beejan grinned and kissed his temple. "I'll wreck you as much as you like, sweetheart."

The way Beejan led them, it was only a few short blocks from the university to the Heron's Bridge. If Eshu kept his gaze straight ahead, he could almost see shops and boulevards wheeling into place in the periphery; cobblestones laid themselves, and trees burst into leaf and blossom. Fires flickered on distant hillsides. Shouts rang over the city, raw with smoke and rage. Behind them, Eshu imagined the city dissolving again into formless sand.

Near the bridge, Beejan put a hand in front of Eshu's chest and pulled him behind a hedge. Peering around the thick leaves, Eshu made out a troop of soldiers guarding the bridge, torchlight gleaming on their mail. He couldn't tell how many there were, but they shifted anxiously in the mist, and they kept their hands on their weapons.

"Is there another way around?" Eshu whispered. "Much as I love watching you fight, I'm afraid this is a bit beyond our caliber."

"Relax," said Beejan, slinging his arm around Eshu's shoulders. "I've been running in this city almost as long as I've been alive. You think I don't know how to keep my head down?" And in a matter of seconds, Eshu watched Beejan transform himself.

He flipped down the collar of his jacket, the way the dockworkers wore theirs, and tied up his trousers at the knee. When he rose, he didn't straighten all the way; he hunched his broad, straight shoulders and let his arms hang heavy at his sides. His jaw slid back, emphasizing the bulge of his double chin.

Something slackened in his face. The keen, inquisitive light seemed to go out of his eyes, and his shapely cheeks hung lax down to his jowls. Before Eshu's eyes, Beejan became just another exhausted working man who'd done a double shift and was looking forward to getting home for a smoke and a meal.

It wasn't magic. It was an art, and one that Beejan had spent his whole life learning. "Ready?" asked Beejan, offering his arm. For a moment, his luminous smile gave him away.

Quelling a traitorous grin, Eshu took his arm and let Beejan escort him across the bridge.

Lady Valikram's soldiers were watching the bridge, and Beejan shuffled right past with a mumbled *Good evening* and a respectful dip of his head. Not one of the soldiers gave Eshu or Beejan a second glance—Beejan's runed club swung against Eshu's knee, and the soldiers seemed not to even see it. They were common folk, and thus they were beneath notice.

They touched down on the far side of the bridge, where troops in some other aristocrat's livery were holding the line. "Good evening, folks," Beejan said again, with a bland and perfunctory deference that worked like sorcery.

"Careful, lads," one soldier said stiffly as they passed. She was a weathered-looking woman with her hair in a tight pigtail, and although her eyes were kind, her voice betrayed no feeling. "We're getting reports of fires in the city. Come running if the fire brigades aren't getting there fast enough."

"Thank you," Beejan answered. "You're a good one."

For half a dozen blocks, Eshu fought the urge to look back over his shoulder for signs of pursuit. At any moment, he expected to hear an outraged cry as the spell broke and the soldiers realized they'd been deceived. But the city wheeled around them, reconfiguring itself as they walked, and eventually Eshu let himself believe that they'd really gotten away with it.

They would have made it all the way back to Beejan's place, if a mob hadn't turned the corner just as they were crossing the street.

The crowd swept them up, a roaring torrent of flame and eyes and banners daubed with blood-red paint. The shouting was so loud that Eshu felt it in his chest. He tasted smoke and blood. Bodies pressed against him from every side, urgent and unrelenting; someone's elbow caught him in the ribs, and he gagged as a red wave of pain washed over him. If he so much as stumbled, he'd be trampled. They wouldn't even notice his body.

Beejan gripped Eshu's arm tighter as the crowd bore them forward, and Eshu let himself be driftwood on their current.

The flood broke at last in a city square lined with soldiers. In the center of the green, beneath a hundred blazing lanterns, stood a platform fluttering with aristocrats' banners. Eshu recognized Lady Valikram's turquoise emblem at the center, the magnolia picked out in thread of gold; the rest he'd never seen before, but there were at least a dozen colors and designs.

He looked uneasily around him. Now that the crowd had begun to still, he could make out the writing on the banners. *Death to the Liar Prince* read one; on another, *Zumera* and *Tisaris* were crossed out, with *Kulmeni* written beneath them.

If anyone here recognized Beejan as Teyam's grandson, they were both of them fucked. "We have to get out of here," Eshu said against Beejan's ear, but the thunder of the crowd swallowed his voice.

A cacophonous cheer rippled through the crowd. At the platform, Lady Valikram mounted the steps with the Anjali River at her side. Some people screamed; others raised their torches; some threw flowers and paper streamers across the stage, showering Valikram with petals. She stood with her arms raised, accepting their praise until the roar of the crowd quieted at last.

She wore all white today, as though their praise had remade her into a pillar of hottest flame. Her spectacles flashed in the torchlight. "My friends," she began, turning to take in the throng. Even from a distance, her face shone with warmth and health. "You have come here today because you know in your hearts what is right. You have heard the lies of the so-called prince, who bought her throne with the head of Prince Vahid—"

"Murderer!" someone shouted, and the crowd took up the chant until Eshu's head rang with it.

When the crowd subsided again, Lady Valikram's expression was solemn. "You have heard her tell you to listen. You have heard her tell you to wait. You have heard her tell you for a month that word from Zumera and Tisaris was coming—but now we know, beyond doubt, that there is no help for us there!"

The answering howl of rage sent birds shuddering from the trees.

"Teyam Acala is a liar and a criminal," Lady Valikram said, and in her voice was all the righteous venom of a woman who'd earned her revenge. "All Kulmeni knows it. She and her brood of thieves have plagued our roads and rivers for decades, pumping vhesha into our slums and money out of our coffers. When the city broke, she rode our disaster like a wave. She played on your fears to claw her way beyond her station. She promised you strength where Prince Vahid had been weak; she promised you freedom where he kept you bound. Now I ask you: *Do you feel free?*"

The answering *No* was a vast wall of sound.

"You have been more than patient," said Lady Valikram. "You are people of the Anjali! You have known floods that swallowed the rice fields and washed the year's silkworms away. You have lost houses! Livestock! Family! And still you have endured. Kulmeni is the lotus of the Anjali, and we will always rise above the muck!"

Someone emptied a basket of roses, and a cascade of petals swirled at Lady Valikram's feet.

"Now, my friends, the wave has receded. We stand in the wreckage left on the shores. Zumera and Tisaris have fallen. There is every reason to expect that Xhonai and Kondala City have, too. Trade is not on the edge of failing; it has already failed. No salt is coming from Tisaris! No lemons are coming from Zumera! No sugar is coming that we didn't grow ourselves!"

A horrified murmur ran through the crowd. *In another life, she could have been a wizard,* thought Eshu through the icy exhilaration of panic. *She plays them like a bone flute.*

"Teyam Acala is out of tricks," said Lady Valikram in clear, belling tones. "She cannot rule because she has never learned any other art but theft and deception. She is the muck that we must rise above. It is time for those who were bred from birth for leadership to return to their rightful place—"

Then a single gunshot sounded, and the crowd went horribly silent.

Even now, with the Anjali River standing sentinel at Lady Valikram's back, the crowd parted for Prince Teyam Acala. She strode across the brick and grass of the courtyard with her chin raised, her pistol handle gleaming in the lamplight.

All around Eshu, the people shifted and whispered. They could sense the conflict brewing, and knew that it might break any moment into bloodshed. Some of them thirsted for it; they had been afraid of shadows for so long that they craved a real monster to tear apart.

Over the rising tide of murmurs, the prince's voice rang out like a knell. "You forget yourself, Lady Valikram," she pronounced. "You forget that these people put me on the throne."

"And we can take you off again!" someone shouted; the prince pretended she hadn't heard.

She spread her arms, turning so that all might see her: plainly dressed in a sailor's short trousers and worn leather boots, with a cotton tunic over her chest. Her thin arms banded with old blue tattoos, and her white hair gleaming against her deep brown skin.

"Look at me and tell me I am not one of you," she said. "Look at me and tell me I didn't grow up in the same piss-streaked alleys you did! Tell me I never went to work in the silk mills, twelve hours a day, even when I'd had nothing to eat for days and my back felt like it was breaking. Tell me my children always had a roof over their heads. If you think I'm like *this* piece of jewel-crusted shit, tell me!" And here she shot a look at Lady Valikram that crackled with lightning. "But you can't. You know I came from the same muck you did. And when she tells you it's time you went back to *your* place, that's where she wants you. In the muck."

Lady Valikram's spectacles flashed. She gripped the hilt of her sword as though she meant to thrust her blade through Teyam's chest and put an end to her—but Teyam only raised her voice and turned to face her.

"But maybe that's what you want. Maybe you *want* a prince who will take your taxes and build herself a pleasure garden or three. Maybe you like buying her silks and jewels and swords—and who could blame you? She's a beautiful woman, is Lady Valikram, if a bit long in the tooth." Teyam turned to the audience, letting them see her sneer. "Maybe you'd rather she have a new marble bath, while your sewers pour into your drinking water and give you all the bloody shits."

The murmur of the crowd grew louder. Eshu found Beejan's hand and pressed it hard.

Lady Valikram clutched her fist to her breast like an actress in a tragedy. Murder glittered in her eyes "How surprising that the conwoman tries to distract you from her crimes! But if you ask her why she kept Tisaris and Zumera a secret, she has no answer. Don't be deceived—she cares for you no more than any other snake does. Your taxes are already in her pockets."

Prince Teyam let her hands fall, one to her pistol and the other to the hilt of her sword. "We won't settle this by shouting at each other in the streets," she said, and though her voice was pitched low, it carried. "There are older ways."

Lady Valikram smiled, and for the first time, Eshu glimpsed the viciousness beneath her polished facade. If she could have torn out Teyam's throat with her teeth, she would have; she craved violence not because she was afraid, but because fear was alien to her. "Do you mean to challenge me to a duel?" she asked.

Prince Teyam unsheathed her sword—the crowd drew a sharp collective breath—and then saluted. "I do."

Lady Valikram gave a matching salute, spare and clean, without the slightest flourish. "Then you must know that, by tradition, I can choose a champion to fight in my stead."

Prince Teyam dipped her head. "As may I."

Turning to the immense figure of the river god looming behind her, Lady Valikram called out in ringing tones, "I name the Anjali River as my champion."

"As you wish." Teyam turned to the crowd, skimming the sea of faces. For a fraction of a second, Eshu thought he saw doubt flash in her eyes—then she locked her gaze with his, and she grinned. His blood ran cold.

Teyam stretched out her sword at Eshu, standing almost a full head above the crowd, and said, "I choose the wizard Eshu as my champion."

CHAPTER 19: THE SMALL HOURS

W e have to find Eshu," said Mnoro, heaving herself over the bottom of the storm drain grate with her gown hiked up around her thighs. "He needs to know what happened to Kondala City."

Fern clambered through behind her and closed the grate. After yesterday's rain, the water rushing through the drain was up to their ankles, and full of dead leaves and soggy newspapers; she was heartily glad to get back onto the solid rock of the shore.

The thought of seeing Eshu again filled her with dread and resentment, but she pushed that feeling all the way down. He'd been cruel because he was afraid of what he'd find when he got home at last, and here she was coming to tell him everything was worse than he'd feared. She could be kinder to him than he had been. "I don't know where he is," she said, a little helplessly. "We had a fight a couple of days ago, and I haven't seen him since. Maybe he's still staying at our old rooms?"

"We can check," said Mnoro. The hem of her gown was soaked. Her fine blue eye paint was smeared from crying. She looked weary beyond measure.

Together they crept south along the Anjali's west bank until they reached the quay. Even from the riverside, they could hear the shouts of protesters—now praising Prince Teyam, now calling for her head. Fires licked the skyline, belching thick black smoke that cut through the blazing mist.

No city's fire brigade could have been ready for the maze that Kulmeni had become. Even as Fern watched, fires dimmed in one place only to blaze anew in another. The distant crown of an amsara tree burst into flame, weeping smoldering leaves; as they fell, a whole row of houses on the far side of the city began to burn.

This is my fault, she thought, aghast. *I did this.*

No, she told herself firmly. Prince Teyam had done this. The aristocrats whose soldiers stalked the streets had done this. They'd had weeks to lie and scheme and prepare themselves for war before she'd come here. Kulmeni had been ready to set itself on fire, and Fern had only been the match.

Mnoro touched Fern's wrist and pointed down the docks, where a group of soldiers was doing a sweep of the boats. *They know we got away somehow, and they're looking for us*, Fern thought.

She gripped her runestone and pulled Mnoro with her off of the wharf. *Rooms for Let*, she chanted to herself, listening for the rhythmic thump of the printing press; she remembered the smell of paper and ink and the sound of the printers shouting. As though she'd imagined it into being, the mists rolled away from the printer's shop, and Fern let herself breathe.

Almost immediately, her relief faded. Behind the *Rooms for Let* sign was a much bigger sign: *Property of the Sovereign Lords' Alliance.* The ink on it still shone as though it was wet.

"Wait here," she told Mnoro in an undertone. "I want to see what's happening."

Mnoro gave her wrist a quick squeeze of reassurance, then let go. Fern stepped back, searching for a trace that Mnoro was there, and saw only a pattern of drips where her gown had shed water. It would have to be good enough.

Fern inhaled, then released her runestone and strode up to the shop. All of its lamps were blazing; the front desk was left unstaffed, and the back room was crowded with people shouting and rolling paper and setting type. "Someone mix more ink!" demanded a broad-shouldered man with his hair in a topknot. "If the Switch Street printers get the story out before we do because our fucking *ink* is dry, I swear to the Sisters I'll fire every last one of you."

Fern heard a tiny, world-weary sigh, and glanced down to see a newspaper girl sitting with her hands folded over her belly and her legs stretched out in front of her. Her empty satchel lay on the floor beside her.

"Hey," said Fern, and came to sit down beside her.

"You've got to interview if you want a job," said the newspaper girl flatly. She couldn't have been more than twelve. "They don't take just anyone."

"I'm renting the rooms upstairs," said Fern, which was still technically true. "What's happening? What's the big news?"

The girl cracked a wry grin and said, in a low parody of her newspaper crier's voice, "Kulmeni in flames! Anjali River backs Lady Valikram for prince! High noon duel for the throne: Anjali River to trade blows with Eshu the wizard!" She took out a bag of candied lemon peel and munched on a piece, adding, "That's all you get for free."

Eshu the wizard. The name hit her like a blow. "What do you mean, a duel?" Fern asked, and didn't care how frantic she sounded.

The girl held out her hand, and Fern wrenched two zil off a cord and put them in her palm. The two zil disappeared into the same pocket the lemon peel had come from. "There was a speech," the girl said. "Lady Valikram made a bid for the throne. Prince Teyam challenged her to a duel, and they both picked champions. It's not sporting to do that—if you want to fight, you should fight for yourself," she opined. "But anyway, the river's going to fight some wizard tomorrow at noon. I'm gonna go watch. I've never seen a wizard duel before. Or a god."

"Where is the wizard?" Fern asked. "Is he here?"

The girl gave her a withering look. "*Obviously* no."

"Thank you," said Fern in a rush, "but I have to go." She clambered back to her feet and dashed outside again, ignoring the girl's indignant shout of "Hey, I thought you lived here!"

On the street, Fern felt a hand slide into hers, and she stifled a squeak before she recognized the shape of Mnoro's palm. "Mnoro," she whispered, gripping her runestone in her free hand. Out here, the rumble of the printing press no longer drowned out the sounds of clashing crowds. "It's bad. Eshu isn't here. He's going to be fighting a duel against a god tomorrow."

Mnoro made a tiny sound of distress. "Then we have to find him. I know it's a bad idea, but if we need to, I can sing a finding song—"

"Do it," said Fern. "If we can find him, maybe we can get him out of here."

"We'll have to let go of our runestones," Mnoro cautioned. "You can't work incantations while you're telling the world not to notice you. And this place is susceptible to magic. We can't know what the second-order effects might be."

"Maybe good ones," said Fern. "Maybe it gets easier for people to find where they're trying to go."

"Or maybe it gets easier for those soldiers to find us. This isn't predictable. No matter how carefully you craft the call, you can't choose how the city's going to answer."

Fern hesitated. "If we don't, I don't know how else to find him."

"Neither do I." The air seemed to shiver, and suddenly, Fern's gaze settled on the place where the world had been telling her not to look. Mnoro stood there, her round face solemn and earnest. "So I'm going to sing, and hope I don't make things worse."

Fern let her runestone go. She met Mnoro's eyes, and nodded. Mnoro closed her eyes and began to sing.

The city unspooled before them. They moved through the streets and alleyways like moths, flitting between the streetlamps, following Mnoro's song. The air tasted of smoke. People ran past them—running to or from, Fern couldn't tell; they all had the same look of agitation. Once, they crossed paths with a fire brigade hustling a wagon uphill with its copper bell clanging, and they ducked into a doorway until the wagon had clattered past.

Still Mnoro sang, and Fern went where she led. They passed under an arch twined with night-blooming jasmine. They crossed a city square, where the grass had been trampled flat and flowers lay crushed into the dirt. The song led them down a long, dark alley, with the sky ablaze above them.

At the far end of the alley, just beyond the streetlamp's glow, something was waiting for them in the darkness. Mnoro's song died on her lips.

Fern froze. The hair on the back of her arms stood up; cold horror washed over her. She tried to tell herself that it was some ordinary animal—a scavenging dog, or a tiger starved out of its hunting grounds. A crocodile, far from the river's edge. But no matter where she looked, her eyes glanced off of the creature as though it were made of glass and shadow.

The hungry ghost paced into the light on clawed hands, bleeding streamers of smoke from its empty eye sockets. For a moment, she glimpsed the porcelain-white mask of the Crowtaker, but this time there were gleaming teeth behind it.

"Run," she said, and dragged Mnoro along by the hand as she fled.

They fled back down the thin dirt alley and onto the paving stones of the main road—Fern stumbled on the wheel ruts, sprawled and scraped her palm bloody, but she caught herself and kept running. The city condensed to a single street, a single lighted way in the darkness. All she could hear was the thunder of her heart, the hammer of her feet on the road, the rasp of her own breath.

She could outrun this thing. She was made for running. But

Mnoro was an anchor at the end of her arm, and if she let go, Mnoro would fall behind.

They dashed across a culvert bridge, where the day's overflow rain washed past in torrents. "We can't keep running," Mnoro said, like a plea. Her breath came in ragged gasps. "We have to fight it. They *can* be fought."

The creature was close now, pacing them with a gale at its back. It carved itself from the shadows, all teeth and eyes and rotting limbs; it took Fern's fear and wore it like a pelt. She saw it and saw her death coming.

As Mnoro stepped in front of Fern with her hands raised, lifting her voice in a warding song, Fern glanced down into the channel.

There, clinging to the mortar just above the waterline, was a cluster of black snails.

Think, she told herself fiercely. *They come from the Mirrorlands. They've spilled into a world that's not their own, just like the snails and the diatoms, and they're trying to find a way to live in it.*

Black talons raked through the air, and Mnoro's song failed. She caught the blow on her wrist and forced it back with a fierce blade of melody, singing a song of knives and broken glass.

They take the shape of what we fear. The Crowtaker. The dead in Sharis. The creatures that lurk in dreams.

Mnoro's sleeve ripped open; her blood sprayed across the road. Shouting, Mnoro fell back.

With all of her focus, Fern closed her eyes and thought of snails.

She heard a soft clatter against the paving stones, and she cracked her eyes open. Before her lay a tiny black river snail with a conical shell—the kind that Sedge had taught her to gather.

"What did you do?" Mnoro asked. She was still panting, and blood gleamed on her arm, but her expression was all rapt curiosity.

Fern stooped down and picked up the snail, looking deep into the opening of the shell. "If these things came from the

Mirrorlands, then they should follow mirror-logic, right? That's how they'd survive there. So they're trying to do that here, shaping themselves to what we're thinking when we're alone and scared of the dark. But if that's true, then you can shape them on purpose into something harmless. Like a snail."

"Another unexpected interplanar traveler," said Mnoro, laughing as she wiped sweat from her brow. "Maybe this one will have better luck here as a snail."

"I hope so," said Fern. She leaned down over the culvert and released the snail, letting the water carry it away.

Mnoro's song led them at last to a building of what looked like one-room apartments, each with a window and a little balcony leaning over the street. On the second story, a few neighbors were leaning over their balcony railings, chatting about a horse race as they passed a clove cigarette across the gap between them. At this hour, all the windows glowed with a rosy light.

"There," said Mnoro. She pointed to a window with the shadow of leaves curling around it. "That's the one."

They climbed the stairs to the second floor, counting doors until they came to the one that matched the window. "Eshu," Fern called, knocking lightly. "Eshu, it's Fern and Mnoro. Are you here?"

There was a pause, then the sound of furniture scraping over a bare wood floor. The locks clicked and turned, and then the door opened on a towering man who nearly filled the frame from one side to the other. "Fern and Mnoro?" he said. He looked them up and down. Mostly down.

Fern stepped back so that she didn't have to crane her neck so much. "We're friends of Eshu. Do you know where he is?"

The man broke into a sudden smile, and it completely

transformed the stern lines of his face. He stepped aside, gesturing them into the apartment. "He's here. My name's Beejan, and you can come on in. Which of you is the one he owes the apology to?"

"Both of them," said Eshu, and to Fern's surprise, he rushed to the door and immediately swept her up in his arms. For a moment she just stood there, not knowing how to answer the desperation in his grip. His thin arms were a vise around her ribs. With his chest pressed to hers, she could feel the hummingbird flutter of his heart, the tremor that went all the way down from his shoulders to his hands. When a sob made his breath hitch, she felt it in her collarbone. Eventually, she just wrapped her arms around him and held him until the last pangs of anxiety ebbed away to nothing.

"I'm sorry," Eshu said against her hair. "I was an asshole. I should never have said those things to you—you were never anything but a friend to me, and I hurt you. And I'm sorry."

"I know you were scared when you said those things," said Fern. "This is scary. I get it. But you shouldn't have taken it out on me. And if you do it again, I'm going."

"That's more than fair." He swallowed, then straightened up and pulled away. "And I'm sorry for just springing on you, too. Obviously I shouldn't have assumed you were in a mood to be hugged."

"You shouldn't have," Fern agreed, stepping into Beejan's room with Mnoro close behind. "But I'm glad you did."

As soon as she was through the door, Eshu wrapped Mnoro up in a hug, too. "I'm sorry I didn't come to see you. When I heard Tuuri was here, I just—"

"No, don't apologize for that." Mnoro ruffled Eshu's locs affectionately. "I don't think either of us knew how—oh."

Her mouth fell shut, and from the inward look in her eyes, Fern knew that she was back in the mirror room again with the world melting around her.

Eshu frowned. "What is it?"

Mnoro didn't answer at once. Instead, she made her way to the table and sat down at an empty place. "Come sit with me," she said. "I've got a lot of bad news for you."

"Not yet," said Eshu. There was a pleading note in his voice that broke Fern's heart. She could almost see the realization dawning over him, grim as a red sun at sea—that she and Mnoro had truly come alone. That Usamkartha wasn't with them. "Please, no."

"Will it be lighter to bear if you hear it tomorrow?" Mnoro asked gently.

"No. No, it won't. But I'm weak today, and I want to imagine that the version of me that wakes tomorrow will be stronger." Sighing, Eshu dropped into the chair beside Mnoro's and brought his temple to rest on his fist. "That's not how it works, though, is it? Tomorrow's version of you is the same as today's; it's just that the list of errata is longer."

"I know there's a lot facing you tomorrow," said Mnoro, giving Fern a look that she didn't know how to interpret. "A duel with a god, they say. If you really do need more time—"

"It's all right." Eshu reached across the table for Mnoro's hand. "You're right. It won't be lighter for me tomorrow. And it would be cruel of me to make you bear it alone."

While Beejan made tea and Fern helped him wash dishes, Mnoro began to unfold the events of the last few days: Usamkartha's abstraction. What they had found beneath the microscope. The arrival of the soldiers, and how Usamkartha had broken the world into sharp-edged shards so that she and Fern could escape. Their flight through the city and into the Mirrorlands. Now and then, when the silences grew long, Fern offered details, theories, memories; mostly, though, she sat sipping her tea and letting Mnoro tell their story.

At long last, though, they reached Njo's Rest and the black crater at its feet.

By then, Eshu sat curled in on himself with his teacup held in both hands. He wasn't weeping anymore. His eyes were fixed on the table, as though he was trying to memorize the grain of the wood. "It's gone, then," he said. "The whole city—just gone."

Mnoro nodded.

"I spent so long trying to get back there," said Eshu. His voice was no more than a whisper. "I stole airships. Crossed jungles. Walked the Mirrorlands. And this whole time, it was gone."

"I'm sorry," said Fern, as though it helped anything for her to be sorry.

Shaking himself, Eshu set his cup down on the table so hard that tea splashed over the edge. "I need to see it. I just—I need to see it with my own eyes."

"Sleep first," said Beejan, resting a hand on Eshu's shoulder. It didn't ease his tremors, but Eshu leaned into the touch all the same like a flower tilting its face toward sunlight.

Oh, thought Fern, awkwardly. She wasn't sure whether she ought to look away; Eshu's gratitude seemed somehow both more private and more vulnerable than his grief.

"We can go at first light," Mnoro said. "But for now, Beejan is right. We could all use some sleep."

When Fern and Mnoro left Beejan's place, the sound of fire brigades' bells still rang through the smoke-cut darkness. All around them, Kulmeni was still burning.

CHAPTER 20: FAR TRAVELERS

Eshu walked down from Njo's Rest and into the black glass crater where his city had been. In the thin light of dawn, he could make out no shape he recognized there—no ruins, no bodies, no gently sloped roads hugging the hillsides. There was only a long hollow of blasted earth, as though a hand of fire had reached down from the sky and gouged Kondala City out of the mountains.

All feeling bled out of him. He felt as frail as a blown-out eggshell, and as empty.

He started singing before he knew he was singing. The words tumbled tuneless out of his lips, sketching the shapes of the city he had lost. He sang the old copper domes and the whitewashed walls, the scent of grapes from the highlands; he sang the grass that swayed along the roadsides and the laughter of schoolchildren. He sang the rise where the Hall of Ways stood with its high white towers, its windows flashing in the sunlight, and he sang how the Grand Assembly chambers rang with debates. He sang fever trees and washing lines and goats bleating on the mountains; wedding processions holding up traffic for blocks as brides promenaded through well-wishers to kiss at last under a yellow awning.

He sang Kondala City, and the black glass answered him. Roads unraveled like vines beneath his feet; houses and hospitals and temples strained toward the sky. Phantoms flickered past him, bright and glorious, dressed in a thousand colors.

Tears tracked down his cheeks. He sang the smell of coffee and spices, and how Asha had painted the ceiling of her room with stars. He sang Sunba wrapping her hair in emerald satin, so anxious to look her best for her first court case. He sang Kiga at their mother's feet, reading poetry aloud while their mother braided her hair into long vine rows.

In the ghost of a city, at the ghost of his mother's house, Eshu sang his family until his throat was raw from singing.

When his voice failed at last, the phantom city faded into nothingness.

Eshu fell to his knees on the black glass, and he wept.

He knelt there a long time, feeling the sunlight slide over his shoulders. He wished he could dissolve into the earth. He wished he'd never asked to see this place.

After what might have been minutes or hours, Fern laid her hand on his shoulder, and he reached for it as though it was a lifeline. Her fingers were small and cool to the touch. "Hey," she said quietly. "The city might not be lost. I thought at first it might be the same kind of black rock from the Mirrorlands, but it's not— this is all smooth and glassy, like obsidian. It breaks in curves. The rocks in the Mirrorlands are rough; they break in straight lines. They're different kinds of rocks. And that means something different happened here."

He tried to swallow, but it felt like his throat had been tied in a knot. "May I—may I see the rocks?" If he could be certain of nothing else, he was certain of this: Fern still had the rocks.

"Sure," she said. With her free hand, she fumbled in her pockets a moment, then placed two pieces of stone into his palm and folded his fingers around them. For a moment, she just held him there, her hand closed around his hand, offering silent reassurance. When at last she let him go, he felt her absence like a wound.

He opened his palm and tried to focus on the two black stones, but his eyes kept swimming with tears. Instead, he traced them with his fingertips: one smooth as glass, sculpted in curving whorls; the other rough against his skin. He ran his thumb over the corners until his tears ran dry.

"I think whatever was happening, they saw it coming," said Fern. She sat down beside him, looping her arms around her knees and gazing down into the crater where Kondala City had been. "They knew the world was going to break, and maybe they only had time to save themselves. Or maybe they managed to get the word to some people—like the missing wizards from Sharis and Kulmeni. I don't know."

"It's a pretty story," Eshu answered. "I'd like to believe it." It was hard to believe in pretty stories, though, with the black glass shadow of his city spread at his feet.

Mnoro came to sit at his other side and put her arm around his back. He leaned against her, the way he had for a hundred other stupid things—a pretty boy who hadn't wanted him, a failed test or a stranger's laughter. She had been a year ahead of him all his life; she had always known more, done more, understood more than he had. And now she understood as little as he did, and it must be cutting her up inside. Eshu wrapped his arm around her shoulder and let her rest her head against his chest.

"You think you're ready for the worst," said Mnoro. Her voice was thick and tight. "They told us what happened to Tisaris, and I was afraid it was like that. I was afraid, but I thought I was ready for it, you know? Even—even in a ruin, you can find something to hold onto. Some piece of your old life that you can keep in your hand. But there's just nothing. Not even bones. Not even ash. There's nothing to bury."

Eshu kissed her brow and stroked her close, tight curls with his fingertips. "Tell me about your mothers? Please?"

Mnoro swallowed. Her arm went tight around him. "You remember Mama's sweet shop, right?"

"Sugar in every color of the rainbow," said Eshu. He could almost smell caramel and almond paste. "Sweet yam rolls full of apricots and cream. She used to chase us out whenever she was frying sesame flower cookies."

"I got too close to the oil once, and it splashed." Mnoro showed him the scar on the back of her arm—he'd seen her arms a thousand, thousand times, and he'd never noticed the scar before. "She was always so afraid I'd hurt myself somehow. Every time, Mother used to tell her to let me make my mistakes. 'Learning forgets, but experience remembers,' she always used to say." She looked down at her arm, and her dark eyes shone with tears. "She didn't want me going to school to be a wizard at all, so of course I had to go halfway to the south pole to show her up."

Eshu managed a little smile. "You mean they didn't have the best incantation school in the world?"

"They did, but that wasn't the point. I wanted to be my own person. See Nanjeer and Cheresse and Ras Kir'uun. I didn't want to be digging yams in my mother's garden until I got old." She sniffled, then wiped her nose on the back of her hand. "I'd give every fucking castle in Cheresse to be digging yams with her right now."

"You wanted to be a far traveler," said Eshu. "So did I. That wasn't wrong of us."

"But that's the thing, isn't it? Njo and her people came sailing in from a land beyond the stars, and when she reached our shores, she found she couldn't return. That's what it means to be a far traveler—it means you can't go home again."

Eshu opened his hand. The two stones lay on the deep-grooved skin of his palm. One, sharp-edged, glittered in the sunlight; it had melted and flowed like candlewax and hardened into a brittle blade. The other was rough and dull as charcoal, and left a black smudge on his hand. Both had been shaped by fire, at some time near or distant. *Njo is the anvil on which the story bends*, he told himself, and he wished he were made of metal. He felt so close to breaking.

"That's why she taught us the Way of Stories," Eshu said softly. "Why she gave us song. If you can't go home again, you make home again, everywhere you go. You remember the people you lost, and the way you lived—you remember it in how you live, until your life becomes a way of telling their story."

"Njo Laughing-Eyed," said Mnoro. She let out a rusty-edged sound; it hurt too much to be laughter. "I never thought to ask how she could laugh again, after everything she lost."

"I don't know," Eshu answered, and laid his head against hers. "I don't even remember how long it's been since I prayed. It reminded me too much of home."

Mnoro raised her gaze to the sun, now riding high over the eastern horizon. It was closer to noon than to dawn—far too late to make the prayer. "Will you pray with me now?" she asked.

Eshu thought of his sisters, kneeling together in a row as the first beams of sunlight spilled over the windowsill. Kiga sleepily mumbling the words while Sunba's warm voice filled the room. Asha racing through her prayers so she could run to school early. His mother, smiling, letting her.

He was the keeper of their story, now. They lived in his remembrance.

"Yes," he said, and turned his face to the east.

They returned to Kulmeni with scant hours to spare before the duel. "You don't have to fight anyone," said Fern, when they parted at the door of Beejan's building. She was chewing at her lower lip; the skin peeled up in flakes under her teeth. "You know that, right? They can't make you. If you want to leave, we can leave."

"Where would we even go?" asked Eshu. "There's nowhere left but Kulmeni."

"We could go back into the forest. Make a really good treehouse. Plant wild ginger and kanan and just live out there in the woods until Kulmeni figures itself out." Fern squeezed his hand hard enough that the bones ached.

She meant it. If he said yes, they'd be back in the forest by noon and have a camp set up by nightfall. They could live out there—not well, but they could live. Digging roots and picking kanan, chasing lantern bees into the darkness. "Please don't take this as a slight on your treehouse-making skills," said Eshu, "but I would quite literally rather let the Anjali drown me."

"At least get some sleep, if your mind's made up," said Mnoro gently. "You're dueling with a god. You'll need all your strength."

"I'll try," Eshu lied.

Once they'd left, Eshu crept upstairs. Beejan's room was unlocked, so Eshu let himself in and closed the door quietly behind him. Beejan lay sprawled on his bed, a thin sheet over his hips and his long curls spread across the pillows. In sleep, all the tension around his eyes eased. His breaths came slow and even, and Eshu stood a long moment watching Beejan's chest rise and fall.

If he sat on the edge of the bed, he knew Beejan would wake as the mattress dipped. He would pull Eshu close and kiss him slow and greedy, as though they could spend the whole day trading kisses. Maybe it would ease Eshu's grief a little to be held and kissed. Maybe it wouldn't.

At the end of that moment, Eshu stepped out again and let Beejan sleep.

He was so tired that his eye sockets ached. He wanted to eat a real breakfast; he wanted to claw at his face with his fingernails. He wanted to throw up. He paced the streets of Kulmeni like a caged tiger, past iron gates and gardens and coffee carts lining the streets, and they blurred together into one long streak of sound and color.

If he won today, Prince Teyam would go on as she had all her life, running confidence schemes where she could and looting outright where she had to. She would turn Kulmeni into an engine for her own profit, and her people would be caught in its gears.

If Lady Valikram won, nothing would change—except now that the world had broken, everything had to change.

When at last his feet grew tired, Eshu found himself at a familiar fountain. A week and a lifetime ago, he and Fern had asked for directions from a baker here. Now, he sat on the edge of it with his eyes closed and listened to the soft splash of water.

Ahead of him, he heard the sound of water birds crying and boats groaning at anchor. *The sounds of the river*, he thought. He wondered if the river wanted to be in this fight any more than he did.

He rose again, and stole down to the quay. At this time of day, the docks were busy and crowded. Shutters clicked on lamps. Dockworkers grunted under the weight of their loads. Eshu walked among them like a ghost, searching for a dock that stretched far into the river.

At the end of the dock, Eshu kicked off his sandals, gathered up the skirts of his robe, and sat with his legs dangling over the water. Pedal boats and catamarans drifted through streamers of mist, laden with fish and bananas, mangos and taro roots; flower sellers came pushing against the current, bearing baskets of lotus flowers and lilies and sweet-scented jalania. In the shallows, men and women picked their way like herons through the reeds, lifting crab traps with long hooked sticks and tossing crabs into buckets.

These were the Anjali's people—not Lady Valikram, and not Prince Teyam. These were the people who lived and died on her waters, who weathered her floods and harvested her bounty. These were the people whose lives would be at stake, when he and the Anjali River faced each other on the battlefield.

Eshu dipped his toes in the water. Curious fish scattered as he parted the surface, then came circling back to investigate. Water broke against his bare skin. "Last time I met you, things were a bit fraught," said Eshu softly. "So let me try again. My name is Kondala m'Barata Eshusikinde. Barata was my mother, and Kondala City was my home, and now both of them are gone." He swallowed. "I still can't get my mind around it. It's too big a loss. There's not enough left of me to keep standing, if they're gone. But Eshusikinde—in your language, it would be 'flowing like a river.' So maybe we're a kind of kinsfolk, after all."

The river sang on over the rocky shore, and didn't answer.

"I don't want to fight you," said Eshu. "I won't presume to know your feelings on fighting me, but I assume you aren't wearing armor for the fun of it. If it means anything to you, I absolutely believe you can demolish me."

Dockworkers shouted to each other; bundles of sugarcane fell clattering to the docks. Shutters rattled down, green to red, as fishermen came in to dock. Beneath Eshu's feet, a giant catfish glided by on business of its own.

Eshu leaned back on his hands and gazed at the high arch of the Heron's Bridge. "I'm not here to beg for your mercy. I suppose I just wanted to ask you whether you really believe that Lady Valikram will be any better for these people than Prince Teyam is."

Somewhere off in the mists, a bird gave a harsh cry. It wasn't an answer, exactly, but it felt like a listening sound.

"I don't know Kulmeni the way you do. I don't know Lady Valikram. Maybe there's some compassion in her that I haven't seen. I really hope there is." He traced slow circles in the water with the tip of his foot, watching the water flow around him. "But— forgive me for saying it—you're an old, old river. You're older than Nanjeer and all of its princes. And whatever comes next, whether it's Prince Teyam's regime or something else, it will be new. I don't blame you for clinging to what you know. I think we all want to believe there's an easy way to put the world back the way it was."

Again, the catfish circled between the piles of the dock, and Eshu's heart quickened.

"The old prince was bad in old, familiar ways," he said. "And maybe you miss them. Maybe you don't know who you are without them." He lifted his legs from the water and stretched out until he lay face-down on the deck, his long locs hanging down around his neck.

Beneath the broken reflection of his face, Eshu thought he saw another face, ageless and solemn. He leaned down until his fingertips grazed the water's surface, and he whispered, "I know how it feels. I've let people hurt me for *years* just because it was familiar—because I didn't know who I'd be without them. And it wasn't my fault that he was an asshole. It wasn't my fault."

A tear slid down his cheek and fell into the rushing waters, but he didn't wipe it away. "It isn't your fault. You deserve better than her. You deserve better than both of them."

The river pressed against his hand, and he lay there a long time and let it.

Under the high noon sun, Eshu and the Anjali River faced each other at the apex of the Heron's Bridge.

Someone had built platforms for Prince Teyam to the west and Lady Valikram to the east, with matching chairs decked with banners and fresh-cut flowers. The west wind swept the scent of tuberose and plumeria between Eshu and his opponent; it nearly drowned out the smell of the hundreds of onlookers crowding onto the bridge at Teyam's back.

He glimpsed Beejan and Fern in the crowd, and grim-eyed Basia, and Sheeram roaring encouragement with a banner gripped like a blade. On the far side, Lady Valikram was flanked by aristocrats garbed in a rainbow of silks and jewels, their shawls embroidered with thread-of-gold and their eyes dark and solemn.

And then there was the Anjali River, standing before them like a prism, breaking their myriad colors into a single spear of light.

From Lady Valikram's side, a potbellied man pulled free of the crowd. He mopped sweat from his dripping brow and tucked his handkerchief in a pocket, then raised his hands to screams and raucous applause. "Quiet!" he shouted, but the crowd couldn't hear him. "Could I have quiet, please!" He lowered his arms, but no one heeded.

Prince Teyam raised her gun skyward, and the crowd quieted fast enough to hear her cock it.

The potbellied man licked his lips, then raised his voice again to fill the silence. "As Mayor of Kulmeni, I serve as witness to this duel between Prince Teyam Acala, first of her name, and Lady Valikram of House Davani." Until this moment, Eshu hadn't known that Kulmeni had a mayor. "The principals are agreed: the victor of this duel will be considered the legitimate prince of Kulmeni, and thereafter, all hostilities between their factions will cease. Do I have your word of honor, as gentlewomen?"

Lady Valikram rose from her chair, and after a moment, Prince Teyam stood, too. "You have my word," said Lady Valikram. "If Teyam Acala's champion defeats mine, I will relinquish all claim to the throne, and I will order my soldiers to stand down."

"You have my word," Prince Teyam agreed. "I've tried to put this city right where others have failed, and I've done better work than the lot of 'em. I'm proud of what I've done for Kulmeni. But I won't linger where I'm not wanted. If the rich bitch from the east side can do better, let her wade through shit for a change!"

Both sides of the bridge howled, praise and rage mingling into one long, convulsive scream.

Again, the mayor raised, then lowered his arms, and this time, the crowd subsided. "Both principals have named champions to fight in their stead: the Anjali River fights as Lady Valikram's champion, and Eshu the wizard as Prince Teyam's. Champions, are you agreed on the terms of the duel?"

Eshu gazed down the bridge to where the Anjali stood, fell and glorious in her mail of scale and sunlight, lotuses tangled in her whitewater hair. He could make out nothing in her expression but calm, clear-eyed determination.

He had no city left but this one. No home left but upon her shores. He made a deep Kondalani bow to her and said, "I agree."

She saluted with her spear and said in a carrying cataract voice, "I agree."

The mayor dipped his head in acknowledgment and backed away. "So witnessed. You may begin."

Alone, now, with the mist spread all around them like a landscape of clouds, Eshu and the Anjali River faced each other again. She circled the cement arch of their arena with her crocodile eyes locked to his. He paced her, studying her face, her weapon, the fish flickering at the hollow of her throat. Songs welled up in him, unsung—songs of warding, of turning, of freezing and breaking; blade-songs, flame-songs, songs of vine and bough. Slowly, the space between them closed, until they stood almost close enough to touch.

"Will you fight with me, wizard?" asked the Anjali. Her voice was so low that Eshu could barely hear it. "Or will you dance around me forever?"

He swallowed down those fierce songs of challenge and extended his hand. "If you insist," he said, "but I'd rather we danced."

Then, like a dam bursting, the Anjali sang.

She sang the sleek silver carp of the river, the fish hook and the line; she sang snails and crabs and catfish, nets flung out into the shallows like a dancer's whirling skirts. She took Eshu's hand in hers and sang him the lotus blooming from the river banks, the broad-leafed taro plants, the river pearls shining in pink and blue and gold.

He let himself be swept up by her and carried—he found her

melody and twined a harmony around it, singing her fisherfolk and her coffee merchants and the Kondalani woman who'd given him ginger just because. Together they sang gardens and bathhouses and street markets hung with lights, wharves and alleyways stretching into the shrouding darkness. They sang the people whom the shadows had devoured, and the gale of the Anjali's grief blew back the mist all around them.

They sang the city, and Kulmeni answered, *Yes.*

Lady Valikram rose from her chair, reaching for her blade. Prince Teyam fired into the close clutch of their dance, and the Anjali batted her shot away as though it were no more than a troublesome fly. She and Eshu were at the heart of a tempest, now, dancing in the hurricane's eye, and no would-be tyrants could touch them.

The Anjali sang him the lineage of princes—the long, broken passage of crowns, hand to hand to clutching hand, down through the centuries. She sang of civil wars that had set the city aflame. She sang cruel princes and kind ones, long years of famine when the river ran dry; she sang soldiers rotting on the riverbanks while crocodiles feasted.

At the heart of the song, cycling like a refrain, was a question that she could not answer: *What else, if not this? Who else, if not them?*

Some of her people had survived, under princes. Those built to survive them had. Princes were a blight she knew how to weather.

She was so tired of weathering blights.

I know, sang Eshu, and turned her around and around. *I know.* He sang her the only answer he knew: the sailors on the *Crest of the Wave*, deciding together to save whom they could. The survivors of Sharis, burying their dead and caring for their children together. Fern with leaves in her hair and dark shadows under her eyes, refusing to leave him alone. He sang his mother on the floor of the Grand Assembly, unmaking unjust laws, and his throat ached with a grief too big to swallow.

A great roaring sound rose from beneath them. The mist rolled and churned; the bridge swayed under Eshu's feet. He tried to let go of the river, but she held him fast with both hands.

Then a wall of roiling water poured over the bridge and swept both Prince Teyam and Lady Valikram away.

When the water subsided, both platforms were gone. The onlookers were soaked to the skin, coughing and wringing out their clothes as tiny fish flopped and flashed on the bridge. Eshu alone was completely dry, and when the river released him, he felt eerily as though he had escaped a drowning.

"Hear me," said the Anjali, her voice echoing over the silent throng. "What has been before, shall not be again. The era of princes is over for Kulmeni. What comes next..." She closed her eyes briefly, as though bracing for a blow. "...what comes next, we must all decide."

The crowd erupted. People swarmed into the center space, shouting at the Anjali—demanding that she bring Prince Teyam back, demanding that she declare herself prince, trying to force her to finish or forfeit the fight. Sheeram and Basia melted back into the crowd, and Eshu lost sight of them.

Mnoro and Fern found him first and hustled him to the pedestrian path at the side of the bridge, where they could start urging him back to the west side and away from the sudden, energetic outburst of politics. "Let's get you out of here now, and you can explain what happened later," Fern said, and for once, he had absolutely no desire to argue.

Beejan caught up with them at the wharf, where the crowd was still thick but not as well-informed. "Hey, wait," he said, pushing through curious onlookers to take Eshu's hand. "You all right?"

"I am really fucking not." Exhaustion weighed him down, as though his veins were full of mercury and his bones were made of lead. "Come here. Let me hold you."

Amid the cramped press of people, Beejan looped his free hand around Eshu's waist and pulled him close enough to hurt.

"I'm sorry about your grandmother," said Eshu, letting his forehead come to rest against Beejan's. "I didn't expect—if there was any way I could've—I'm sorry."

Beejan just squeezed his hand. "I'm not."

The four of them returned to Beejan's place, where Eshu promptly fell asleep face-down on the couch and didn't wake for hours. By the time he roused himself, the lamps were lit, and the room smelled of ginger and garlic and dark, earthy kicha root.

Fern grinned at him as she spooned rice out of a steamer and into a serving dish. "You're awake! We thought we were going to have to eat without you."

"I see—the hero's reward is leftovers," grumbled Eshu. He shuffled across the floor to drape himself over Beejan's back, resting his chin on Beejan's shoulder. The warm solidity of him was restorative in a way that the nap hadn't been. For just a moment, Eshu longed to stand here forever with his arms around Beejan's waist.

Beejan turned to kiss his cheek. "Taste?" he said, and brought a piece of kicha up to Eshu's lips. The edges had caramelized, leaving a burnt sweetness on Eshu's tongue that cut through the heat of the ginger.

"It's amazing," said Eshu honestly.

Mnoro snorted and set down the last bowl on the table. "If you're done canoodling, maybe you can help him get dinner on the table. Some of us have been waiting."

They settled around the table, passing around rice and pepper sauce and a bowl of pickled greens to go with the kicha. At first, everyone ate in silence, just dipping their kicha into pepper sauce with the mechanical determination of people who hadn't had a proper meal all day. Eventually, though, Mnoro said, "Fern and I have been talking, and we'd like to see whether we can find out what happened to Kondala City. Are you in?"

Hearing the name of his city still sent a knife of grief straight through his gut. Eshu swallowed his rice, forcing it past the lump in his throat. "What's there to find out? It was obliterated. All of it. Gone."

"We don't think that's true," said Fern. "But anyway, we'd like to go to Xhonai and see what we can find there. If we're right, and Kondala City did something to avoid getting destroyed like every other city, maybe Xhonai will have records of it. And if not Xhonai, maybe Morra. Yelayo. Somewhere."

"If they had records, then wouldn't they have done the same?" asked Eshu.

Mnoro looked tired. In all the years he'd known her, Eshu had never really seen her look tired; even when they'd been suffering through exams together, she had always risen early to paint her face with immaculate highlights and bright lips and eyes. She always looked fresh and composed. He didn't quite know how to look at her, when she was so fragile and human.

"I'm not giving up on my home," said Mnoro after a long, heavy silence. "Fern's evidence gives me hope. Maybe more evidence will kill that hope—but until I find it, I'm not giving up."

Fern set down her spoon. "I also want to go back to Matis. I've spent so long running in the other direction, afraid of what I'm going to see there. But I need to see it. Bury my dead, if there are dead. See if there's anyone left to help."

Again, the image of the black glass plain of Kondala City flashed across Eshu's mind, and the vertiginous ache of it made him feel sick. He'd crossed a continent to get there, dragging Fern and being dragged by her, and found no answers.

If he could help her find her own answers, maybe the journey would be worth it. "I'd like to go with you," he said. "Matis. Usbaran. Xhonai, and all the rest." *Find out where the* Crest of the Wave *landed, or if it's traveling still.*

"Not tonight, though," said Beejan. "I could knock you all down with a blade of grass."

"Not tonight," agreed Fern. "Tomorrow, maybe."

"Or maybe in a week," said Mnoro wryly. "I don't know about you two, but I need a long rest. If you want to go to Matis without me, I will not feel the slightest bit left out."

"And what about you?" Eshu asked, turning to Beejan.

Eshu saw how Beejan's posture shifted as he felt Eshu's attention on him—how he sat up straighter, smiled brighter, tilted his head just so. It was a masterful performance, so convincing that it nearly hurt to watch. "I'll find something to occupy myself," said Beejan breezily. "There are still hungry ghosts roaming the streets. I assume you haven't turned all of them into snails."

"Not yet," said Fern.

Eshu reached out under the table and found Beejan's hand. "Not tonight, though," he said.

The brightness in Beejan's smile faded, but the warmth remained. "Tonight, I just want to fall asleep on your shoulder." And after Fern and Mnoro had cleared out for the night, that was exactly what he did.

Beejan's door slammed open without so much as a knock to give them warning, and Lali stormed through. She barely spared Eshu a glance; she went straight to the kitchen and started slinging jars into a satchel. One slipped from her hands and shattered, spilling dried beans across the bare wood floor. "Pack your clothes, Bee," she snapped. "Anything else you want to bring, pack it—but pack light, because we're going to have to leg it through the city."

"What are you doing?" Beejan rose from the couch, sweeping a hand back through his sleep-tangled hair. "Put those back. I'm not going anywhere."

Lali whirled on him. Her eyes were bloodshot—with tears or sleeplessness, Eshu couldn't tell. "The fuck you aren't! You saw what happened back there. They'll be after us next. We've got to get out of Kulmeni. Make a new start somewhere. Xhonai, maybe; no one knows us there—"

Picking his way through broken glass and scattered beans, Beejan laid a hand on Lali's arm. "I saw what happened. I'm not going."

Her eyes flashed, and she yanked her arm away. "You're an idiot, then."

"Maybe so." Beejan's voice was steady, sure as stone. "Tell me something, Lali. What happened to the old prince's family? The ones we sent to the mulberry orchard?"

Lali shook her head. "Don't play dumb, Bee," she said softly. "Please."

"What happened?" he asked again, sharper this time. "Did Granny put a gun to their heads? She always did love waving her pistol around. Or did she ask you to do it? You would've, too; any one of us would've, we were so fucking desperate for her approval—"

"It doesn't fucking matter," said Lali. "They're dead, all right? If you care so much, you can dig them up."

"I care about Kulmeni." Beejan planted his feet; his back was straight, his shoulders squared as though he was daring her to strike him down. For a moment, Eshu almost thought she would. "This was our place, Lali. We grew up on these streets. These people trusted us to help them, and instead we held our city up by the ankles and shook it until the money fell out."

"Fuck Kulmeni," Lali said, and spat on the floor. "You think we were any different from the last prince? Or whoever the fuck comes after us? The aristocrats will stay rich, the poor will stay poor, and the merchant folk will play us against each other until we forget we're tearing each other apart for scraps from their tables. Fuck Kulmeni. Fuck everyone. We'll take what's ours."

"Maybe that's true," Beejan began, but Lali didn't let him finish. She dropped her bag of jars with a clash of glass, raising herself up to her full height.

"It's true," she snarled. "And even if it isn't, think for one second about what's going to happen to you if you stay. People here know you. They know what family you come from. You think you have friends here? They'll slam the door in your face, Bee. You think you can just go back to being a runner? See if some vhesha-pusher or pimp has work for you? Not fucking likely. Even the criminals won't want you after this shit."

"Maybe not," said Beejan, "but if I run now and do the same shit in a different city, I won't want me, either."

Slowly, Lali's shoulders slumped. When she reached out for Beejan, he put his arms around her and held her tight. "I'm worried about you, Bee," she said against his neck. Her voice was so small that Eshu could barely make it out. "I don't know what these people are going to do to you. I don't want to hear how you got strung up and hanged off the Heron's Bridge."

Beejan heaved a sigh. "Well, if I didn't want that on the table, I should've made different choices."

"Can you *please* just come with us?" Lali pulled back just far enough to look Beejan in the eyes. "Safi and Tir are already on the road. They've got the stuff from Tisaris and the palace—we can build a new life on that. There's got to be someone who will buy it."

Beejan kissed her cheek, then let her go. "I hope there is. I hope you get away clean. But I'm not going, Lali."

She blinked hard, then wiped her nose with the back of her wrist. When she spoke again, her voice was thick. "Take care of yourself. I mean it, Bee. If I hear anything happened to you, I'm going to come back and tear this city apart."

"Love you, Lali," he said, low.

"Love you, Bee." One last time, she wrapped him in her arms for a crushing hug, then she took her leave without saying goodbye.

In the silence that followed, Eshu climbed to his feet. He wasn't sure whether Beejan wanted to talk to him right now—he wasn't sure whether Beejan wanted him *here* right now, after everything that had happened today. They'd hardly known each other a week, and most of that had been fucking or being afraid for their lives. They weren't friends.

But Eshu had said that before, and been wrong.

He gathered up Beejan's broom and a dustpan, and he started sweeping up the beans and the broken glass. After a moment, Beejan fetched down an empty jar, and together, they picked the beans out of the pile until only the glass remained.

While Beejan tied a scrap of cloth over the mouth of the jar, Eshu sat back on his heels. He hesitated, then asked, "If it's not indelicate of me, why are you going to stay?"

Beejan smiled weakly. His eyes were shadowed; there was a sunken cast to his features that spoke to an exhaustion deeper than grief. "I'm wondering that, myself. She's right—people won't forgive me. Or they will, and I'll hate that they did. There's so much work still to be done here, but maybe I'm not the right person to do it. Maybe the best thing for me to do is get out of the way." He blew out a breath between his lips, then stood to put the beans back on the shelf. "Anyway. I want to stay, and fix what I can. Maybe that's enough."

Eshu rose, too, and scooped up a couple of jars from the floor. He passed them to Beejan one by one, letting him settle peppercorns and star anise and powdered turmeric in their places. "I can't tell you whether what you're doing is right, or enough," said Eshu, when they'd put everything away. "I'm not sure what I did was right, either. But I'm glad you're staying. Whatever that means."

Beejan raised his brows. "Are you planning to stay?"

"I don't know," said Eshu honestly. "Fern and I still need to go to Matis. And I need to see what's left of Usbaran. And my father's village, if we can even—"

Beejan grazed his fingertips over Eshu's cheek, and Eshu subsided. Some aching knot in his chest eased at the touch. It must have shown on his face, because Beejan smiled—a real smile that went to his eyes. "What I meant is, I'd like it if you stayed."

CHAPTER 21: THE ROAD HOME

Fern and Eshu set out early in the morning, while the mist lay golden over the Anjali. Beejan made sure they had breakfast and coffee before they left; Mnoro came with them all the way to the university, and kissed both of them on their cheeks even though she had to stand on tiptoe to reach Eshu's. "Come back to me," she said, and gripped Eshu tight. "Promise me you're coming back."

"I promise," said Eshu. He held her a long time in the doorway, arms around her shoulders and chin tucked against her brow.

Then it was through the mirror again, into the starless dark.

"It feels different," said Fern as they set off along an outcropping of black stone. A low wind sighed over the spine of the ridge, but their footfalls nearly drowned it out.

"Different?" asked Eshu.

Fern shrugged. "From the last time we were here together. I don't know—maybe it's just that I know more about it now."

"I suppose it's hard to see a place as sublime after you've put its sand under a microscope." At the top of the ridge, Eshu paused, his face turned toward the distant mountains. For a moment, he looked unmoored and lonely, with the wind catching in his robe like a torn sail. "I'm still not sure we should even be here. If the mirror network really did break the world..."

Fern stepped up beside him and felt the wind ruffle her hair.

"I don't think it's us being here that's the problem," she said. "Maybe I just don't understand magic, but it feels like the problem was treating this place like it wasn't real. Like you could just do anything to it, open a door to anywhere in our world you wanted, and it wouldn't matter."

"As though the fact that it responded to our wills just proved how powerful our wills were. And it wasn't even as though we didn't think there would be consequences—runecrafters *knew* there would be consequences. They just decided that the convenience was worth the risk." Eshu closed his eyes and drew in a long breath. "There used to be so many mirrors here. Njo, we were so fucking *stupid*."

Fern didn't have an answer for that, so she just stood with him until he was ready to start walking again.

She focused her thoughts on Matis: the busy boardwalk, fishermen mending nets and thick-waisted women frying fish balls with green onions and coconut mixed in. Whitewashed houses on curving cobbled roads. Moss roses and creeping zilia spilling out of every window box; doors and window frames painted red and green and blue. The lighthouse to the north, still alight as dawn broke over the eastern lowlands and spilled down to the Kirami Sea. She gathered the scattered fragments of her memories and pieced them together, until the image of Matis came together whole.

Fern remembered the door to her favorite teashop, painted blue as the ocean, with windows of textured glass in amber and bottle-green. She reached out her hand and felt the curve of its brass handle fit perfectly into her palm. Then she swung the door open and stepped out of the Mirrorlands.

Something had burrowed under the indigo tiles of the teashop floor, scattering chairs and tables in its wake. The tiles bulged obscenely over the ridge; some had broken, and others lay pushed apart on the swell of the mound, like the scales of a snake that had swallowed a man whole. The sight went through Fern like a knife. *So it happened here, too.*

The cashbox had been pried open, and the jars of tea behind the counter were broken or missing. Over everything lay a film of dust. Even the scavengers' fingerprints were softening again at the edges. Eshu picked his way over scattered chairs to the window and pried it open—the wall had shifted, and it stuck in the frame at first, but he kept pushing until it slid up with a horrible rattling jar. He bent down, peering through the opening until his eyes seemed fixed on the sky. "Fern," he said softly. "Come look at this."

She came, setting chairs upright as she went. It was a stupid thing to do. No one was coming back here. When she reached the window, Fern craned her neck to see what Eshu had seen.

Beyond the window, a forest of silver trees grew strange and wild.

Fern ran to the door and flung it open, gazing down the hill toward the sea. All through the city, silver trees had burst up from the streets and splintered through ceilings, rising hundreds of times her height into the sky to spread their shining leaves. Their roots stood proud from the earth like walls of steel. In the harbor, a ship hung impaled on a massive trunk, its sails speared through with silver boughs. The forest stretched down in the deep water, where the waves crashed against their towering boles with a sound like cannonfire.

She swallowed hard. It would have been beautiful, if it hadn't been Matis. She would have loved to wander for days between the shining trees, as though they were immense columns in some legendary queen's palace. Or at least—Fern would have loved it. Because Fern didn't have a family here. She tried to speak, but her voice failed her, and she only made a caught, ugly sound like a mouse being stepped on.

Eshu rested his arm around her shoulders and pulled her against his side. "Hey," he said. "I know. It's hard."

"This looks survivable," Fern managed at last. "Maybe not for everyone. But for a lot of people."

"Then we'll go looking for them," said Eshu. "Where do your parents live?"

Fern swallowed again and wiped her eyes on her sleeve. It wouldn't help anything to cry. "Up closer to the lighthouse. North. A ways back from the sea."

"Then let's go."

They walked the cobbled streets together, climbing carefully over roots and wreckage, listening for any signs of life. The place smelled of death, but it was old death—none of the putrid urgency of Sharis. Whoever lay buried beneath the rubble, they had been there for a month or more.

Now and then, she saw strangers crossing the road at far-away intersections, but never close enough to hail. *Some people survived*, she told herself to quell the clawing misery in her gut. *There's still hope.*

In the middle of the road, a little white cat lolled on its side, sunning itself on the cobblestones. "Hey," said Fern, kneeling and offering her hand. The cat thumped its tail against the road, then rose and trotted toward her to give her fingertips a sniff. After a few seconds of nosing at her fingers, it let her scratch behind its ears, and she felt like she would crack with joy at the living warmth of it. When she stroked its ribs, the cat was still sleek beneath her hands. Someone must be feeding it; it wore a collar that looked clean and new. "I'm glad you have someone to take care of you," she said, and ruffled the cat's fur one last time before she climbed to her feet again. The cat meowed in protest at being abandoned, then followed her and Eshu for a few blocks before getting distracted by a sunbeam.

High above her, the leaves rustled and sighed like a second sea.

They reached her parents' neighborhood about half an hour after they'd set out. The Masreens owned the corner house in a handsome terrace, of which Fern's father had always been very proud, and he'd refused to move even though the south-facing windows never got any light and the back wall had settled so badly that they couldn't get some of their doors to shut all the way.

Her parents had just taken the doors off their hinges and planed them until they fit their frames, then put them back in place without a word of complaint. That was the kind of people they were. They never fussed when they met with trouble; they just found the tools they needed to take care of things, and got on with it. She missed them so much it felt like someone had scraped her ribs out with a spindle gouge.

At the far end of the street stood a towering tree with her parents' house and part of their neighbors' caught in the crook of its branches. The boughs alone were at least as wide as a city boulevard; fifty men couldn't have circled the trunk with their arms. As she watched, the house rocked gently in the breeze.

"It—it's that one," she said, raising her hand to point. Eshu tracked the line of her finger until his gaze found the wreck of the house, suspended in the sky.

"I'm so sorry," said Eshu. He sounded as defeated as she felt.

No one could have survived. If they'd fallen from that height, they would have broken like glass on the houses below. Some stubborn part of Fern, though, refused to accept that. "I'm going to climb up there," she said, and lowered her pack to the ground to take out her climbing rope and her pitons. "It's all right if you stay here. But I have to see it for myself."

"Is there anything I can do?" Eshu asked.

She hesitated, then wrapped her arms around his waist and held him tight. He held her back, stroking her close-cropped hair. "Just be here for me when I come back down, all right?"

"Promise," he said.

With that, Fern let him go and set out for the tree.

She canvassed the ground beneath the trunk at first, searching for bodies or bones. The detritus of her parents' lives lay broken on the ground: their red-painted porcelain dishes from Ras Kir'uun, their sweetgrass baskets and conch shells the size of Fern's head. A single umbrella lay crushed beneath a hunk of brick, like some strange wounded bird.

There were no bodies she could find, but that meant nothing. The ground here was piled with rubble too heavy for her to shift.

Taking out her hammer and pitons, she began to climb the silver tree. The pitons rang on the tough bark as though she was trying to pierce through metal, and they came out dented when she pried them free. She would have to get new ones after she finished this climb. She wondered if they sold climbing gear in Kulmeni, or if she'd have to find a blacksmith and commission a set.

It was easier to distract herself with practicalities. To think of the next step, rather than let herself live in a world where her parents were probably dead.

It took her a long time to scale the side of the tree, and by the time she reached the crook between two massive boughs, her hands were red and trembling. *Breathe*, she told herself. *Remind yourself where you are. Tell it to yourself like a story until you're calm again.*

She secured her rescue line to an offshoot branch the size of a thirty-year-old tree, then made sure it was hitched tightly to her belt. "I'm standing in a great big tree over Matis," she said. Her voice shook. She placed one foot carefully in front of the other, edging down the silver bough while the silver leaves rang like chimes all around her. "The wind is very strong. I'm walking toward my parents' house, which is in this tree, and the wall is broken off, and—"

She put a tentative foot on the parquet floor of her parents' living room and felt the whole house sway in the wind. All of the shells and sextants and statuettes in her parents' collections, all the articulated bird skeletons and pieces of coral, lay scattered across the floor. The dust sheets on the furniture flapped like sails.

Someone was sitting in her mother's chair. Over the threadbare green upholstery, Fern saw dark, matted hair and the corner of a sleeve.

No, thought Fern. She swallowed. She hadn't wanted to find this. She hadn't wanted to know this. As long as she didn't know, maybe her mother wasn't really dead. That was what hope was, wasn't it? Not knowing the worst yet. With slow, halting steps, Fern approached the chair. The floor groaned and tilted underfoot.

She saw the bone-white mask an instant before the Crowtaker rose from her mother's place. "You!" Fern shouted, snatching up a fallen candlestick and holding it like a club. "Get out of here! Leave me *be!*"

"Would you drive me from my home?" the Crowtaker asked, and in her voice was the rattle of death.

"You're fucking right I would! This place is *mine!*" Rage licked through Fern like a flame. Hot tears pricked at her eyes. "Why won't you leave me alone?"

Through her tears, she thought she saw the Crowtaker smile. "You have heard the people of Kulmeni speak my name. You have felt my shadow on Zumera and Sharis. Wherever there is death, there am I—and there has been death here, my child."

"No," said Fern, but she couldn't make herself mean it. The candlestick fell from her fingers and rolled away.

"You feel it," the Crowtaker said. "You *feel* how the trees tore them apart, and roots wound through their bones."

Fern couldn't hold back a sob. She did feel it. She heard her parents screaming as the ground erupted beneath them; she felt branches and roots spearing them through, breaking bones, shredding flesh. In the part of her that had never wanted to come here, she knew that the Crowtaker was speaking only the ugly truth.

Then the wind caught in the dust sheets over the furniture, and she remembered. Her parents only put the dust sheets up when they were sailing.

It was a lie.

"You aren't Death," said Fern softly. She smeared away her tears and stared straight into the eyeless sockets of the Crowtaker's mask. "If you were Death, you'd be long gone. You don't come for the dying—you come for the people who are trying to live. You're something else. You're despair."

The Crowtaker laughed, low and swelling—a hideous, bubbling laugh, thick with blood and water. Her laughter was an avalanche, a flood, a lava flow pouring down a mountainside; it was a firestorm. It was a war. By the time the Crowtaker began to sing, Fern already felt death's cold hand around her.

Her lungs burned. Her heart strained, each beat a slow sucking pump that throbbed in her chest. Her ribs were made of broken glass. Her heart was a stone. She fell to her knees, retching as the world went grey at the edges.

A little sample vial fell from her breast pocket and rolled under her hand. She watched the water wash against the sides of the bottle. *Diatoms*, she thought dizzily, her numb fingers closing on the slick glass. *Arroyos. Aquifers somewhere under the sand.* The way the world snapped into focus when the lenses of the microscope aligned just right. There were still a thousand questions that no one had ever thought to ask, and she would not let the Crowtaker steal the answers from her.

Perhaps her parents were dead. Perhaps everything she had feared had already come to pass. But there was still more work to be done, and *that* was hope.

Despair could not have her. With her last breath she cried, "My name is Rukha Masreen, and I will not be taken!"

In a furor of feathers, a tumult of black wings, the Crowtaker shuddered and burst into nothingness.

Slowly, Rukha's breath came back to her. She flattened her hand against her chest, feeling her heartbeat grow steady under her palm. When at last she had the strength to stand, she heaved herself to her feet and nearly fell over again from vertigo. She closed her eyes until the lightheadedness faded. The floor swayed. The world righted itself. Rukha opened her eyes.

Where the Crowtaker had been, only a white bone mask lay on the floor. Rukha stared at it a long time, then crushed it under her boot.

The climb back down was long, and quiet. Rukha took her time, making sure her rope harness was secure, checking every piton before trusting it as an anchor point. There was something calming about the ritual of it, and after what she'd just been through, she needed that calm.

When at last her feet touched the ground, Eshu was waiting for her. "Are you all right? What happened up there?" he asked. Worry lined his brows.

"I need to tell you something," she said. "My name is Rukha. Rukha Masreen. And I don't care if the Crowtaker hears it."

"Rukha." He seemed to test the name, seeing how it felt in his mouth. "Well, Rukha, are you all right?"

She thought about how to answer as she unhooked her climbing harness. It was in her to say yes. She'd just bested the Crowtaker. She'd unsung her songs, broken her mask, driven her back to wherever she lurked between calamities.

She didn't feel all right.

"No, not really," said Rukha at last. "My city is ruined. I'm still afraid of what comes next. I don't know where my parents are or if they're all right, and I haven't even started looking for Heza and Kufa. And there's so much I still don't know about what happened or why."

"We'll find answers," Eshu said. He held out his arms to her, but she shook her head, and he let them fall. "I promise you, F— Rukha. I promise you, we'll find your family."

Rukha looked down at her hands. The green glass ring on her finger caught the sunlight. "I hope so. But I'm afraid that if

I promise myself that, I'll turn out like Shell. Diving down again and again, looking for bones."

Eshu wrapped his arms around his chest. The stiff sea breeze stirred his hair. "What do you want to do next? After we look for your friends, where do we go?"

"I don't know," said Rukha. "I want to learn more about the Mirrorlands. I want to find out what happened to Kondala City. And I want to do what I can for Kulmeni—someone there told me that even if things got bad, the work was still the same. We had to take care of each other. And I really believe that. With my whole heart, I believe it."

This time, when Eshu offered his hand, Rukha took it. Both of them were cold, but where their palms touched, a slow, sure warmth grew between them. "I used to think I hated people," said Eshu softly. "But I don't. I don't think I ever really did. I just hated not knowing how to be with them. And more than anything, I want to learn."

"We'll figure it out together," said Fern. "Maybe we don't know what comes next. No one does. But together, maybe we can find a way forward."

"Together," said Eshu, and stood with her under the silver canopy until she was ready to go on.

EPILOGUE

In Kondala City, the sun no longer rose; no moon turned overhead, and no stars wheeled through the firmament. Only the song of the city bells and the rumble of prayer drums at dawn and dusk marked the passage of time, and even dawn and dusk soon bled together. Lamps burned through the day and dimmed when the city slept.

Against the marble walls of the Grand Assembly, the night-blooming jasmine never faded. Their heady perfume was thick on the air as Barata and Sunba climbed the stairs to the assembly chamber.

Barata bore herself with the ease and dignity of a woman who had spent decades making laws. Her hair was twisted up in an elaborate crown of braids, woven through with wefts of purple and gold. She wore a white gown with embroidery tracing the severe slit of the neckline, and a deep violet shawl over her shoulders against the unnatural cold.

Sunba was here as an observer only—still a plum position for a junior counselor, and she was conscious that without her mother's considerable pull, she wouldn't have been permitted to sit in on this trial at all. She had dressed in somber blue with only the faintest of black print, the better to let her mother shine.

They settled into their seats beneath the blazing wheel of the chamber's chandelier. When she'd been very small, Sunba had loved to climb all up and down the tiered seats when the Assembly was in recess; she'd played skipping games on the intricate geometry of the tiled floor and laughed at how her footsteps echoed through the empty room. She'd stood with her nose pressed against the great glass window at the back of the chamber, looking for her friends' houses on the hillside.

Today, though, the Assembly was in session, and Sunba couldn't help staring at the wizards chained up in the witnesses' gallery.

In the center of the chamber, the Speaker of the Assembly rose from his chair. "Welcome, honored friends," he said, in a voice that rolled and carried. "We are accustomed to coming together to make laws; it is rare that we are called to serve as tribunal. But these are rare times." He gestured back toward the chamber's window. In the darkness, it threw back the light of the chandelier, reflecting the Assembly to themselves. The Speaker paused to let the Assembly members make peace with their own reflections. Then, deliberately, he said, "Today we are gathered to try the Keepers of the Hall of Ways on charges of treason."

Beyond their reflections, beyond the window glass, the long black mountains of the Mirrorlands rolled on to infinity.

ACKNOWLEDGMENTS

This book was a journey that I could not have completed alone. I would especially like to thank Caroline Pruett, whose early comments on this book were critical in helping me understand the emotional logic and the shape of its narrative, and Kavita Mudan Finn, whose sensitivity read for this novel was both immensely helpful and very kind. I'd also like to thank Beck Maier, Laura Bitely, Waverly March, and Christopher and Jennifer Pipinou for talking through the trickier parts with me and encouraging me to keep going. These wonderful people have rescued the story from at least seven different kinds of disaster; any remaining errors are my own.

I have also been immensely grateful for those who have supported me in the ever-more-fraught work of living: my wife, my family, my tabletop roleplaying group, and the network of friends who have never stopped reaching out to me during the isolation of the pandemic. One day, I hope we will see each other face to face again.

ABOUT THE AUTHOR

A.M. Tuomala lives in western New York, somewhere between Niagara Gorge and the Eternal Flame. In addition to hiking those sublime landscapes, Tuomala enjoys researching eighteenth-century science, collecting rocks, and building new worlds.

Lightning Source UK Ltd.
Milton Keynes UK
UKHW012104221222
414360UK00004B/33

9 781952 456121